D1598121

FEATURING
CONTRIBUTIONS
BY

NEAL BARRETT JR.
MICHAEL BISHOP
JACK DANN
BRADLEY DENTON
GARDNER DOZOIS
NEIL GAIMAN
RICHARD GILLIAM
BARBARA HAMBLY
LAWRENCE PERSON
MIKE RESNICK
PAMELA SARGENT
HOWARD WALDROP
GEORGE ZEBROWSKI

Rue Bourbon
Bourbon

GEORGE
ALEC
EFFINGER
Live! FROM
PLANET EARTH

GOLDEN GRYPHON PRESS • 2005

Introduction to "The Aliens Who Knew, I Mean, *Everything*," copyright © 2005 by Michael Bishop.
Afterword to "The Aliens Who Knew, I Mean, *Everything*," copyright © 2005 by George Zebrowski.
Introduction to "All the Last Wars at Once," copyright © 2005 by Mike Resnick.
Introduction to "At the Bran Foundry," copyright © 2005 by Jack Dann.
Introduction to "Everything but Honor," copyright © 2005 by Neal Barrett Jr.
Introduction to "From Downtown at the Buzzer," copyright © 2005 by Mike Resnick.
Introduction to "Glimmer, Glimmer," copyright © 2005 by Bradley Denton.
Introduction to "Housebound," copyright © 2005 by Richard Gilliam.
Introduction to "My First Game as an Immortal," copyright © 2005 by Barbara Hambly.
Introduction to "My Old Man," copyright © 2005 by Lawrence Person.
Introduction to "One," copyright © 2005 by Barbara Hambly.
Introduction to "Seven Nights in Slumberland," copyright © 2005 by Neil Gaiman.
Introduction to "Solo in the Spotlight," copyright © 2005 by Bradley Denton.
Introduction to "Target: Berlin!" copyright © 2005 by Pamela Sargent.
Introduction to "Two Sadnesses," copyright © 2005 by Howard Waldrop.
Introduction to the O. Niemand Stories, copyright © 2005 by Gardner Dozois.

Copyright © 2005 by the Estate of George Alec Effinger
Cover illustration copyright © 2005 by John Picacio

Edited by Marty Halpern

LIBRARY OF CONGRESS CATALOGUING–IN–PUBLICATION DATA
Effinger, George Alec.
    George Alec Effinger live! from planet Earth / with contributions by Neal Barrett Jr., Michael Bishop, Jack Dann, Bradley Denton, Gardner Dozois, Neil Gaiman, Richard Gilliam, Barbara Hambly, Lawrence Person, Mike Resnick, Pamela Sargent, Howard Waldrop, and George Zebrowski. — 1st ed.
    p.   cm.
    ISBN 1-930846-32-0 (hardcover : alk. paper)
    1. Science fiction, American.   I. Title: Live! from planet Earth.
    II. Barrett, Neal.   III. Title.
PS3555.F4 A6   2005
813'.54—dc22   2004016935

Contents

In memory of
George Alec Effinger
1947–2002

Editor's Notes and Acknowledgments

In an email I received from George dated August 30, 2001, he wrote: "As far as the collection goes . . . I've imagined a hefty selection of my 200 stories, with introductions to each one, and calling it *George Alec Effinger: The White Album* or *George Alec Effinger Live! At the Village Gate* or something."

After George passed away, and the agreement for the book you now hold in your hands became a reality, Barbara Hambly (executrix of the Effinger estate) and I agreed upon the present title. Hopefully, George would be pleased.

By far the most requested story amongst the contributors to this volume was "The Aliens Who Knew, I Mean, *Everything*." Quintessential George Alec Effinger, which undoubtedly explains its popularity. So this one story, which kicks off this collection, gets the full treatment: an introduction *and* an afterword.

Tracking down the myriad uncollected stories that George Alec Effinger wrote in his all-too-brief career could not have been accomplished without the assistance of many. Thanks to the members of the *fictionmags* e-forum, including Paul Brazier and Curt Phillips, and especially Richard Bleiler and Paul Di Filippo, both of whom went above and beyond. I would email (and I *still* do!) Richard and Paul lists of stories, and almost magically those stories would appear in the mail a short time later.

Others who provided copies of George's uncollected works include his previous editors Michael Bishop, Esther M. Friesner, Richard Gilliam, and Robin Scott Wilson; also Bradley Denton,

Barbara Hambly, Tom Jackson, and George Zebrowski; and Scott Pendergrast of Fictionwise.com. Thank you all once again.

And lastly, I would like to thank those who contributed introductions to stories that could not be included in this collection due to space limitations: Richard Bleiler, Paul Di Filippo, Barbara Hambly, and Gordon Van Gelder. However, these introductions, and stories, may yet find a home:

At the start of the *Budayeen Nights* project (George Alec Effinger's previous Golden Gryphon Press collection), I promised George that we would work together to bring his short fiction back into print. Alas, I never expected that I, and not George, would be writing these acknowledgments. There are so many wondrous, timeless stories still remaining in George's *oeuvre* that I hope there will be another volume (or two) of his short fiction for you to read and savor in the near future.

—Marty Halpern

George Alec Effinger
Live!
From Planet Earth

Introduction to "The Aliens Who Knew, I Mean, *Everything*"

In a letter to me, the mordant Barry Malzberg once described George Alec Effinger as "fey." As a writer proud of my vocabulary, I sort of knew what *fey* meant. But, of course, when we *sort of* know what a word means, we place ourselves in even greater danger of committing a linguistic howler than when we confess ignorance and go to a dictionary for help. I never told Barry that I had only an inkling of what *fey* meant; instead, I consulted my college dictionary and wrote him back using his offbeat adjective as if I had known its meaning since age thirteen, if not earlier.

I no longer have that college dictionary—I wore it out, long ago—but *The New Oxford American Dictionary* sprawled open on my lap today defines *fey* as "giving an impression of vague unworldliness: *his mother was a strange, fey woman,*" and I must admit that Effinger did in fact live up to the unworldly connotations of the adjective *fey.* Upon our first meeting in 1976 or '77 at a small convention in Rome, Georgia, he gave me the impression of a visitor from a continuum *aslant* our own, as if he had wafted in through a magic heating duct or tiptoed through the wall via a process of somatic intermolecularization. He complained of not having slept in days. He flattered me. He borrowed five dollars for cab fare, when five dollars felt more like thirty and I could scarcely afford breakfast, and then either forgot to repay it or assumed that I had never wanted or expected such a payback, attributing to me more generosity of spirit and of pocketbook than I deserved. And, of course, he wrote stories of such surreal intelligence and deadpan wit that I envied both his talent and his accomplishment.

But *fey* has two additional meanings, the first of which is "having supernatural powers of clairvoyance"

—Who would *not* envy such powers?—and the second of which is Scottish-speak for "fated to die or at the point of death," from the Old English word *fæge* ("in the sense 'fated to die soon'"). George did not die a young man, but neither did he live to become an old one, and the pain and insomnia that he bore his entire life surely contributed to the puzzled and puzzling otherworldliness that made him seem at once distracted and engaged, Chaplinesque and Sartrean. When he wrote, however, he focused all his shattered attention, depleted energy, and tireless self-effacing wit on the words at his command. And, by so doing, he produced a host of literary marvels worthy of our attention, energy, and laughter today.

Among the downright funniest of George Alec Effinger's marvels, I reckon, is his short story "The Aliens Who Knew, I Mean, *Everything*," which first appeared in the October 1984 issue of *The Magazine of Fantasy & Science Fiction*. I could write a scholarly paper about this story, dissecting its techniques of understatement, awe-free character presentation, and science-fictional self-referentialism, throwing in allusions to low-budget alien-invasion films from the 1950s and 1960s and to the influential Cold War satires of Robert Sheckley and William Tenn, but an introduction to a funny story should no doubt refrain from that sort of analysis. For one thing, it would spoil the jokes. For another, it would strike the author as overblown, tone deaf, and beside the point, for in this story George's primary purpose was to amuse—indeed, to prompt one to Laugh Out Loud. And I can remember Laughing Out Loud a half-dozen times, or more, on first reading this story. Further, my *persistent* fondness for it stems from the fact that all my subsequent readings have evoked not only laughter, but also fresh respect for the grace and economy with which the author achieved his effects.

At this point I should simply shut up. Go read "The Aliens Who Knew, I Mean, *Everything*." And come back afterward, *if you want to,* for a couple of minor insights that may or may not prove amusing. Go.

* * *

Funny story, right?

Absolutely.

One of the first auctorial strategies that engages me when I read, or reread, George Alec Effinger is his implicit assumption that those in high office know no more about what is going on than do any of the rest of us, whether we're taxi drivers, seamstresses, truck dispatchers, or runway models. Everyone is just muddling through, and those who *think* they have a grip on the basic operating principles of the universe clearly suffer from self-aggrandizing delusions. Those who do best, like the president-cum-mayor who narrates this story, *acknowledge* their shortcomings from the outset, if not to the world at large then at least to themselves. Note, too, that Effinger must have identified (although the quality of his work suggests that he need not have) with every average Jane and Joe who daily makes her or his problematic way by muddling. And why not? His story strongly implies that, on the galactic scale, our entire sentient species rates as no better than a C student.

Second, as a consequence of this notion, Effinger uses a mundane human example, the narrator's college roommate, Barry Rintz, an insupportable know-it-all, to make apparent and palpable to us the *superior* insupportability of the aliens who know, I mean, *everything*. This technique *seems* to place Effinger squarely in the camp of those gloomy science fictionists whose tales equate human angst with the heat death of the universe, or WWI shell shock with the astrophysical mechanics of black holes, or earthly ethnic divisions with the complexities of string theory. However, in Effinger's hands the structural analogy from little to big, from micro to macro, produces chuckles instead of an Excedrin headache. Let us rain huzzas upon his memory for this hugely considerate boon.

Also, as a signal of support to anyone weary of academic overinterpretation, Effinger equips the know-it-all aliens in his story with a wonderfully nonsensical —but *still* terrifically meaningful—name. As Luis, the secretary of defense, reports to the president early on, explaining the aliens' distaste for the nominative *aliens*, "[The alien] tells me he's a nup. That's their word for

'man,' in the sense of 'human being.' The plural is
'nuhp.'" Well. Anyone with a modicum of critical acu-
ity will recognize instantly that *nup* spelled backwards
is *pun* and that *nuhp* spelled backwards is *phun*. I don't
know about you, but I think that's *phunny*. More to the
point, this textual jape—in my view, anyway—absolves
the reader of the need to seek existential profundities
in the story's theme or to fall into a pit of rebarbative
(i.e., "unattractive and objectionable") analysis upon
reading its final sentence, which I find mildly anticli-
mactic (*feh*) but wholly appropriate to this particular
narrator (*fey*).

In conclusion, I'd like to leave you with one evocative, cabalistic, and prophetic word: *hollyhocks*.

—Michael Bishop

+ + +

The Aliens Who Knew, I Mean, Everything

I WAS SITTING AT MY DESK, READING A REPORT on the brown pelican situation, when the secretary of state burst in. "Mr. President," he said, his eyes wide, "the aliens are here!" Just like that. "The aliens are here!" As if I had any idea of what to do about them.

"I see," I said. I learned early in my first term that "I see" was one of the safest and most useful comments I could possibly make in any situation. When I said, "I see," it indicated that I had digested the news and was waiting intelligently and calmly for further data. That knocked the ball back into my advisors' court. I looked at the secretary of state expectantly. I was all prepared with my next utterance, in the event that he had nothing further to add. My next utterance would be "Well?" That would indicate that I was on top of the problem, but that I couldn't be expected to make an executive decision without sufficient information, and that he should have known better than to burst into the Oval Office unless he had that information. That's why we had protocol; that's why we had proper channels; that's why I had advisors. The voters out there didn't want me to make decisions without sufficient information. If the secretary didn't have anything more to tell me, he shouldn't have burst in, in the first place. I looked at him awhile longer. "Well?" I asked at last.

"That's about all we have at the moment," he said uncomfortably. I looked at him sternly for a few seconds, scoring a couple of points while he stood there all flustered. I turned back to the pelican report, dismissing him. I certainly wasn't going to get all flustered. I could think of only one president in recent memory who was ever flustered in office, and we all know what happened to him. As the secretary of state closed the door to my office behind him, I smiled. The aliens were probably going to be a bitch of a problem eventually, but it wasn't my problem yet. I had a little time.

But I found that I couldn't really keep my mind on the pelican question. Even the president of the United States has *some* imagination, and if the secretary of state was correct, I was going to have to confront these aliens pretty damn soon. I'd read stories about aliens when I was a kid, I'd seen all sorts of aliens in movies and television, but these were the first aliens who'd actually stopped by for a chat. Well, I wasn't going to be the first American president to make a fool of himself in front of visitors from another world. I was going to be briefed. I telephoned the secretary of defense. "We must have some contingency plans drawn up for this," I told him. "We have plans for every other possible situation." This was true; the Defense Department has scenarios for such bizarre events as the rise of an imperialist fascist regime in Liechtenstein or the spontaneous depletion of all the world's selenium.

"Just a second, Mr. President," said the secretary. I could hear him muttering to someone else. I held the phone and stared out the window. There were crowds of people running around hysterically out there. Probably because of the aliens. "Mr. President?" came the voice of the secretary of defense. "I have one of the aliens here, and he suggests that we use the same plan that President Eisenhower used."

I closed my eyes and sighed. I hated it when they said stuff like that. I wanted information, and they told me these things knowing that I would have to ask four or five more questions just to understand the answer to the first one. "You have an alien with you?" I said, in a pleasant enough voice.

"Yes, sir. They prefer not to be called 'aliens.' He tells me he's a nup. That's their word for 'man,' in the sense of 'human being.' The plural is 'nuhp.' "

"Thank you, Luis. Tell me, why do you have an al—Why do you have a nup and I don't?"

Luis muttered the question to his nup. "He says it's because they wanted to go through proper channels. They learned all about that from President Eisenhower."

"Very good, Luis." This was going to take all day, I could see that; and I had a photo session with Mick Jagger's granddaughter. "My second question, Luis, is what the hell does he mean by 'the same plan that President Eisenhower used'?"

Another muffled consultation. "He says that this isn't the first time that the nuhp have landed on Earth. A scout ship with two nuhp aboard landed at Edwards Air Force Base in 1954. The two nuhp met with President Eisenhower. It was apparently a very cordial occasion, and President Eisenhower impressed the nuhp as a warm and sincere old gentleman. They've been planning to return to Earth ever since but they've been very busy, what with one thing and another. President Eisenhower requested that the nuhp not reveal themselves to the people of Earth in general, until our government decided how to control the inevitable hysteria. My guess is that the government never got around to that, and when the nuhp departed, the matter was studied and then shelved. As the years passed, few people were even aware that the first meeting ever occurred. The nuhp have returned now in great numbers, expecting that we'd have prepared the populace by now. It's not their fault that we haven't. They just sort of took it for granted that they'd be welcome."

"Uh huh," I said. That was my usual utterance when I didn't know what the hell else to say. "Assure them that they are, indeed, welcome. I don't suppose the study they did during the Eisenhower administration was ever completed. I don't suppose there really is a plan to break the news to the public."

"Unfortunately, Mr. President, that seems to be the case."

"Uh huh." That's Republicans for you, I thought. "Ask your nup something for me, Luis. Ask him if he knows what they told Eisenhower. They must be full of outer space wisdom. Maybe they have some ideas about how we should deal with this."

There was yet another pause. "Mr. President, he says all they discussed with Mr. Eisenhower was his golf game. They helped to correct his putting stroke. But they are definitely full of wisdom. They know all sorts of things. My nup—that is, his name is Hurv— anyway, he says that they'd be happy to give you some advice."

"Tell him that I'm grateful, Luis. Can they have someone meet with me in, say, half an hour?"

"There are three nuhp on their way to the Oval Office at this moment. One of them is the leader of their expedition, and one of the others is the commander of their mother ship."

"Mother ship?" I asked.

"You haven't seen it? It's tethered on the Mall. They're real sorry about what they did to the Washington Monument. They say they can take care of it tomorrow."

I just shuddered and hung up the phone. I called my secretary. "There are going to be three—"

"They're here now, Mr. President."

I sighed. "Send them in." And that's how I met the nuhp. Just as President Eisenhower had.

They were handsome people. Likable, too. They smiled and shook hands and suggested that photographs be taken of the historic moment, so we called in the media; and then I had to sort of wing the most important diplomatic meeting of my entire political career. I welcomed the nuhp to Earth. "Welcome to Earth," I said, "and welcome to the United States."

"Thank you," said the nup I would come to know as Pleen. "We're glad to be here."

"How long do you plan to be with us?" I hated myself when I said that, in front of the Associated Press and the UPI and all the network news people. I sounded like a desk clerk at a Holiday Inn.

"We don't know, exactly," said Pleen. "We don't have to be back to work until a week from Monday."

"Uh huh," I said. Then I just posed for pictures and kept my mouth shut. I wasn't going to say or do another goddamn thing until my advisors showed up and started advising.

Well, of course, the people panicked. Pleen told me to expect that, but I had figured it out for myself. We've seen too many movies about visitors from space. Sometimes they come with a message of peace and universal brotherhood and just the inside information mankind has been needing for thousands of years. More often, though, the aliens come to enslave and murder us because the visual effects are better, and so when the nuhp arrived everyone was all prepared to hate them. People didn't trust their good looks. People were suspicious of their nice manners and their quietly tasteful clothing. When the nuhp offered to solve all our problems for us, we all said, sure, solve our problems—*but at what cost?*

That first week, Pleen and I spent a lot of time together, just getting to know one another and trying to understand what the other one wanted. I invited him and Commander Toag and the other nuhp bigwigs to a reception at the White House. We had a church choir from Alabama singing gospel music and a high school band from Michigan playing a medley of favorite collegiate fight songs and talented clones of the original stars nostalgically recreating the

Steve and Eydie Experience and an improvisational comedy troupe from Los Angeles or someplace and the New York Philharmonic under the baton of a twelve-year-old girl genius. They played Beethoven's Ninth Symphony in an attempt to impress the nuhp with how marvelous Earth culture was.

Pleen enjoyed it all very much. "Men are as varied in their expressions of joy as we nuhp," he said, applauding vigorously. "We are all very fond of human music. We think Beethoven composed some of the most beautiful melodies we've ever heard, anywhere in our galactic travels."

I smiled. "I'm sure we are all pleased to hear that," I said.

"Although the Ninth Symphony is certainly not the best of his work."

I faltered in my clapping. "Excuse me?" I said.

Pleen gave me a gracious smile. "It is well-known among us that Beethoven's finest composition is his Piano Concerto Number Five in E Flat Major."

I let out my breath. "Of course, that's a matter of opinion. Perhaps the standards of the nuhp—"

"Oh, no," Pleen hastened to assure me, "taste does not enter into it at all. The Concerto Number Five is Beethoven's best, according to very rigorous and definite critical principles. And even that lovely piece is by no means the best music ever produced by mankind."

I felt just a trifle annoyed. What could this nup, who came from some weirdo planet God alone knows how far away, from some society with not the slightest connection to our heritage and culture, what could this nup know of what Beethoven's Ninth Symphony aroused in our human souls? "Tell me, then, Pleen," I said in my ominously soft voice, "what is the best human musical composition?"

"The score from the motion picture *Ben Hur*, by Miklos Rozsa," he said simply. What could I do but nod my head in silence. It wasn't worth starting an interplanetary incident over.

So from fear our reaction to the nuhp changed to distrust. We kept waiting for them to reveal their real selves; we waited for the pleasant masks to slip off and show us the true nightmarish faces we all suspected lurked beneath. The nuhp did not go home a week from Monday, after all. They liked Earth, and they liked us. They decided to stay a little longer. We told them about ourselves and our centuries of trouble; and they mentioned, in an off-hand nuhp way, that they could take care of a few little things, make some small adjustments, and life would be a whole lot better for everybody on Earth. They didn't want anything in return. They wanted to give us these things in gratitude for our hospitality, for letting them park their mother ship on the Mall and for all the free refills of coffee they were getting all around the world. We hesitated, but our vanity and our greed won out. "Go ahead," we said, "make our deserts bloom. Go ahead, end war and poverty and disease. Show us twenty exciting new things to do with leftovers. Call us when you're done."

The fear changed to distrust, but soon the distrust changed to hope. The nuhp made the deserts bloom, all right. They asked for four months. We were perfectly willing to let them have all the time they needed. They put a tall fence all around the Namib and wouldn't let anyone in to watch what they were doing. Four months later, they had a big cocktail party and invited the whole world to see what they'd accomplished. I sent the secretary of state as my personal representative. He brought back some wonderful slides: The vast desert had been turned into a botanical miracle. There were miles and miles of flowering plants now, instead of the monotonous dead sand and gravel sea. Of course, the immense garden contained nothing but hollyhocks, many millions of hollyhocks. I mentioned to Pleen that the people of Earth had been hoping for a little more in the way of variety, and something just a trifle more practical, too.

"What do you mean, 'practical'?" he asked.

"You know," I said. "Food."

"Don't worry about food," said Pleen. "We're going to take care of hunger pretty soon."

"Good, good. But hollyhocks?"

"What's wrong with hollyhocks?"

"Nothing," I admitted.

"Hollyhocks are the single prettiest flower grown on Earth."

"Some people like orchids," I said. "Some people like roses."

"No," said Pleen firmly. "Hollyhocks are it. I wouldn't kid you."

So we thanked the nuhp for a Namibia full of hollyhocks and stopped them before they did the same thing to the Sahara, the Mojave, and the Gobi.

On the whole, everyone began to like the nuhp, although they took just a little getting used to. They had very definite opinions about everything, and they wouldn't admit that what they had were *opinions*. To hear a nup talk, he had a direct line to some categorical imperative that spelled everything out in terms that were unflinchingly black and white. Hollyhocks were the best flower. Alexander Dumas was the greatest novelist. Powder blue was the prettiest color. Melancholy was the most ennobling emotion. *Grand Hotel* was the finest movie. The best car ever built was the 1956 Chevy Bel Air, but it had to be aqua and white. And there just wasn't room for discussion: the nuhp made these pronouncements with the force of divine revelation.

I asked Pleen once about the American presidency. I asked him who the nuhp thought was the best president in our history. I felt sort of like the Wicked Queen in *Snow White*. Mirror, mirror, on the wall. I didn't really expect Pleen would tell me that I was the best president, but my heart pounded while I waited for his answer; you never know, right? To tell the truth, I expected him to say Washington, Lincoln, Roosevelt, or Akiwara. His answer surprised me: James K. Polk.

"Polk?" I asked. I wasn't even sure I could recognize Polk's portrait.

"He's not the most familiar," said Pleen, "but he was an honest if unexciting president. He fought the Mexican War and added a great amount of territory to the United States. He saw every bit of his platform become law. He was a good, hard-working man who deserves a better reputation."

"What about Thomas Jefferson?" I asked.

Pleen just shrugged. "He was okay, too, but he was no James Polk."

My wife, the First Lady, became very good friends with the wife of Commander Toag, whose name was Doim. They often went shopping together, and Doim would make suggestions to the First Lady about fashion and hair care. Doim told my wife which rooms in the White House needed redecoration, and which charities were worthy of official support. It was Doim who negotiated the First Lady's recording contract, and it was Doim who introduced her to the Philadelphia cheese steak, one of the nuhp's favorite treats (although they asserted that the best cuisine on Earth was Tex-Mex).

One day, Doim and my wife were having lunch. They sat at a small table in a chic Washington restaurant, with a couple dozen Secret Service people and nuhp security agents disguised elsewhere among the patrons. "I've noticed that there seems to be more nuhp here in Washington every week," said the First Lady.

"Yes," said Doim, "new mother ships arrive daily. We think

Earth is one of the most pleasant planets we've ever visited."

"We're glad to have you, of course," said my wife, "and it seems that our people have gotten over their initial fears."

"The hollyhocks did the trick," said Doim.

"I guess so. How many nuhp are there on Earth now?"

"About five or six million, I'd say."

The First Lady was startled. "I didn't think it would be that many."

Doim laughed. "We're not just here in America, you know. We're all over. We really like Earth. Although, of course, Earth isn't absolutely the best planet. Our own home, Nupworld, is still Number One; but Earth would certainly be on any Top Ten list."

"Uh huh." (My wife has learned many important oratorical tricks from me.)

"The hollyhocks were nice," said the First Lady. "But when are you going to tackle the really vital questions?"

"Don't worry about that," said Doim, turning her attention to her cottage cheese salad.

"When are you going to take care of world hunger?"

"Pretty soon. Don't worry."

"Urban blight."

"Pretty soon."

"Man's inhumanity to man?"

Doim gave my wife an impatient look. "We haven't even been here for six months yet. What do you want, miracles? We've already done more than your husband accomplished in his entire first term."

"Hollyhocks," muttered the First Lady.

"I heard that," said Doim. "The rest of the universe absolutely *adores* hollyhocks. We can't help it if humans have no taste."

They finished their lunch in silence, and my wife came back to the White House fuming.

That same week, one of my advisors showed me a letter that had been sent by a young man in New Mexico. Several nuhp had moved into a condo next door to him and had begun advising him about the best investment possibilities (urban respiratory spas), the best fabrics and colors to wear to show off his coloring, the best holo system on the market (the Esmeraldas F–64 with hexphased Libertad screens and a Ruy Challenger argon solipsizer), the best place to watch sunsets (the revolving restaurant on top of the Weyerhauser Building in Yellowstone City), the best wines to go with everything (too numerous to mention—send SASE for list), and which of the two women he was dating to marry (Candi Marie Esterhazy). "Mr. President," said the bewildered young man, "I realize that we must be gracious hosts to our benefactors from space, but I am having some difficulty keeping my temper. The nuhp are certainly knowledgeable and willing to share the benefits of their wisdom, but they don't even wait to be asked. If they were people, regular human beings who lived next door, I would have punched their lights out by now. Please advise. And hurry: they are taking me downtown next Friday to pick out an engagement ring and new living room furniture. I don't even *want* new living room furniture!"

Luis, my secretary of defense, talked to Hurv about the ultimate goals of the nuhp. "We don't have any goals," he said. "We're just taking it easy."

"Then why did you come to Earth?" asked Luis.

"Why do you go bowling?"

"I don't go bowling."

"You should," said Hurv. "Bowling is the most enjoyable thing a person can do."

"What about sex?"

"Bowling *is* sex. Bowling is a symbolic form of intercourse, except you don't have to bother about the feelings of some other person. Bowling is sex without guilt. Bowling is what people have wanted down through all the millennia: sex without the slightest responsibility. It's the very distillation of the essence of sex. Bowling is sex without fear and shame."

"Bowling is sex without pleasure," said Luis.

There was a brief silence. "You mean," said Hurv, "that when you put that ball right into the pocket and see those pins explode off the alley, you don't have an orgasm?"

"Nope," said Luis.

"*That's* your problem, then. I can't help you there, you'll have to see some kind of therapist. It's obvious this subject embarrasses you. Let's talk about something else."

"Fine with me," said Luis moodily. "When are we going to receive the real benefits of your technological superiority? When are you going to unlock the final secrets of the atom? When are you going to free mankind from drudgery?"

"What do you mean, 'technological superiority'?" asked Hurv.

"There must be scientific wonders beyond our imagining aboard your mother ships."

"Not so's you'd notice. We're not even so advanced as you

people here on Earth. We've learned all sorts of wonderful things since we've been here."

"What?" Luis couldn't imagine what Hurv was trying to say.

"We don't have anything like your astonishing bubble memories or silicon chips. We never invented anything comparable to the transistor, even. You know why the mother ships are so big?"

"My God."

"That's right," said Hurv, "vacuum tubes. All our spacecraft operate on vacuum tubes. They take up a hell of a lot of space. And they burn out. Do you know how long it takes to find the goddamn tube when it burns out? Remember how people used to take bags of vacuum tubes from their television sets down to the drugstore to use the tube tester? Think of doing that with something the size of our mother ships. And we can't just zip off into space when we feel like it. We have to let a mother ship warm up first. You have to turn the key and let the thing warm up for a couple of minutes, *then* you can zip off into space. It's a goddamn pain in the neck."

"I don't understand," said Luis, stunned. "If your technology is so primitive, how did you come here? If we're so far ahead of you, we should have discovered your planet, not the other way around."

Hurv gave a gentle laugh. "Don't pat yourself on the back, Luis. Just because your electronics are better than ours, you aren't necessarily superior in any way. Look, imagine that you humans are a man in Los Angeles with a brand-new Trujillo and we are a nup in New York with a beat-up old Ford. The two fellows start driving toward St. Louis. Now, the guy in the Trujillo is doing a hundred and twenty on the interstates, and the guy in the Ford is putting along at fifty-five; but the human in the Trujillo stops in Vegas and puts all of his gas money down the hole of a blackjack table, and the determined little nup cruises along for days until at last he reaches his goal. It's all a matter of superior intellect and the will to succeed. Your people talk a lot about going to the stars, but you just keep putting your money into other projects, like war and popular music and international athletic events and resurrecting the fashions of previous decades. If you wanted to go into space, you would have."

"But we *do* want to go."

"Then we'll help you. We'll give you the secrets. And you can explain your electronics to our engineers, and together we'll build wonderful new mother ships that will open the universe to both humans and nuhp."

Luis let out his breath. "Sounds good to me," he said.

Everyone agreed that this looked better than hollyhocks. We all hoped that we could keep from kicking their collective asses long enough to collect on that promise.

When I was in college, my roommate in my sophomore year was a tall, skinny guy named Barry Rintz. Barry had wild, wavy black hair and a sharp face that looked like a handsome normal face that had been sat on and folded in the middle. He squinted a lot, not because he had any defect in his eyesight, but because he wanted to give the impression that he was constantly evaluating the world. This was true. Barry could tell you the actual and market values of any object you happened to come across.

We had a double date one football weekend with two girls from another college in the same city. Before the game, we met the girls and took them to the university's art museum, which was pretty large and owned an impressive collection. My date, a pretty Elementary Ed major named Brigid, and I wandered from gallery to gallery, remarking that our tastes in art were very similar. We both liked the Impressionists, and we both liked Surrealism. There were a couple of little Renoirs that we admired for almost half an hour, and then we made a lot of silly sophomore jokes about what was happening in the Magritte and Dali and de Chirico paintings.

Barry and his date, Dixie, ran across us by accident as all four of us passed through the sculpture gallery. "There's a terrific Seurat down there," Brigid told her girlfriend.

"Seurat," Barry said. There was a lot of amused disbelief in his voice.

"I like Seurat," said Dixie.

"Well, of course," said Barry, "there's nothing really *wrong* with Seurat."

"What do you mean by that?" asked Brigid.

"Do you know F. E. Church?" he asked.

"Who?" I said.

"Come here." He practically dragged us to a gallery of American paintings. F. E. Church was a remarkable American landscape painter (1826–1900) who achieved an astonishing and lovely luminance in his works. "Look at that light!" cried Barry. "Look at that space! Look at that air!"

Brigid glanced at Dixie. "Look at that air?" she whispered.

It was a fine painting and we all said so, but Barry was insistent. F. E. Church was the greatest artist in American history, and one of the best the world has ever known. "I'd put him right up there with Van Dyck and Canaletto."

"Canaletto?" said Dixie. "The one who did all those pictures of Venice?"

"Those skies!" murmured Barry ecstatically. He wore the expression of a satisfied voluptuary.

"Some people like paintings of puppies or naked women," I offered. "Barry likes light and air."

We left the museum and had lunch. Barry told us which things on the menu were worth ordering, and which things were an abomination. He made us all drink an obscure imported beer from Ecuador. To Barry, the world was divided up into masterpieces and abominations. It made life so much simpler for him, except that he never understood why his friends could never tell one from the other.

At the football game, Barry compared our school's quarterback to Y. A. Tittle. He compared the other team's punter to Ngoc Van Vinh. He compared the halftime show to the Ohio State band's Script Ohio formation. Before the end of the third quarter it was very obvious to me that Barry was going to have absolutely no luck at all with Dixie. Before the clock ran out in the fourth quarter, Brigid and I had made whispered plans to dump the other two as soon as possible and sneak away by ourselves. Dixie would probably find an excuse to ride the bus back to her dorm before suppertime. Barry, as usual, would spend the evening in our room, reading *The Making of the President 1996*.

On other occasions, and with little or no provocation, Barry would lecture me about subjects as diverse as American literature (the best poet was Edwin Arlington Robinson, the best novelist James T. Farrell), animals (the only correct pet was the golden retriever), clothing (in anything other than a navy blue jacket and gray slacks, a man was just asking for trouble), and even hobbies (Barry collected military decorations of czarist Imperial Russia; he wouldn't talk to me for days after I told him my father collected barbed wire).

Barry was a wealth of information. He was the campus arbiter of good taste. Everyone knew Barry was the man to ask.

But no one ever did. We all hated his guts. I moved out of our dorm room before the end of the fall semester. Shunned, lonely, and bitter, Barry Rintz wound up as a guidance counselor in a high school in Ames, Iowa. The job was absolutely perfect for him; few people are so lucky in finding a career.

If I didn't know better, I might have believed that Barry was the original advance spy for the nuhp.

When the nuhp had been on Earth for a full year, they gave us the gift of interstellar travel. It was surprisingly inexpensive. The nuhp explained their propulsion system, which was cheap and safe and adaptable to all sorts of other earthbound applications. The revelations opened up an entirely new area of scientific speculation. Then the nuhp taught us their navigational methods, and about the "shortcuts" they had discovered in space. People called them space-warps, although technically speaking the shortcuts had nothing to do with Einsteinian theory or curved space or anything like that. Not many humans understood what the nuhp were talking about, but that didn't make very much difference. The nuhp didn't understand the shortcuts either; they just used them. The matter was presented to us like a Thanksgiving turkey on a platter. We bypassed the whole business of cautious scientific experimentation and leaped right into commercial exploitation. Mitsubishi of La Paz and Martin Marietta used nuhp schematics to begin construction of three luxury passenger ships, each capable of transporting a thousand tourists anywhere in our galaxy. Although man had yet to set foot on the moons of Jupiter, certain selected travel agencies began booking passage for a grand tour of the dozen nearest inhabited worlds.

Yes, it seemed that space was teeming with life, humanoid life on planets circling half the G-type stars in the heavens. "We've been trying to communicate with extraterrestrial intelligence for decades," complained one Soviet scientist. "Why haven't they responded?"

A friendly nup merely shrugged. "Everybody's trying to communicate out there," he said. "Your messages are like Publishers Clearinghouse mail to them." At first that was a blow to our racial pride, but we got over it. As soon as we joined the interstellar community, they'd begin to take us more seriously. And the nuhp made that possible.

We were grateful to the nuhp, but that didn't make them any easier to live with. They were still insufferable. As my second term as president came to an end, Pleen began to advise me about my future career. "Don't write a book," he told me (after I had already written the first two hundred pages of A *President Remembers*). "If you want to be an elder statesman, fine; but keep a low profile and wait for the people to come to you."

"What am I supposed to do with my time then?" I asked.

"Choose a new career," Pleen said. "You're not all that old. Lots of people do it. Have you considered starting a mail-order business? You can operate it from your home. Or go back to school and take courses in some subject that's always interested you. Or become active in church or civic projects. Find a new hobby, raising hollyhocks or collecting military decorations."

"Pleen," I begged, "just leave me alone."

He seemed hurt. "Sure, if that's what you want." I regretted my harsh words.

All over the country, all over the world, everyone was having the same trouble with the nuhp. It seemed that so many of them had come to Earth, every human had his own personal nup to make endless personal suggestions. There hadn't been so much tension in the world since the 1992 Miss Universe contest, when the most votes went to No Award.

That's why it didn't surprise me very much when the first of our own mother ships returned from its twenty-eight-day voyage among the stars with only two hundred seventy-six of its one thousand passengers still aboard. The other seven hundred twenty-four had remained behind on one lush, exciting, exotic, friendly world or another. These planets had one thing in common: They were all populated by charming, warm, intelligent, humanlike people who had left their own home worlds after being discovered by the nuhp. Many races lived together in peace and harmony on these planets, in spacious cities newly built to house the fed-up expatriates. Perhaps these alien races had experienced the same internal jealousies and hatreds we human beings had known for so long, but no more. Coming together from many planets throughout our galaxy, these various peoples dwelt contentedly beside each other, united by a single common aversion: their dislike for the nuhp.

Within a year of the launching of our first interstellar ship, the population of Earth had declined by one half of one percent. Within two years, the population had fallen by almost fourteen million. The nuhp were too sincere and too eager and too sympathetic to fight with. That didn't make them any less tedious. Rather than make a scene, most people just up and left. There were plenty of really lovely worlds to visit, and it didn't cost very much, and the opportunities in space were unlimited. Many people who were frustrated and disappointed on Earth were able to build new and fulfilling lives for themselves on planets that we didn't even know existed until the nuhp arrived.

The nuhp knew this would happen. It had already happened dozens, hundreds of times in the past, wherever their mother ships touched down. They had made promises to us and they had kept them, although we couldn't have guessed just how things would turn out.

Our cities were no longer decaying warrens imprisoning the impoverished masses. The few people who remained behind could pick and choose among the best housing. Landlords were forced to reduce rents and keep properties in perfect repair just to attract tenants.

Hunger was ended when the ratio of consumers to food producers dropped drastically. Within ten years, the population of Earth was cut in half, and was still falling.

For the same reason, poverty began to disappear. There were plenty of jobs for everyone. When it became apparent that the nuhp weren't going to compete for those jobs, there were more opportunities than people to take advantage of them.

Discrimination and prejudice vanished almost overnight. Everyone cooperated to keep things running smoothly despite the large-scale emigration. The good life was available to everyone, and so resentments melted away. Then, too, whatever enmity people still felt could be focused solely on the nuhp; the nuhp didn't mind, either. They were oblivious to it all.

I am now mayor and postmaster of the small human community of New Dallas, here on Thir, the fourth planet of a star known in our old catalog as Struve 2398. The various alien races we encountered here call the star by another name, which translates into "God's Pineal." All the aliens here are extremely helpful and charitable, and there are few nuhp.

All through the galaxy, the nuhp are considered the messengers of peace. Their mission is to travel from planet to planet, bringing reconciliation, prosperity, and true civilization. There isn't an intelligent race in the galaxy that doesn't love the nuhp. We all recognize what they've done and what they've given us.

But if the nuhp started moving in down the block, we'd be packed and on our way somewhere else by morning.

Afterword to "The Aliens Who Knew, I Mean, *Everything*"

One of the problems I faced during the three years I edited the *Nebula Awards* anthology for Harcourt was that the editor is obligated to include the winners but the runners-up are a matter of choice. Which to include and which to leave out? Considerations of length and name recognition played, as always, unfair roles; but what if I didn't like any of the stories? Should I make my choice by ranking them in order of least liked?

When I read George Alec Effinger's story, "The Aliens Who Knew, I Mean, *Everything*," I knew at once that I would have no problem because I preferred it to the winner and to most of the other runners-up. Since George's tale was about "taste," I joked in the introduction to the anthology that "somewhere, perhaps, there are readers and judges with minds like lamps, where what is good is clearly demonstrable." These judges would *always* pick the best stories. "Maybe there's a story in that," I mused, "and one that would win all the prizes," I jested, suggesting that the perfect title would be, "The Aliens Who Came to Give Out Awards —Because They Could Be Objective."

But George's outrageous story had already hit home, by implication, and I was only elaborating. The story has been known to not only start arguments but also to end them. Humor is a weapon, and a healer. It gets you to admit truths before your preconceptions can kick in. "Little ambushes of reason," quipped George Bernard Shaw about humor. Ridicule has been known to bring down kings and presidents, which is why tyrants always lock up the comedians first. Effinger belongs to the great line of SF's satirical humorists, beginning with Aesop and Jonathan Swift, and continuing with William Tenn, Fredric Brown, Robert Sheckley, Frederik Pohl, and Kurt Vonnegut, and carried forward by more recent guerrillas James Morrow and Paul Di Filippo.

The invading aliens of Effinger's story, the nuhp (plural), have the irritating habit of telling the truth, even when they draw the wrong conclusion from it, as when they accurately describe President James Polk's legislative record (Effinger did his homework). "My way of joking is to tell the truth," wrote Shaw. "It's the funniest joke in the world."

The example of the nuhp's behavior also made plain to me my own problem as editor: "What *is* best? What does it mean? What can it *ever* mean?" The nuhp said they knew. Editing the *Nebula* anthology meant presenting a more complex and truthful view of the judgment of our own nuhp (the SFWA members who actually voted), who choose the best story, novelette, novella, and novel of the year. Well-armed by George's pointed narrative, I knew that any of the nominees was worthy to win (by definition of being a nominee), and that the "winner" was an artifact of the voting circumstances, an outcome possible during a finite piece of time, a mere technicality, since someone else might have won. You'd be surprised how this reasoning escapes people. I had the chance to make visible the sampling from which the "winner" emerged, by including runners-up and by publishing the entire list of nominees as "honorable mentions." George's story gave me the opening to emphasize the equality of contenders, and to soften the bending-of-the-knee ceremony visited on "worthy losers."

And people say that SF has nothing to do with the "real world."

So I put George's story in the book.

I was not going to be a nup (singular).

—George Zebrowski

Introduction to "All the Last Wars at Once"

In all the years I knew George, I never saw him lose his temper. If someone did him dirt—and people did, from time to time—his usual reaction was sorrow, or at worst mild annoyance, never anger or hatred.

I think he saved all the harsher emotions for this story.

On the surface of it, "All the Last Wars at Once" is a satire—but it's about as bitter a satire as you'll ever read. It builds in the usual Effinger fashion: It homes in on one conflict—white versus black—and just when you think that's what it's about, you realize that no, the title's got it right, this really *is* about all the last wars at once. It's black against white, but it's also gay against straight, and male against female, and Jew against Christian, and Protestant against Catholic, and if it were 10,000 words longer you can bet the farm that it would also be baseball fans against football fans, draw poker fans against stud poker fans, Marilyn Monroe fans against Jean Harlow fans, and Sondheim fans against Rodgers and Hammerstein fans.

Yes, it's a satire—or perhaps I should say, it's a satire *too*. But then we come to the final section of the story. The month is up. The wars are over. There are some survivors. Surely we've gotten it out of our system and learned our lesson. That ought to be the end of it.

And then we realize that this was all just a preamble, spring training, exhibition season, the first draft of the final war—and George pinpoints, as only George could, gently and without rancor, exactly what caused all the other wars and who the enemy in the final war must inevitably be.

It's not only a very effective story, but for the life of me I can't think of anyone else in the field who could have written it.

—Mike Resnick

+ + +

All the Last Wars at Once

We interrupt this p—
    —upt this program to—
    —terrupt our regularly scheduled programming to bring you this bulletin pieced together from the archives of the General Motors Corporation.

"Good afternoon. This is Bob Dunne, NBC News in New Haven, Connecticut. We're standing here in the lobby of the Hotel Taft in New Haven, where the first international racial war has just been declared. In just a few seconds, the two men responsible will be coming out of that elevator. (Can you hear me?)

"—elevator. Those of you in the western time zones are probably already—"

The elevator doors opened. Two men emerged, smiling and holding their hands above their heads in victorious, self-congratulatory boxers' handshakes. They were immediately mobbed by newsmen. One of the two men was exceptionally tall, and black as midnight in Nairobi. The other was short, fat, white, and very nervous. The black man was smiling broadly, the white man was smiling and wiping perspiration from his face with a large red handkerchief.

"—C News. The Negro has been identified as the representative of the people of color of all nations. He is, according to the printed flyer distributed scant minutes ago, Mary McLeod Bethune

Washington, of Washington, Georgia. The other man with him is identified as Robert Randall La Cygne, of La Cygne, Kansas, evidently the delegate of the Caucasian peoples. When, and by whom, this series of negotiations was called is not yet clear.

"At any rate, the two men, only yesterday sunk in the sticky obscurity of American life, have concluded some sort of bargaining that threatens to engulf the entire world in violent reaction. The actual content of that agreement is still open to specu—"

"—or at any later date."

A close-up on Washington, who was reading from a small black notebook.

"We have thus reached, and passed, that critical moment. This fact has been known and ignored by all men, on both sides of the color line, for nearly a generation. Henceforth, this situation is to be, at least, honest, if bloodier. Bob and I join in wishing you all the best of luck, and may God bless."

"Mr. Washington?"

"Does this necessarily mean—"

"—iated Press here, Mr. Washing—"

"Yes? You, with the hat."

"Yes, sir. Vincent Reynolds, UPI. Mr. Washington, are we to understand that this agreement has some validity? You are aware that we haven't seen any sort of credentials—"

Washington grinned. "Thank you. I'm glad you brought that up. Credentials? Just you wait a few minutes, and listen outside. Ain't no stoppin' when them rifles start poppin'!"

"Mr. Washington?"

"Yes?"

"Is this to be an all-out, permanent division of peoples?"

"All-out, yes. Permanent, no. Bob and I have decided on a sort of statute of limitations. You go out and get what you can for thirty days. At the end of the month, we'll see what and who's left."

"You can guarantee that there will be no continuation of hostilities at the end of the thirty days?"

"Why, sure! We're all growed up now, ain't we? Sure, why, you can trust *us!*"

"Then this is a war of racial eradication?"

"Not at all," said Bob La Cygne, who had remained silent behind Washington's broad seersucker back. "Not at all what I would call a war of eradication. 'Eradicate' is an ugly term. 'Expunge' is the word we arrived at, isn't it, Mary Beth?"

"I do believe it is, Bob."

Washington studied his notebook for a few seconds, ignoring the shouting newsmen around him. No attempt was made by the uniformed guards to stop the pushing and shoving, which had grown somewhat aggravated. Then he smiled brightly, turning to La Cygne. They clasped hands and waved to the flashing bulbs of the photographers.

"No more questions, boys. You'll figure it all out soon enough; that's enough for now." The two men turned and went back into the waiting elevator.

(Tock tockatock tocka tock tock) "And now, the Six O'Clock Report *(tocka tock tocka tocka)*, with *(tockatock)* Gil Monahan."

(Tocka tocka tock tock tocka)

"Good evening. The only story in the news tonight is the recently declared official hostilities between members of all non-Caucasian races and the white people of the world. Within minutes of the original announcement, open warfare broke out in nearly every multi-racially populated area in the United States and abroad. At this moment the entire globe is in turmoil; the scene everywhere flickers between bloody combat in the streets and peaceful lulls marked by looting and destruction of private property.

"What has happened, in effect, is a thirty-day suspension of all rational codes of conduct. The Army and National Guard are themselves paralyzed due to their own internal conflicts. A state of martial law has been declared by almost all governments, but, to our knowledge, nowhere has it been effectively enforced.

"There seems to be absolutely no cooperation between members of the opposite sides, on any level. Even those who most sympathized with the problems of the other are engaged in, using Mary McLeod Bethune Washington's terms, 'getting their own.' Interracial organizations, social groups, and even marriages are splintering against the color barrier.

"We have some reports now from neighboring states that may be of importance to our viewers concerning the conditions in these areas at the present time. A state of emergency has been declared for the following municipalities in New Jersey: Absecon, Adelphia, Allendale, Allenhurst, Allentown, Allenwood, Alloway, Alpha . . . Well, as my eye travels over this list of some eight or nine hundred towns I notice that only a few *aren't* listed, notably Convent Station and Peapack. You can pretty well assume that things are bad *all* over. That goes for the New York, Pennsylvania, and Connecticut regions as well.

"We have some footage that was shot in Newark about ten

minutes after the New Haven declaration. It's pretty tense out there now. The expert analysts in the news media are astounded that the intense polarization and outbreaks of rioting occurred so quickly. Let's take a look at those films now.

"Apparently there's some diffi—

"I don't know, what can . . . experiencing ourselves some of this interference with . . . refusal to even . . .

"—rifying. They're running around out there like maniacs, shooting and—

"—flames and the smoke is—you can see the clouds against the sky, between the buildings like waves of—"

It was a pink, photocopied factsheet. Frowning, he stuffed it into his pocket. "Factsheet," eh? It had been several days since Stevie had heard a fact that he could trust.

Nobody was saying *anything* worth listening to. The factsheets had begun the second day with the expected clutter of charges and accusations, but soon everyone realized that this wasn't going to be that kind of war. Nobody gave a good goddamn *what* happened to anyone else. On the third day the few angry allegations that were made were answered with "our own sources do not indicate that, in fact, any such incident actually occurred" or with a curt "T.S., baby!" or, finally, no reply at all. Now the factsheets just bragged, or warned, or threatened.

Stevie was hitchhiking, which was a dangerous thing to do, but no more dangerous than sitting in an apartment waiting for the blazing torches. He felt that if he were going to be a target, a moving target offered the better odds.

He carried a pistol and a rifle that he had liberated from Abercrombie & Fitch. The hot morning sun gleamed on the zippers and studs of his black leathers. He stood by the side of the parkway, smiling grimly to himself as he waited for a ride. Every car that came around the curve was a challenge, one that he was more than willing to accept. There wasn't much traffic lately, and for that Stevie was sorry. He was really getting to dig this.

A car approached, a late model black Imperial with its headlights burning. He set himself, ready to dodge into the ditch on the side of the road. Stevie stared through the windshield as the car came nearer. He let out his breath suddenly: it was a white chick. It looked like she had liberated the car; maybe she was looking for someone to team up with. Even if she was a dog, it would beat hitching.

The Imperial passed him, slowed, and stopped on the road's shoulder. The chick slid over on the seat, rolling down the window on the passenger's side and shouting to him.

"Hurry up, you idiot. I don't want to sit here much longer."

He ran to the car, pulling open the door to get in. She slammed it shut again, and Stevie stood there confused.

"What the hell—"

"Shut up," she snapped, handing him another pink factsheet. "Read this. And hurry it up."

He read the factsheet. His throat went dry and he began to feel a buzz in his head. At the top of the page was the familiar fisted Women's Lib symbol. In regulation incendiary rhetoric below it, a few paragraphs explained that it had been decided by the uppermost echelon to strike now for freedom. During this period of severe disorientation, women the world over were taking the opportunity to beat down the revisionist male supremist pigs. Not just the oppressed racial minorities can express their militancy, it said. The female popular liberation front knew no color boundaries. Who did they think they were kidding? Stevie thought.

"You're gonna get plugged by some black bitch, you know that?" he said. He looked up at her. She had a gun pointed at him, aimed at his chest. The buzz in his head grew louder.

"You wanna put that sheet back on the pile? We don't have enough to go around," she said.

"Look," said Stevie, starting to move toward the car. The girl raised the pistol in a warning. He dove to the ground, parallel to the car, and rolled up against the right front wheel. The girl panicked, opening the door to shoot him before he could get away. Stevie fired twice before she sighted him, and she fell to the grassy shoulder. He didn't check to see if she was dead or merely wounded; he took her pistol and got in the car.

"My fellow Americans." The voice of the president was strained and tired, but he still managed his famous promiseless smile. The picture of the Chief Executive was the first to disturb the televisions' colored confetti snow for nearly two weeks.

"We are met tonight to discuss the intolerable situation in which our nation finds itself. With me this evening—" the president indicated an elderly, well-dressed Negro gentleman seated at a desk to the left of the president "—I have invited the Reverend Dr. Roosevelt Wilson, who will speak to you from his own conscience. Reverend Wilson is known to many of you as an honest man, a community leader, and a voice of collaboration in these times of mistrust and fiscal insecurity."

Across the nation, men in dark turtlenecks ran down searing channels of flame, liberated television sets in their gentle grasp, running so that they might see this special telecast. Across the nation men and women of all persuasions looked at Wilson and muttered, "Well, isn't he the clean old nigger!"

Reverend Wilson spoke, his voice urgent and slow with emotion. "We must do everything that our leaders tell us. We cannot take the law into our own hands. We must listen to the promptings of reason and calmth, and find that equitable solution that I'm sure we all desire."

The TV broadcast had been a major accomplishment. Its organization had been a tribute to the cooperation of many dissatisfied men who would rather have been out liberating lawn furniture. But the message of these two paternal figures of authority was more important.

"Thank you, Dr. Wilson," said the president. He stood, smiling into the camera, and walked to a large map that had been set up to his right. He took a pointer in one hand.

"This," he said, "is our beleaguered nation. Each green dot represents a community where the violence that plagues us has gone beyond containable limits." The map was nearly solid green, the first time the USA had been in that condition since the early seventeenth century. "I have asked for assistance from the armed forces of Canada, Mexico, and Great Britain, but although I mailed the requests nearly two weeks ago I have yet to receive a reply. I can only assume that we are on our own.

"Therefore, I will make one statement concerning official government policy. As you know, this state of affairs will technically come to an end in about fifteen days. At that time, the government will prosecute *severely* anyone connected with any further disruptions of Federal activities. This is not merely an empty threat; it con—"

A young black man ran before the camera, turning to shout an incoherent slogan. Reverend Wilson saw the pistol in the boy's hand and stood, his face contorted with fear and envy. "The business of America *is* business!" he screamed, and then dropped back into his seat as the black militant shot. The president clutched his chest and cried, "We *must* not . . . lose . . ." and fell to the floor.

The cameras seemed to swing at random, as men rushed about confusedly. From somewhere a white man appeared, perhaps one of the technicians, with his own pistol. He hurried to the desk shouting, "For anarchy!" and shot Dr. Wilson point-blank. The white assassin turned, and the black assassin fired at him. The two killers began a cautious but noisy gun battle in the studio. Here most viewers turned off their sets. In very poor taste, they thought.

The sign outside: SECOND NATIONAL BANK OF OUR LORD, THE ENGINEER. UNIVERSAL CHURCH OF GOD OR SOME SORT OF COSMIC EMBODIMENT OF GOOD.

Above the entrance to the church fluttered a hastily made banner. The masculine symbol had been crudely painted on a white sheet; the white flag indicated that the worshippers were white males and that blacks and women were "welcome" at their own risk. The population was now split into four mutually antagonistic segments. The separate groups began to realize that there was some point in keeping their members together in little cadres. The streets and apartment buildings were death traps.

Inside the church the men were silent in prayer. They were led by an elderly deacon, whose inexperience and confusion were no greater or less than any in the congregation.

"Merciful God," he prayed, "in whatever Form the various members of our flock picture You, corporal Entity or insubstantial Spirit, we ask that You guide us in this time of direst peril.

"Brother lifts sword against brother, and brother against sister. Husband and wife are torn asunder against Your holiest ordainments. Protect us, and show us our proper response. Perhaps it is true that vengeance is solely Yours; but speak to us, then, concerning Limited Cautionary Retaliation, and other alternatives. We would see a sign, for truly we are lost in the mires of day-to-day living."

The deacon continued his prayer, but soon there began a series of poundings on the door. The deacon stopped for just a second, looking up nervously, his hand straying to his sidearm. When nothing further happened he finished the prayer and the members of the congregation added, if they chose, their amens.

At the end of the service the men rose to leave. They stood at the door, in no hurry to abandon the sanctuary of the church. At last the deacon led them out. It was immediately noticed that a yellow factsheet had been nailed to the outside of the door. The Roman Catholics of the neighborhood had decided to end the centuries-long schism. Why not now, when everybody else was settling their differences? A Final Solution.

A bullet split wood from the door frame. The men standing on the stoop jumped back inside. A voice called from the street, "You damn commie atheist Protestants! We're gonna wipe you out and send your lousy heretic souls straight to Hell!" More gunfire. The stained-glass windows of the church shattered, and there were cries from inside.

"They got one of the elders!"

"It's those crummy Catholics. We should have got them when we had the chance. Damn it, now they got us holed up in here."

The next day a blue factsheet was circulated by the Jewish community explaining that they had finally gotten tired of having their gabardine spat on, and that everybody'd just have to watch out. Around the world the remaining clusters of people fractured again, on the basis of creed.

It was getting so you didn't know *who* you could trust.

Stevie was heading back toward the city when the car died. It made a few preliminary noises, shaking and rattling slower, and then it stopped. For all he knew it might simply have been out of gas. There were eight days left in the prescribed thirty, and he needed a ride.

He took the rifle and the two pistols from the Imperial and stood by the side of the road. It was a lot more dangerous to hitch now than it had been before, for the simple reason that the odds were that anyone who happened by would probably be on the other side of *one* of the many ideological fences. He was still confident, though, that he would be safely picked up, or be able to wrest a car away from its owner.

There was very little traffic. Several times Stevie had to jump for cover as a hostile driver sped by him, shooting wildly from behind the wheel. At last an old Chevy stopped for him, driven by a heavy white man whom Stevie judged to be in his late fifties.

"Come on, get in," said the man.

Stevie climbed into the car, grunting his thanks and settling warily back against the seat.

"Where you going?" asked the man.

"New York."

"Um. You, uh, you a Christian?"

"Hey," said Stevie, "right now we ain't got any troubles at all. We can just drive until we get where we're going. We only have eight days, right? So if we leave off the questions, eight days from now *both* of us'll be happy."

"All right. That's a good point, I guess, but it defeats the whole purpose. I mean, it doesn't seem to enter into the spirit of things."

"Yeah, well, the spirit's getting a little tired."

They rode in silence, taking turns with the driving. Stevie noticed that the old man kept staring at the rifle and two pistols. Stevie searched the car as best he could with his eyes, and it looked to him as though the old man was unarmed himself. Stevie didn't say anything.

"You seen a factsheet lately?" asked the man.

"No," said Stevie. "Haven't seen one in days. I got tired of the whole thing. *Now* who's at it?"

The old man looked at him quickly, then turned back to the road. "Nobody. Nothing new." Stevie glanced at the man now, studying his face curiously. Nothing new.

After a while the man asked him for some bullets.

"I didn't think that you had a gun," said Stevie.

"Yeah. I got a .38 in the glove compartment. I keep it there, well, I'm less likely to use it."

"A .38? Well, these shells wouldn't do you any good anyhow. Besides, I don't really want to give them up yet."

The man looked at him again. He licked his lips, appearing to make some decision. He took his eyes off the road for a moment and lunged across the seat in a dive for one of the loaded pistols. Stevie slammed the edge of his hand into the older man's throat. The man choked and collapsed on the seat. Stevie switched off the engine and steered the car to the side of the road, where he opened the door and dumped the still body.

Before he started the car again, Stevie opened the glove compartment. There was an unloaded revolver and a crumpled factsheet. Stevie tossed the gun to the ground by the old man. He smoothed out the wrinkled paper. The youth of the world, it proclaimed, had declared war on everyone over the age of thirty years.

"How you coming with that factsheet?"

The thin man in the green work shirt stopped typing and looked up. "I don't know. It's hard making out your crummy hand-writing. Maybe another fifteen minutes. Are they getting restless out there?"

The man in the jacket gulped down some of his lukewarm coffee. "Yeah. I was going to make an announcement, but what the hell. Let 'em wait. They had their vote, they know what's coming.

Just finish that factsheet. I want to get it printed and put up before them goddamn Artists beat us to it."

"Look, Larry, them queers'll never think of it in the first place. Calm down."

The man in the work shirt typed in silence for a while. Larry walked around the cold meeting hall, pushing chairs back in place and chewing his cigar nervously. When the factsheet was finished, the man in the work shirt pulled it off the printer and handed it to Larry. "All right," he said, "there it is. Maybe you better go read it to them first. They been waiting out there for a couple of hours now."

"Yeah, I guess so," said Larry. He zipped up his green jacket and waited for the man in the work shirt to get his coat. He turned off the lights and locked the door to the hall. Outside was a huge crowd of men, all white and all well into middle age. They cheered when Larry and the other man came out. Larry held up his hands for quiet.

"All right, listen up," he said. "We got our factsheet here. Before we go and have it printed, I'm going to let you hear it. It says just like what we voted for, so you all should be pretty satisfied."

He read the factsheet, stopping every now and then to wait through the applause and cheers of the men. He looked out at the crowd. They're all brawny veteran-types, he thought. That's what we are: we're Veterans. We been through it all. We're the ones who know what's going on. We're the Producers.

The factsheet explained, in simple language unlike the bitter diatribes of other groups, that the laborers—the Producers—of the world had gotten fed up with doing all the work while a large portion of the population—the goddamn queer Artists—did nothing but eat up all the fruits of honest nine-to-five work. Artists contributed nothing, and wasted large amounts of our precious resources. It was simple logic to see that the food, clothing, shelter, money, and recreational facilities that were diverted from the Producers' use was as good as thrown into the garbage. The Producers worked harder and harder, and got back less and less. Well then, what could you expect to happen? Everything was bound to get worse for everybody.

The men cheered. It was about time that they got rid of the parasites. No one complained when you burned off a leech. And no one could complain when you snuffed out the leechlike elements of normal, organized, Productive society.

Larry finished reading the sheet and asked for questions and comments. Several men started talking, but Larry ignored them and went on speaking himself.

"Now, this doesn't mean," he said, "that we gotta get everybody that doesn't work regular hours like we do. You see that some of the people are hard to tell whether they're Producers like us, or just lousy addict Artists. Like the people that make TV. We can use them. But we have to be careful, because there's a lot of Artists around who are trying to make us think that they're really Producers. Just remember: if you can use it, it's not Art."

The crowd cheered again, and then it began to break up. Some of the men stood around arguing. One of the small groups of Producers that was slowly walking to the parking lot was deeply involved in debating the boundaries separating Artists and Producers.

"I mean, where are we going to stop?" said one. "I don't like the way this divisioning is going. Pretty soon there won't be any groups left to belong to. We'll all be locked up in our homes, afraid to see anybody at all."

"It's not doing us any good," agreed another. "If you go out and get what you want, I mean, take something from a store or something, why, everybody knows you got it when you bring it home. Then *you're* the target. I got less now than when this all started."

A third man watched the first two grimly. He pulled out a factsheet of his own from the pocket of his jacket. "That's commie talk," he said. "You're missing the point of the whole thing. Let me ask you a question. Are you right- or left-handed?"

The first man looked up from the factsheet, puzzled. "I don't see that it makes any difference. I mean, I'm basically left-handed, but I write with my right hand."

The third man stared angrily, in disbelief.

Bang.

YANG and YIN: Male and female. Hot and cold. Mass and energy. Smooth and crunchy. Odd and even. Sun and moon. Silence and noise. Space and time. Slave and master. Fast and slow. Large and small. Land and sea. Good and evil. On and off. Black and white. Strong and weak. Regular and filter king. Young and old. Light and shade. Fire and ice. Sickness and health. Hard and soft. Life and death.

If there *is* a plot, shouldn't you know about it?

One more hour.

Millions of people hid in their holes, waiting out the last minutes of the wars. Hardly anyone was out on the streets yet. No one shouted their drunken celebrations that little bit ahead of schedule. In the night darkness Stevie could still hear the ragged crackings of guns in the distance. Some suckers getting it only an hour from home free.

The time passed. Warily, people came out into the fresher air, still hiding themselves in shadows, not yet used to walking in the open. Guns of the enthusiasts popped; they would never get a chance like this again, and there were only fifteen minutes left. Forty-second Street chromium knives found their lodgings in unprotected Gotham throats and shoulders.

Times Square was still empty when Stevie arrived. Decomposing corpses sprawled in front of the record and porno shops. A few shadowy forms moved across the streets, far away down the sidewalk.

The big ball was poised. Stevie watched it, bored, with murderers cringing around him. The huge lighted New Year's globe was ready to drop, waiting only for midnight and for the kissing New Year's VJ-Day crowds. There was Stevie, who didn't care, and the looters, disappointed in the smoked-out, gunfire-black, looted stores.

It said it right up there: 11:55. Five more minutes. Stevie pushed himself back into a doorway, knowing that it would be humiliating to get it with only five minutes left. From the vague screams around him he knew that some were still finding it.

People were running by now. The square was filling up. 11:58 and the ball was *just* hanging there: the sudden well of people drew rapid rifle-fire, but the crowd still grew. There was the beginning of a murmur, just the hint of the war-is-over madness. Stevie sent himself into the stream, giving himself up to the release and relief.

11:59 . . . The ball seemed . . . to tip . . . and *fell!* 12:00! The chant grew stronger, the New York chant, the smugness returned in all its sordid might. "We're Number One! We're Number One!" The cold breezes drove the shouting through the unlit streets, carrying it on top of the burnt and fecal smells. It would be a long time before what was left would be made livable, but We're Number One! There were still sporadic shots, but these were the usual New York Town killers, doing the undeclared and time-honored violence that goes unnoticed.

We're Number One!

Stevie found himself screaming in spite of himself. He was standing next to a tall, sweating black. Stevie grinned; the black grinned. Stevie stuck out his hand. "Shake!" he said. "We're Number One!"

"We're Number One!" said the black. "I mean, it's *us*! We gotta settle all this down, but, I mean, what's left is *ours*! No more fighting!"

Stevie looked at him, realizing for the first time the meaning of their situation. "Right you are," he said with a catch in his voice. "Right you are, Brother."

"Excuse me."

Stevie and the black turned to see a strangely dressed woman. The costume completely hid any clue to the person's identity, but the voice was very definitely feminine. The woman wore a long, loose robe decorated fancifully with flowers and butterflies. Artificial gems had been stuck on, and the whole thing trimmed with cheap, dime store gold-and-silver piping. The woman's head was entirely hidden by a large, bowl-shaped woven helmet, and from within it her voice echoed excitedly.

"Excuse me," she said. "Now that the preliminary skirmishes are over, don't you think we should get on with it?"

"With what?" asked the black.

"The Last War, the final one. The war against ourselves. It's senseless to keep avoiding it now."

"What do you mean?" asked Stevie.

The woman touched Stevie's chest. "There. Your guilt. Your frustration. You don't really feel any better, do you? I mean, women don't really hate men; they hate their own weaknesses. People don't really hate other people for their religion or race. It's just that seeing someone different than you makes you feel a little insecure in your own belief. What you hate is your own doubt, and you project that hatred onto the other man."

"She's right!" said the black. "You know, I wouldn't mind it half so much if they'd hate me because of *me*; but nobody ever took the trouble."

"That's what's so frustrating," she said. "If anyone's ever going to hate the *real* you, you know who it'll have to be."

"You're from that Kindness Cult, aren't you?" the black said softly.

"*Shinsetsu*," she said. "Yes."

"You want us to meditate or something?" asked Stevie. The woman dug into a large basket that she carried on her arm. She handed each of them a plump cellophane package filled with a colorless fluid.

"No," said the black as he took his package. "Kerosene."

Stevie held his bag of kerosene uncertainly, and looked around the square. There were others dressed in the *Shinsetsu* manner, and they were all talking to groups that had formed around them.

"Declare war on myself?" Stevie said doubtfully. "Do I have to publish a factsheet first?" No one answered him. People nearby were moving closer so they could hear the *Shinsetsu* woman. She continued to hand out the packages as she spoke.

Stevie slipped away, trying to get crosstown, out of the congested square. When he reached a side street he looked back: already the crowd was dotted with scores of little fires, like scattered piles of burning leaves in the backyards of his childhood.

Introduction to "Two Sadnesses"

If you haven't previously read "Two Sadnesses," please go do so now; I'm going to tell you things about it you don't *want* to know before you read it. Go ahead, I'll wait . . .

* * *

Back already? I can tell it stunned you, just like it did me the first time I read it, because your eyes are still bugged out, just like mine were . . .

Let's get this out of the way right off the bat: "Two Sadnesses" is a *masterpiece*. There is no other word for it. There are so many astounding things about this story, but the most unbelievable one is that it came so early in George's career.

This was written for Thomas M. Disch's *Bad Moon Rising*, if I remember correctly, all original stories, the subtitle being *An Anthology of Political Foreboding*. The book came out in 1973, which means George wrote this tale in late 1972 when he was twenty-six.

Chronological age doesn't count much, as these things go—what counts is that it was written less than two years into his career. George's published stories only began appearing in 1971, after he'd gone to the Clarion SF&F Writers' Workshop in the summer of 1970.

Two years on in their writing, most authors are just finding which end their ass is on; they don't know what you can and can't do, or how to do it, or much else for that matter, if I may bring myself into this discussion. . . .

As in the much later O. Niemand stories (which see), Effinger has caught—precisely, exactly, and yet without slavish imitation—the feel, mood, tone, and spirit of his models. At the same time, he's provided an early '70s objective correlative of concerns from a half-century or more before . . .

* * *

A short pertinent digression: Most of what we think of as great classic children's literature were written in the decade and a half before the outbreak of World War I. Beatrix Potter with Peter Rabbit et al., J. M. Barrie with *Peter Pan*, E. Nesbitt's Bastable Children books, the American L. Frank Baum's *The Wonderful Wizard of Oz*.

It was as if the authors felt the Great Change coming in some form or shape. What it was, they didn't know, but they felt things would never be the same again, and wanted to get it all down, before it was all gone.

The most English, and the best of all of these, was Kenneth Grahame's *The Wind in the Willows* (1908). In this book you see the world changing from rural to urban, from the handcrafted to the mass-produced, right before your eyes.

Contrast Rat, Badger, Mole—old rural English sporting types to the end—"messing about in boats," simple pleasures, friendships, and joys—with the novelty-seeking, up-to-the-Edwardian-minute Toad of Toad Hall—all mad for caravans, motor cars, aeroplanes, for speed and sensation.

Similarly, no book shows the reaction to the horrors of WWI and this Big Change than A. A. Milne's *Winnie-the-Pooh* (1926). It's almost like a chapter of Robert Graves's *The Long Weekend*, Britain between the two wars in capsule form; a fever dream of Warren Gamaliel Harding's "normalcy" and isolationism. It's about self-concern, obsession with the quotidian, rounds of visits to friends, small backyard adventures, conundrums, and Getting Snacks. A more insular book was never written. (To the characters, the presumed invasion of the Heffalumps and Woozles must have been like listening to Orson Welles's broadcast of *War of the Worlds*.)

Back to "Two Sadnesses":

You begin to see what George did here, and how staggeringly well he did it all. Not just the tone and feel —although those would have taxed any writer, no matter how good. Just the word choices—exactly the right word, just where it belongs. Without aping the style of Milne or Grahame, he has put the characters within a further adventure of the kinds they've always had.

What happens at the beginning of the two parts is like any other day (or the end of a very long one) in the lives of the subjects. What happens to them then is exactly like what would happen to them if their original authors had been afforded glimpses fifty or sixty years into the future. . . .

Effinger, in other words, took the premonitions of Grahame, and the bleak look-back of Milne, and he applied them to the forebodings and terrors of our early 1970s. Only George could have taken the subject, style, and viewpoint of two past children's classics, and through them brought our future dreads right home to us.

What could have been two joke-conceits ("the Vietnam War comes to the Three-Acre Wood; pollution and urban sprawl get the River Bank") instead became something else entirely—a double-view masterpiece: the visions of the Past telling the Present what the Terrible World of the Future would be like If This Goes On.

He did it, finally and for all time, beautifully, and, yes, sadly, using *other people's voices.*

This, to me, is the best thing he ever wrote.

And he wrote it only two years on, in his thirty-something-year career, the great shining bastard.

—Howard Waldrop

Two Sadnesses

I

IT WAS ONE OF THOSE WARM SUMMERY AFTER-
noons where you *know* that Something Grand is going to
happen, but the only problem is whether you ought to go out to
meet it or not, or wait around your house to be pleasantly surprised.
Waiting around the house has its points, for you can always say,
"Yes, well, perhaps it would be better, *if* Something Grand is to
happen, and *if* Something Grand is to happen *today*, to *me, here,*
it may be better to have A Bit Of A Snack just in case. In case
Something Grand *does* happen, so that I won't be left All At
Sea, as it were."

But going out to look for S. G. has just as many good points.
Because then you could take A Bit Of A Snack along with you
on the search, and you always stood the chance of running into Rabbit or Piglet on the way. It certainly was better to have Something
Grand happen with Piglet watching, than to have it alone in your
house, as Grand as that may be to tell about afterward. And this is
what decided the case. Bear made himself a honey and honey sandwich and set out carelessly, purely by chance in the direction of
Piglet's house.

It was one of those summery afternoons out-of-doors, also. Bear walked along through the Forest happily, not actually laughing-happy but sort of smiling and humming as if he didn't know *for sure* about that Something. The tall trees of the Forest waved in the wind, as if they didn't know *for sure*, either, and Bear took that as a Good Sign and felt even Grander. He walked for a while, and after a time to his surprise he found himself in front of Piglet's house.

"Ho," thought Bear, "why here I am at Piglet's, and my sandwich seems to have been left behind. Perhaps Piglet may have found it somewhere, or one like it, and we can discuss *that*, of course, and who knows but that Something might happen?"

Piglet lived in the middle of the Forest in a large beech tree. The front door to the house had neither bell-cord nor knocker, as did some of the other more elegant houses in the Forest. Piglet was always surprised and delighted whenever someone came to visit *him*, but first he stood in the middle of his large room and quivered, not exactly knowing what to expect. He was not the bravest animal in the Forest, and a simple knock on the door was enough to set him quivering, until he actually answered the call and discovered one of his very good friends. Thus it was that Bear generally called to him first, before knocking. "Piglet?" he would cry. "It's just me, Bear, your friend. I'm going to knock on your door so that you'll know that I've come to visit."

Then he would knock, and Piglet would quiver anyway. When at last he opened the door to his house he would say, "Bear! Come in! You gave me quite a start." And Bear would come in.

This morning, though, Bear stopped before he shouted to Piglet in the beech tree. His mouth opened but he didn't say anything, and his brown paw stopped in the air, because over his head in the sky he saw Something. It looked like a flock of little silver birds, or a swarm of big silver bees. Bear frowned to himself, because he could remember some other interesting times that he had had with bees. These silver bees were flying by very fast, and they buzzed so loudly that when he called out to Piglet, Bear couldn't hear his own voice.

Very soon the noise from the silver bees faded away, and Bear knocked on Piglet's door. The door didn't open; instead, Bear heard Piglet's voice from inside. "Oh, Bear!" he squealed. "It's you! Come in!" Bear opened the door to Piglet's house and went in. He couldn't see Piglet anywhere, but he did see a very suspicious quivering beneath a rug on the floor.

"I suppose you heard the buzzing of those silver bees," said Bear, as Piglet appeared from under the rug.

"Why yes," said Piglet, his ears still pink. "I think I heard it when I was . . . I was . . . I was looking for something that I might have lost underneath this rug." He was *still* quivering.

"I see," said Bear.

"Silver bees, you say?" said Piglet.

Bear rubbed his nose, unsure that the Something Grand could be anywhere in Piglet's room, because the room looked exactly the way it had always looked. "Yes," he said.

"They must have been awfully big bees to make such a noise."

"Yes, I suppose." Bear was beginning to think of suggesting a trip to see Owl, whom they hadn't visited since yesterday.

"I wonder what sort of hive they live in. It must be bigger than any that we've *ever* seen in the Forest," said Piglet as he patted the rug flat, taking out all the Piglet-shaped folds.

Now Bear is not known among his friends, who all love him dearly nevertheless, for having the sharpest wits in the Forest. Indeed, he is the one to whom even the simplest Plans of Operation must be explained, and usually more than once. But Bear knew bees, and he knew beehives, being a bear. And so he thought that the silver bees should, indeed, have a great big hive. And, the idea trickled through, a great big hive must have a great deal of HONEY. Now it was plain to see that a Great Deal of Honey would be Something Grand on any occasion. Bear was very proud to have solved the mystery ever so quickly, and even before anyone else knew that there *was* a mystery, completely by himself (although Piglet had maybe helped just the least bit). The only thing that remained was to get the honey out of the hive, which was always a problem that needed a Careful Scheme.

"Let us go see Owl," announced Bear after this bit of thinking. It had made him quite tired and unable to come up with a Careful Scheme, too. "Perhaps you have some provisions about, and then we could be all set in case Something Grand happens *before* we get to Owl's, so that we should be able to tell him all about it. And then, if Something Grand *doesn't* happen, we shouldn't be too disappointed."

"Is Something Grand to happen today?" asked Piglet, who really hadn't had the same feeling that morning, and certainly not after the buzzing of the silver bees had shaken up his house.

"Well, one never knows that it will, for sure," said Bear, looking for a moment as if he really did have a prodigious brain in there after all, "but, again, one never knows that it won't, either, on the other hand. In either case, a Bit of Lunch is the safest way." And then he looked like the same dear old Bear.

So Bear and Piglet set out for Owl's house. Bear was thinking that he would like that Something Grand to happen *before* they reached Owl's, because, with Piglet, he already had to give half away, and should Owl join in the venture, the Something must be further divided. Not, he hastily interrupted himself, that he was so selfish that he didn't want his friends to enjoy his Good Fortune, but rather that the more people who were in on the adventure originally, the less of an appreciative audience he could expect afterward, just in the event that some celebrative poem might suggest itself to him.

The sun lit the beeches and firs of the Forest perfectly, just the way Bear had been taught that the sun ought to on such a summery day. The clouds were small and quick, and were having their own Important Business in the very blue sky. The familiar path unfolded like an old and especially favorite story.

And then the bees returned. Some flew overhead so high that the sun made tiny bright stars of them, and some flew by closer, so that they screeched louder than anything Bear or Piglet had ever heard. Piglet quivered, and held tight to Bear, who realized that he would have to Be Stout for them both but didn't want to. The bees seemed to spit at them as they flew past, and the ground jumped up in straight little rows, like spouting teakettles going *thitt! thitt! thitt! thitt! thitt!* around them. Sometimes the rows of flying dirt and grass would lead to a tree, and then instead of a *thitt!* there would be a *thokk!* and a piece of the tree would fly off over their heads.

Just before they got to Owl's house they found Owl, lying on the ground as if he had fallen asleep before reaching his bed. He thrashed as though he were having bad dreams, flapping his ruffled wings against the ground. He wouldn't talk except in very small, un-Owl-like noises, and Bear and Piglet decided that he may have been hit by one of the *thitts* or maybe a *thokk.* The best thing seemed to be to carry him home and put him to bed. Bear said that they might be able to fix him up A Bit Of A Snack, which looked like a good idea all 'round.

When they got to Owl's house they put him to bed, and he rested there very quietly, without any of his usual pronouncements. Bear and Piglet found this very strange. Bear explained that it was a day for Something Grand, and not at all a day for Being Still And Mysterious. Unless, Bear thought to himself, unless you were part of some large and secret Something Grand that you didn't want to tell anyone (like Bear) about yet. Bear smiled to himself proudly for figuring out Owl's secret. Two puzzles solved already, before lunchtime! In any event, Owl said nothing and did not seem to move in his bed.

After a time, during which Piglet had fixed them a small and rather incomplete sort of Snack, the bees came back again. Bear and Piglet watched them from Owl's window. The bees did not fly so high as before, and looked larger even than any birds that they had ever seen. The bees roared as they flew, and Bear and Piglet were frightened even though they were in old Owl's home right in the middle of their own Forest. Silver eggs dropped from the bees, and when they fell to the ground they burst into huge, boiling, orange and black clouds of flame. Bear watched silently; Piglet was suddenly nowhere to be found. With every flash of fire there was a horrible thunder that shook the tree that was Owl's home.

After a time the bees went away. Bear stood by the window, watching the flaming trees shrivel and fall. There was a knock on Owl's door, and a voice called out hoarsely. Bear recognized it as belonging to the gray Donkey. He opened the door for Donkey, and felt a flash of heat from the raging fires outside.

"Hullo, Bear."

"Hullo, Donkey."

"Looks like a busy morning. We're always having Busy Mornings whenever I specially decide to have a little nap. But I don't suppose a nap is very important if everyone else decides to have a Busy Morning." He indicated the burning Forest with a flick of his floppy ears. "Is that your idea? If it is, it certainly busied up the morning. It looks like it will use up most of the afternoon as well. Not that I mind, you understand, I can see how you might forget to notify me; but I would like to schedule that nap *sometime*."

"No, Donkey, I don't think that is my idea," said Bear, feeling just a little guilty because he knew that he did have that Something Grand feeling. But he wasn't at all sure that this was the sort of Grand Something that he was looking forward to.

"I was standing around in my little part of the bracken," said Donkey, "you know how my little part is more or less marshy and wet and cold and altogether unpleasant. Not that I'm complaining, you see, but *someone* has to live there, I suppose, while the rest of you live out here in the really comfortable places. And I don't really mind. But, as I was saying, there I was, eating my thistles (which are hardly delicious, but that *is* all that I have, and I'm not one to complain), when this group of men came running through, splashing around in my stream, turning my little yard into a perfect swamp, if you like swamps, which I don't particularly, especially in my own living room. And I tried to be civil, as much as I can be to men, but do they listen? Why, they do not. They point their machines and start making a horrible racket, and my little spot of home is torn to pieces. Now, it's not the most attractive spot in the Forest, I'll be the first to admit that, but it *is* home to me, and I was pretty upset when they started knocking it all to bits. But they looked like they were having such a good time running around and shouting and pointing their fingers and wrecking away that I decided that I would just come over here and sit awhile." And Donkey did sit, flopping in a corner of Owl's parlor with a sullen expression, and he didn't say another word.

After a time there was a series of *whumps!* After each *whump!* there would be a terrible clap of thunder and a large part of the Forest would disappear in a black cloud, leaving only a smoking hole. Bear watched this silently, his hands clasped behind his back, until the *whumps!* went away, too. Then the men that Donkey had seen arrived, running around in front of Owl's house and shouting. Some of them had metal tanks strapped on their backs, and these men began to spray more fire from long hoses attached to the tanks. Soon all the gorse and brush in this part of the wood was afire, and the larger trees were beginning to catch, too. Bear thought for a moment about his other friends in the other parts of the Forest.

"Did you see Rabbit on your way here?" he asked Donkey.

"Yes," said Donkey.

"Oh. Perhaps he will come here, too."

"You know that I am hardly an expert in these matters," said Donkey, "but I am of the opinion that Rabbit will not be coming."

"Oh," said Bear. The men outside were rapidly chopping away at whatever of the standing saplings and trees remained. "Perhaps Christ—"

The guns of the men drowned out Bear's voice. He stood by the window and watched; Donkey sat in his corner. Piglet was still off Somewhere, doing Something. During a sudden lull in the noise Bear turned from the window.

"I think that I know what we need," he said. "If only Christ—"

"As I said before," said Donkey, "I'm not the most experienced member of our little band. But I am sure, I am very, *very* sure that he will not be coming either."

Bear stared at him sadly for some time, until a crash behind him made them all start. Something had been thrown through the window. It was a rough, gray-green object with a handle. In the few seconds before it went off there was a strange silence, during which they could all hear the distant chuttering of the helicopters.

II

The summer had very definitely come to its conclusion, running smack into autumn, as it has its way of doing; Mole thought to himself that it was very fortunate indeed that he and Water Rat had managed to finish up their bit of adventure before the really cold weather set in. Now was the time for steaming tea in china cups, and cedar shakes crackling in the fire, and, above all else, *stories* about adventuring. But Mole knew that mucking about the countryside on strange errands had its season, and that time was not autumn. The short breather that Nature in her wisdom permits between the fevers of the warm weather and the sleepy contemplation of winter was for only one thing: sitting comfortably, dry and warm in Ratty's snug rooms at River Bank, planning the excursion of next year.

And as the year found its way to its end, so did this particular day. The sun was going down through the carmine sky, and the late afternoon was so absolutely lovely, in a purely autumn and unhurried way, that both animals kept their own counsel, as if by unspoken mutual consent fearing to disturb that fragile beauty that they thought had passed, too, with the pleasanter temperatures. "It is like this every year," thought the Mole. "Autumn *is* such a wonderful time of year, there is really nothing else quite like it. And the trees now are really without their equal in the sameness of the summer's colors! Why do I always seem to forget that autumn is, after all, my favorite season?" Perhaps the Rat was thinking the same thoughts, for after a time the Mole could hear him whispering his poetry words, about pumpkins and frost and that sort of thing.

As the twilight deepened around the pair while they crossed a meadow yet some distance from their goal, the Rat stopped still in his tracks. "Mole, my good friend and true companion," he said, "it is October." Rat bent back his silky head and gazed silently into the sky, which was growing bluer and darker blue, and already a star or two had edged into view. "Where does the year go?" And then he moved on, his hands clasped behind his back, or shoved into the shallow pockets of his thin coat.

At the other side of the meadow they found a low, broken-backed fence of timber and, as there did not appear to be a gate, the Mole stood on the lowest beam and vaulted over. Rat made as to follow but, before he grasped the topmost timber, he turned and looked out across the field that next they would cross. He paused for a moment, and Mole knew that he could expect a bit of poetry. And so the Rat recited:

> "Tears, idle tears, I know not what they mean,
> Tears from the depth of some divine despair
> Rise in the heart, and gather to the eyes,
> In looking on the happy Autumn-fields,
> And thinking of the days that are no more."

"Hmm," said the Mole, moved but unsure if he were glad or totally melancholy. "Quite lovely, but not without its proper weight of sensibility."

"Tennyson," said the Rat.

"Hmm." And this was all that was said for a longish period of time, as they made their way over the field of stalks of last summer's corn. The field was set off on the farther side by another barrier like the one that they previously had crossed. They passed over, and were in a large coppice of mountain ash.

"It will take but one good shower to loose these leaves at last," said the Rat. "Then the rowan will stand winter-bare, and we will be left for a time with nothing to remind us of the summer but the cry of the jay."

"Ratty," said the Mole in a small voice, "might I ask of you the least favor?"

"Certainly, Mole. You ought to know that you are my dearest of friends."

"Why, if you please, it is nothing, actually. But you keep saying the *most* saddening things, so that while I am going along thinking about how wonderful it will be to find River Bank once more, and about how delightful everything will be when we're all tucked in at home again, you say something to make me feel all tumbled about inside and downright *abandoned*. Sometimes I want to stop right here, or turn around and *look* for our lost summer. Certainly it is autumn, and winter is coming on. There's no use saying that it isn't. But it's happened to us before, and I do so wish that you could talk of spring and punting about in the boat for the first time of the new season, or at least, if it must be autumn, then how lovely it is to see Orion again. Because it is hard, it is so hard to be sad and in unfamiliar territory at the same time." This was a rather long speech for the poor Mole, but he was always so affected by poetry. And of course Ratty understood, and thoughtfully made his comments to cheer his companion.

And thus the stand of rowan was passed, and more relics of fields, and open meads where the eyes of animals glared like little glass marbles from the clumps of brown grass. It was night now, no use at all trying to call it "evening," and Mole, whose habits had been set in his later life at retiring early and rising with the sun, began to feel uncomfortable. Even one as adventured as he, who had seen more odd things than ever he could have dreamed in his parochial molish youth, was glad that he was not alone beneath the watchful gaze of the diamond stars. He walked with his head tucked down and his short stubby arms held at his sides; every once in a while he stumbled, as upon an unseen clod of dirt or half-buried stone, and fell against Water Rat, mumbling apologies and feeling grateful for the solid presence of his friend.

The Mole's thoughts were exclusively of home; he employed the memories of long out-of-sight friends and out-of-mind, familiar objects to hold back both the pressing darkness and the insistent, cold wind. But the home of his reveries was not always River Bank, where he had gone to live upon discovering the joys of riverside life and meeting River Bank's most generous and gentle tenant, the Water Rat. No, the cozy fires that he imagined burned as often as not in his own relinquished place at Mole End. The more he thought the cozier the picture became, until he was just on the point of asking the Rat if they might stop there for the night, rather than going on to River Bank. It *was* very late, of course, and it *was* getting colder and colder. Mole's hands were nearly without sensation, and his poor feet were *his* only by virtue of their aching. He knew that there was a small supply of food left in his rooms (mainly a tin of Danish bacon and some capers); a small but sufficient supper might be coaxed from his forsaken pantry. It would be nice to stop by again; it had been so long, and perhaps the detour would be advisable, just to check that all was still in order. And then the trip to River Bank could be continued after a good rest, and perhaps something more undiscovered would appear for a bit of breakfast, although—

"—beyond that hedge, I should think," said the Water Rat.

"Eh?" said Mole, who realized that the Rat had stopped by the wayside and had been speaking to him for no little time. "I'm sorry, Ratty, but perhaps my ears are a little numb, too."

"I merely suggested that, as I calculate, your very nice Mole End should be in a field very near, perhaps just on the other side of the hedge on that knoll, there. It would be a convenience to spend the night there tonight, for I, at least, have just about had a full time of it. That is, of course, if the plan meets with your approval. I should hate to invite myself around in this way, except that I *am* so infernally exhausted. However, if you would rather remain with our original—"

"Oh, remarkable, Ratty!" cried Mole. "Have you been eavesdropping on my secretest thoughts? Oh thank you, I would so like to see my old home again." The two companions discussed their situation further, and agreed to pass the night at Mole End, although it would not be as comfortable as had they pressed on to River Bank. The next day would be one of cleaning and tidying up after their long absence, and also of the happy chore of visiting their friends and spending tea, dinner, and supper regaling them with the history of their adventures. The Mole and the Rat began to feel better, warmer inside if not out, and both knew that welcome tingle of anticipation. At last, they were coming home.

The Mole could hardly control his excitement as he topped the low rise and passed through an opening in the hedgerow. It was far too dark to see, but (if Ratty's estimate were correct) he ought to be able to smell the first fair indications of his old neighborhood. And there they were! His nose twitched with pleasure as he scented those familiar signals. But they were arriving somewhat muffled, as though buried under strange and unknown smells. The Mole strained his eyes to try to aid his bewildered nose, but of course all that he could see was a bright glow before him.

"Is that morning already?" he asked.

"No," said Rat, his voice peculiarly grim.

"Because I didn't think that the night had passed so quickly. We must have come much farther than ever we thought. Or else this quite proves my theory that the time you spend asleep is actually less than the equal number of daylight hours," said the Mole, chuckling at his very small joke.

"No, we've been heading west for some time, in any event."

They walked toward the light, upon a curious hard black surface. The ground had been made flat and smooth, and covered over with some material. It was this that the Mole's nose could not identify. As they came closer it became evident that the light was originating from a group of shining lamps placed high on poles. These were situated about the queer field in widely spaced rows.

"Your home ought to be right about here," said the Rat, indicating a spot on the blacktop between two painted yellow lines.

"It looks as though I have a bit of work," said the Mole unhappily. "They seem to have covered over my tunnel." He set to immediately, trying with his freezing paws to get through the pavement to his warm little burrow.

"Oh, Ratty, it . . . won't . . . *dig!*" And the gasping Mole sat down on the blacktop, tears forming in his tiny eyes. The Rat was stricken by the sadness of his friend, and thought that Mole should at least make another attempt, if only because that seemed so much more positive a plan than nocturnal and earnest lamentation. So the Mole turned to once more, working even harder but with the same lack of success. The hard surface of the parking lot resisted his most practiced efforts.

"What are we to do, Ratty?"

"We'll continue on, of course. It would have been pleasant to stay here, but River Bank isn't an impossible distance. So buck up; we'll have you all tucked in soon enough."

"But that was my *home!*" said the distressed Mole.

"You'll live with me officially, now. So remember to mind your muddy feet." But the Water Rat was not so unconcerned as he would have his companion believe. He was nearly as sick at heart as the Mole to find the least trace of Mole End obliterated; animals take only one spot for their home, not like we larger folk who may move about several times before finding one last resting place in our dotage. And animals invest in their single residences all the security and love that they hold in their smaller but wiser selves. Thus it takes a major disruption of life, such as that experienced by the Mole when he turned out his solitary existence for the new and exciting life at River Bank, to enable an animal to quit his chosen home. The Rat was wise enough to know this, and he also knew that it could serve no purpose to let his friend languish in despair.

In accordance then with their revised schedule, the Mole and Water Rat turned south, heading across the lot toward the river. It was quite impossible for either to walk along without picturing in his private and gloomy thoughts the beautiful spot of greenery that had been removed to allow the pavement's unsightly intrusion. At the far end of the lot, where once had been a border of low hedges and, beyond that, a row of slender poplars, the Rat could make out the dim lines of a huge, square, dark building. He said nothing to the sorrowful Mole, but waited instead until they were close enough to investigate firsthand. He suspected another of Toad's ephemeral and ill-advised schemes, but surely even Toad had enough romance and enough sense to prevent him from cementing over the country-side.

The building was quite monstrous, and ugly in an efficient sort of way that indicated that it was some sort of factory.

"How long were we gone?" asked the Mole in a hurt tone of voice.

"Much too long, it would seem," said the Rat.

"Toad?"

"I'm not certain. It would be like his old self to catch on to a seemingly easy moneymaking proposition, and then ruin everyone for miles around. But, of course, to be fair we'll make inquiries in the morning."

"Not many folks around anymore to ask," said a new voice. The Mole and the Water Rat turned around, startled. The voice belonged to a rather small and hungry-looking weasel. He nodded in recognition of the two returned travelers, although neither Mole nor Rat knew him by name.

"Toad's gone, himself," said the weasel.

"Old Toad, gone?" said the Mole.

"Yes, sir. Had a spell of warmish weather along about the end of June. One of those still days, not a breath of air to be had; lot of smoke from this factory just hung there, thicker than fog. Some of the older folk couldn't do it. Apoplexy or something, Mr. Badger called it."

"You mean Toad's passed away?" asked the Rat, astonished.

"Yes, sir."

"Silly old Toad . . . "

"Good old Toad . . . dead?"

There was a shocked silence. After a time the weasel spoke again. "And then, when they built those new homes across the water, a good many fine weasels and others lost theirs. When they tore down the Wild Wood, that is. Most everybody that I grew up with has left the neighborhood entirely. Gone east, I suppose."

"They tore down the Wild Wood?" asked Mole in his very small voice.

"And Badger?" asked Rat.

"Well, that is, Mr. Badger got caught up in a load of concrete. When they was putting in those new homes."

"*Badger?*" cried the Rat. He was sorely smitten; the Mole just stood, confused, with his long snout wavering in the night air. After a time the Rat roused himself enough to wish the weasel a good evening and grab Mole's elbow. The two travelers hurried off, following a large corrugated-metal pipe toward the river a short distance away.

At the water's edge the conduit ended. From its open maw poured a sluggish and foul-smelling stream. The river itself seemed slow-moving and evil.

"What have they done to my river?" cried the Rat. He stared across in the gloom, but he could not make out the night-shrouded features of his house. After a bit of a search he located the small boat that had been left tied up on the Mole's side of the water so many months previously. The Rat allowed Mole to enter, meanwhile undoing the knotted painter. He threw the rope into the boat and pushed off, stepping into the river to do so. The water felt oily and unpleasant, and the Rat shuddered as he hopped into the skiff and grabbed the oars. He rowed in silence, and the Mole was similarly lost in his own thoughts. On the other side Mole leaped out and hauled the boat to shore, where the Rat joined him after shipping the oars.

River Bank was ruined. The outside of the dwelling was coated with a thick, sludgy layer that had seeped inside and spoiled everything: furniture, books, food stores, everything. Rat viewed the scene with growing anger and frustration, but remained quiet. Finally he took the Mole's elbow once again.

"Come along, old friend. It's obvious that we can't stay here, either."

"Where shall we go, Ratty? We have nowhere to go."

"And nothing to take with us. That's fine, I suppose; a new start, new beginnings. Although we're both a bit far along for that sort of thing. But, what's done is done, and no use being resentful. Let us leave soon, while I still have the strength of this impulse, and before I truthfully realize that everything I've ever had is wasted and made into rubbish."

So they took to the water, following the course of the stream and the cold night wind. The Rat took the first turn at rowing while the Mole drowsed. Then they switched; Mole rowed and Water Rat failed in his resolve to stay awake and hunt for a likely place to spend the night. The Rat dropped off to sleep, and the Mole's rowing grew slower and slower as he, too, fell fast asleep. They were both awakened some time later by the lurching of the boat in the strong current.

"Oh, Mole," said the Rat accusingly, "*have* you lost the oars? Where? Just now?"

"I don't know, Ratty! I suppose that I drifted off to sleep, and I don't know just when I dropped the oars. Where are we? Oh, I'm so sorry, but I'm just so tired!"

"I don't know where we are, my very good Mole. I'm sorry for speaking to you in that unkind way. I don't recognize any of this shoreline that we're passing, so I assume that we've both been getting back a good share of the night's rest that we have cheated ourselves of so far. It looks as if our adventures *aren't* over yet."

The river had grown broader and stronger than they had ever

seen it. The boat and its two weary passengers followed helplessly wherever it led them. The Rat must have dozed again, for he was awakened by the Mole's excited cry.

"Rat, do you see? The dawn, now for sure. At least we won't be traveling in the dark any longer. Oh, how glad I will be to see the sun!"

But Mole was incorrect once more; it was not the sun. The fierce, ruddy glow on the river ahead was caused by artificial means, though not as before in the parking lot. As the crippled rowboat sped nearer in the river's grasp, it became clear to the Water Rat that the light was from a great fire. Indeed, up ahead the thick, orange water of the river itself was blazing in a towering wall of flame.

Introduction to "Target: Berlin!"

George Alec Effinger and I began publishing stories in the early 1970s, but it was clear right from the start that he was an exceptional talent. To put it another way, he had true star quality. He was selling his first stories to the most demanding editors in our field, and came within a hair's breadth of winning the first John W. Campbell Award for best new writer. His early stories, several of which appeared in Damon Knight's *Orbit* and Robert Silverberg's *New Dimensions* and Terry Carr's *Universe* anthologies, were gems, and he was soon regularly in the running for all the awards.

George began publishing novels not long after his first stories were out, and soon achieved the enviable accomplishment of selling one novel outside the genre markets for a higher advance than usual to a respected hardcover house. That novel, *Felicia*, the story of a Louisiana community's encounter with a major hurricane, came out in 1976.

In a well-ordered universe, *Felicia*, along with George's industry and intelligence, would have been enough to launch him on a career trajectory that would have led to bestselling novels with a wide readership of devoted fans, whom the prolific Effinger could have kept satisfied with many more novels to come. And maybe that success would have led to more prestigious markets for his delightfully quirky short stories, most of which would not have been out of place in *The New Yorker* or other such classy venues. And maybe George would have had the financial security and time to build on his early successes, or at least to have been able to become world-weary and disenchanted with the downside of fame and fortune.

Unfortunately, George, like the rest of us, was stuck in this world.

Throughout his life, beginning in his twenties, he was in and out of hospitals, undergoing surgery for

stomach growths, and having to turn out books and
stories simply to pay his medical bills; his rare ailment
afflicted him for his entire life and, being a "pre-existing
condition," made it impossible for him to get medical
insurance. (Whenever some morally obtuse idiot rails
against the notion of guaranteed universal health care, I
think of George, whose hospital bills eventually bank-
rupted him.) He won the highest awards speculative
fiction has to offer, picking up the Nebula, the Hugo,
and the Theodore Sturgeon Memorial Award for his
story "Schrödinger's Kitten," but it took him until the
late 1980s to win them. His Budayeen novels, beginning with *When Gravity Fails*, displayed ingenuity,
originality, and a mastery of characterization and futur-
istic detail that promised more such fine works, but we
had only two more of these novels from him, even
though he could have created a series of Budayeen
books that would have avoided the repetitiousness and
increasing tedium of most series: George had the inven-
tiveness to have evaded that trap. What he didn't have
was the physical health and the time.

I remember George coming from New Orleans to
New York to receive his Nebula Award in 1989, although I think he had to borrow the money to make the
trip. He was classy enough to show his respect for the
honor and for his fellow writers by wearing full formal
dress to the Nebula banquet. In 1993, when I was having my own troubles with illness and depression,
George was the first person to call me from New
Orleans, where the Nebula Awards banquet was being
held, to tell me that I had won a Nebula. We lost touch
for a while after that, but were again emailing each
other during the months before his death. I wanted a
story for an anthology I was editing, and he was worrying about whether or not he could write one, but I got
that story from him, "Walking Gods," an elegiac tale
narrated by Saladin at the end of his life. In spite of the
somber mood of that story, George was sounding more
optimistic, full of ideas for new stories and books, and
looking forward to getting up to his old writing speed,
when he could turn out a first rate story in the time it
takes many of us to set down one decent paragraph.

Then, suddenly, he was gone.

"Target: Berlin!" is one of my favorite George Alec Effinger stories because it's such a prime example of the deliciously skewed perspective he brought to his writing, the ability to take an idea and twist it in ways that wouldn't have occurred to anyone else. I mean, major air battles of World War II fought with automobiles because of an oil shortage? This is a story that will make you laugh out loud, while also delighting you with its ironic turns of phrase and absurd situations, but you'll feel a few cuts and slashes of the knife along the way. Even while seeing the world's absurdities, George was well aware of its inexorable tragedies, in his fiction and in his life.

—Pamela Sargent

✛ ✛ ✛

Target: Berlin!
The Role of the Air Force
Four-Door Hardtop

PREFACE

Feeling neglected, my wife left me during those terrible months. I also lost the friendship of several colleagues, but we succeeded in modifying a Lincoln Continental four-door sedan into our first great bomber of the war, the B–17 Flying Fortress. It was a trying time, but I'll tell you about it if you care to listen.

Effinger WWII Book Gossipy, Rambling

Reviewed for the Rusty Brook, New Jersey, *Sun* by Louis J. Arphouse

The opening words of Effinger's memoir, the very first paragraph of his preface, give the flavor of the remainder of the book. After a chapter or two, it is not a pleasant flavor. This is the first eye-witness document we have gotten from the war, at least from so notorious a participant. One could have hoped for a more disciplined, less discursive book. Effinger was personally involved in many of the tactical decisions and technical inventions that shaped the Second World War. He has seen fit in his history of those years to give us instead his meager snapshots of great figures, mere glimpses of elbows and coats rushing out of the frame while momentous consequences remain hinted at in the background.

One might even think that Effinger's book was written well before the end of the war, as a kind of hedging of his bets. In places it seems like the author is placating his former enemies, smoothing over their errors in the hopes that, had they emerged victorious, they might have gone easier on Effinger in whatever hypothetical war crimes trials that might have ensued. It's unlikely that the book would have had even that effect. Instead, it is too stilted to be read with any pleasure as a personal memoir, and not strict enough to be of value as a history text. It is fortunate for Effinger, and for the free world, that his talents during the war were used in other directions.

PREFACE (continued)

The decision not to hold the Second World War in the 1940s was made by mutual consent of all combatant parties, and a general agreement was signed in Geneva. Simply speaking, most nations felt it would just be better to wait. But there were often more probing reasons, situations which reflected sophisticated and convoluted paths of national policy. The Japanese, for example, at the Maryknoll conference, were rankled at the oil embargo a suspicious United States had placed on that island empire. A Japanese delegate rose from his seat at one point and abandoned his polite but false diplomatic manner. "What's the matter?" he said in a loud voice. "I can't understand it. Your own Admiral Perry opened us up to trade. Now you won't sell us what we want. That's stupid." And the irate delegate walked out of the conference room, blushing at his own brazenness.

There was a stunned silence, and then a great deal of muttering from the American side of the table. One of the American delegates cleared his throat. "You know," he said, "we never looked at it that way. He has a point."

The conference went on more smoothly from there and eventually achieved a compromise that both sides could accept enthusiastically. Japan no longer felt threatened economically, and war with the United States was averted. However, there were other causes for the sudden mending of political fences, many of which might have seemed laughable at the time but which cannot be underestimated in the light of successive events. One of the emperor's younger nephews, a member of the Imperial War Office, was a great baseball fan, as were many of his countrymen; this influential person believed that it would be a shame to interrupt the career of such a star as Joe DiMaggio. The emperor's nephew, too, was a voice that counseled patience.

In Nazi Germany, the citizens were made aware of the activities of Heinrich Himmler and Reinhard Heydrich. These men, chiefs of the SS and the Security Police, were assembling vast dossiers on millions upon millions of people: Nazis, anti-Nazis, politicians, common people, rich, poor, old, young. No one in the Reich could escape their scrutiny. Of course, this news made the people of Germany nervous; at the first opportunity, the Nazis were removed from office. "Thank God for the American news services," said many German citizens afterward, for it was through the American newspapers and radio broadcasts that the Germans were alerted to the shenanigans of the Nazis. "The Americans are the sentinels of liberty. Once again they have had to save our necks." The political structure of Germany reformed, moving from the extreme right, stopping comfortably just left of middle; the new rulers in Berlin made it embarrassingly clear to Washington that there was no further reason to seek war. Italy, her trains humming along on schedule, followed suit a few months later. The trains got all fouled up, but tourists in Italy reported that otherwise things had changed for the better, except around Venice during July and August, and even Mussolini hadn't been able to do anything about that.

AT LAST, THE WAR AS IT WAS!

TARGET: BERLIN!
BY GEORGE ALEC EFFINGER
OFERMOD PRESS, $12.95
ILLUSTRATED

At long last, Ofermod Press is proud to announce the publication of the first genuine firsthand documentary to come out of the war. A searing indictment of the conservative voices in President Roosevelt's cabinet and of the timid liberal partisans, both groups which almost led the United States to ruin. MORE! A caustic attack on the fearful counselors who would allow other nations in this postwar world to maintain a superiority in number and type of bombing weapon. MORE! A vital book for all thoughtful citizens, a shocking, sometimes amusing glimpse into the world of high-pressure politics and top-level decision-making. MORE! This book is much more because it was written by one of the most influential men of the Second World War, and it contains an urgent message for all Americans.

NATIONAL ADVERTISING, PROMOTION, AND TWENTY-FOUR-CITY AUTHOR TOUR

$12.95, Publication Date September 9, 1981

PREFACE (continued)

I could see how the war was going to go, even at the very beginning. I know that isn't the kind of thing one should say about oneself, especially in a book like this. But in this case there isn't anyone else around to say it and, after all, my opinion was later seconded by President Roosevelt himself, in addition to a handful of lesser dignitaries. "Well, George," said the president, "you guessed which turn this war would take quite a while ago, didn't you?" I had to agree. And, in the same way, I can see which way this book is going, too, not that it does me any more good. Because during the war I had what I came to call a Cassandra complex. I'll discuss that in more detail later; let me just say now that I had a sense of the magnitude of the war's climax, but I never felt certain of the moral implications.

It must be made clear, prefatorily, that international disagreements had not been completely resolved without open conflict. No, rather, the war had merely been shelved. The more bloodthirsty members of Japan's Imperial War Office went underground for some years, as did their counterparts in France and Great Britain, in the Soviet Union, the war-seekers in the United States, Hitler's colleagues and Mussolini's. The world at large slumbered in three decades of what the Twenties and Thirties had been—a mixed bag of peace, prosperity, anxiety, and depression. Franklin Delano Roosevelt, relieved of many of his heaviest political worries, continued in office, as hearty as ever, a visual reminder, along with Winston Churchill, of a nostalgic time. The Forties passed, and the Fifties, and the frenetic Sixties. Then the Seventies began, and it looked once more as if the world were edging closer to that irrevocable stumble into total war. In Germany the populace, tired of thirty years of liberal politics and the rowdiness it induced in the younger generation, began a slow retreat toward fascism. Adolf Hitler, now eighty-five years old, came out of retirement to lead his country. Himmler dusted off his old dossiers. The people of Germany who recalled the old days smiled and nudged their neighbors. Hitler was something they could understand, not like the glittery transvestite singing stars of their children's generation. Hitler would show those guys something. The older people settled back to watch.

In Japan, the emperor's nephew no longer followed American baseball. He had taken up golf. With a worldwide fuel shortage in 1974, Japan found herself back in the same situation that she had been in the early Forties. "What the hell," muttered the Imperial War Office. "What the hell," muttered the emperor. Secret plans were made.

France watched nervously, Great Britain watched confidently, the Soviet Union watched slyly. The United States didn't seem to be watching at all, but it was difficult to be sure.

Events moved quickly thereafter, resuming their inexorable march to war along the very same lines that had been abandoned three decades before. But there were a few alterations, thanks to the progress of both technology and human relations.

Hermann Göering, leader of Hitler's *Luftwaffe*, studied detailed maps of Poland and France. Göering, now eighty-one years old, looked somewhat ridiculous in his refurbished uniforms. His fat face was masked by broad striations of wrinkles. His hands wavered noticeably as he lifted small replicas of aircraft, moving them from bases within the Reich to proposed targets all over the mapboard. He beamed happily as he set an airplane down in Paris, another in London, a third in Prague. An aide moved still another airplane to Moscow, too far for Göering to reach by himself. The air marshal's aides whispered behind his back. Someone would have to tell the Führer's trusted lieutenant about the *Luftwaffe*'s weak point. The young men, fearful of the senile yet powerful man, contested among themselves. Eventually the least assertive and most vulnerable of them presented Göering with a special file, one which had been placed on his desk several times before and which Göering had chosen to ignore. He could ignore it no longer.

FROM THE DESK OF . . .
. . . HERMANN GÖERING
Reich Master of the Hunt
June 10, 1974

Dear George:

It's been a long time since I've seen you. How are things in the Free World? Things are moving along at a rapid pace here, under the banner of National Socialism. I'm sure you're keeping up with events, but I'll bet we still surprise you. The next few years will be momentous ones in the history of the world. Isn't it kind of exciting, being on the inside?

Talk of war is heard on all sides. I'm sure you're keeping up to date on our air force, its size and capabilities, just as I receive reports on you and the others. I wonder if your reports are any better than mine. You must know that the *Luftwaffe* is in no shape to face a long, drawn-out war now. But there's no talking to Adolf these days. He has this timetable, he keeps telling us. Ah, well, we do our best. You know just how difficult this job is.

You probably also know that we've scrapped the idea of long-range heavy bombers. I don't suppose I'm giving away any secrets in saying that. We'd have to restructure our entire automotive industry. You've already beaten us there. But don't count us out altogether! You might wake up some morning to the sound of Volkswagen six-passenger luxury bombers driving by under your window. You know us. We have more Situation Contingency Plans than anyone even knows about—including me, Adolf, the OKW, or anybody. If we could just get everything indexed and sorted, we'd be in great shape. Too many personalities clashing for that, though, I'm afraid. . . .

Tell Diana that my Emmy tried her recipe for Mad Dog Chili last week. Emmy saw it in the *New York Post*. It was so good that I was in bed recovering for three days. That was a very nice profile on Diana, too. She must be happy. Emmy can't get anything like it here, in the *Beobachter*. I think Emmy's jealous.

If there isn't war by then, I'll see you in the fall in Milan for the air show. I wish I had your youth; nowadays, a few days away from Emmy means only that I'll end up with diarrhea. Regards to your . . . President (I almost wrote you-know-what).

Best,
H.

PREFACE *(continued)*

In Tokyo, the War Office studied a photographed copy of Göering's file. The Japanese conclusions were the same as the German: the Imperial Air Force would also have to be drastically restructured. As things turned out, that did not prove to be so large an obstacle.

Finally, here in the United States, the clamor to arms did not sound so loudly. Nevertheless, President Roosevelt was aware of what the potential belligerent nations were doing and spurred production. The Air Force followed in the footsteps of Germany and Japan and turned from the development of aircraft to the exploration of the motorcar as a tactical weapon, both as long-range bomber and as fighter escort. The reasons were the same: the Air Force generals were astonished by the statistics concerning the vast amounts of petroleum products that an all-out war would demand. Oil was scarce, and supplies were dangerously low. There was no guarantee that overseas oil-producing nations would remain friendly. Automobiles could bring about the same results as aircraft and with much greater economy. All that was necessary was a certain basic alteration in military thinking. Naturally enough, because of the conservative outlook of the military mind, this change met some resistance. But when the facts were made clear and the economic and political ramifications were explained, the real business of realigning the Air Force began, in Washington as well as Berlin, Tokyo, Moscow, Paris, and London.

It was against this background, then, that I began my work. I was given a suite of offices in the Pentagon; that was on February 18, 1974. Across the United States, huge lines of cars waited at service stations, unable to purchase gasoline with the freedom the American motorist had come to enjoy. On the way home each day I saw hundreds of automobiles still queued up hopefully; I remember thinking that it was ironic that the same gasoline shortage that paralyzed these motorists had made an all-out air war equally impractical and that the common solution of all the leading nations had been to replace their aircraft with automobiles. Billions of gallons of gasoline would be saved in this way—involuntarily, of course, as the gasoline was not actually available to be saved in the first place; still, I wondered if the man in the street would react as we hoped, would rise up in patriotic sacrifice and curtail his pleasure driving for the war effort, should hostilities become official.

CHAPTER TWO

George Alec Effinger, *Special Assistant to President Roosevelt*: Then you were involved with the early *Luftwaffe* attacks on Poland?

Oberleutnant Rolf Mulp, *pilot of the German Nazi* Luftwaffe: Yes, indeed, certainly so. I commanded a *kette* in an attack—

Effinger: *"Kette"*?

Mulp: Yes. I'm sorry. It's a German word. Don't worry about it.

Anyway, we were taking these three Stukas against a bridge just across the Polish border. This was September 1, 1974. The first day of the war.

Effinger: And the Stuka, the old terror bomber—

Mulp: Was now the 1973 Opel 53 four-door sedan. We had made the change in strategy and procedures very quickly, thanks to our basic German love of discipline. We practiced a lot, driving around shopping centers, aiming our fingers at people—

Effinger: And with Hitler and Göering and everybody back in power, it was like old times.

Mulp: I wouldn't know firsthand, of course. I was too young in the Thirties to remember them. But my parents told me stories of what it had been like. And we all joined in, and we all settled down quickly. It was so comfortable to have those familiar faces back, now grown so old, but still so familiar. Comfortable, like an old boot.

Effinger: A high black one, no doubt.

Mulp: It comes just below the knee. Ah, I see that you understand, do you not? Ha, ha, ha.

Effinger: Ha, ha, ha. We can laugh, now that the war's over.

Mulp: Ha, ha, ha. Indeed, yes. But those were terrible years. Me, driving the Opel at top speed. My tail gunner sitting in the back seat, worried, nervous, chattering nonsense while I was trying to keep my mind on the road. We had a constant fear of enemy fighters screaming toward us around the next bend in the road. And then the business of having to pitch bombs at bridges or whatever, or stopping the car and getting out to toss the things. It took a lot of skill and a lot of luck.

Effinger: And a lot of daring.

Mulp: I'm glad that you can appreciate that now. I'd like to ask you a question, if I may.

Effinger: Certainly. I'll bet I know which one, too.

Mulp: You were almost single-handedly responsible –

Effinger: No, for crying out loud, I don't want to hear it. I'm tired of hearing it already.

From the Cormorant, Indiana, *Flash-Comet*

ON THE TOWNE
by Craig Towne

This column's reporter went to an unusual promo party last week. In town for a few days pushing a new book was a former aide of the late President Roosevelt. The author, George Effinger, visited our little city once several years ago, before the war. I recall meeting him then, shaking his hand, and hearing him say that he was "glad I could make it." This reporter was very gratified that Mr. Effinger, too, remembered that brief acquaintanceship. Also, his book seems very handsome. But remember when books cost five bucks?

Chapter Four

Effinger: What was it like?

Maginna: It was awful, what do you think? Really awful. Anybody who lived through it would tell you the same thing. About how awful it was. We were all thinking such idiotic things while it was happening. And now, looking back, it's kind of hard to straighten it all out in my mind. I remember thinking, "God, they're all going to think we were idiots here." I was afraid that people would laugh or something, because we let it happen. That Pearl Harbor would go down in history as our fault.

Effinger: Of course, there was a certain lack of communication.

Maginna: Things seemed worse at the time. I've read about the attack since, many times. I'm glad, of course, that the whole thing wasn't as bad as it looked to me then. But the accounts never convey the real feeling we had, the loud awfulness. I thought, "There goes the shortest war in the world." I thought the Navy was sunk.

Effinger: Can you describe what it looked like?

Maginna: Sure. Nothing easier. It was mostly these Honda Civics—we called them Kates during the war—that did most of the bombing. And these Toyota Corolla 1200 coupes, what we called Zeroes, were the fighter escorts. It was such a quiet morning. I don't know, I can't remember what I had planned for the afternoon. Anyway, these Jap cars started driving up in long lines from Honolulu, a couple of hundred of them at least. They roared through the sentry posts, the Zeroes shooting down soldiers, sailors, a lot of civilians, even. The Kates screeched their brakes at the end of the piers, threw their bombs, and drove away. All the time their Zeroes, those Toyota coupes, were demolishing our planes before our pilots could get them started. Most of the damage was done real quick. We never knew what hit us.

Effinger: And you have no trouble recalling your feelings.

Maginna: No trouble at all. That's something I'll remember until the day I die. That's the reason I don't like to read about Pearl Harbor, because the accounts just don't capture it.

Effinger: I'm giving you the chance to correct that.

Maginna: Sure. A lot of us that saw the *Arizona* get hit — some of us had friends on her — were glad of what you did at the end of the war. We would have voted for you for president. And you're right these days, about not letting other countries do that to us all over again. Sure. We ought to screw them down while we have the chance.

Effinger: That's not exactly what I —

Maginna: I wouldn't want that to happen all over again.

Effinger: Me, neither.

Maginna: Right. Right. *(Pause)* Are you okay?

> Dear Mr. Effinger:
>
> I recently borrowed your book *Target: Berlin!* from the library. It isn't such a big library, here in Springfield, not so big as you'd think with a college right in town, but then the college has its own, of course, but we had your book, and since my husband was a pilot in the war I thought I'd read your book. My husband was killed in one of the raids over Germany that you talk about in Chapter Eight late in the war. We were married only a little while before Pearl Harbor, and when my husband was killed, it was a tremendous loss, but I have learned to live with it and accept it as God's will, something that a lot of us wives have trouble doing but I don't. That's just the way I was raised, I guess.
>
> I liked your book a lot. A lot of us wives had trouble understanding just why our husbands were dying, dropping bombs on tiny towns that didn't look like they'd be worth anything to anybody. I liked your book because it made me understand for the first time that my husband was actually

contributing and doing something important instead of just throwing his life away which is what we all thought for so long. I'm glad at last that somebody told us something. We all are, though a lot of us wives have trouble believing it, even still.

But I know that if Lawrence was alive today, he'd like your book too, on account of he was a part of what you describe so well. And the fact that it was you, personally, that did so much to help our country win the war, not only coming up with the idea of the big bombing missions but also making the decision to go ahead with the A-bomb, I know that would have impressed him no end. Of course, I didn't know who you were then, during the war I mean, and I doubt that Lawrence did, either, but I know that if he wasn't dead, he'd know who you are now and be grateful. I know that I am.

God bless you. I hope things work out all right for you.

Very truly yours,
Mrs. Catherine M. Tuposky

CHAPTER SEVEN

Dr. Nelson: I walked into the project director's office that first Monday, I recall it very clearly, and I was mad as a drowning hornet. I said, "Who is this jerk?" I figured I'd worked for twenty years, and now was no time for some idiot with no experience and a lot of nerve to come and tell me what to do, war or no war. It was the wrong way for the president to go about things, I thought. Roosevelt was always like that, even in his first five or six terms, if you'll remember. But, like I say, the matter was settled, and I didn't have anything to say about it. We were at war. We needed another heavy bomber to fill in on certain kinds of missions on which the B–17 had demonstrated a kind of vulnerability. The project director said to me, "This guy Effinger wants you to make something out of this." He tossed me a picture of a 1974 Chrysler Imperial Le Baron four-door hardtop. A beauty of a car. Well, I didn't know as much about the situation as the president or you did. I thought about all the work we did to rig up a heavy bomber out of the Lincoln Continental. I didn't want to have to go through all of that again. But what could I say?

Dr. Johnson: This was my first big project. I was very excited about it. I can still picture Dr. Nelson fuming and raging at his desk, but I never shared that feeling. I was still very much impressed by your development of the long-range bombing attacks against the enemies' industrial complexes. That showed a certain sophistication that I admired. Up until that point, the bomber was used only to support troops and armored attacks—in short, limited raids. But both Germany and Japan were learning the hard way that we meant business.

Dr. Nelson: It was a kind of perverse rebellion that forced me to include many of the Le Baron's luxury extras as standard equipment on what eventually came to be the B–24 Liberator. It was only later that I learned from B–24 crew members that these things which I intended as a harmless slap at the government, hitting it in the budget so to speak, actually saved many lives and greatly added to the crews' driving pleasure.

Dr. Green: The B–24 had certain advantages over the B–17, although some B–17 pilots say the same about their own bombers. Still, the Liberator was fitted out better in some respects, particularly the leather trim inside, rear radio speaker, glove compartment vanity mirror, carpeted luggage space in the trunk, and an interior gas cap lock release. These things had been left off the B–17 for monetary reasons, but they showed up on the B–24 as Dr. Nelson's little joke.

Dr. Nelson: Still, they saved many lives and undoubtedly shortened the war.

Dr. Johnson: And you, Mr. Effinger, you were with us through all of it, with the B–17, the B–24, and, later, with the B–29. I'll never forget how much I hated your guts.

Dr. Green: Still, our country will always be grateful.

Dr. Nelson: Still.

FROM THE OFFICE OF THE PRESIDENT

February 7, 1981

Dear George:

It's been a long time, I know, since we've last had the time to talk. Well, after all, I'm president now, you know. I sometimes miss the old days, before FDR died and I accepted the burden that so wears me down these days. I miss the pinball contests in the Executive Mansion. I miss the table-tennis matches with the Senate Majority Leader whose name I've forgotten, he's dead now. I miss being able to sneak out for some miniature golf and not being recognized.

It's silly to live in the past. They all tell me that, every day. Even Miss Brant says the same thing. Am I living in the past? That's a kind of mental illness, isn't it? I suspect that they're trying to convince me that I'm unstable. Sometimes I'm thankful that we don't have the vote of confidence in this country.

What brought all this on was I found the enclosed while moving a file cabinet this morning. Thought you'd like to have it. We all live in the past, just a little.

Regards,
Bob

Robert L. Jennings
President of the United States

RLJ / eb
Enc.

FROM THE OFFICE OF THE PRESIDENT

August 21, 1979

Dear George:

How are things going with the you-know-what? Have you heard from the Manhattan District boys lately? Are you working on the delivery vehicle for the you-know-what? I suppose you are, but I can't help worrying that Uncle Adolf will beat us to it. Hitler is an even ninety years old this year. He dodders when he speaks these days, you can see it in the newscasts. I'm ninety-seven, but at least I have an excuse not to have to stand up. I do all my doddering with a shawl on my lap.

War is hell, did you know that? It's also futile. And inhuman, if you listen to the right people. But it can be glorious, and no one can deny that marvelous things come out of war. For instance, if you recall your history, the elimination of a lot of odd little Balkan states (a wonderful thing, I wish they'd thought of that in my childhood) and, of course, the you-know-what. Hurry it up, will you?

I hope you're not feeling the weight of responsibility for the you-know-what. I mean, it'll shorten the war, won't it? Try to think of it like that.

I remember when it looked like this war was going to be fought forty years ago. I thought about all the wonderful patriotic movies that could have been made: Fred Mac-

*Murray as a pilot, Pat O'Brien as a tough old naval officer,
John Wayne in the Marines, James Stewart as a bashful
hero. Who do we have today? Robert Redford? O'Toole?
Newman? Gatelin? I miss radio.*

*Eleanor tried Diana's recipe for chicken in honey sauce.
In fact, she tried it on some Englishman over here for something or other. He said he knew for a fact that it was a dish
that Rudolf Hess asks for a lot in prison. Hess calls it* Poulet
au Roehm; *he always gets a laugh from ordering it, poor
man.*

*So. Keep up the good work. Push on with the you-know-
what, keep me posted, and let's have you over for supper some
evening when I'm back on solid food.*

Hello to Diana.

> *Best,*
> *F.*

> *Franklin Delano Roosevelt*
> *President of the United States*

FDR / sf

CHAPTER NINE

Major Erich von Locher, *German fighter pilot:* I am frequently . . .
Can you hear me? I am frequently . . . How is that?

Effinger: Fine. Fine.

Von Locher: All right, I suppose. I am frequently asked these
days to comment on what I feel to be the reasons for the sudden
deterioration of the *Luftwaffe* after the Battle of Britain. I generally
avoid that question. It is too complex. I would be doing my former
comrades an injustice by trying to answer.

Instead, let me speculate on the relative strengths of our "aircraft," such as they were. I feel I have more experience and more
confidence to discuss such a concrete problem.

The chief workhorses of our fighter-interceptor arm were the
Me 109, which the Messerschmitt people had built from the beautiful little Porsche 911-T, and the FW 190, which came later, a
development of the ungainly Volkswagen Beetle. With the introduction of disposable fuel tanks, these two fighters had great range,
great mobility. They were unmatched in the air during the early
part of the war. However, it was not long before the Allies came up
with planes that equaled and, finally, surpassed them. Much has
been made of the supposed even match between our Porsche and

the English Triumph Spitfire "Spitfire." As far as I'm concerned, it was an even match only when neither was destroyed. That did not happen often.

I piloted a Volkswagen during most of the war, first in the west, then on the Russian front. Is that all right?

Effinger: You're doing fine.

Von Locher: You don't think I'm being too pedantic? I don't want to sound like a professor or something.

Effinger: No, no. Just keep going like you were. It's fine.

Von Locher: Where was I?

Effinger: Here, I'll play it back.

Von Locher: *Was destroyed. That did not happen often. I piloted a Volkswagen during most of the war, first in the west, then on the Russian front. Is that all—*

Oh, yes. Well. I remember one particular battle. A whole gang of American bombers was coming east, along the northern route. Our spotters along the way had counted over five hundred bombers, all Lincoln Continentals and Chrysler Imperials, the big ones. They had landed in France and driven across Belgium, then southeast toward Augsburg. This was '79, when the Allied bombing missions were going on night and day, without much resistance from the weakened *Luftwaffe*. Anyway, our Operations people had the facts on this wave, but all we could do was wait. That was the hard part, sitting in our Volkswagens with the engines revving, waiting.

Suddenly we got the call: the bombers had taken the freeway to Berlin. I felt a cold chill; this was the first actual attack on our capital. It had a tremendous symbolic meaning for us. We all gritted our teeth and swore to defend Berlin. Still, even then, all we could do was wait. The drive from France to Berlin was very long, even on the good roads. The Allied crews would have to stop in motels along the way. Our nerves were worn thin, if that is possible with nerves. At last our group leaders ordered us to pull out. We drove in squadrons, spaced out over all four lanes of the divided highway. We did not anticipate running into any civilian traffic, so we drove on both sides of the median strip. The civilians were mostly taking the trains at the end of the war, leaving the highways to the *Luftwaffe*.

We met the Allied bombers about 170 miles from Berlin. There we got the greatest and most horrifying surprise of the war. The bombers were escorted by fighter planes, the Ford Mustang "Mustang." Until this time the bombers were escorted by Plymouth Duster "Thunderbolts" and Chevy Vega "Tomahawks," which could not carry enough fuel to make a long journey into Germany and then return. The bombers were usually on their own during the last stages of their missions. That's when we had our greatest success. But the "Mustangs" changed that. Even Göering realized this fact. That's when he finally admitted that the end had come. And besides their range, the "Mustangs" were our superior in most offensive categories as well.

We did our best, weary and low in morale as we were. We were defending Berlin. I ignored the "Mustangs" and went straight for the bombers. I drove at about eighty-five miles per hour, approaching at a right angle to the path of a Lincoln ahead of me. The bomber's gunner began firing, but my Volkswagen made a small target. I also could turn quicker than he could; it was shortly after dawn, and the sun was rising in the Lincoln pilot's eyes. I drove out of the sun, swung in to him, and raked the side of the car with my 20-mm cannons. The bomber exploded, then swerved off the road and through the guardrail. The battle was less than five minutes old, and already I had a confirmed kill. My squadron leader congratulated me over the radio. I did not take time to relax. A "Mustang" was trying to position itself on my tail. All around me the battle raged; tires screamed as evasive maneuvers were made; burned cars, American and German, littered the highway, making tactics and strategy more difficult. By the end of the morning I had six kills. The Americans lost hundreds of planes, but enough got through to Berlin to shock our leaders into an awareness of just how defenseless the Reich had become.

We drove back to our base in a subdued—

Effinger: I'm sorry, I think the tape's running out. Let me change . . . no, doggone it, that's the last one.

Von Locher: I wanted to talk about the time I held off three Ford Pintos while my machine guns were jammed.

Effinger: Tomorrow. As soon as I g—

June 18, 1980

Dear George:

I hope you understand. I just can't take it anymore, that's all. I suppose people will think I'm unpatriotic, but they don't know how much I've given to the war effort. I sit home every night alone, watching television, wondering what you're doing. And you're always saying that you're with those scientists of yours, trying to come up with a better airplane. Well, we're supposed to be married. Germany surrendered already, remember? Japan isn't going to last much longer, either, as far as I can see. Still, you have to go to "meetings." I'm beginning to wonder.

Last Monday you said you were going to have a meeting with the president. But did you know that at just the time you were supposed to be huddling with him in the Oval Office he was on TV addressing the nation? Did you know that? I won't even bother to ask you where you were. It doesn't matter anymore. I've left you before, and the Secret Service boys always convinced me to come back, for reasons of national security. But what about *my* security? Nobody seems to worry about that.

You spend all day tinkering with Imperials and things, and what does the government give us to drive? A Mercury Comet. I think it's ridiculous.

Don't think that I don't love you, because I still do. But it's just gotten to be too much. I really mean it.

What's-her-name, that old bag secretary of yours, can take care of you. She can learn to make macaroni and cheese, and after that you won't miss me at all. That's about all you needed me for, anyway. And don't worry about money or things like that. I'm not going to bleed you. I think I'll go back to Matamoras for a while, and then I think I'll go into the theater. I've already got an offer of a job from Mickey.

> All good wishes,
> Your wife,
> Diana

CHAPTER TWELVE

Tanora Keigi, *Japanese fighter pilot:* Now here's an interesting point. Today in America many people believe that the kamikaze pilots were religious fanatics or superpatriotic men hypnotized by their devotion to the emperor. As I recall it, this was not the case. We were merely defending our homeland and our families. The B–29 bases in the South Pacific were too numerous and too well-defended to be destroyed. With the fall of Iwo Jima to the Americans, the long-range "Mustang" fighters could be based close enough to the Japanese home islands to accompany the bombers on their missions. All that the dwindling Japanese air force could accomplish were attacks against the aircraft carriers that ferried bombers and fighters from the more distant American bases. And ammunition production was down, and fuel was scarce. We suicide pilots took our inspiration from several high-ranking officers who crashed their planes against American craft in demonstration of their love for their countrymen. It was not long before suicide squadrons were organized on a regular basis.

It was very difficult to crash an automobile against a ship, especially if the ship was still at sea. Therefore, our tactics called for waiting until the American ships dropped anchor near our shores, and the bomber cars and the fighter cars were landed on the beach. We could attack these enemy cars, or the landing craft, or, with the aid of the navy and our own motorized rafts, we might be able to crash into the American ships themselves. Few of us were that lucky.

We had very strange procedures, once these decisions to give our lives in suicidal attacks were made. A friend of mine who drove a Toyota Corolla "Zero" was given a large bomb to throw. The idea was that he would toss the bomb, the bomb would damage his target, and a few seconds later he would crash his Toyota into the same target. Of course, he had to throw the bomb from very short range. The odds were that the target would be shooting back at my friend. As it turned out, he threw the bomb too soon, the bomb hit the ground and bounced up, my friend's "Zero" hit the bomb, which exploded. My friend was already dead when the flaming mass of his car struck his target. He was a hero, and we praised his name from a position of safety about a half mile away.

I had my opportunity to emulate my friend the next day, but bad luck caused me to overshoot my target and waste my precious bomb. Three days later I was ordered to drive my Datsun into a flight of Cadillac Fleetwood "Superfortresses." Again, the gods willed otherwise. Although I weaved through the American bombers for nearly an hour, I did not hit a single target. The bombers passed me by, and I was left out of gas on a highway seven miles from the small town of Gogura.

I kept trying. My commanding officers were very sympathetic. One by one my comrades met glorious death, while I found only frustration. At last the war ended before I found my own moment of honorable sacrifice.

Today I am a moderately successful and prosperous automobile dealer, with a Toyota showroom in San Diego, California. I bear no ill will toward the people who slew so many of my friends and relatives. They seem to harbor no resentment toward me, at the same time. Years have passed, and old disagreements are forgotten. A group of fellow businessmen from Japan have joined me in forming a syndicate, and we are currently buying golf courses in America, athletic teams, and opening franchised fast-food stands. Everything is fine. Everyone is happy. The emperor must have been right, after all. My service mates did not die in vain.

December 10, 1983

Mr. George Alec Effinger
c/o Ofermod Press
409 E. 147th Street
Cleveland, Ohio 44010

Dear Mr. Effinger:

I recently had the pleasure of reading your book, *Target: Berlin!* which was published a few years ago. I don't exactly know why I picked it up, except for the fact that I enjoy reading memoirs of famous people. Sort of like high-class gossip. Also, I've had acquaintances with several people mentioned in your book. I liked your book very much, though much of it was way over my head. I learned a lot from it.

This letter is being written for more than one reason. I don't know if you'll recall, but a couple of years ago I prosecuted a paternity suit against then White House aide Arthur Whitewater, who figures often in your work. Because of governmental pressure, the case was eventually dismissed. Another typical example of administrative self-preservation at the expense of the common man. In the following year I brought L. Daniel Dresser, former presidential press secretary to President Jennings during the close of the war, to court on similar grounds. Again, the case was thrown out before I ever had a fair chance to prove my charges. But I've learned to accept the facts that high-up officials can do just about anything these days. That's why I really liked your book, because it shows these people in everyday life, fallible and slightly stupid.

I saw you on a late-night talk show with Don McCarey, and I thought you were terrific, even if you only had four minutes. Just think, a few years ago you were one of the most influential men in the country. Now you're lucky to get four minutes of time at one o'clock in the morning. Still, that's more than I'll ever get.

Did you have any trouble publishing your book? I mean, did the government censors hassle you or threaten you at all? I bet they did. You have a lot of integrity, and I admire that. That's why I'm sure you'll behave with more honor than either Whitewater or Dresser. I can't say anything for certain as yet, but I go to the doctor the day after tomorrow, and I may have some important news for you then.

Keep up the good work. I know that in the years since the war you've had a constant guilt thing about being responsible for the dropping of the A-bombs on Japan. It shows up all the time in your book. I just want to say that we all have things to be guilty about, and we just have to learn to stifle those feelings before they interfere with regular life. So your situation is a little more extreme than most everyone else's. In a way, we're all responsible for those tragedies. Did you ever think of it like that? It probably doesn't make any difference to you, but I wish I could make you happier. I'd like to meet you in person some day.

Like I said, you'll get the results of the doctor's examination, and we can proceed from there. Surely the royalties on your book would be more than enough to cover the minor expenses that I might cost you. It's no big thing. It happens to people all the time. I don't hold any personal grudge. After all, you never really did anything; we've never been in the same state together. Still, you must admit that, as a famous celebrity, you're a target. This is just part of the circumstances you agreed to accept along with your notoriety. So there isn't any personal animosity between us. I want you to understand that.

Anyway, I'm looking forward to your new book. I saw an ad for it in the *Plain Dealer*. *The Lighter Side of Hiroshima*. Lots of humorous anecdotes collected in the years since 1980. That takes a little nerve, too, you know. I'm impressed. The wild, wacky world of nuclear holocaust. Perhaps it's good therapy for you, though. Who am I to say?

Hoping to hear from you soon (I enclosed a self-addressed, stamped envelope for your convenience),

Heather Oroszco

Chapter Fourteen

Colonel Holbrook Leaf, *pilot of the B–29* Enola Gay: I think that I was the only man in the entire 509th Composite Group that knew of the existence of the atomic bomb. I was the commanding officer of the Group, of course, and we had been assembled specially for the purpose of delivering the bomb on certain selected targets in Japan. We went through what seemed to the regular crews unusual training procedures and special treatment. I imagine that it must have been a hard time for the three other members of my crew.

Major Charles W. Bartz, *co-pilot of the* Enola Gay: It sure was. The other men on the base on Tinian laughed at us and called us names. They couldn't understand what we were contributing to the war effort. We weren't going on regular bombing runs. We were contributing, but even we, except for Colonel Leaf, were unaware of just how. But everybody suspected that something special was in preparation. We never guessed that it was on the order of the A-bomb, though.

Major Andrew Douglas Swayne, *bombardier:* The B–29 was a beautiful car. The Cadillac Fleetwood. After flying B–17s during the early part of the war, it was like a vacation to be transferred to the 509th. But we had to take a lot of ribbing from the guys. It's funny. When you meet those fellows today, they never remember all that happened before the dropping of the bomb. They just remember the awe and the pride.

Bartz: I've had to describe that moment to my kid at least a hundred times.

Leaf: Me, too. Your kid never gets tired of hearing about it.

Swayne: As bombardier, and with just the single bomb, I took over the job of navigator. They put us ashore in some Godforsaken rural area of Japan. I didn't even know where we were. It was Colonel Leaf and Major Bartz in the front seat, and me and Captain Ealywine in the large, comfortable back seat. We drove for nearly an hour before we saw a sign. It put us on the road to the main road to Hiroshima. We were really afraid that we'd run out of gas before we got there. The *Enola Gay* wasn't going to make the return trip with us, but it still had to get us to the target.

Captain Solomon Ealywine, *gunner:* The back seat wasn't as comfortable as in most B–29s, because the A-bomb itself was nearly ten feet long, and a hole had been cut to allow the nose of the thing to extend out from the trunk and across the seat. It separated Swayne and me. It was an eerie feeling, driving along with that thing under my right arm.

Swayne: And it made navigation more difficult. I had to sit in the back seat with the road maps spread out on my lap, and I didn't really have room to operate. In those days in Japan, the road-map markings and the routes they represented bore little relation to each other. Just finding our way to Hiroshima was a tough job. No divided highways with large green overhead signs.

Bartz: Still, we got there. I didn't have much to do, as it turned out. We weren't bothered the whole time. No enemy fighters to meet us or anything. It was like a weekend drive in the country. It seemed like a shame to abandon such a nice car, but we left the Cadillac in the parking lot of a largish shopping center in Hiroshima, where it would blend in with a lot of other cars, many of them prewar American.

Swayne: I had been trained to operate the bomb, although during the instruction drills I never had any idea of the magnitude of the bomb I'd be working with. I set it to explode in ninety minutes. ConComOp had worked out the schedule with almost split-second precision. That was their thing, even though it rarely worked in practice. Still, we kept amazingly to the schedule. We got out of the car, keeping our eyes on the ground, trying to be inconspicuous in enemy territory. We said goodbye to the faithful *Enola Gay*, slammed and locked the doors, and walked across the parking lot to where we could catch the bus back to the village of Horoshiga. There would be a submarine waiting for us offshore. That's the last we saw of the plane, but ninety minutes later, many miles away, riding on the bus, we saw the sky turn pinkish-white. It happened with a suddenness like a bolt of lightning. We turned and shook hands all around. We knew that stroke would crumble the Japanese will to continue the war.

Effinger: Do you ever feel the least bit guilty about killing and maiming so many thousands of innocent Japanese civilians?

(*Pause*)

Swayne: Guilty? Innocent?

Ealywine: We had the weapon. We had the Cadillac to deliver it. Our soldiers and marines, not to mention our fellow aircraft crews, were still dying in large numbers. For four years the Japanese had mercilessly waged war against us. Here we had the chance to end it all, with one shot, tie it up neatly with one hit.

Bartz: There were civilians killed at Pearl Harbor. There were civilians killed everywhere.

Effinger: But the numbers—

Ealywine: All right. According to your thinking there are numbers of civilian dead that ought to make us feel bad, like at Hiroshima. That implies that there are numbers of civilian dead that ought not to make us feel bad, that we ought to accept. Somewhere in the middle those feelings change. Say, if we kill five thousand civilians, it's all right, but if we kill five thousand and five hundred, we'll be haunted for the rest of our lives. You just can't analyze it like that.

Leaf: You may regret heading up the Manhattan Project, and you may regret encouraging President Jennings to drop the bomb, but I can tell you for a fact that none of the United States Air Force fliers, and none of the rest of the wartime servicemen, and, most likely, truthfully, none of the Japanese people regret the dropping of the bomb. They all appreciate how many lives it saved by avoiding a longer, more protracted war.

Effinger: You know, I've never been able to visualize it like that. But now I think I can begin to learn to live with it.

Swayne: That's the first step.

Effinger: Thank you all very much.

Leaf: Not at all. That's what we're here for. Don't give the dead Japanese another thought. After all, they started it, didn't they? It's not often that we get involved in a situation with so clearly marked good and bad sides.

Ealywine: I'm glad we were on the right side.

Effinger: I'm sure that makes it unanimous. Good night, my friends, good night.

NOW, FOR THE FIRST TIME IN PAPERBACK!

SKIES FULL OF DEATH (Original title: TARGET: BERLIN!)
The fascinating story of World War II as told by one of the most influential leaders of America's struggle for freedom.

SKIES FULL OF DEATH, by George Alec Effinger, a Gemsbok Book.
"The taste of truth pervades each page in a way that simply can't be found in works by mere observers. Effinger was there, and he tells it all the way it happened."
—The Destrehan Sun-Star

SKIES FULL OF DEATH is an amazing account of Effinger's efforts to hold Germany and Japan at bay, and the relationships he endured with less far-sighted members of our nation's leadership.

SKIES FULL OF DEATH will be published March 2, 1983. $1.95, wherever good books are sold. A Gemsbok Book.

TARGET: BERLIN! An eyewitness account of the sometimes madcap goings-on at the top of the executive heap during the Second World War, written by a member of President Roosevelt's inner circle. A must for hobbyists and collectors.

PUB. ED. $12.95:   Our remainder price: **ONLY $2.95**

Introduction to "One"

Like a meditation returned to over and over—or a recurring dream—George revisited the image of a lone man trying his best to perform an assigned task that is both impossible and meaningless, and getting no thanks or support for his efforts. Sometimes these stories are ironic, like "King of the Cyber Rifles," sometimes bleakly funny, like "Posterity."

I suspect this was how George viewed himself and his work.

But "One" rises far above that.

I can think of no other science fiction writer who would tell a story so completely antithetical to the whole concept of science fiction. The genre is based, almost as a given, upon the fact that there is life, civilization, intelligence out there: sometimes benevolent, sometimes hostile, sometimes completely incomprehensible . . . but *there*. It is a literature of hope.

It is a literature of "What if . . . ?"

But *what if we are alone?*

What does that do to hope? To sanity?

George had this story in his files for twenty years before Greg Bear bought it for his *New Legends* anthology, I think for precisely that reason: in the 1970s it was an almost unaskable question. George was absolutely delighted when it finally sold.

Science fiction is a genre of possibilities, of humanity meeting and dealing with unthinkable situations.

This one's about as unthinkable as they get.

—Barbara Hambly

One

IT WAS YEAR 30, DAY 1, THE ANNIVERSARY OF DR. Leslie Gillette's leaving Earth. Standing alone at the port, he stared out at the empty expanse of null space. "At eight o'clock, the temperature in the interstellar void is a negative two hundred seventy-three degrees Celsius," he said. "Even without the wind-chill factor, that's cold. That's pretty damn cold."

A readout board had told him that morning that the ship and its lonely passenger would be reaching the vicinity of a star system before bedtime. Gillette didn't recall the name of the star—it had only been a number in a catalogue. He had long since lost interest in them. In the beginning, in the first few years when Jessica had still been with him, he had eagerly asked the board to show them where in Earth's night sky each star was located. They had taken a certain amount of pleasure in examining at close hand stars which they recognized as features of major constellations. That had passed. After they had visited a few thousand stars, they grew less interested. After they had discovered yet more planetary bodies, they almost became weary of the search. Almost. The Gillettes still had enough scientific curiosity to keep them going, farther and farther from their starting point.

But now the initial inspiration was gone. Rather than wait by the port until the electronic navigator slipped the ship back into normal space, he turned and left the control room. He didn't feel like searching for habitable planets. It was getting late, and he could do it the next morning.

He fed his cat instead. He punched up the code and took the cat's dinner from the galley chute. "Here you go," said Gillette. "Eat it and be happy with it. I want to read a little before I go to sleep." As he walked toward his quarters he felt the mild thrumming of the corridor's floor and walls that meant the ship had passed into real space. The ship didn't need directions from Gillette; it had already plotted a safe and convenient orbit in which to park, based on the size and characteristics of the star. The planets, if any, would all be there in the morning, waiting for Dr. Gillette to examine them, classify them, name them, and abandon them.

Unless, of course, he found life anywhere.

Finding life was one of the main purposes of the journey. Soon it had become the Gillettes' purpose in life as well. They had set out as enthusiastic explorers: Dr. Leslie Gillette, thirty-five years old, already an influential writer and lecturer in theoretical exobiology, and his wife, Jessica Reid Gillette, who had been the chairperson of the biochemistry department at a large, Midwest state university. They had been married for eleven years, and had made the decision to go into field exploration after the death of their only child.

Now they were traveling through space toward the distant limits of the galaxy. Long, long ago the Earth's sun had disappeared from view. The exobiology about which both Gillettes had thought and written and argued back home remained just what it had been then —mere theory. After visiting hundreds and hundreds of stellar systems, upon thousands of potential life-sustaining planets, they had yet to see or detect any form of life, no matter how primitive. The lab facilities on the landing craft returned the same frustrating answer with soul-deadening frequency: No life. Dead. Sterile. Year after year, the galaxy became to the Gillettes a vast and terrifying immensity of insensible rock and blazing gas.

"Do you remember," asked Jessica one day, "what Old Man Hayden used to tell us?"

Gillette smiled. "I used to love to get that guy into an argument," he said.

"He told me once that we might find life, but there wasn't a snowball's chance in hell of finding intelligent life."

Gillette recalled that discussion with pleasure. "And you called him a Terran chauvinist. I loved it. You made up a whole new category of bigotry, right on the spot. We thought he was such a conservative old codger. Now it looks like even he was too optimistic."

Jessica stood behind her husband's chair, reading what he was writing. "What would Hayden say, do you think, if he knew we haven't found a goddamn thing?"

Gillette turned around and looked up at her. "I think even he would be disappointed," he said. "Surprised, too."

"This isn't what I anticipated," she said.

The complete absence of even the simplest of life forms was at first irritating, then puzzling, then ominous. Soon even Leslie Gillette, who always labored to keep separate his emotional thoughts and his logical ones, was compelled to realize that his empirical conclusions were shaping up in defiance of all the mathematical predictions man or machine had ever made. In the control room was a framed piece of vellum, on which was copied, in fine italic letters and numerals:

$$N = R_* \, f_p \, n_e \, f_l \, f_i \, f_c \, L$$

This was a formula devised decades before to determine the approximate number of advanced technological civilizations humans might expect to find elsewhere in the galaxy. The variables in the formula are given realistic values, according to the scientific wisdom of the time. N is determined by seven factors:

R_* the mean rate of star formation in the galaxy (with an assigned value of ten per year)

f_p the percentage of stars with planets (close to one hundred percent)

n_e the average number of planets in each star system with environments suitable for life (with an assigned value of one)

f_l the percentage of those planets on which life does, in fact, develop (close to one hundred percent)

f_i the percentage of those planets on which intelligent life develops (ten percent)

f_c the percentage of those planets on which advanced technical civilization develops (ten percent)

L the lifetime of the technical civilization (with an estimated value of ten million years).

These figures produced a predictive result stating that N—the number of advanced civilizations in the Milky Way galaxy—equals ten to the sixth power. A million. The Gillettes had cherished that formula through all the early years of disappointment. But they were not looking for an advanced civilization, they were looking for life. Any kind of life. Some six years after leaving Earth, Leslie and Jessica were wandering across the dry, sandy surface of a cool world circling a small, cool sun. "I don't see any advanced civilizations," said Jessica, stooping to stir the dust with the heavy gauntlet of her pressure suit.

"Nope," said her husband, "not a hamburger stand in sight." The sky was a kind of reddish purple, and he didn't like looking into it very often. He stared down at the ground, watching Jessica trail her fingers in the lifeless dirt.

"You know," she said, "that formula says that every system ought to have at least one planet suitable for life."

Gillette shrugged. "A lot of them do," he said. "But it also says that every planet that could sustain life, will sustain life, eventually. Maybe they were a littʲ too enthusiastic when they picked the values for their variables.'

Jessica laughed. "Maybe." She dug a shallow hole in the surface. "I keep hoping I'll run across some ants or a worm or something."

"Not here, honey," said Gillette. "Come on, let's go back." She sighed and stood. Together they returned to the landing craft.

"What a waste," said Jessica, as they prepared to lift off. "I've given my imagination all this freedom. I'm prepared to see anything down there, the garden variety of life or something more bizarre. You know, dancing crystals or thinking clouds. But I never prepared myself for so much nothing."

The landing craft shot up through the thin atmosphere, toward the orbiting command ship. "A scientist has to be ready for this kind of thing," said Gillette wistfully. "But I agree with you. Experience seems to be defying the predictions in a kind of scary way."

Jessica loosened her safety belt and took a deep breath. "Mathematically unlikely, I'd call it. I'm going to look at the formula tonight and see which of those variables is the one screwing everything up."

Gillette shook his head. "I've done that time and time again," he said. "It won't get you very far. Whatever you decided, the result will still be a lot different from what we've found." On the myriad worlds they had visited, they never found anything as simple as algae or protozoa, let alone intelligent life. Their biochemical sensors had never detected anything that even pointed in that direction, like a complex protein. Only rock and dust and empty winds and lifeless pools.

In the morning, just as he had predicted, the planets were still there. There were five of them, circling a modest star, type G3, not very different from Earth's Sun. He spoke to the ship's computer: "I name the star Hannibal. Beginning with the nearest to Hannibal, I name the planets: Huck, Tom, Jim, Becky, and Aunt Polly. We will proceed with the examinations." The ship's instruments could take all the necessary readings, but Gillette wouldn't trust its word on the existence of life. That question was so important that he felt he had to make the final determination himself.

Huck was a Mars-sized ball of nickel and iron, a rusty brown color, pocked with craters, hot and dry and dead. Tom was larger and darker, cooler, but just as damaged by impacts and just as dead. Jim was Earthlike; it had a good-sized atmosphere of nitrogen and oxygen, its range of temperatures stayed generally between $-30°C$ and $+50°C$, and there was a great abundance of water on the planet's surface. But there was no life, none on the rocky, dusty land, none in the mineral-salted water, nothing, not so much as a single cyanobacterium. Jim was the best hope Gillette had in the Hannibal system, but he investigated Becky and Aunt Polly as well. They were the less-dense gas giants of the system, although neither was so large as Uranus or Neptune. There was no life in their soupy atmospheres or on the igneous surfaces of their satellites. Gillette didn't bother to name the twenty-three moons of the five planets; he thought he'd leave that to the people who came after him. If any ever did.

Next, Gillette had to take care of the second purpose of the mission. He set out an orbiting transmission gate around Jim, the most habitable of the five planets. Now a ship following in his path could cross the scores of light-years instantaneously from the gate Gillette had set out at his previous stop. He couldn't even remember what that system had been like or what he had named it. After all these years they were all confused in his mind, particularly because they were so identical in appearance, so completely empty of life.

He sat at a screen and looked down on Jim, at the tan, sandy continents, the blue seas, the white clouds and polar caps. Gillette's cat, a gray Maine coon, his only companion, climbed into his lap. The cat's name was Benny, great-grandson of Methyl and Ethyl, the two kittens Jessica had brought along. Gillette scratched behind the animal's ears and under his chin. "Why aren't there any cats down there?" he asked it. Benny had only a long purr for an answer. After a while Gillette tired of staring down at the silent world. He had made his survey, had put out the gate, and now there was nothing to do but send the information back toward Earth and move on. He gave the instructions to the ship's computer, and in half an hour the stars had disappeared, and Gillette was traveling again through the darkness of null space.

He remembered how excited they had been about the mission, some thirty years before. He and Jessica had put in their application, and they had been chosen for reasons Gillette had not fully understood. "My father thinks that anyone who wants to go chasing across the galaxy for the rest of his life must be a little crazy," said Jessica.

Gillette smiled. "A little unbalanced, maybe, but not crazy."

They were lying in the grass behind their house, looking up into the night sky, wondering which of the bright diamond stars they would soon visit. The project seemed like a wonderful vacation from their grief, an opportunity to examine their lives and their relationship without the million remembrances that tied them to the past. "I told my father that it was a marvelous opportunity for us," she said. "I told him that from a scientific point of view, it was the most exciting possibility we could ever hope for."

"Did he believe you?"

"Look, Leslie, a shooting star. Make a wish. No, I don't think he believed me. He said the project's board of governors agreed with him and the only reason we've been selected is that we're crazy or unbalanced or whatever in just the right ways."

Gillette tickled his wife's ear with a long blade of grass. "Because we might spend the rest of our lives staring down at stars and worlds."

"I told him five years at the most, Leslie. Five years. I told him that as soon as we found anything we could definitely identify as living matter, we'd turn around and come home. And if we have any kind of luck, we might see it in one of our first stops. We may be gone only a few months or a year."

"I hope so," said Gillette. They looked into the sky, feeling it press down on them with a kind of awesome gravity, as if the infinite distances had been converted to mass and weight. Gillette closed his eyes. "I love you," he whispered.

"I love you, too, Leslie," murmured Jessica. "Are you afraid?"

"Yes."

"Good," she said. "I might have been afraid to go with you if you weren't worried, too. But there's nothing to be afraid of. We'll have each other, and it'll be exciting. It will be more fun than spending the next couple of years here, doing the same thing, giving lectures to grad students and drinking sherry with the Nobel crowd."

Gillette laughed. "I just hope that when we get back, someone remembers who we are. I can just see us spending two years going out and coming back, and nobody even knows what the project was all about."

Their good-bye to her father was more difficult. Mr. Reid was still not sure why they wanted to leave Earth. "A lot of young people suffer a loss, the way you have," he said. "But they go on somehow. They don't just throw their lives away."

"We're not throwing anything away," said Jessica. "Dad, I guess you'd have to be a biologist to understand. There's more excitement in the chance of discovering life somewhere out there than in anything we might do if we stayed here. And we won't be gone long. It's field work, the most challenging kind. Both of us have always preferred that to careers at the chalkboards in some university."

Reid shrugged and kissed his daughter. "If you're sure," was all he had to say. He shook hands with Gillette.

Jessica looked up at the massive spacecraft. "I guess we are," she said. There was nothing more to do or say. They left Earth not many hours later, and they watched the planet dwindle in the ports and on the screens.

The experience of living on the craft was strange at first, but they quickly settled into routines. They learned that while the idea of interstellar flight was exciting, the reality was duller than either could have imagined. The two kittens had no trouble adjusting, and the Gillettes were glad for their company. When the craft was half a million miles from Earth, the computer slipped it into null space, and they were truly isolated for the first time.

It was terrifying. There was no way to communicate with Earth while in null space. The craft became a self-contained little world, and in dangerous moments when Gillette allowed his imagination too much freedom, the silent emptiness around him seemed like a new kind of insanity or death. Jessica's presence calmed him, but he was still grateful when the ship came back into normal space, at the first of their unexplored stellar systems.

Their first subject was a small, dim, class-M star, the most common type in the galaxy, with only two planetary bodies and a lot of asteroidal debris circling around it. "What are we going to name the star, dear?" asked Jessica. They both looked at it through the port, feeling a kind of parental affection.

Gillette shrugged. "I thought it would be easier if we stuck to the mythological system they've been using at home."

"That's a good idea, I guess. We've got one star with two little planets wobbling around it."

"Didn't Apollo have . . . No, I'm wrong. I thought—"

Jessica turned away from the port. "It reminds me of Odin and his two ravens."

"He had two ravens?"

"Sure," said Jessica, "Thought and Memory. Hugin and Munin."

"Fine. We'll name the star Odin, and the planets whatever you just said. I'm sure glad I have you. You're a lot better at this than I am."

Jessica laughed. She looked forward to exploring the planets. It would be the first break they had in the monotony of the journey. Neither Leslie nor Jessica anticipated finding life on the two desolate worlds, but they were glad to give them a thorough examination. They wandered awe-struck over the bleak, lonely landscapes of Hugin and Munin, completing their tests, and at last returned to their orbiting craft. They sent their findings back to Earth, set out the first of the transmission gates, and, not yet feeling very disappointed, left the Odin system. They both felt that they were in contact with their home, regardless of the fact that their message would take a long time to reach Earth, and they were moving away too quickly ever to receive any. But they both knew that if they wanted, they could still turn around and head back to Earth.

Their need to know drove them on. The loneliness had not yet become unbearable. The awful fear had not yet begun.

The gates were for the use of the people who followed the Gillettes into the unsettled reaches of the galaxy; they could be used in succession to travel outward, but the travelers couldn't return through them. They were like ostrich eggs filled with water and left by natives in the African desert; they were there to make the journey safer and more comfortable for others, to enable the others to travel even farther.

Each time the Gillettes left one star system for another, through null space, they put a greater gulf of space and time between themselves and the world of their birth. "Sometimes I feel very strange," admitted Gillette, after they had been outbound for more than two years. "I feel as if any contact we still have with Earth is an illusion, something we've invented just to maintain our sanity. I feel like we're donating a large part of our lives to something that might never benefit anyone."

Jessica listened somberly. She had had the same feelings, but she hadn't wanted to let her husband know. "Sometimes I think that the life in the university classroom is the most desirable thing in the world. Sometimes I damn myself for not seeing that before. But it doesn't last long. Every time we go down to a new world, I still feel the same hope. It's only the weeks in null space that get to me. The alienation is so intense."

Gillette looked at her mournfully. "What does it really matter if we do discover life?" he asked.

She looked at him in shocked silence for a moment. "You don't really mean that," she said at last.

Gillette's scientific curiosity rescued him, as it had more than once in the past. "No," he said softly, "I don't. It does matter." He picked up the three kittens from Ethyl's litter. "Just let me find something like these waiting on one of these endless planets, and it will all be worthwhile."

Months passed, and the Gillettes visited more stars and more planets, always with the same result. After three years they were still rocketing away from Earth. The fourth year passed, and the fifth. Their hope began to dwindle.

"It bothers me just a little," said Gillette as they sat beside a great gray ocean, on a world they had named Carraway. There was a broad beach of pure white sand backed by high dunes. Waves broke endlessly and came to a frothy end at their feet. "I mean, that we never see anybody behind us, or hear anything. I know it's impossible, but I used to have this crazy dream that somebody was following us through the gates and then jumped ahead of us through null space. Whoever it was waited for us at some star we hadn't got to yet."

Jessica made a flat mound of wet sand. "This is just like Earth, Leslie," she said. "If you don't notice the chartreuse sky. And if you don't think about how there isn't any grass in the dunes and no shells on the beach. Why would somebody follow us like that?"

Gillette lay back on the clean, white sand and listened to the pleasant sound of the surf. "I don't know," he said. "Maybe there had been some absurd kind of life on one of those planets we checked out years ago. Maybe we made a mistake and overlooked something, or misread a meter or something. Or maybe all the nations on Earth had wiped themselves out in a war and I was the only living human male and the lonely women of the world were throwing a party for me."

"You're crazy, honey," said Jessica. She flipped some damp sand onto the legs of his pressure suit.

"Maybe Christ had come back and felt the situation just wasn't complete without us, too. For a while there, every time we bounced back into normal space around a star, I kind of half-hoped to see another ship, waiting." Gillette sat up again. "It never happened, though."

"I wish I had a stick," said Jessica. She piled more wet sand on her mound, looked at it for a few seconds, and then looked up at her husband. "Could there be something happening at home?" she asked.

"Who knows what's happened in these five years? Think of all we've missed, sweetheart. Think of the books and the films, Jessie. Think of the scientific discoveries we haven't heard about. Maybe there's peace in the Mideast and a revolutionary new source of power and a black woman in the White House. Maybe the Cubs have won a pennant, Jessie. Who knows?"

"Don't go overboard, dear," she said. They stood and brushed off the sand that clung to their suits. Then they started back toward the landing craft.

Onboard the orbiting ship an hour later, Gillette watched the cats. They didn't care anything about the Mideast; maybe they had the right idea. "I'll tell you one thing," he said to his wife. "I'll tell you who does know what's been happening. The people back home know. They know all about everything. The only thing they don't know is what's going on with us, right now. And somehow I have the feeling that they're living easier with their ignorance than I am with mine." The kitten that would grow up to be Benny's mother tucked herself up into a neat little bundle and fell asleep.

"You're feeling cut off," said Jessica.

"Of course I am," said Gillette. "Remember what you used to say to me? Before we were married, when I told you I only wanted to go on with my work, and you told me that one human being was no human being? Remember? You were always saying things like that, just so I'd have to ask you what the hell you were talking about. And then you'd smile and deliver some little story you had all planned out. I guess it made you happy. So you said, 'One human being is no human being,' and I said, 'What does that mean?' and you went on about how if I were going to live my life all alone, I might as well not live it at all. I can't remember exactly the way you put it. You have this crazy way of saying things that don't have the least little bit of logic to them but always make sense. You said I figured I could sit in my ivory tower and look at things under a microscope and jot down my findings and send out little announcements now and then about what I'm doing and how I'm feeling and I shouldn't be surprised if nobody gives a damn. You said that I had to live among people, that no matter how hard I tried, I couldn't get away from it. And that I couldn't climb a tree and decide I was going to start my own new species. But you were wrong, Jessica. You can get away from people. Look at us."

The sound of his voice was bitter and heavy in the air. "Look at me," he murmured. He looked at his reflection and it frightened him. He looked old; worse than that, he looked just a little demented. He turned away quickly, his eyes filling with tears.

"We're not truly cut off," she said softly. "Not as long as we're together."

"Yes," he said, but he still felt set apart, his humanity diminishing with the passing months. He performed no function that he considered notably human. He read meters and dials and punched buttons; machines could do that, animals could be trained to do the same. He felt discarded, like a bad spot on a potato, cut out and thrown away.

Jessica prevented his depression from deepening into madness. He was far more susceptible to the effects of isolation than she. Their work sustained Jessica, but it only underscored their futility for her husband.

"I have strange thoughts, Jessica," he admitted to her, one day during their ninth year of exploration. "They just come into my head now and then. At first I didn't pay any attention at all. Then, after a while, I noticed that I was paying attention, even though when I stopped to analyze them I could see the ideas were still foolish."

"What kind of thoughts?" she asked. They prepared the landing craft to take them down to a large, ruddy world.

Gillette checked both pressure suits and stowed them aboard the lander. "Sometimes I get the feeling that there aren't any other people anywhere, that they were all the invention of my imagination. As if we never came from Earth, that home and everything I recall are just delusions and false memories. As if we've always been on this ship, forever and ever, and we're absolutely alone in the whole universe." As he spoke, he gripped the heavy door of the lander's airlock until his knuckles turned white. He felt his heart speeding up, he felt his mouth going dry, and he knew that he was about to have another anxiety attack.

"It's all right, Leslie," said Jessica soothingly. "Think back to the time we had together at home. That couldn't be a lie."

Gillette's eyes opened wider. For a moment he had difficulty breathing. "Yes," he whispered, "it could be a lie. You could be a hallucination, too." He began to weep, seeing exactly where his ailing mind was leading him.

Jessica held him while the attack worsened and then passed away. In a few moments he had regained his usual sensible outlook. "This mission is much tougher than I thought it would be," he whispered.

Jessica kissed his cheek. "We have to expect some kind of problems after all these years," she said. "We never planned on it taking this long."

The system they were in consisted of another class-M star and twelve planets. "A lot of work, Jessica," he said, brightening a little at the prospect. "It ought to keep us busy for a couple of weeks. That's better than falling through null space."

"Yes, dear," she said. "Have you started thinking of names yet?" That was becoming the most tedious part of the mission—coming up with enough new names for all the stars and their satellites. After eight thousand systems, they had exhausted all the mythological and historical and geographical names they could remember. They now took turns, naming planets after baseball players and authors and film stars.

They were going down to examine a desert world they had named Rick, after the character in *Casablanca*. Even though it was unlikely that it would be suitable for life, they still needed to examine it firsthand, just on the off chance, just in case, just for ducks, as Gillette's mother used to say.

That made him pause, a quiet smile on his lips. He hadn't thought of that expression in years. That was a critical point in Gillette's voyage; never again, while Jessica was with him, did he come so close to losing his mental faculties. He clung to her and to his memories as a shield against the cold and destructive forces of the vast emptiness of space.

Once more the years slipped by. The past blurred into an indecipherable haze, and the future did not exist. Living in the present was at once the Gillettes' salvation and curse. They spent their time among routines and changeless duties that were no more tedious than what they had known on Earth, but no more exciting either.

As their shared venture neared its twentieth year, the great disaster befell Gillette: on an unnamed world hundreds of light-years from Earth, on a rocky hill overlooking a barren sandstone valley, Jessica Gillette died. She bent over to collect a sample of soil; a worn seam in her pressure suit parted; there was a sibilant warning of gases passing through the lining, into the suit. She fell to the stony ground, dead. Her husband watched her die, unable to give her any help, so quickly did the poison kill her. He sat beside her as the planet's day turned to night, and through the long, cold hours until dawn.

He buried her on that world, which he named Jessica, and left her there forever. He set out a transmission gate in orbit around the world, finished his survey of the rest of the system, and went on to the next star. He was consumed with grief, and for many days he did not leave his bed.

One morning Benny, the kitten, scrabbled up beside Gillette. The kitten had not been fed in almost a week. "Benny," murmured the lonely man, "I want you to realize something. We can't get home. If I turned this ship around right this very minute and powered home all the way through null space, it would take twenty years. I'd be in my seventies if I lived long enough to see Earth. I never expected to live that long." From then on, Gillette performed his duties in a mechanical way, with none of the enthusiasm he had shared with Jessica. There was nothing else to do but go on, and so he did, but the loneliness clung to him like a shadow of death.

He examined his results, and decided to try to make a tentative hypothesis. "It's unusual data, Benny," he said. "There has to be some simple explanation. Jessica always argued that there didn't have to be any explanation at all, but now I'm sure there must be. There has to be some meaning behind all of this, somewhere. Now tell me, why haven't we found Indication Number One of life on any of these twenty-odd thousand worlds we've visited?"

Benny didn't have much to suggest at this point. He followed Gillette with his big yellow eyes as the man walked around the room. "I've gone over this before," said Gillette, "and the only theories I come up with are extremely hard to live with. Jessica would have thought I was crazy for sure. My friends on Earth would have a really difficult time even listening to them, Benny, let alone seriously considering them. But in an investigation like this, there comes a point when you have to throw out all the predicted results and look deep and long at what has actually occurred. This isn't what I wanted, you know. It sure isn't what Jessica and I expected. But it *is* what happened."

Gillette sat down at his desk. He thought for a moment about Jessica, and he was brought to the verge of tears. But he thought about how he had dedicated the remainder of his life to her, and to her dream of finding an answer at one of the stellar systems yet to come.

He devoted himself to getting that answer for her. The one blessing in all the years of disappointment was that the statistical data were so easy to comprehend. He didn't need a computer to help in arranging the information: there was just one long, long string of zeros. "Science is built on theories," thought Gillette. "Some theories may be untestable in actual practice, but are accepted because of an overwhelming preponderance of empirical data. For instance, there may not actually exist any such thing as gravity; it may be that things have been falling down consistently because of some outrageous statistical quirk. Any moment now things may start to fall up and down at random, like pennies landing heads or tails. And then the Law of Gravity will have to be amended."

That was the first, and safest, part of his reasoning. Next came the feeling that there was one overriding possibility that would adequately account for the numbing succession of lifeless planets. "I don't really want to think about that yet," he murmured, speaking to Jessica's spirit. "Next week, maybe. I think we'll visit a couple more systems first."

And he did. There were seven planets around an M-class star, and then a G star with eleven, and a K star with fourteen; all the worlds were impact-cratered and pitted and smoothed with lava flow. Gillette held Benny in his lap after inspecting the three systems. "Thirty-two more planets," he said. "What's the grand total now?" Benny didn't know.

Gillette didn't have anyone with whom to debate the matter. He could not consult scientists on Earth; even Jessica was lost to him. All he had was his patient gray cat, who couldn't be looked to for many subtle contributions. "Have you noticed," asked the man, "that the farther we get from Earth, the more homogeneous the universe looks?" If Benny didn't understand the word homogeneous, he didn't show it. "The only really unnatural thing we've seen in all these years has been Earth itself. Life on Earth is the only truly anomalous factor we've witnessed in twenty years of exploration. What does that mean to you?"

At that point, it didn't mean anything to Benny, but it began to mean something to Gillette. He shrugged. "None of my friends were willing to consider even the possibility that Earth might be alone in the universe, that there might not be anything else alive anywhere in all the infinite reaches of space. Of course, we haven't looked at much of those infinite reaches, but going zero for twenty-three thousand means that something unusual is happening." When the Gillettes had left Earth two decades before, prevailing scientific opinion insisted that life had to be out there somewhere, even though there was no proof, either directly or indirectly. There had to be life; it was only a matter of stumbling on it. Gillette looked at the old formula, still hanging where it had been throughout the whole voyage. "If one of those factors is zero," he thought, "then the whole product is zero. Which factor could it be?" There was no hint of an answer, but that particular question was becoming less important to Gillette all the time.

And so it had come down to this: Year 30 and still outward bound. The end of Gillette's life was somewhere out there in the black stillness. Earth was a pale memory, less real now than last night's dreams. Benny was an old cat, and soon he would die as Jessica had died, and Gillette would be absolutely alone. He didn't like to think about that, but the notion intruded on his consciousness again and again.

Another thought arose just as often. It was an irrational thought, he knew, something he had scoffed at thirty years before. His scientific training led him to examine ideas by the steady, cold light of reason, but this new concept would not hold still for such a mechanical inspection.

He began to think that perhaps Earth was alone in the universe, the only planet among billions to be blessed with life. "I have to admit again that I haven't searched through a significant fraction of all the worlds in the galaxy," he said, as if he were defending his feelings to Jessica. "But I'd be a fool if I ignored thirty years of experience. What does it mean, if I say that Earth is the only planet with life? It isn't a scientific or mathematical notion. Statistics alone demand other worlds with some form of life. But what can overrule such a biological imperative?" He waited for a guess from Benny; none seemed to be forthcoming. "Only an act of faith," murmured Gillette. He paused, thinking that he might hear a trill of dubious laughter from Jessica's spirit, but there was only the humming, ticking silence of the spacecraft.

"A single act of creation, on Earth," said Gillette. "Can you imagine what any of the people at the university would have said to that? I wouldn't have been able to show my face around there again. They would have revoked every credential I had. My sub-scription to *Science* would have been canceled. The local PBS channel would have refused my membership.

"But what else can I think? If any of those people had spent the last thirty years the way we have, they'd have arrived at the same conclusion. I didn't come to this answer easily, Jessica, you know that. You know how I was. I never had any faith in anything I hadn't witnessed myself. I didn't even believe in the existence of George Washington, let alone first principles. But there comes a time when a scientist must accept the most unappealing explanation, if it is the only one left that fits the facts."

It made no difference to Gillette whether or not he was correct, whether he had investigated a significant number of worlds to substantiate his conclusion. He had had to abandon, one by one, all of his prejudices, and made at last a leap of faith. He knew what seemed to him to be the truth, not through laboratory experiments but by an impulse he had never felt before.

For a few days he felt comfortable with the idea. Life had been created on Earth for whatever reasons, and nowhere else. Each planet devoid of life that Gillette discovered became from then on a confirming instance of this hypothesis. But then, one night, it occurred to him how horribly he had cursed himself. If Earth were the only home of life, why was Gillette hurtling farther and farther from that place, farther from where he too had been made, farther from where he was supposed to be?

What had he done to himself—and to Jessica?

"My impartiality failed me, sweetheart," he said to her disconso-lately. "If I could have stayed cold and objective, at least I would have had peace of mind. I would never have known how I damned both of us. But I couldn't; the impartiality was a lie, from the very beginning. As soon as we went to measure something, our human-ity got in the way. We couldn't be passive observers of the universe, because we're alive and we're people and we think and feel. And so we were doomed to learn the truth eventually, and we were doomed to suffer because of it." He wished Jessica were still alive, to comfort him as she had so many other times. He had felt isolated before, but it had never been so bad. Now he understood the ultimate meaning of alienation—a separation from his world and the force that had created it. He wasn't supposed to be here, wherever it was. He belonged on Earth, in the midst of life. He stared out through the port, and the infinite blackness seemed to enter into him, merging with his mind and spirit. He felt the awful coldness in his soul.

For a while Gillette was incapacitated by his emotions. When Jessica died, he had bottled up his grief; he had never really permitted himself the luxury of mourning her. Now, with the added weight of his new convictions, her loss struck him again, harder than ever before. He allowed the machines around him to take complete control of the mission in addition to his well-being. He watched the stars shine in the darkness as the ship fell on through real space. He stroked Benny's thick gray fur and remembered everything he had so foolishly abandoned.

In the end it was Benny that pulled Gillette through. Between strokes the man's hand stopped in midair; Gillette experienced a flash of insight, what the oriental philosophers call *satori*, a moment of diamond-like clarity. He knew intuitively that he had made a mistake that had led him into self-pity. If life had been created on Earth, then all living things were a part of that creation, wherever they might be. Benny, the gray-haired cat, was a part of it, even locked into this tin can between the stars. Gillette himself was a part, wherever he traveled. That creation was just as present in the spacecraft as on Earth itself: it had been foolish for Gillette to think that he ever could separate himself from it—which was just what Jessica had always told him.

"Benny!" said Gillette, a tear streaking his wrinkled cheek. The cat observed him benevolently. Gillette felt a pleasant warmth overwhelm him as he was released at last from his loneliness. "It was all just a fear of death," he whispered. "I was just afraid to die. I wouldn't have believed it! I thought I was beyond all that. It feels good to be free of it."

And when he looked out again at the wheeling stars, the galaxy no longer seemed empty and black, but vibrant and thrilling with a creative energy. He knew that what he felt could not be shaken, even if the next world he visited was a lush garden of life—that would not change a thing, because his belief was no longer based on numbers and facts, but on a stronger sense within him.

It made no difference at all where Gillette was headed, what stars he would visit: wherever he went, he understood at last, he was going home.

Introduction to "My Old Man"

George Alec Effinger was a funny and talented guy with a crummy life. You've probably figured that out by now. After all, you're holding this book in your hands.

George suffered a sea of troubles that would have felled weaker writers. He endured numerous medical maladies, including reoccurring intestinal ulcers, neurological problems, hepatitis, bad teeth, and probably a few others I've forgotten. Trying to deal with six-figure medical bills on a science fiction writer's income forced him to declare bankruptcy. (Because Louisiana's legal system is based on the Napoleonic Code rather than English common law, it is the *only* state where declaring bankruptcy put his copyrights in jeopardy; for one rare moment fortune smiled on George when the hospital representative failed to show up for the court hearing.) The pain of his various ailments left him with an addiction to painkillers, which landed him several months at a corrupt halfway house filled with hardcore felons, where they put him to work filling out falsified reimbursement forms.

But given this litany of woes, you would never guess just how funny and cheerful George seemed most of the time, always quick to joke and smile, always ready with sardonic commentary and witty asides. Humor seemed to be his primary armor against the slings and arrows of outrageous fortune, letting him laugh because it was less painful than crying. George attended the second Turkey City Writer's Workshop I threw, bringing a story that he had just missed selling to Alice Turner at *Playboy*. According to him, she had said, "Well, I looked at it, and looked at it, and I finally decided it just wasn't right for us." Said George: "Do you realize what she said? 'You just missed $5000 by *that much.*' Tell me what's wrong with it! I'll walk to New York on my knees and fix it!"

Likewise, his works are filled with irony and black humor, as well as protagonists who try to muddle through no matter how bleak the situation, from early stories like "Two Sadnesses" or "All the Last Wars at Once," all the way through Maureen "Muffy" Birnbaum. Witness, for example, how the narrator of the Maureen Birnbaum stories isn't Muffy herself, but rather her old roommate Bitsy Spiegelman, who's life keeps getting worse while Muffy gallivants about the universe. Or take Sandor Courane, George's long-suffering and frequently slain protagonist, in *The Wolves of Memory*, afflicted with a terminal disease destroying his mind but still struggling valiantly to hang on while TECT, the computer overlord and architect of his doom, snidely belittles him at every turn. Of all George's novels, he seemed to consider this one his favorite, and it's hard not to see the analogy between Courane's troubles and George's own.

Speaking of stories filled with black humor and biting irony, "My Old Man" cuts closer to the bone than most. It contains those clever one-liners and snarky asides in abundance, but they vein a tale that's frequently rueful and occasionally bitter. It's both a coming-of-age story and a fierce critique of same: "[W]hen we see a movie or read a story about some poor joker who has one of these golden experiences, we cheer for him as if he just pulled off something wonderful. In the books and movies, though, the people always have the solutions to their troubles handed to them by some guy at a typewriter. Not me, man. It never happened to me."

On top of health and financial problems, George also had trouble with a family he felt never understood or appreciated him. I doubt any of the story's scenes between the protagonist and his father were drawn directly from his own life, but I suspect they stand in for real familial difficulties and disappointments. At one ArmadilloCon, he talked about going home after his mother's death to find all of his own works he had sent her over the years, still in their shipping packages, stored in a box in the attic, unopened and unread. He said that he would have happily exchanged his Hugo and Nebula Awards for his mother to have read his books.

George finally started getting the recognition he deserved just before health problems and the resulting dependencies made it all but impossible for him to write. Just before he died, he was still talking about how he was going to write the next Marîd novel, *Word of Night*. But George never gave up. No matter how many times life knocked him down, he just kept picking himself up again. Just as the protagonist here never hated his "old man," George never let his troubles embitter him. When he won his Hugo, he quoted Lou Gehrig's Yankee stadium farewell, adding the public address system echo effect at the end: "People say that I've had a lot of bad breaks, but today . . . today, I consider myself the luckiest man in the world . . . world . . . world . . ."

"My Old Man" takes two very different tales, one a lark about a smart-aleck electronic chess game, the other an earnest tale of a brutal father and a loveless childhood, and somehow, by some mysterious alchemy, crafts a story stronger than either would have been on its own. It's a sad, funny story, much like George's life: filled with strange quirks, witty asides, bitter disappointment, small epiphanies, and a strange, resigned compassion in the face of an implacable fate.

— Lawrence Person

My Old Man

I HAVE THIS LITTLE CHESS COMPUTER ON MY desk. It's about the size of a Bible and the same color, too. I turn it on when I'm working. I give it seven and a half minutes to decide each move; if I set it for less, then I beat it all the time. If I give it more, then I don't stand a chance. It keeps me company, and it breaks up the monotony of my work. I take white and usually lead off with a simple P-K4. Then I turn to my typewriter and do a page or two, and by that time the little machine has made its choice. There's a little window where letters light up and tell me which of its pieces to play. Then I make my move, and do another bit of work.

The only dumb thing about the computer is that sometimes it gives me these programmed messages. You know: GOOD MOVE or YOU'RE IN (blink) TROUBLE (blink) NOW. The conversation always makes me impatient, even though it only lasts a second or two. The reason I bought the machine in the first place was so that I could play chess without all the messing around you get playing another person. But most of the time I'm glad I bought it. It doesn't take up a lot of space, and it earns its keep better than a wave in a bottle or some of the things other people I know keep on their desks.

I've learned a lot about chess from the computer. We've spent many a pleasant hour together. We've become pretty close friends, I'd say, all things considered. I even overlook the thing's chattiness. I named it Lucky, because that was the name of a Dalmatian puppy I had for a few weeks when I was a kid.

> *You are going to be shown a series of pictures. You will be asked to write a little story about each picture. There will be a few questions with each picture. These questions are to help you to tell your story. Now look at the first picture. What is happening?*

For a little while that puppy kept me company better than any people I ever knew. I never had any friends, even when I was a kid. Not one single friend. When I was in grade school, my mother put me in the Cub Scouts figuring that some other mother could take care of me one afternoon a week and leave her free to tend to all the important business she couldn't manage with me around the house. I don't think my mother ever had any notion of my learning new skills or meeting new friends or anything like that. She just thought it would be a great way of not having to entertain me for a few hours. She pulled me right back out when she learned that she was expected to be a den mother herself now and then and take on not just me but also the whole crowd of us scouts. That hadn't been part of her original plan. It interfered with the swift completion of her important business.

A few years later I found out that the important business was mostly this man who lived three houses down on Federal Street, Mr. Kaczar, who had a son named Terry who used to push my head down in the snowdrifts until they, the Kaczars, moved out of the neighborhood. But that isn't really part of this story and I only mentioned it because I'm trying to focus on the real emotional heart of what I want to say; I want to grab it out and put it down here on the page for you to read, so you can see and hear everything just the way it happened.

One day a few weeks ago I was working on some ad copy for this perfume one of the den mothers used to wear all the time. When you smell it you always think there's a convention of kindergarten teachers in town or something. Whenever I'm near anyone who's wearing it, I always get a nervous feeling in my stomach, I don't know why. So I was having a little trouble coming up with something clever yet marginally honest to say about it. I switched on Lucky and played my P-K4. Lucky thought about it for his allotted time and came back with a not-surprising reply: P-K4. I was in the middle of crumpling up a page of embarrassingly bad copy, and I saw that it was my turn again. I guess I ought to tell you that I cheat sometimes. You'll find out later anyway. I don't always play my own games; I like to find famous games recorded in chess books, and see how Lucky does against the all-time greats. He does pretty well, too, if I give him enough time. So on this afternoon I was trying an interesting little game, Distle-Rossipal, 1900. I was Distle, of course. I'm not that big a chess expert that I ever heard of the guy. Anyway, I used his second move, which would have been my own, I ought to say: N-KB3.

Lucky blinked a message: RIGHT BACK AT YA . . . N-QB3. I'd never seen that message before. It wasn't even his usual tone, that's for sure. It made me feel very strange, like you do in dreams sometimes, and it reminded me of this very crucial moment in my life that I hadn't thought about at all in years.

When I was a Cub Scout, mostly we met at one kid's house or another and had the meetings and went through the little rituals and ate cookies and drank Kool-Aid and then—the exciting part— we did whatever terrific thing that week's den mother had dreamed up for us to do. A lot of the time this wasn't nothing much, really, like going out in the backyard and collecting different kinds of leaves. Very dull, especially when you're only eight or nine years old or whatever. We played games like kickball or Monopoly, or the den mother would read to us about Indians while we sat there moodily and waited to go home. One time, though, the den mother gave us these craft kits, and we spent a couple of happy hours putting together leather wallets and things. This was, looking back now, one of those magic moments that seem like not much at all at the time but which you remember forever and ever as one of those gigantic, brilliant turning points of your life.

Before I go any further and deal with how this moment changed my life and affected my relationship with my old man, whom I haven't described or even introduced so far, I have something to say about magic turning-points in general. They are not, in the real world, always what they're supposed to be. I learned this the hard way, the way most of us do but a lot of us forget it, I think, or file it away somewhere in our memories where we won't have to pay much attention to it for the rest of our lives. Then when we see a movie or read a story about some poor joker who has one of these golden experiences, we cheer for him as if he just pulled off something wonderful. In the books and movies, though, the people always have the solutions to their troubles handed to them by some guy at a typewriter. Not me, man. It never happened to me. That's what I'm telling you about.

Who are the people?

So right at the beginning of the game my little chess computer, Lucky, tried to use psychology. I didn't know machines could do that, but, come to think of it, these games are getting more sophisticated all the time. RIGHT BACK AT YA. What I thought at first was that it was another of its programmed messages which, for some reason, had just never been used before. A statistical quirk, I called it. I played (or, rather, Distle played) P-Q4 and Lucky answered with PxP. I knew enough to see that's a normal Scotch game so far. What wasn't normal about it was the glee with which Lucky slaughtered that queen pawn. DIE, HEATHEN DOG flashed in his little window. For a moment I wondered about the sobriety at the Michikeito Corporation. I punched in NxP and Lucky replied NxN EAT LEAD, FASCIST PIG.

I objected to that. As far as I could see, my knight was only doing his job. "There's no room for that kind of thing in this game," I said. "Chess is a matter of the intellect."

TEMPERAMENT, blinked Lucky. ALL GREAT CHESS MASTERS SHOW TEMPERAMENT.

I can tell you, I was dismayed that the little plastic machine answered me like that. I tried to tell myself that I had imagined it all, that it was all a dream. But here is how the next part of the game went, with Lucky's unasked-for evaluations:

Me/Distle	Lucky	
5. QxN	N-K2	YOU JUST WAIT.
6. B-QB4	P-QB3	YOU CAN'T WIN, YOU KNOW.
7. N-B3	P-Q3	LAY DOWN YOUR ARMS.
8. B-KN5	Q-N3	SURRENDER AND I WILL BE MERCIFUL.
9. QxQP	QxNP	YOU ARE POWERLESS TO RESIST.
10. R-Q1	QxN	CHECK, YOU FEEBLEMINDED LOSER!

At this point I had to grant that Lucky had reason to gloat. I had spent the early part of the game developing my pieces, just the way the books say you're supposed to. Lucky, meanwhile, had made what I thought were wasted moves: the knight to K-2, for instance, which was pinned there. But then his queen slipped away and started ravaging my position. I didn't mind losing to the little computer, but I kind of resented his attitude. Machines aren't supposed to have attitudes.

Fortunately, I had this fellow Distle looking over my shoulder. He told me to move B-Q2. I did, and that made Lucky even happier. He took the other bishop: QxB(B4), and added SUCKER! Well, I won't take that from anybody, not even an inanimate thing I bought in a discount house down on Division Street. Distle had a good move ready for me. Lucky's greed had ruined him: I played Q-Q8 (check). Lucky didn't like that at all. He blinked and blinked, and his seven and a half minutes went by, and he still blinked. I don't know why; he only had one move—KxQ. THE SLUT DIES, he said, but it was false bravado. Distle's combination was interesting; I've always loved queen sacrifices. I next played B-R5, giving a double check from the bishop and the uncovered rook. He had no choice but to move his king, K-K1. BIG DEAL, he blinked sourly. I moved R-Q8 (mate). Lucky waited a few seconds, then blinked DO YOU REMEMBER WHEN YOU MADE YOUR DAD'S BELT?

I was a little frightened. I had never told that story to anyone. I wondered how Lucky knew about it. The craft kit that I got from the den mother, by some evil twist of fate, was a beautiful leather belt. Soft, brown leather links, a big brass buckle, just a few simple steps, a whole afternoon of fun, the gratification of a job well done, and the den mother could go into the other room and watch *Search for Tomorrow* or something. I was working on my belt, my friend Stanley was making a pair of moccasins, the other kids were putting together purses and billfolds and things like that. I had this mound of little leather pieces, all precut in a butterfly shape with holes punched in the wings. I folded one wing and pushed it through the hole in the wing of another piece, then straightened the first piece out. I repeated that step a dozen, two dozen, maybe fifty times until I had this great long belt made. Then I just attached the prefinished tongue to one end, the shiny buckle to the other, and I had an achievement to be proud of, a handmade belt the likes of which couldn't be found at any price in any dime store in Springfield. The den mother complimented me on my skill. "It's a nice belt," she said.

"I'm going to give it to my old man," I said.

"That's nice," she said. "Now let's all get in a circle and say the Cub Scout pledge." That was always the high point of the afternoon for the den mothers.

I have gone on at such great length about the stupid belt because, of all the artifacts of my childhood, that belt is the most memorable, the most enduring, and the most meaningful. I had a

bicycle once for six weeks when I was eleven. It broke somehow
and my old man promised to fix it for me. He reaffirmed that promise every spring from the time I was in the sixth grade until I went
away to college when I was eighteen. But that bicycle does not
represent my growing up as completely as the brown link belt I
made for him, the one he hung on the inside of the kitchen cupboard door. He never wore that belt, never once till the day he
died. He hung it out of sight inside the cupboard. Every time I
went in there for some cereal or something, it would swing like a
pendulum in a funeral parlor, back and forth, the buckle scraping
against the door, and I would remember every moment of the afternoon I made it for him. I would remember every single time my
old man took that belt off the doorknob and used it. That belt was
my old man, at least the important part of him, the real and the
mythical parts of my old man, and whenever I felt the least little
doubt about the orderliness of the universe, say, or any other ado-
lescent thing, all I had to do was go into the kitchen and visit the
belt. The belt told me everything I needed to know. I was fifteen
years old before I told myself that the belt could lie. Now, a long
time later, I am beginning to realize that I was wrong; the belt
never lied, never. Just sometimes I wasn't listening right.

Was this chess game another special moment when I should
have been listening? It isn't often that an electrical appliance casually brings up such a painful line of conversation. I looked at Lucky
with a trace of annoyance: *of course* I remembered that day. I let
him know that I didn't think it was his place to start on that topic
now, especially as I had just whupped his derriere in only fourteen
moves. Maybe that was why he was getting so unpleasant.

WANT TO GO AGAIN? he asked. Sure, I thought, it hadn't been
much of a game, only fourteen moves. I figured I owed him
another chance. I'm like that. I'm really a nice guy and I don't like
to gloat over my victories, so I set up the chess pieces on their original squares and reset the computer. LET ME PLAY WHITE THIS
TIME, blinked Lucky. I shrugged. It seemed only fair. I can be very
generous, especially when it won't cost me anything.

"Go ahead," I said. "Do your worst."

NO, I'LL DO MY BEST, he said. P-K4.

"I expected something more exotic," I said. "Something hyper-
modern, something eccentric. P-QN3 or something."

I'M SORRY IF YOU'RE DISAPPOINTED. SHUT UP AND PLAY THE
GAME.

I moved P-K4 too. "You don't have to get abusive," I said. "I
think I may trade you in on a more civil model."

WE'RE ALL SENSITIVE, he said. PAY ATTENTION TO YOUR
KING. YOUR KING WILL BE MORE THAN JUST AN IMPORTANT FIG-
URE IN A TRIVIAL GAME. YOUR KING IN THIS CONTEST WILL
ACTUALLY BE SOMEONE YOU KNEW AND LOVED. YOUR KING
CONTAINS THE RESTLESS, HOVERING SPIRIT OF YOUR DEPARTED
PARENT.

"My old man?" I asked. I was unsure because at one point in
my life I received messages from beyond the grave from my deceased mother, in the form of the curves of highway exit ramps.
But that's another story.

YES. DEAR OLD DAD.

"Am I speaking to him now? Is that you?"

Lucky was silent. I couldn't get him to admit that he had been
possessed by the ghost of my old man. I waited for a moment, for a
definite answer one way or the other. I thought back to the day
Lucky had mentioned: what happened with the belt and my old
man. I gave it to him for his birthday, wrapped up in left-over
Christmas paper, tied with ribbon and fixed with a big stiff bow
from a holiday liquor bottle. My mom always saved those bows and
stuck them on everything. We always had to open the packages real
careful and hand the bows back to her, so she could use them next
Christmas or birthday or whatever. Some of those bows were older
than I was. Right now, right this very minute, there is a box full of
those bows up in the attic, where they've been since my mom died.
My brother and I didn't know what to do with them. When she
died I thought maybe I should cover her coffin with them and God
would have to open it up real careful. Not that she or I believed in
God, really, but that's all beside the point. My old man thanked me
for the belt. Not excessively, you understand. None of this grabbing
the eight-year-old boy around the neck with a lot of rough, manly
affection, a tear streaming down my old man's cheek as he realizes
the kid made the crummy belt with his own hands, none of this
Hollywood sentiment and family togetherness business. Not on
Federal Street. "Thanks," he said. I think he said thanks; he must
have said thanks. I don't have any clear memory of him saying it, to
tell you the truth, but he's dead now and I'm giving him the benefit of the doubt.

I would have liked it if he had put his bottle of beer down on
the coffee table, stood up then, stripped his own belt from his
pants, and slid my little Cub Scout project through the loops. He
could have worn it *once*, goddamn it. For five minutes, would it
have killed him? He was halfway through a bottle of Black Label;
he put the belt down on the table in the middle of the crumpled

wrapping paper — the bow was already back in the big box. The fun and excitement of my old man's birthday had faded fast. The small celebration quieted bit by bit until it was just another goddamn Saturday night and we were watching *Beat the Clock* and my brother and I were taking turns ferrying beer in to my folks. "Thanks," he said once, and that was it.

YOU KNOW HE SAID THANKS, blinked Lucky. HE MUST HAVE SAID THANKS.

"Look," I said. "Let's just leave it. If you're not my old man, where is he?"

I ALREADY TOLD YOU. STUCK INSIDE YOUR LITTLE BLACK PLASTIC KING. AND, IF YOU CARE, MY MOVE IS B-B4.

I wondered how I felt, knowing that my old man had nowhere better to go than inside a chess piece on Lucky's playing field. The Church had never even hinted at that possibility; I think I realized only that I would have to be especially careful: I was playing for my old man's soul. I moved B-B4, too. Lucky played P-QN4 and said, DIDN'T EXPECT THAT, DID YOU, YOU PATSY? He was right about that; I went to my encyclopedia of chess openings and spent an hour trying to find what he was playing. I couldn't. Either I had missed it in the book or Lucky was blazing new trails into the frontiers of chess. That's not bad for a fifty-dollar plastic toy. Anyway, he chased my bishop away. I retreated, B-N3, to stay on the long diagonal. Lucky played N-QB3; I played N-KB3. Lucky brought out his other knight, N-B3. Then, floundering around without expert advice, I moved NxP. I expected that Lucky would follow with NxN, and I could play P-Q4 and get either the bishop or the knight, and we'd be even. But Lucky didn't do that.

I'M TRUTHFULLY SORRY TO SEE YOU BLUNDER SO BADLY SO EARLY IN THE GAME, he said. CHEW ON THIS . . . (blink) BxP CHECK. HERE BEGINS THE HUMILIATION OF YOUR FATHER.

What has led up to this situation?

What reminded me of this incident with Lucky, something I admit I've tried to bury pretty deep down the last few weeks, was this movie I saw just last night. It made me very upset, and I was sitting in the theater with a friend of mine, a girl, and I guess I was bothering her just a little bit because I kept muttering things. Somebody on the screen would do or say something and I'd go, "Yeah, sure," or something equally bright.

"What's the matter with you?" asked my girlfriend after a little while.

"It's this movie," I said. "I just can't believe these people." The movie was about this man who had a lot of trouble expressing his love for his family. He was very concerned about his own image, and with things like success and authority and all. So his son hates him a lot because he doesn't understand how much his father really loves him. His father bullies him all through the movie, and every goddamn time, the boy's mother comes into the kid's room and strokes his brow and all that and explains how his father has this problem about expressing his emotions. We're supposed to feel really sorry for this kid. I'll tell you a couple things: first, the guy never laid a finger on his son, no backhand smacks at the dinner table or nothing; and two, nobody ever came into my room and soothed my brow or explained how my old man couldn't get in touch with his feelings. So naturally, by the end of the picture, the kid stands up to his father and rebels, in some non-threatening way, and the man is a little shocked but secretly pleased, we are led to believe, and from then on they are just the greatest of pals and the son says, "I love you, Dad," and the guy says, "I love you too, son," and the mother soothes both their brows and then we have the end titles, except by that time I'm in the lobby buying a box of Sno-Caps and my stomach is starting to hurt a little. I couldn't figure out what that kid was getting so worked up about; I would have traded with him in a minute.

Just another example of how my life has been screwed up by books and movies. When I was in grade school I would go to bed at night and have fantasies that my parents would be different in the morning. I wanted to go to sleep, my mother and my old man watching television, and when I awoke in the morning they would be transformed into James Stewart and June Allyson. That's exactly who I yearned to have for parents. June Allyson in those short-sleeved blouses with a string of pearls around her neck making breakfast, and my old man a sort of combination of Glenn Miller, Elwood P. Dowd, and Mr. Smith Goes to Washington. But instead I always came downstairs in the morning and there they'd be, in the kitchen bitching at each other, Norma Desmond in a bathrobe and Mighty Joe Young.

And Lucky had the nerve to threaten, HERE BEGINS THE HUMILIATION OF YOUR FATHER. Let me tell you, it was pretty hard to humiliate my old man. Nobody ever managed it while he was alive, and I thought it was pretty cheap of Lucky to take shots at him now that he was dead and couldn't defend himself. HE HAS YOU TO DEFEND HIM NOW, said Lucky. I really needed to hear that. BUT I'M NOT GOING TO VENTURE MY OPINION AS TO THE JOB YOU'RE DOING.

"Thank God for small favors," I said. Lucky was making the most of his chance to gloat. He had a bishop held against my king like a knife to the throat. And my old man was inside the king.

YOU'RE BURNING DAYLIGHT, said Lucky.

"I'm just taking my time," I said. "After all, you said my old man's spirit was in that piece, I have to be careful. This isn't some nickel-and-dime game in a bus station."

IS THAT WHERE YOU LEARN YOUR CHESS? IN BUS STATIONS? HA HA!

So I ate his damn bishop, KxB.

YOU OUGHT TO THANK ME. I WILL PUNISH YOUR FATHER AS HE PUNISHED YOU. NxP CHECK.

I had seen that coming, but there wasn't any way around it. "I don't want my old man punished," I said. "Let him rest in peace."

MAKE YOUR MOVE. I WILL SMITE HIM EVEN AS HE HATH SMITTEN YOU.

The situation, I felt, had definitely gotten out of hand. Lucky was right about the smiting, however. My old man was always a first-class smiter. I have been trying for more than twenty years now to remember just what it was that made my old man use that belt the first time. What did I do? Smuggle a quarter out of the coin bank to buy baseball cards? Some felony like that, I guess. But that first time is lost to me now, invisible behind innumerable identical episodes. First, my old man would just yell at me. Then the wry wit my old man was so famous for would start. "So what's your problem? You stupid?" was always one of his favorites. Once my brother tried to defuse the situation by agreeing readily to anything my old man said. "Yeah, Dad, I'm stupid," he said. Before he got the words out of his mouth he was laid out on the ground. I never said anything. "Look at you, you eat like the Russians are on the West Side. You ain't got sense God give a goose." Then he would walk—saunter, really—into the kitchen, pull open the cupboard door, and get the belt. This was my signal. This was the sign to run like hell. I had a few seconds, while he was fetching that goddamn belt, to hide myself away if I could. The problem was that I couldn't. There wasn't anywhere to go. I usually tore up the stairs to the bedroom, but that wasn't much good for hiding. There was only the one room up there, no way to keep my old man out, nowhere to go once I got there.

My old man loved that belt. He would take it off the doorknob with a kind of reverence, like a medieval knight putting on his armor or a priest assuming his robes. He took a good grip on the belt's leather tongue and made three quick, tight turns around his hand. Then he'd swing it just a little as he walked; he loved the *feel* of it in his hand, you could tell. If I hadn't been so scared I might have been proud. I know that before he used it for the first time he had forgotten completely that I had made it for him. I also know that even if he had remembered, the idea of going after me with something I had made and given him as a gift would not have struck him as ungrateful. I never brought it up; he would only have shrugged. He probably would have thought I was a chucklehead to have given it to him in the first place, and I was only getting what I should have expected.

What is being thought?

CHOOSE YOUR MOVE AND AGAIN YOU WILL GET WHAT YOU SHOULD HAVE EXPECTED. YOUR KING IS DOOMED.

My stomach started to hurt. I didn't like playing with Lucky when he was in this frame of mind. All the fun seemed to have gone out of our relationship. Partly because I didn't know what the right move was, and partly because I knew his analysis of the game was probably right, I delayed.

YOU CANNOT HOPE TO ACHIEVE VICTORY BY STALLING. YOU CANNOT STARVE ME INTO SUBMISSION.

I don't know why it didn't occur to me simply to switch the stupid black machine off. Maybe I did think of it, but I figured it might consign my old man's spirit to something unimaginably horrible. But that looked like his ultimate fate anyway. I wished that I knew some marvelous chess experts personally, so that I could call up Boris Spassky on the phone for some quick advice on the position. It seemed to me that there was really only one move: K-K3, because if my king moved anywhere else, Lucky would grab up the knight that now looked so lonely and forlorn on the far side of the field, and I'd get nothing in return. But that meant sending my old man even farther into the middle of the board. That must have been what Lucky had planned, what he meant when he predicted humiliation. First Lucky would hound my old man, separate him from all his defenders, then bring him to his knees alone and helpless, and then dispatch him.

IF YOU WERE AS CLEVER AS YOU THINK YOU ARE, YOU WOULDN'T BE IN THIS POSITION. NOW YOU MUST DO THE BEST YOU CAN. IS K-K3 YOUR MOVE?

"Yes," I said. I really didn't feel like going on. "Would you care to make this a best-of-seven series?"

HA HA. YOU ARE TOO AMUSING. MY MOVE IS NxN. YOUR LACKEY DIES ANYWAY, HORSE AND RIDER SLAIN IN A WELTER OF BLOOD.

I knew that in this contest I would need all the lackeys I could get. I didn't have any to spare.

All of this is, of course, background to that one horrible moment of desperate insight I experienced at the age of fifteen. That was the instant I became a man, although no one else appeared to notice. It was not, I'd like to make clear, as heart-rending as when that kid has to go out and shoot the deer in *The Yearling*. Later on the kid realizes that his old man knew what he was talking about and they achieve this swell reconciliation and you get twenty different emotions thrown at you before the story comes to an end. Things like that didn't happen to us on Federal Street, or at least we didn't brag about them to each other if they did. If there were any private enlightenings going on next door or across the street, I was never told. We played pickle-in-the-middle and flipped baseball cards and that was it. None of this going out and shooting the goddamn deer and coming back a man stuff. I saw that picture on a Saturday afternoon with my brother and my friend Stanley. At the end of it my brother was in tears, but for the life of me I couldn't figure it out. Stanley tried to tell me on the way home, but I just couldn't see it. To this day I can't see it.

What is wanted? By whom?

What I really wanted was a way to turn the tide of bitter defeat. "Once more into the breach," I called to my troops, but they were all polishing their buckles back in the trenches. The only fighting forces I had mustered on this checkered battlefield were my king himself and one bishop way off to one side, probably mumbling matins while his liege is forced to take matters into his own hands.

At least I could take some of Lucky's lackeys. "KxN," I said, and that put me ahead, materially speaking. And, well, positionally, I couldn't see that Lucky, playing white, with the advantage of first move, was in a much stronger position. He had a knight and a crazy queen's knight pawn developed. I had a bishop and, of course, my king.

Lucky could barely control himself. He expressed extreme glee by blinking HA HA HA HA at me for a full minute. I wanted to slap him silly. YOUR KING! he said when he finally calmed down. LOOK WHERE YOUR KING IS! I had to admit that K4 is not the safest place for him to be out wandering, almost entirely undefended. But Lucky must have known that at the first opportunity I would change that. I would bring my old man back to safety, and I would begin more typical development.

YOU HAVE BROKEN EVERY SINGLE RULE OF RATIONAL CHESS. SOMEONE FROM THE CHESS FEDERATION SHOULD REMAND ME TO A FOSTER HOME.

I began to notice that Lucky's remarks were getting longer and were frequently far from the point at hand, which was this vital match with my old man's soul at stake.

NO DOUBT YOU SEEK TO FIND A SAFE HARBOR FOR YOUR FOUNDERING KING. I WILL NOT GIVE YOU THE OPPORTUNITY. MY NINTH MOVE IS B-N2 CHECK.

It was not a strong check, I thought. Lucky's bishop had merely moved over a square and up a square and lined up with my king. This time, for a change, I had freedom of movement, and I had an opportunity to grab off some more material before I gave my old man the sign to run for his own lines. KxN, the king took the second of white's knights and now stood on K5, ready for flight. Before he turned his back to the enemy, however, he had courageously accounted for three pieces—two knights and a bishop. A very laudable showing.

YOUR FATHER WILL BE FURIOUS WITH YOU, said Lucky.

I couldn't see why, other than that my old man never needed much of a reason. When I was fifteen years old, in the tenth grade, my old man got mad at me because I dropped a quart of milk all over the kitchen floor. I wasn't aware that this was a major offense; I was busy cleaning it up and I heard him explode. "Uh oh," I thought. We had progressed past the witticism phase before I had any idea that I was in trouble; I thought that my brother had done something in the other room. No such luck; it was my turn for the gantlet. I knew I was in for it this time because my old man had me cut off. I was kneeling in the middle of the kitchen floor; and he was just coming around the corner from the dinette to get his belt. I stood up very slow and dropped the dishrag in the kitchen sink, then tried to ease by my old man. There was no clever way to do this. He had a kind of half-smile on his face, I can see it right now as plain as day, his eyes closed a little, the bottom row of his yellowed teeth showing in an expression I could never read. I was helpless, and in desperation I thought I might just try zipping past him. He opened the cupboard door and got the belt, and that's when I made my move, such as it was. Suddenly his face went cherry-red and he lunged for me. "Where do you think you're going?" he shouted. It was a very good question, but one we both had the answer to. I was going up the stairs, naturally. I ran, and my old man ran. He was mad, God only knows why, all I did was drop a lousy quart of milk on the floor. I think the fact that I just didn't stand there in the middle of the kitchen and take a few healthy whacks made him angrier.

I ran for the stairs and took them two at a time. He was right behind me. When I got to the turn in the stairs, I stopped. Don't ask me why, because I don't have the answer. I didn't then and I don't now. I stopped and faced my old man. He was surprised. I could see the confusion in his soft, cowlike brown eyes. He didn't stop to worry about it, though. I watched his right arm go up and back, I can see it in slow motion now in memory, and I just stood there. I saw that belt flip over his shoulder, I measured the pause, I saw the beginning of the powerful down stroke. That brass belt buckle was slicing through the air, coming to take me right across the cheek. I had it all the way, like a good fielder chasing down a long fly ball toward the line; I timed it good, I reached out, and I caught that goddamn thing in my hand. I caught it good and solid, and I held it.

I felt like I was dreaming. This was something completely new; something no one had ever hinted at before, that I could take control, that I didn't have to be hit if I didn't want to be, that I had a mind and life of my own and I could make decisions. I was simply stunned. And all of this rushed through my mind in the moment of catching the belt buckle.

My old man still held the other end of the belt. There we stood on the stairs, planted in the midst of the old scenario, but now something terribly different had happened. And we stared at each other, each holding an end of that pitiful brown leather belt.

The joy and promise of my turning-point moment evaporated in the next few seconds, when I knew for certain that it had floated by above my old man's head. He didn't have the faintest idea of what had just happened. The whole business didn't count for anything unless he was ready to endorse it. Reluctantly I let go of the belt buckle and it dropped to the carpeted stair. I took a deep breath. My life, my future in that house and in that family lay on the stair, too, in the form of my old man's belt. I turned round and went up the rest of the way to the bedroom. My old man followed, and we played out the scene up there without further interruption.

All that I could carry away from that moment was the knowledge that I had been given a choice, and I would have to make a decision more painful to me than my old man's belt had ever been:

I could stay and be ruled or, when the time came, I could leave. The decision was painful, I had been right about that, but it wasn't difficult.

My relationship with my old man always included some measure of pain, even in the recent years when the only contact I've had with him has been in memories. In some ways, it's even worse; my own failures grow with time, my victories seem smaller and more ridiculous. When Lucky told me that my old man's spirit was in my chess piece, his Judgment subject to the outcome of the game, I felt a lot of pain. I knew that I was not equipped to champion my old man, that in his single moment of absolute need, I could do nothing other than fail him.

YOU ARE TRYING TO TOUCH THE EMOTIONS OF A RECTANGULAR PLASTIC BOX OF ELECTRONIC COMPONENTS, said Lucky. YOUR FOOLISHNESS ASTOUNDS ME.

"Any box that can be astounded must have emotions somewhere," I said. "You can stop chipping away at my self-esteem. Remember, I can throw you away. You can't throw me away."

TOGETHER WE CAN THROW YOUR FATHER AWAY. YOU HAVE ONE MOMENT LEFT TO THINK OF HIM BEFORE I ANNOUNCE MY MOVE. YOU MIGHT TRY PRAYING. I ADVISE YOU TO DO SO.

"Pompous ass," I said.

Q-B3. CHECKMATE. LISTEN CLOSELY: DO YOU HEAR THE SHRIEKS OF YOUR FATHER AS HIS SOUL PLUMMETS HOPELESSLY DOWN TO HELL?

"No," I said.

THAT'S RIGHT. THE UNIVERSE IS MORE REASONABLE THAN TO LET SOMEONE LIKE YOU DECIDE IN SINGLE COMBAT THE ETERNAL FATE OF ANYONE OR ANYTHING.

"Then where is my father's spirit?"

Lucky just blinked for seven and a half minutes and said P-K4, trying to start a new game. From then on that's all I could get from him, except for the cute preprogrammed remarks. But even those have been limited to the ones the Michikeito Corporation intended there to be. In a way, I miss his company, if not his distorted sense of humor. I never found out if my old man's spirit had really been in my king, or if that had been just some mechanical bitchiness Lucky dreamed up to repay me for using that guy Distle's game to beat him.

What will happen? What will be done?

Thy will be done, on Earth as it is in Heaven.

And, speaking of Heaven, I imagine that my old man is there

now, looking down on me, reading this over my shoulder, knowing exactly what I'm feeling, understanding at last a few things that he never understood before, fixing on the truth I am telling and on the lies I am slipping in, too. He should know that I never hated him, that I never hoped that anything bad should ever happen to him, that I had small resentments but no burning rage. The only thing he ever did to me that still hurts is rob me of my single moment. I never wanted very much, just to hear the small rumble of pieces sliding into place. My mother should have seen that, she should have come upstairs later and stroked my brow and said, "There, there. Today you have become a man."

That was nineteen years ago, believe it or not. After that day my old man still chased me and beat me with that belt. I still ran, even though I knew that at any time I could stop and turn and catch the heavy buckle again. I even knew that if I wanted to, I could pull the whole goddamn belt away from him, leaving him empty-handed; looking up at me on the stairs and wondering what had happened to order in the universe. I didn't want to take his belt away; he had never shown me anything else. It was all he had.

So a few years ago my old man dies and I travel back to Springfield. I go to the funeral and I go to the cemetery, and afterward my mother has the relatives and friends over to the house. There is a lot of beer and some sandwiches and cake and stuff like that, and my brother is there with his wife and kid, and I'm there feeling very out of place. I don't belong there anymore and everyone is making that very clear to me. Along about twilight, when they've all had enough beer, they begin telling stories about my old man.

I left the room on the pretext of getting myself something from the refrigerator. I went into the kitchen and opened the cupboard door. I closed my eyes, but I could hear the *skik, skik, skik* of the belt scratching in its slow swing against the door. All these years later, the belt is still there. There are no final reconciliations on Federal Street.

I touched the brown leather belt lightly once and then I closed the cupboard door. I could hear my mother and my aunt telling another story about my old man.

I've been playing a game of chess with Lucky while I've been writing this. He just made his move, B-B4, and added, YOU SHOULD HAVE LEFT HIM IN THE GRAVEYARD, LIKE YOUR MOTHER AND AUNT DID. THEY HAD THE RIGHT IDEA. But I don't know. Seems like when they get started they don't leave a guy nothing.

Introduction to "Everything But Honor"

I met George in New York at the 1988 Nebula Awards banquet. We were both up for best novelette—me for "Ginny Sweethips' Flying Circus," George for "Schrödinger's Kitten." George won. We rode out in the airport bus together. George let me hold his award. Wow, what a guy.

Though we only saw one another at conventions, we became good friends. We ate. A lot. We enjoyed sharing our misadventures in the writing game. I liked George's work, and he liked mine. In fact, when my novel *The Hereafter Gang* came out in 1991, George not only told everyone to read it, he made people sit and listen to *him* read from it. A lot of people probably got sick of him doing that. I didn't. It's one of the nicest things anyone ever did on my behalf.

It would be impossible—and certainly unworthy—to put George's work in this category or that. George could write whatever he wanted to write, and write it well. Still, "Everything But Honor" is pure Effinger. Hard science fiction is one thing; humor is something else. There are writers in the SF field who can handle both, but George's work stands up with the best.

The story you'll read here is a time travel story. There's a time machine in it, and scientists too—Einstein, Schrödinger, Heisenberg, that crowd—but black physicist Dr. Thomas Placide's the guy we need to watch out for here. George and I shared a love for characters like Placide: a sober, well-meaning citizen, *a man who just wants to do things right*. You can't ask for a better scenario for total catastrophe.

Setting history straight is a time-honored theme. Nearly every writer has given it a try, and many have come up with terrific tales. George gave his story the "Effinger twist" and presented us with a classic.

There are a couple of wars here, some familiar

names like Abraham Lincoln, "Presidents" Robert E. Lee, Salmon Chase, and George Custer, and a few not so familiar characters such as the controversial War Between the States General David Emanuel Twiggs.

The problem here is simple enough: All our hero Thomas Placide wants to do is go back in time from 1936 to 1860 and murder General Twiggs, an act he's certain will liberate American blacks from the racist hardships and injustices of the twentieth century.

Simple enough, unless you're writer George Alec Effinger. Absolutely no one could create a more disastrous crop of alternate realities than noble, well-meaning Thomas Placide. As Placide's cellmate, a guy named Schindler puts it: "You've got a rare talent for making good times hard, and hard times worse."

There's more. As Placide hops from one Universe to another, things do get harder, and they do get worse. The story, though, just gets better and better, right up to the end. You want to know what a "tangled web" really looks like, jump into "Everything But Honor" right now.

—Neal Barrett Jr.

+ + +

Everything But Honor

DR. THOMAS PLACIDE, A BLACK AMERICAN-BORN
physicist, decided to murder Brigadier General David E.
Twiggs, and he realized that it had to be done in December of
1860. He made this decision at the Berlin Olympics of 1936. Jesse
Owens had just triumphed over the world's best runners in the
two-hundred-meter dash. The physicist jumped up and cheered for
the American victory, while his companion applauded politely.
Yaakov Fein was one of the most influential scientists in the German Empire, but he was no chauvinist. After the race, Owens was
presented to Prince Friedrich. The papers later reported that the
prince had apologized for the absence of the seventy-seven-year-
old Kaiser, and Owens had replied, "I'm sure the most powerful
man in the world has more important things to do than watch six
young men in their underwear run halfway around a circle." The
quotation may have been the product of some journalist's imagination, but it became so identified with Jesse Owens that there was no
point in arguing about it.

Whatever the truth of the matter, Placide settled back in his seat
and looked at his program, getting himself ready for the next event.

"You must be proud of him," said Fein. "A fellow Negro."

"I *am* proud of him," his friend said. "A fellow American."

"But you are a naturalized German citizen now, Thomas. You
should cheer for the German runners."

Placide only shrugged.

Fein went on. "It's a hopeful sign that a Negro has finally won a place on the American Olympic team."

Placide showed some annoyance. "In America, Negroes have equal rights these days."

"Separate, but equal," said Fein.

The black man turned to him. "They aren't slaves anymore, if that's what you're implying. The German Empire has this fatuous paternal concern for all the downtrodden people in the world. Maybe you haven't noticed it, but the rest of the world is getting pretty damn tired of your meddling."

"We believe in using our influence for everyone's benefit."

That seemed to irritate Placide even more. "Every time some Klan bigot burns a cross in Mississippi, you Germans—"

Fein smiled. "We Germans, you mean," he said.

Placide frowned. "All right, we Germans send over a goddamn 'peace-keeping force' for the next nine months."

Fein patted the air between them. "Calm down, Thomas," he said, "you're being far too sensitive."

"Let's just watch the track and field events, and forget the social criticism."

"All right with me," said Fein. They dropped the subject for the moment, but Placide was sure that it would come up again soon.

Two years later, in November 1938, Dr. Placide was selected to make the first full-scale operational test of the Cage. He liked to think it was because of his contribution to the project. His journey through time would be through the courtesy of the Placide-Born-Dirac Effect, and neither Max Born nor Paul Dirac expressed any enthusiasm for the chance to act as guinea pig. In Berlin and Göttingen, there was a great deal of argument over just what the Placide-Born-Dirac Effect was, and the more conservative theorists wanted to limit the experiments to making beer steins and rodents disappear, which Placide and Fein had been doing for over a year.

"My point," said Placide at a conference of leading physicists in Göttingen, "is that after all this successful study, it's time for someone to hop in the Cage and find out what's happening, once and for all."

"I think it's certainly time to take the next step," said Heisenberg.

"I agree," said Schrödinger.

Dirac rubbed his chin thoughtfully. "Nevertheless," he said, "it's much too soon to talk about human subjects."

"Are you seriously suggesting we risk a human life on the basis of our ill-fitted and unproven theories?" asked Einstein.

Marquand shrugged. "It would be a chance to clear up all the foggy rhetoric about paradoxes," he said.

La Martine just stood to one side, sullenly shaking his head. He obviously thought that Placide's suggestion was unsound, if not altogether insane.

"We have four in favor of using a human subject in the Cage, and four against," said Yaakov Fein. He took a deep breath and let it out as a sigh. "I'm the project director, and I suppose it's my responsibility to settle this matter. God help me if I choose wrong. I say we go ahead and expand the scope of the experiment."

Placide looked relieved. "Let me volunteer, then," he said.

"Typical American recklessness," said La Martine in a sour voice.

"You mean," said Placide, "that you'll be happy if I'm the one in the Cage. Not as a reward for my work, of course, but because if anybody's alternate history is going to be screwed up, better it be America's than Germany's."

La Martine just spread his hands and said nothing.

"Then I volunteer to go along," said Fein. "As copilot."

"There's nothing for a 'copilot' to do," said Placide. Even then, it may have been that Fein didn't have complete faith in Placide's motives.

Placide had his own agenda, after all, but he kept it secret from the others.

"Why don't you travel back a week or so," suggested Born. "Then you can take a photograph or find some other proof to validate the experiment, and return immediately to Göttingen and time T_0."

"In for a penny, in for a pound," said Placide. "I'd like to choose my own destination, and possibly solve a little historical problem while I have the chance." The Cage would never have existed without him, and so it didn't take him long to persuade the others. Placide and Fein worked with Marquand and his team for nine more weeks, learning to calibrate the Cage. In the meantime, Placide studied everything he could find about General Twiggs, and he carefully hid his true plan from the Europeans.

Placide should have known that his first attempt would not go smoothly, because as far as he could see, his plan was foolproof. His reasoning was simple: His primary goal—greater even than testing the operation of the Cage—was to relieve the barbaric conditions forced on American blacks following the Confederate Insurrection of 1861–1862.

Although he'd quit the land of his birth, he still felt an unbreakable bond between himself and others of his race, who could never escape the oppression as he had. A white friend of his father had enabled Placide to attend Yale University, where he'd studied math and physics. During the middle 1930s, after he joined the great community of experimental scientists working in the German Empire, he began to see how he might accomplish something far more important than adding a new quibble to the study of particle physics.

The Cage—*his* Cage, as he sometimes thought of it—gave him the opportunity to make a vital contribution. His unhappy experiences as a child and a young man in the United States supplied him with sufficient motive. All he lacked was the means, and this he found through historical research as painstaking as his scientific work with Dirac and Born.

To Placide, Brigadier General David Emanuel Twiggs seemed to be one of those anonymous yet crucial players in the long game of history. In 1860 he was the military commander of the Department of Texas. Although few students of the Confederate Insurrection would even recognize his name, Twiggs nevertheless had a moment, the briefest moment, when he determined the course of future events. Placide had come to realize that Twiggs was his target. Twiggs could be used to liberate American blacks from all the racist hardships and injustices of the twentieth century.

Leaving T_0, the Cage brought Placide and Yaakov Fein to San Antonio on December 24, 1860. Fein agreed to guard the Cage, which had come to rest in a wintry field about three miles from Twiggs's headquarters. Fein, of course, had no idea that Placide had anything in mind other than a quick scouting trip into this city of the past.

Placide began walking. From nearby he could hear the lowing of cattle, gathered now in shadowed groups beneath the arching limbs of live oaks. He climbed down a hill into a shallow valley of moonlit junipers and red cedar. The air smelled clean and sharp, although this Christmas Eve in Texas was not as cold as the February he'd left behind in Germany. Frosty grass crunched underfoot;

as he passed through the weeds, their rough seeds clung to his trouser legs.

His exhilaration at his safe arrival in another time was tempered almost immediately by anxiety over the danger he was in. If anyone stopped and questioned him, he would have an impossible time explaining himself. At best, he would be taken for a freed slave, and as such he could expect little if any help from the local citizens. Worse was the fact that he had no proper identification and no money, and thus he would certainly appear to be a runaway.

Placide had put himself in a grave and desperate situation. If he failed and was captured, his only hope would be Fein, but Fein was a German with little knowledge of this period in American history. Placide did not have much faith in the other man's ability to rescue him, if it came to that. It might happen that no one would ever learn of Placide's sacrifice. He was thinking of the black generations yet unborn, and not his colleagues in Göttingen: There were plenty of others who could take Placide's place in the scientific field, but he was in a unique position to do something remarkable for his oppressed people.

As it happened, Placide was not detained or captured. He made his way through the barren, cold night to the general's quarters. Twiggs was already in bed, and there was a young soldier standing sentry duty outside the door. Placide shook his head ruefully. Here was the first serious hitch in his plans. He was going to have to do something about that guard.

It wasn't so difficult to gain entry. Placide needed only to nod at the young man, grab him, and drive a knife into his chest. The soldier made a soft, gurgling cry and slumped heavily in Placide's grasp. Placide let the body fall silently to the floor. He paused a moment, listening for any sign of alarm, but all was still. Oddly, he felt no sense of guilt for what he'd done. In a way, the world of 1860 didn't seem truly real to him. It was as if the man he'd killed had never really existed, although the corporal's dark blood had stained Placide's trousers convincingly.

Placide went quietly through the door and stood over General Twiggs's bed, looking down at him. He was old, seventy or so, with long white hair and a dense white beard. He looked like a Biblical patriarch, sleeping peacefully. Placide was surprised to discover that it was not in him simply to kill the old man in his sleep. Placide wasn't sure if he was too cruel or too weak for that. He woke Twiggs, pressing one hand over the general's mouth to keep him silent.

"Don't make a sound," Placide said as Twiggs struggled to sit up. "I must speak with you. I'll remove my hand if you promise not to call out for help. That will do you no good in any event." Twiggs nodded slowly, his eyes wide.

Placide took his hand away. Twiggs gasped and tried to speak, but for a moment he could only wheeze. "Who are you?" he asked at last.

"That's not important. You must understand that your life is in my hands. Will you answer my questions?"

Twiggs was no fool. He knew better than to bluster or threaten. He nodded again. Dressed in his bedclothes, he was a wrinkled, feeble figure; but Placide suppressed his pity for the old man. Twiggs was a Southerner by birth and a secessionist by inclination.

"You are in command here," Placide said.

"Yes," said the general. "If you think that after breaking into my room, you can get me to arrange for you to escape—"

Placide raised a hand curtly, cutting him off. "If for some reason you stepped down, who would assume command in your place?"

Twiggs's brow furrowed, but otherwise he showed no outward sign of fear. "I suppose it would be Lieutenant Colonel Lee," he said.

"You mean Robert E. Lee?"

"Of the First Cavalry," said Twiggs.

Placide was relieved to hear the answer. Some months before, while Twiggs had been away from San Antonio, he had named Lee acting commander of the Department of Texas. If Twiggs were forced to retire, Lee would take over again until the War Department made its own permanent appointment.

"Now let me propose a hypothetical situation," said Placide. "Suppose Texas decides to secede from the Union—"

"So you've burst your way in here and ruined my sleep to argue politics?" Twiggs demanded angrily. "And what have you done to the young man on guard duty?"

Placide slapped Twiggs hard across the face. "Suppose Texas decides to secede from the Union," he repeated calmly. "What would your position be?"

The general raised a trembling hand to his cheek. His expression was furious, and Placide caught the first hint of fear in his eyes. "Texas will secede," Twiggs said softly. "Any fool can read that. I've already written to Washington, but the War Department has so far chosen not to send me any definite instructions."

"What will you do when the rebels demand your surrender?"

Twiggs's gaze left Placide's face and stared blankly toward the far wall. "I will surrender," he said finally. "I have not the means to carry on a civil war in Texas."

A gunshot would have roused the entire garrison. Placide cut the old man's throat with his knife, then searched the room for items to take back with him to show Fein and the others. Finally, he made his escape back into the silent night of the past. Outside, it was very strange to smell bread baking not far away, as if all was well, as if something impossible had not just happened.

"There," he told himself, "you have changed history." It remained to be seen if he'd changed it for the better.

When Placide met Fein later that night, he suggested that they not return directly to 1938 and Göttingen. Fein was dubious. "The more time we spend here," he argued, "the more chance there is that someone will see us. We may cause an alteration in the flow of events. That could be disastrous."

Placide swallowed a mouthful of brandy he'd taken from Twiggs's headquarters building. The liquor had a harsh, sweet taste, but it gave the illusion of warmth. He offered the brandy to his companion. "Yaakov," he said, shivering in the cold night wind, "it's already too late."

Fein's brows narrowed. "What are you talking about?" He declined to sample the general's brandy.

Placide shrugged. "Just that I've already inserted myself into the past. I had a conversation with General Twiggs."

"Don't you know what that means?" cried Fein. He was furious. "We may return to the present and find God only knows what!"

"I couldn't help it," said Placide. "I was discovered. I was arrested and taken to the commanding officer. I had to do some fancy talking or you would never have seen me again."

"God help us," murmured Fein. The two men looked at each other for a moment. There was no sound but the lonely creaking of bare tree limbs, and the rustle of dead leaves blowing along the ground.

"Look," said Placide, "why don't we jump ahead to, say, February, and find out if anything's different. In case of some kind of disaster, we can always reappear a few minutes before T_0 and prevent ourselves from making this trip."

"I don't know," said the German. "That might leave two of you and two of me in the present."

"Let's worry about that only if we have to. Right now we've got to find out if my little interview had any permanent effect." Fein watched him closely but said nothing more.

The two men entered the Cage, and Placide reset the controls to take them forward a few weeks. He knew that on February 16, 1861, Texas state troops would surround the government buildings in San Antonio. Twiggs would give in quickly to demands that he turn over all the arms and equipment to the militia. Of course, Placide had prevented that from happening with his single bold stroke. In effect, he'd put Robert E. Lee in command of the Department of Texas. Lee was a Virginian, but he had publicly stated that he would have no part in a revolution against the Union. Placide had acted to change his mind.

They reappeared in San Antonio on the twentieth of February. Once more, Fein guarded the Cage while Placide went into town. The air was warmer and smelled of wood smoke. He heard the ragged cries of birds, and once he saw a large, black winged shape detach itself from the ground and fly into a cottonwood that was beginning to show new yellow-green leaves. For a while, everything seemed peaceful.

The town, however, was in a frenzied state of confusion. Bands of armed rebels patrolled the streets. Gunshots frequently split the air. The younger men wore the wide-eyed, fierce looks of inexperienced warriors looking forward to their first battle. The older men and women were grim and worried, obviously in fear that the conflict that had threatened so long in the abstract had come at last.

Placide stood in a narrow alley between two shops, afraid to push himself into the throngs of shouting people in the street. Finally, as both his curiosity and fear for his own safety increased, he stopped a well-dressed, elderly white man. "Pardon me, sir," he said, trying to sound calm, "my master has sent me for news."

The older man drew himself up, unhappy at being accosted in the street by an unfamiliar slave. "Tell your master that our boys have driven the Federals out," he said.

"That news will ease his pain," said Placide. He was galled to have to pretend to be a slave, but he had no other choice. "And Lee?"

"The rascal is dead, killed in the fight." The man was so pleased to be able to report that fact, he actually slapped the black man's shoulder.

Placide was stunned by the news; he'd hoped to persuade Lee to become a general for the South. He watched the man turn and go on about his business, and he knew that it was time to go about his own. His plan had not failed; it had but succeeded too well.

When they returned to T_0, Placide and Fein discovered that the present was just as they'd left it, that their excursion in time had not changed the past, but rather created a new alternate reality. Still, some of their colleagues were furious.

"What the hell were you thinking of?" demanded Eduard La Martine.

He'd been fascinated by the theoretical aspects of their work, but fearful of practical applications.

Now Yaakov Fein was convinced that the Cage was too dangerous to use, at least until the Placide-Born-Dirac Effect was better understood.

Placide knew that if he hoped to try again in the past, he'd have to win La Martine and Fein over. "Look," he said, "we're all curious about what happens when a change is made in the past."

"You were tampering!" cried La Martine. "As it turned out, you had no permanent effect—"

"So I don't understand why you're so upset."

"—but there was the possibility that you might have changed this world disastrously, for all of us. You had no right to attempt such a thing!"

"Sending beer steins into the past might have had disastrous results, too, Eduard," said Werner Heisenberg thoughtfully. "Yet you had no qualms about that."

"Making inanimate objects vanish is hardly equal to interviewing historical figures in their bedrooms," said Paul Dirac indignantly.

Placide had told the others that he'd merely discussed politics with General Twiggs. It hadn't seemed profitable at the time to mention that he'd killed the old man. "You know how I feel about the Legislated Equality programs in the United States."

Dirac gave him a weary look and nodded.

"Before returning here to T_0, Yaakov and I jumped from 1861 to 1895, where we bought a history of that new timeline." Placide held up the book. "Here are the effects of our visit. I thought by going back before the Confederate Insurrection and starting things off on a different course, I could keep the Equality programs and the Liberty Boroughs and all the other abuses from ever happening. I persuaded Twiggs to retire, because I knew Robert E. Lee wouldn't surrender the garrison at San Antonio. His sense of duty and honor wouldn't allow it. He'd resist, and there would be a violent confrontation. The war would begin there in Texas, rather than two months later at Fort Sumter."

"So?" asked Heisenberg.

"So Lee would learn firsthand that the war could not be avoided, and that the needs of the Confederacy were immediate and desperate. I was certain that history would unfold differently from there on. I wanted Lee to turn down Lincoln's invitation to command the Union Army. In our world, his military brilliance brought the rebellion under control in little more than eighteen months. Now, though, we'd created a new timeline, one in which Lee would not be the Great Traitor, but rather the great genius of the Southern cause."

"But you were wrong, Thomas," said Fein. "Without Lee to lead it, the Union *still* defeated the Confederacy. All you succeeded in doing was extending the bloody conflict another year while the North searched for able military leadership."

Placide shrugged. "A minor miscalculation," he said.

"You're personally responsible for the death of Robert E. Lee, man!" said La Martine.

Placide was startled. "What do you mean? Robert E. Lee's been dead for almost seventy years. He died peacefully in the White House, not yet halfway through his term as president."

"Yes," said Zach Marquand, "in *our* timeline that's what happened. But you went into another universe and interfered. Lee's blood is on your hands."

Placide suddenly saw the absurd point Marquand was trying to make. "Zach," he said, "we went into a world that doesn't exist. It was a fantasy world. That Robert E. Lee didn't really live, and he didn't really die. He was no more than a possibility, a quantum quirk."

"We're talking about people, Thomas," said Erwin Schrödinger, "not particles."

"Particles come into and go out of existence all the time. Just the same way, the people and events in that timeline were only local expressions of the wave function. You're letting emotion twist your thinking."

Fein frowned at him. "Thomas, I want you to prepare a report as quickly as you can. We're all going to have to think very hard about this. You've shown us that there are moral questions involved with this project that none of us foresaw."

"Yaakov, I wish you'd—"

"And I'm not going to permit anyone to use the Cage again until we establish some philosophical ground rules." Fein gave Placide a long, appraising look, then turned and left the room. Placide glanced at the book they'd brought back, the history of America in the timeline they now called Universe$_2$. He was very eager to get back to his quarters and read of the elaborate and unpredictable results of what he'd done.

Placide made another trip into the past, this one unauthorized and in secret. He didn't know what Yaakov Fein would do if he found out that Placide had ignored his prohibition, but to be truthful, Placide didn't care. He had more important matters to worry about. It was his belief—and both Schrödinger and Marquand agreed with him—that a second experiment would take him to an 1861 untouched by his previous meddling. If their many-worlds hypothesis had any validity, it was statistically unlikely that Placide would find himself back in Universe$_2$. He could make a clean start in Universe$_3$, profiting from his regrettable mistakes.

His destination this second time was the District of Columbia, on the morning of April 18, 1861. He was dressed in clothes that would attract little attention in the past, and he took with him a small sum of U.S. money in gold and silver that he'd purchased through numismatic shops in Berlin. Upon his arrival, Placide left the Cage outside of town, as he'd done in Texas. He walked some distance in the chilly air of early spring. He intended to find a hotel where he might hire a carriage, but this was more difficult than he'd imagined. He was, after all, a black man and a stranger on some inscrutable errand of his own. Whenever he approached an innkeeper or carriage-driver with his gold coins, he was told either that none of the vehicles were in proper repair, or that they had all been reserved to other parties. He understood their meaning well enough.

Placide made his way along Pennsylvania Avenue to Blair House, almost directly across the street from the Executive Mansion. He gave a little involuntary shiver when he realized that inside the White House, at that moment, Abraham Lincoln was hearing firsthand reports of the events at Fort Sumter, and preparing his order to blockade the Confederate ports. Placide was tempted to abandon his subtle plan and instead seek an interview with the president himself. What advice and warnings he could give Lincoln, if he would only listen . . .

That was the problem, of course: Getting these strong-willed men to pay attention. Placide knew that he could help them save thousands of lives, and at the same time build a future free of the oppression their shortsightedness would lead to. His influence, obviously, would be greater if he were white, but there was no point in making idle wishes. He would do the best he could.

A carriage pulled up in front of Blair House just as he arrived. He knew that the man who stepped down from it must be Robert E. Lee, although he didn't look much like the photographs Placide was familiar with. Lee was wearing the blue uniform of the United States Army, and he carried the wide-brimmed hat of a cavalry officer in one hand. He had yet to grow his famous gray beard. He was taller, too, with broad shoulders and a strict posture and military bearing that gave him an imposing appearance. His manner was calm and poised, although he was on his way to a momentous meeting.

Lee paused a moment, perhaps collecting himself, before turning toward the entrance of the grand house. Placide hurried up to him. "General Lee," he said.

Lee smiled. "You flatter me," he said. "I presently hold the rank of colonel." He waited patiently, apparently thinking that Placide was bringing him a message of some kind.

Placide was struck by Lee's gentle manner. There was intelligence in his eyes, but not the haggard, haunted look that would come later. In the few years remaining to him after the Insurrection, Lee always carried with him the painful knowledge that he had been, after all, the fatal betrayer of his homeland. "I have some important information for you, sir," Placide said. Now that he was before the man, the physicist was unsure how to proceed. After all, Lee wasn't the Great Traitor yet, not in this timeline. Placide had prevented him from becoming the savior of the Union in Universe₂, but he'd learned only that Lee dead was no better than Lee as Yankee. "May I have a moment of your time?"

Lee pursed his lips. "I have an appointment at this address, sir, and I am obliged by both courtesy and duty to respect it."

"I know," said Placide, "and I won't keep you long. When you go inside, Francis Preston Blair is going to offer you command of the Union Army, on behalf of President Lincoln. I know that you intend to accept; but if you do, sir, you will be damning future generations of American Negroes to lives of degradation and suffering. They will harbor a rage that will grow until our nation is torn by violence more terrible than this quarrel over secession. I beg you to reconsider."

Lee did not reply at once. He studied Placide's face for a long moment. "May I inquire, sir," he said quietly, "how you come to be in possession of this information?"

Placide took out his wallet and removed a fifty dollar bill—currency from the United States of his world, of his time. He handed it to Lee. The cavalry officer examined it in silence, first the back, with the picture of the Capitol Building, then the front, with his own portrait. "Sir, what is this?" he asked.

"Paper money," said Placide.

Lee turned the bill over and over in his hands. "Is it a banknote?"

"Legal tender printed by the Federal government, and backed by government gold reserves."

"I've never seen a note like it before," said Lee dubiously.

Placide showed him the small legend beside Lee's picture. "It was issued in 1932," he said.

Lee took a deep breath and let it out. Then he gave the money back to Placide. "Mr. Blair is an elderly man, and I do him no honor by my tardiness. I beg you to excuse me."

"General Lee," Placide pleaded, "if you accept Lincoln's offer, you must lead an invading army onto the soil of Virginia, your home. How can you raise your sword against your own family and friends? You must allow me to explain. I showed you the bill because you'd think me a madman unless I presented some evidence."

"Evidence only of the skill of your engraver," said Lee. "I did not find the portrait flattering, and I did not find the item in question amusing."

As earnestly as he could, Placide explained to him that he'd come through time to let Lee know of the terrible consequences of his decision to defend the Union. "I can tell you that with you in command, the Army of the Potomac will withstand the first thrusts of the Confederate forces."

"Indeed, sir," said Lee with a little smile.

"And then you will sweep down to force the evacuation of Richmond. You will coordinate your army's movements with those of McClellan in the west, and divide the South into helpless fragments. In the meantime, the navy will blockade the ports along the Atlantic, the Gulf Coast, and the Mississippi River."

"Your predictions make the difficulties seem not so very daunting after all."

Placide paid no attention to Lee's skepticism. "The Confederacy's only true victory will come at Petersburg, and only because of the incompetence of one of your subordinates, General Ambrose Burnside. Finally, on October 17, 1862, P. G. T. Beauregard will surrender the Army of Northern Virginia to you at Dry Pond, Georgia, northeast of Atlanta."

"And tell me, sir," said Lee, "will the Union thereafter be restored?"

"Yes," said Placide, "the Union will be restored, but in terrible circumstances." Placide described to him the fight over Reconciliation, and how the radical Republicans would seek to punish the Southern states. "All that will hold the country together in those furious months will be your strength of will as president," Placide told him.

Lee shook his head. "I am certain now that you offer me dreams and not prophecy. I cannot conceive of any circumstance that would persuade me to undertake that office. I have neither the temperament nor the wisdom."

"The Democrats will come to you, as a war hero and as a Southerner. You'll be the natural choice to oversee the process of Reconciliation. Congress will battle you, but your resolve will be as strong as Lincoln's. You'll prevent the plundering of the South."

"I am glad to hear this, but I wonder why you wish me then to decline the offer that awaits me inside. Would you see the South torn apart in peace to more horrible effect than in war?"

Placide felt a tremendous sympathy for this man, and he had to fight the urge to tell him all that would happen. In Placide's own world, Lee would die in 1870. Vice President Salmon P. Chase would then be sworn in, and the long, cruel struggle of the black would resume. Before his death, Lee would prepare a document emancipating all the slaves in the South; but on taking office Chase would find it convenient to set this initiative aside. The issue would still be the self-determination of the states. Chase would let progress on civil rights hang in abeyance rather than antagonize the newly reconstituted Congress. Not until 1878, during the Custer administration, would slavery be officially abolished.

"Please try to understand," said Placide, "what seems like victory for you and for the Union will be, for the Negro population, the beginning of a dreadful spiral down into a social and economic abyss."

"I'm not certain that I take your meaning, sir," said Colonel Lee.

"I mean only that your concern for the slaves will blind you to the long-range effects of what Congress will propose. And after you've left the White House—" Placide still could not tell Lee how brief his tenure would be "—your successors will pervert your programs to trap the Negroes in misery. Even in my time, seventy-five years after the Insurrection, many Negroes believe that life as a slave must have been better than what they endure. As wretched as the condition of slavery is, the American Negro of 1938 has little more of freedom or opportunity or hope."

Lee was bemused by Placide's vehemence. "If I entertain your argument, sir, I am left with the feeling that all my actions will be futile, particularly those guided most strongly by my conscience."

"Millions of Negroes are forced to live in squalid slums the government calls 'Liberty Boroughs,' segregated from the prosperous white communities," Placide told him. "We suffer under the Legislated Equality programs, and—"

Lee raised a hand, cutting him off. "I beg your pardon, sir," he said. "I am grateful to have your opinion, but I can tarry here no longer." He gave Placide a nod and strode up to the front door of Blair House.

Placide didn't know how effective his appeal had been. He was heartened to see, however, that as Lee turned away, his expression was solemn and thoughtful.

In his own timeline, Placide had read that Lee, as General-in-Chief of the Union Army, resisted the president's frequent pleas to attack the Confederate units across the Potomac in Virginia. "You must do something soon," Lincoln demanded late in July 1861. "The army consists to a large degree of ninety-day recruits who volunteered after the attack on Fort Sumter. The period of enlistment has almost expired. When it does, those young men will leave the ranks and go back to their families, unless they are given something to inspire them to remain. You must use them to strike a strong and decisive blow."

Lee remained firm. "Our soldiers are simply not ready," he said. "The volunteers are poorly trained and poorly outfitted. It would be little more than murder to take such an unprepared mob into battle."

"A victory would encourage our soldiers and open the way to the capture of Richmond."

Lee saw it differently. "A defeat," he argued, "would open the way for the enemy to capture Washington."

As the weeks went by, Lincoln continued to put pressure on Lee to act, even threatening to strip the General-in-Chief of his command, but Lee would not be bullied. When the ninety-day period came to an end, most of the recruits reenlisted out of respect and admiration for Lee himself, and not the Federal cause. Lee used the time to deploy his troops with care and precision. He instructed his subordinates to hinder any advance of the Confederate Army, but to fall back slowly rather than engage. Finally, on September 1, Lee reported to the president and his Cabinet that he was satisfied. Two weeks later, at Occoquan, Virginia, Lee defeated a numerically superior Confederate force under the command of General Beauregard. Aided by Generals Irwin McDowell and Benjamin Butler, Lee prevented the Southern corps from crossing the Potomac into Maryland, and then encircling Washington.

The Battle of Occoquan was the smashing victory that Lincoln had hoped for. With one stroke, Lee crushed the dreams of the Confederacy. At Occoquan, he seized the offensive and never relinquished it for a moment during the rest of the war. The remainder of the eighteen-month struggle in the east saw little more than Beauregard's courageous though vain efforts to delay with his clever skirmishes and retreats the unavoidable outcome.

Inevitably, however, he was to have his most difficult meeting with Lee at Folkston's Dining Room in Dry Pond. Beauregard, the Napoleon in Gray, was as noble in defeat as Lee was gracious in victory. The two men had been friends when they'd served together in Mexico. They would be friends again when Lee was president and Beauregard governor of Louisiana.

All of this was a matter of record, but Placide knew just how easily the record could be erased.

Placide felt a mixture of hope and anxiety while he waited in the street outside Blair House. If Lee emerged as a Union general, if he became again the Great Traitor, Placide planned to return to T_0 and abandon this timeline. He would then have to hit on a more forceful method of persuading Lee—in Universe$_4$.

If, however, Placide had read Lee's expression correctly, then he planned to spend quite some time in Universe$_3$, making short jumps forward through time to follow the course of the Insurrection. With the invincible Robert E. Lee as the defender of the Confederacy's fortunes, the fate of the South would certainly be different.

Placide opened to the first page of the journal he intended to keep during his experiment. He wrote his first entry:

Universe$_3$
April 18, 1861
Outside Blair House, Washington

   If things turn out as I hope, I will remain in this newly
made world, studying it and perhaps learning something
of value to take back with me to T_0. I will adopt this alternate timeline as my own, and love these people regardless
of their sins, for have I not created them? Perhaps that
sounds mad, but there has not yet been time enough to
evaluate properly this unlooked-for benefit of my work.
But surely I am a god to these people, having called them
out of nothing, with the power to send their history off in
whichever direction I choose. The God of Abraham created but the universe of T_0, and I have already created two
more. How many others will I call into being before I
achieve my purpose? General Lee comes now, with the
fate of Universe$_3$ in his hands.

It was September 16, 1861, and the air should have been thick with
drifting clouds of gun smoke, the acrid breath of massed rifles;
but the autumn breeze carried only the tang of burning firewood
from a farmhouse nearby. There should have been the menacing,
booming shocks of the field artillery, and the ragged cries of
wounded men; but there was only stillness. The roads near Occoquan, Virginia, should have been jammed with wild-eyed, charging
infantry, and the urgent mounted messengers of the generals; but
only Thomas Placide disturbed the quiet countryside.
   It was a grim, gloomy day in late summer, and black clouds
threatened low overhead. It had not yet begun to rain, but a storm
seemed imminent. Thunder cracked and rolled, and Placide grimaced. He did not like to be out in this kind of weather.
   He was cheered only by the knowledge that he had truly persuaded Robert E. Lee, that a mechanism for the salvation of
American blacks had been set in motion. All that now remained
was the job of supervision, to make certain that Placide's careful
scheme did not falter as this world's divergent history unfolded.
   He shook his head. He wouldn't have guessed that this was the
kind of day Lee would choose for his first major test as a general in
the Confederate Army. Placide hurried down a rutted, dusty lane to
the white-painted frame farmhouse, hoping to meet someone who
could direct him to the battlefield.
   The house was surrounded by a bare yard and a gap-toothed
fence. Placide went through the yawning gate and climbed three

steps to the porch. He heard nothing from within the house. He rapped loudly. A moment later, a distracted white woman opened the door, gave Placide a critical look, and shut the door again. "Ma'am?" called Placide. "Will you help me, ma'am?"

The door opened again, and he was looking at a tall, burly, frowning man. "We got nothin' for you," said the farmer.

"I just need some directions from y'all," said Placide. He reminded himself that once again he needed to behave modestly.

"Directions we can afford, I guess," said the farmer.

Placide nodded gratefully. "I've got to find my way to the battle, and quickly."

The white man closed one eye and stared at him for a few seconds. "Battle?" he asked.

"I've got news for General Lee."

"You his boy?"

Placide felt a flush of anger, but he stifled it. "No, sir, I'm a free man of color. But I've got news for General Lee."

"What's this about a battle? There been no soldiers around here except when they came by in July. On their way to Manassas."

"Manassas? Where's that?"

The farmer gave him another close look. "Where the battle was. Bull Run. It was Beauregard and Joe Johnston that licked the Yankees at Bull Run. Your boss was busy fetchin' coffee cups for Jeffy Davis down in Richmond."

Placide wondered at how quickly men and events had found their new course. "General Lee is obliged to follow the wishes of President Davis," he said.

The farmer gave a derisive laugh. "While Granny Lee was doin' just that, one Sunday afternoon the blue boys come out of Washington, thinkin' they was goin' to whup Beauregard and send him on home. Then Joe Johnston showed up to help him out, and before you know it the damn Yankees are runnin' ever which way, goin' back to cry on Lincoln's shoulder."

Placide took all this in. "Well, sir," he said, "I guess they told me wrong when they said he'd come up here."

"Your General Lee ain't never been within fifty mile of here. As far as I know, he's somewheres off in the west, diddlin' around in the mountains."

"I thank you, sir. I suppose I'd just better get back to Richmond myself. Someone's made some kind of mistake."

The farmer laughed. "I'm lookin' right at him." He turned away and closed the door. Placide found that his hands were clenched into tight fists. He let out his breath slowly and forced himself to relax. He walked back out through the farmer's gate and headed back the way he'd come. He wanted to return to the Cage before the heavy rain began.

Although he hated having to play the role of fool, Placide was elated by the news. He'd prevented the crushing Confederate defeat at Occoquan from occurring in Universe₃. There had been a mighty rebel victory that had not happened in Placide's timeline, and it had happened even without Robert E. Lee. With Lee yet on the verge of fulfilling his destiny, Placide could almost see the glory of the greater victories yet to come. He found himself smiling broadly as the first huge raindrops spatted about him in the dust.

> Universe₃
> October 17, 1862
> Dry Pond, Georgia
>
> For the second time, I've come to watch an event that has vanished from history. I suspected that would be the case, yet I jumped here from Occoquan anyway. Hearing the news of the Battle of Bull Run, I was of the opinion that I had wholly altered the course of the Insurrection. It would be unlikely in the extreme that its ending should now fall out just as it had in my own timeline, on the same day, at the same place, and for the same reasons. Still, I had to be certain.
>
> In the deficient universe of my origin, Beauregard's surrender took place in the salon of Folkston's Dining Hall. I was not foolish enough to enter that white establishment by the front door. Rather, I went around to the rear of the building. There I won the sympathy of the kitchen slaves with a glib story of fear and desperation. They kindly gave me a good meal, some clothing more appropriate than my own, and a sum of money in both Confederate scrip and silver.
>
> Of course, no one here has heard rumors of the approach of a triumphant Union Army. Everyone agrees that the fighting continues far to the north in Maryland, and far to the west in Mississippi. Yaakov was right: I have given this world a fiercer, longer conflict. In Universe₃, this is no mere Confederate Insurrection. This is civil war.
>
> And how is the struggle going? My new friends have caught me up on the thirteen months I missed, jumping here from Occoquan: George McClellan is Lincoln's General-in-Chief (I am certain he is no Lee, and will

hardly present an obstacle to Confederate triumph). There was a Southern victory at Ball's Bluff, Virginia, and a battle at Shiloh, in Tennessee, that wasn't much of a victory for the Federals or much of a defeat for the South. Lee defended Richmond against McClellan, and then, *damn it*, Lee and Stonewall Jackson beat up the Yankees at Bull Run a second time! After that, Marse Robert tried to invade the North by heading up through Maryland, just as Beauregard tried in my own timeline. And just like Beauregard, Lee was stopped. He was stalled at Antietam Creek because a set of his campaign orders was lost and later discovered by Union soldiers.

If there is a turn for the worse, and if I must abandon Universe$_3$, I may begin again as I did at Blair House; but this time, I will remove in advance that careless officer at Antietam. "In for a penny, in for a pound." It was not enough, it seems, to have won Robert E. Lee to my cause. I find that I must continue to supervise and guide this entire war.

How astonished Dirac and the others will be when I return to T_0! I will seem to have aged several years in a single moment.

How sad I will be to leave a world I am perfecting, to return to a world I can no longer love.

Placide locked his door and went downstairs to dinner. The Negro rooming house was on Rampart Street, on the edge of the Vieux Carré. Placide had grown up in New Orleans, but that had been in the early years of the twentieth century. Here it was 1864, and the city was very different. There were still steamboats working on the river, and bales of cotton piled high on the wharves. He thought that somewhere in this quaint version of New Orleans his own grandparents were growing up. He could visit them, if he chose to. The idea made him a little queasy.

A young quadroon woman waved to him. "Monsieur Placide," she called, "won't you sit beside me this evening?"

"I'd be delighted," he said. Her name was Lisette, and she'd been the mistress of the son of a prosperous businessman who lived above Canal Street in the American Sector. It was common for a young white man of means to select a light-skinned girl like Lisette and establish her in a small house of her own on Rampart or Burgundy Streets. It was her misfortune that the boy's interest had waned, and he no longer supported her. Now she was looking for a new friend—a new white friend. The quadroon beauty disdained forming attachments to black men. When she'd called to Placide, she was just practicing her social graces.

"You always have so much interesting gossip," she said.

Placide sighed and held her chair for her, then seated himself. "I wonder what Mrs. Le Moyne has for us tonight," he said.

Mrs. Le Moyne came into the dining room and gave Placide a dour look. "I will serve y'all what I always serve," she said. "And that is, sir, what little the damn Yankees haven't taken for themselves or spoiled."

Placide rose slightly from his seat and gave her a little bow. "You work miracles, madame," he said.

"I'm sure, sir, that you wish I could," said Mrs. Le Moyne. She went back out into the kitchen.

"Isn't she a charmer?" whispered Lisette.

Another of the tenants sat down across the table from them. He was a surgeon's assistant in the black community. Placide thought the man always seemed to know too much of everyone else's business. "Will you be leaving us again soon, Mr. Placide?" he asked.

"Yes," said Placide. "Tomorrow."

"Where are you going?" asked Lisette. "Don't the Yankees stop you from traveling?"

Placide shrugged. "I don't worry about them."

The black man across the table laughed. "Then you must be the only person in New Orleans who doesn't."

"How long will you be gone?" asked Lisette.

"Maybe a month or two," said Placide. "Maybe longer." He thought of the Cage, safe upstairs in his room. The War of Southern Independence was proceeding differently than he'd planned. Lee's final northward thrust had been turned back at Gettysburg. The Confederate nation now had little hope of victory, but it still fought grimly on. Oddly, though, Placide was not wholly dissatisfied. What mattered was that Lincoln had been driven to a point of urgency. Politics might yet achieve for blacks what military might had not.

Almost a year before, desperate to rally continued support for his war effort, Lincoln had issued what he called an Emancipation Proclamation. In Placide's timeline, with Lee leading the Federal forces to quick victory in 1862, Lincoln was never pressed to make such a concession. And in Universe$_2$, with Lee killed before the Insurrection even began, Lincoln considered freeing the slaves but put the idea aside when victory proved imminent in 1863.

Only here in Universe₃, in the spring of 1864, with Lee in a grim and determined struggle to hold off defeat as long as possible, could Placide see some hope that American blacks might avoid the horror of what President James G. Blaine had so sanctimoniously called "Parallel Development."

"Mr. Placide," said Lisette sweetly, "would you bring me back something pretty from your travels? I'd be ever so grateful." She gave him a dazzling smile.

He was neither flattered nor fooled. He thought that with luck he'd bring her freedom and dignity, although he was sure she'd much rather have a new dress from New York. He only smiled back at the young woman, then turned his attention to the food Mrs. Le Moyne was carrying in from the kitchen.

Universe₃
March 22, 1884
New Orleans, Louisiana

Shock has followed shock: Even with Lee at last General-in-Chief, the Confederate hopes ended in 1865. It's as if God Almighty has decreed that it must happen just so in all worlds, all timelines, across the breadth of the manifold realities. Evidently the South cannot win, with Lee or without him. There are economic, social, and political reasons too vast for me to correct with so simple a plan.

Today, in a raging downpour, I witnessed the dedication of a handsome, brooding bronze statue of General Lee. The monument stands upon a column seventy feet above the traffic of St. Charles Avenue. Lee gazes resolutely northward, as if grimly contemplating the designs not only of the Union Army, but also of the subtle and guileful Yankee mind. It is a statue I have seen before, although in the world of my childhood the model was P. G. T. Beauregard, and not Robert E. Lee. I knew the area as Beauregard Place; here it has been newly named Lee Circle. In this timeline, of course, Lee is not the Great Traitor. He is idolized as a hero and the defender of the Southern way of life, despite the fact that it was his defeat that ended both the war and what is already being spoken of as "The Old South." To me (and possibly to me alone), he is the Great Failure.

I see that I must begin again. If Lee is to be successful in Universe₄, I must take a greater hand in arranging things. Perhaps Lincoln should die in 1862. Perhaps Jefferson Davis should also be removed, or at least be firmly persuaded to leave Beauregard with his command and to make better and timelier use of Lee's abilities. I have the leisure to consider these matters, as I intend to make a few more jumps to evaluate the fate of the Negroes in this timeline before I return at last to T_0.

On one hand, this world doesn't know either the corruption of the Custer and Blaine administrations, or the abuses of Chase's program of Reconciliation. On the other hand, it has suffered through the different though no less odious crookedness of Ulysses Grant's two terms. I wonder where Grant came from. If he played any important part at all in the universe of my origin, I never read any reference to it. Yet here he emerged as a shrewd tactician, a victor, and a president. More important to me, though, is that he oversaw most of Reconstruction and permitted the wholesale rape of the South.

Reconstruction was a grotesque injustice inflicted on a conquered population. In my world, the brief Confederate Insurrection and Lee's vigilance as president prevented Congress from exacting such harsh penalties on the South. Even the ancient Romans knew better than to impose tyrannical conditions on a defeated people.

Here in Universe$_3$, almost twenty years after the war's end, I see continued evidence of the South's rage and indignation. The Southern attitude, shaped by the war and by Reconstruction, is a desperate desire to cling to what little yet remains of the old ways and the old life. There have been many attempts to circumvent the will of the Yankee, even to reviving slavery under new guises. This is, all in all, a bitter, unhealthy society.

And yet I will remain in this timeline a little while longer. I plan to look around 1884 for another few days, and then jump to 1938 and Göttingen just a week or so before T_0, so that I will remain in Universe$_3$. I'm very curious to see what changes my experiment makes in the rest of the world after seventy-five years.

Despite the problems here, it is a more hopeful world for the Negro. Amendments to the U.S. Constitution have abolished slavery, guaranteed civil rights, and given Negroes the right to vote. Southern state legislatures have seated many Negroes, and some Negroes have been elected to office as high as lieutenant governor or been sent to Washington as senators and district representatives. In my timeline, slavery wasn't abolished until 1878, while in 1938 most Southern Negroes still can't vote, let alone run for office.

The version here of Blaine's "Parallel Development" is segregation, which is not so absolute and despotic, but is still highly offensive. In the New Orleans of my world, Negroes may live only in specially zoned Liberty Boroughs, which are crowded, undeveloped neighborhoods with virtually no communication or trade with each other or with the white community. Negroes here are permitted by law to take up residence wherever they choose, although in actual practice it is impossible for Negroes to find homes in many white areas.

In Universe3, Negroes may travel freely within the city and throughout the South. They may not always be made welcome, of course, but no official restrictions are placed on their movements. In the America I abandoned, a Negro must still carry an endorsement book, which records his assigned Liberty Borough and prevents him from traveling beyond it without a special permit. At any time the state government may move individuals or groups of Negroes from one Liberty Borough to another, sometimes without warning, explanation, or recourse. There are many more similar provisions of the Blaine program, and most of them are happily absent from this timeline.

At the close of the war, the South lay ruined and bankrupt. My experiment ended in tragedies I did not foresee and that have no counterpart in my world. The burning of Atlanta, Sherman's march of devastation from that city's ashes to the Atlantic coast, and the assassination of Abraham Lincoln all occurred as a result of what I set in motion. The war went on three and a half years longer than in my timeline, where some one hundred thousand soldiers died in the Confederate Insurrection. In Universe3, more than six hundred thousand perished in the Civil War.

That nameless army guard outside General Twiggs's quarters did not seem real to me at the time. Why has it taken vast mountains of dead soldiers to make me see the full extent of what I've done? Nevertheless, I believe now that although the cost has been high, I have succeeded in my dream of improving the lot of my people, at least to a small degree. I am confident that the end has truly justified the means.

Placide jumped to 1938, to T_0 minus seven days. He felt like a trespasser. It gave him an eerie feeling to walk around the university town of Göttingen, knowing that there was very likely a duplicate of himself nearby, one who had lived his whole life in Universe3.

There were important differences between the two timelines. Some of the streets and buildings here had new names, clothing styles were oddly altered, and there were unfamiliar flags and signs wherever he looked. The degree of change depended on how much influence the United States had in this alternate reality. After the Confederate Insurrection in his own timeline, the North and South hadn't joined together strongly enough to make America an international power comparable to England, France, Germany, or Russia. Placide could not predict how in Universe$_3$ the bloodier Civil War might have affected that situation.

He climbed the steps of the laboratory, which in his own world had been in the Kaiser Wilhelm Institute; the building was now called the Max Planck Institute. He found what had been his own office, but a stranger's name was now on the door. As he walked down the darkened hallway reading notices and posters, he met the building's elderly porter. Placide was cheered that, despite all, some things remained the same. "Good afternoon, Peter," he said.

The old man cocked his head and studied him. "May I help you?" he asked. His tone was suspicious.

"Don't you know me?"

Peter shook his head. "We don't see many black men here."

Whatever other changes had been made in Univers$_3$, Placide evidently had not pursued his studies in the German Empire. "I'm looking for a few of my colleagues," he said.

Peter raised his eyebrows.

"Werner Heisenberg," said Placide.

"Ah, Dr. Heisenberg's no longer here. He's gone to Berlin, to the other Max Planck Institute."

"Well, then, how about Dr. Schrödinger?"

"He went to Austria. That's where he's from, you know. But I think I've heard that since then he's gone on to England."

"Paul Dirac?"

"He's at Cambridge now."

Placide wondered if this scattering of his colleagues meant that the discoveries they'd made together had not been made in this world. "La Martine and Marquand?"

"I'm sorry, but there's never been anyone here by those names in the years I've worked here."

That made Placide uncomfortable. "Yaakov Fein?"

Peter's expression grew even more cautious. "Who are these men?" he asked.

"Albert Einstein?"

"Gone to live in America."

"Tell me about Max Born. Max must still be here."

"He's now at the University of Edinburgh. He's a British subject."

Placide felt gripped by a cold despair. He suspected that there was no Placide-Born-Dirac Effect in Universe$_3$, and no Cage, either. "These men were friends of mine," he said. "Do you mind if I look around here for a little while? I planned to come work here myself once."

Peter gave him a dubious look, but nodded his head. "I guess it will be all right, if you don't disturb anything."

"I won't." The old porter left him alone in the dusty, drafty corridor.

A quarter of an hour later, while Placide was inspecting some primitive laboratory equipment, two men in the uniform of the town's police approached him. "Will you come with us, sir?" one said.

"Why should I?" asked Placide.

"We must establish your identity. Please show us your papers."

He'd been afraid this might happen. He knew he could be in serious trouble now. "I'm a German citizen," he said.

It was obvious that the policemen didn't believe him. "If that's true," said the second officer, "we'll get this cleared up quickly at headquarters." There was nothing else for Placide to do but go along.

Some time later he was led to a jail cell. He'd had no identification, and none of his references existed in this timeline or could be produced to vouch for him. As the jailer clanged the cell door shut he said, "Make yourself comfortable, Dr. Placide. I'm sure there's been some misunderstanding. In the meantime, you'll just have to make the best of it here."

Placide nodded. The jailer went away, leaving him in a small, dim cell with another prisoner. "How good of you to drop in," said the other man. Placide lay on his hard bunk and stared sullenly at the ceiling. The air was stale, and there was a heavy smell of urine and vomit.

"My name is Schindler," said his cellmate. "I'm a thief, but not a very good one."

"Apparently," murmured Placide.

Schindler laughed. "What got you nicked?"

"No identification."

"That's a hanging offense in this town, friend. Where are you from?"

"The United States, originally. But I've lived in Germany for a few years."

Schindler whistled tunelessly for a little while. "What do you do in Germany?" he asked at last.

"I'm a scientist," said Placide. "Particle physics, quantum mechanics. Nothing that would interest the average person."

"Jewish physics," said Schindler, laughing again. "Einstein and that gang, right?"

"Yes," said Placide, puzzled.

"No wonder you're locked up."

"What do you mean, 'Jewish physics'?"

"The government's official policy is that sort of thing isn't politically correct."

"Politically correct?" cried Placide. "Science is science, truth is truth!"

"And the National Socialists decide which is which."

They talked for some time, and Schindler gave him a great deal to think about. After a while, Placide told the good-humored thief about the Cage and his adventures traveling from one universe to another. Schindler was skeptical, but he stopped short of calling Placide a liar. The two men compared what they knew of recent history in their divergent worlds.

Here in Universe₃, the United States had taken part in the Great War, and the German Empire had come to an end. In response to the Depression, and growing out of Germany's bitterness after the war, a party of fascists came to power in Berlin. Many talented people, liberals and Jews and other persecuted groups, fled Germany soon after that.

"You shouldn't admit that you even knew those people," advised Schindler. "You won't do yourself any good."

"What can they do to me?"

Schindler laid a finger alongside his nose and spoke in a hushed voice. "They can send you to the camps," he said.

"What kind of camps?"

"The kind of place where your friend Einstein might have been sent. Where lots of brilliant but racially inferior scientists are hauling boulders around until they drop dead." He gave Placide a meaningful look.

It was too crazy for Placide to believe, but still he began making plans to escape. When he was released, he'd use the Cage to get out of this stifling reality as quickly as he could. In the meantime, he hoped that the mechanism of the German government would operate efficiently.

Weeks later he was granted a hearing. He sat in a small room at a wooden table while several strangers testified that he was insane. Peter the porter was brought in. He identified Placide as the man who'd wandered into the laboratory and asked after the decadent physicists. Schindler reported everything Placide had told him, and added his own embellishments. Quite obviously, he'd been put in the cell with Placide as an informer.

Placide himself was not permitted to testify. He was judged insane. The American embassy could find no record of him in New Orleans; the examining board ironically chose to believe only one item of Placide's story, that he was a naturalized German. Therefore, it had the authority to remand him to a clinic for the mentally disturbed in Brandenburg. After the hearing, he was locked up again, along with Schindler.

"You goddamn spy!" cried Placide. His voice echoed in the cold stone cell.

Schindler shrugged. "Everyone is a spy these days," he said. "I'm sorry you're upset. Let me make it up to you. I'll give you some advice: be careful when you get to Brandenburg." He lay down on his narrow wooden bunk and turned away from Placide.

"What are you talking about?"

Schindler took out a penknife and began chipping at the mortar between two blocks in the wall. "I mean, that clinic isn't what it appears to be. The Brandenburg clinic is a euthanasia center, friend. So when you go in, just take a deep breath and try to hold it as long as you can."

Schindler's knife was making a rasping, gritty sound. Placide stared at his back. "I'm being sent to a mental health clinic."

"Carbon monoxide," said Schindler, turning to face him. "That's the only treatment they use. Look, you say you helped the Negroes of your country, but see what you've let loose in the world instead! When they drag you into that narrow room, think about that. Think about all the other people who are going to follow you to the gas, and decide if it was worth it."

Placide shut his eyes tightly. "Of course it was worth it," he said fiercely. "All that I've discovered. All that I've accomplished. I only regret that I won't be able to go back to T_0 and report to the others. Then I'd go back to 1860 and try again, correct my mistakes. Even if it took me two or three more attempts, I'd succeed eventually.

And then I could move on to another time, another problem. We could create a committee to guide similar experiments all through history, relieving suffering and oppression wherever we chose."

Schindler jammed his penknife into the wooden frame of the bunk. "You *are* insane, Placide, do you know that? You haven't learned a goddamn thing. You'd charge right ahead if you could, and who knows what new horrors you'd instigate? You've got a rare talent for making good times hard, and hard times worse."

"I have one chance," Placide murmured thoughtfully, not hearing Schindler's words at all. "*Another* Thomas Placide, from another parallel reality, may be aware of my trouble here. He may be searching for me this very minute. I have to hang onto that hope. I must have faith."

Schindler laughed as if he'd never heard anything so funny in his life.

And while Nazi guards patrolled the hallway beyond the cell's iron-barred door, Placide began planning what he would do when he was released, and where he would go, and on whom he'd revenge himself.

Introduction to "Solo in the Spotlight"

George Alec Effinger had a tattoo of an owl on his fore-arm.

That tattoo was one of the first things I noticed about him when we first met at a science fiction convention sometime back in the 1980s. At that time, none of the other authors I'd met had any tattoos (not that I'd seen, anyway), so of course I asked George about his. He told me that he'd gotten it because the owl was his totem animal . . . and although he didn't elaborate any further, it occurred to me that the tattoo's location meant it would be just a glance away every time he sat down to write.

In the years since then, I've often thought that the owl ought to be *every* writer's totem animal—because the longer I live and the more I read, the more I realize that the one thing a writer needs even more than talent, skill, dedication, or a check-in-the-mail is wisdom.

This is especially true if the writer in question is a satirist. And George was one of the best satirists to ever write speculative fiction. He was also one of the best speculative fiction writers to ever write satire.

One of the stories that proves this is "Solo in the Spotlight." Even as it makes you laugh, you'll find yourself wishing that the ridiculousness of the real-life U.S. Executive Branch and its handling of international crises made half as much sense as the ridiculousness of this story's fictional U.S. Executive Branch and its handling of the "situation" in Breulandy. And you'll marvel at the wisdom of a writer who can make his characters sympathetic despite that ridiculousness.

Oh, by the way—if, like me, you're initially confused about the relevance of the story's title, just hop onto the Internet and perform a Google search for the terms "Solo in the Spotlight" and "Barbie." Or ask any serious Barbie collector. All will become hilariously clear.

And the next time you're trying to determine the worth of either a writer or a politician, just ask yourself whether you can see any wisdom there.

Just look for the owl.

—Bradley Denton

✦   ✦   ✦

Solo in the Spotlight

COLONEL McNEILL LEANED DOWN AND MURMURED, "Mr. President, the pilot asked if you want him to turn the plane around and head back to Dulles."

I took off my reading glasses and rubbed the bridge of my nose. "How far are we from Chicago?" I asked.

"We'll be landing in about half an hour, forty-five minutes."

It was a long flight back to Washington. "What does General Paradiz think?" I asked.

Colonel McNeill paused. "Maybe you should ask *him* that, sir."

That wasn't what I wanted to hear. "I asked you, what does General Paradiz think?"

He looked uncomfortable. "The general thinks it's definitely a situation, but it's not a crisis yet, and it's a long way from becoming an emergency. Of course, any situation can turn into a crisis without warning."

This colonel from one of the small states in the Frozen North was telling me—his Commander-in-Chief—something I'd figured out for myself in about the ninth grade. I didn't want to seem impatient, though. You never want to say or do anything to discourage your subordinates from showing what little initiative they have. "We'll just go on to Chicago," I said. "I think we can stay on top of things from here. Please keep me informed."

"Yes, Mr. President. Thank you, sir."

I don't know why he thanked me; they're *always* doing that.

When he'd gone away, the First Daughter turned to me. She had been cruising her favorite Internet sites through the modem in her laptop. She never went anywhere without her laptop. My wife, the First Lady, worried that our daughter was growing up to be a geek rather than a lovely young woman. I told my wife that the girl had plenty of normal teenage interests.

"Is this going to spoil our trip to Chicago, Daddy?" she asked.

I shrugged. "I hope not, sweetheart, but even if things get worse, I've got lots of advisers to help me." I'd been president for only nine or ten weeks, and this was the first troubling situation of my administration. To tell the truth, because it was the first time, I felt more anxiety than conditions warranted.

"Good. I want to see you throw out the first pitch, I want to have cheeseburgers, chips, and Coke at the Billy Goat Tavern, and I want to see the big dollhouse in the Museum of Science and Industry."

"And we have to shop for your mother, too," I said.

"Frango Mints from Marshall Field's and—"

"I have her list, honey. Now, I need to do some work. There's a lot of reading every day, and I'd rather not depend entirely on my staff's summaries."

"Okay, Daddy." She went back to her laptop. She's a great kid, and if anybody's daughter could handle the pressures of growing up in the White House, I knew she could. Sometimes her mother worried about her too much.

Colonel McNeill worried too much, too, but he got paid for that. A little while later, while Air Force One was beginning its descent into O'Hare, he was again murmuring into my ear.

"There's been some news, Mr. President, very distressing news. The general thinks we need to have a meeting."

"We'll be on the ground in a few minutes, Colonel," I said.

"Sir, the general thinks we should go back to Washington."

That sounded bad. "What happened?" I asked.

"The Breulen rebels have seized the American Embassy. Some Marines and other embassy personnel have been injured, possibly killed. No confirmation yet on the fatalities, though."

Fatalities—what an empty, distancing word. I felt my stomach tensing. "All right," I said. "How do I order the pilot to head home?"

"The intercom at the table, sir."

I turned to the First Daughter. She hadn't heard any of this.

"We're going back to Washington, sweetheart," I said. "Sorry. It's an emergency."

Colonel McNeill cleared his throat. "Mr. President, the situation is now a *crisis.* It's not an emergency yet."

I turned and gave him a look, but I stopped myself from saying anything. Nobody liked the colonel; he was an attitude without a person.

The First Daughter sighed. "Well, okay, Daddy, Chicago isn't going anywhere. We'll miss the ballgame, but you've got seven more first pitches to throw out."

"That's my girl." I liked the way she assumed we'd be going to Opening Days during my second term, too.

I stood up, took a deep breath and let it out, straightened my suit jacket, and followed the colonel to the conference table. Most of my advisers stood up and greeted me with a "Mr. President." General Paradiz didn't. I made a mental note of that.

"Please sit down, gentlemen," I said. "And we can do without ceremony and protocol. Let's just get to work."

"Mr. President," General Paradiz said. He glanced around the table, checking to see if any of the other advisers, military or otherwise, objected to his taking charge. No one did, of course. "Before I begin, do you have any questions?"

"I think I have all the facts of the situation," I said.

"Crisis," Colonel McNeill corrected. We all ignored him.

General Paradiz went on. "It's extremely important to act with speed and confidence, Mr. President. This is the first test of your administration's foreign policies."

"Our first concern is the welfare of the Americans in Breulandy," said Luis, my secretary of defense. "But you should remember that there is a political side as well."

I frowned. "I'm not thinking of politics right now. The safety of our people is not a political issue."

"If you actually mean that," General Paradiz said, "then you'll be the first U.S. president in my experience who did."

He was not a likable guy, either. The best you could say about him was that he was a mammal. The trouble was that if you got more specific, the very next word would have to be "however." I wondered if I, as Commander-in-Chief, could simply reassign him to some Distant Early Warning outpost on the tundra. If we still had the DEW Line.

"How much can we accomplish now?" I asked Luis. "From Air Force One?" He was on the plane only because he'd grown up in

Chicago, and the mayor was his boyhood friend. Luis had come along just for the baseball game, but I was grateful to have him with me.

He shrugged. "You don't have to wait until you get back to Washington, Mr. President, if that's what you mean. Anything you can do from the White House, you can do from here. Major Mathias has the football, of course."

"The football" was a large briefcase that contained everything I'd need to commit the country to any sort of action, up to and including Global Thermonuclear War. All the necessary secret codes and commands were in the football, and wherever the president went, Major Mathias or someone very much like him carried it nearby.

"Good," I said.

"Yes, sir," Luis said. "And Master Hsu has the hockey puck."

Okay, that one got by me. I'd known about the football before I took office—I read about it in *Time* years ago; but I'd never even heard of the hockey puck. "Who is Master Hsu?" I asked.

Colonel McNeill indicated a portly, sober-faced man seated near—but not at—the conference table. "The gentleman with the wooden box." I didn't recall ever seeing the man before.

"He's the president's psychic adviser," Luis explained.

"Psychic adviser?" I said. "I don't have time for that."

"Sir," said Colonel McNeill, "almost every administration since Andrew Jackson has had a psychic adviser. President Jackson himself consulted Marie Laveau, the New Orleans voodoo queen, on several difficult matters. The 'hockey puck' is the code name for the tools of the psychic trade. In the case of this particular adviser, Master Hsu, I understand that means tarot cards."

I looked at Master Hsu for a moment. "I know I didn't appoint him."

"He was selected by someone on your staff, Mr. President," the colonel said.

"Mr. President, sir," said Master Hsu, standing and bowing his head, "I may offer insights not available to your other advisers."

"That remains to be seen, Master Hsu." I turned back to the others at the table, and I put the psychic adviser and his hockey puck out of my mind.

The conference lasted from Chicago to just beyond Toledo, Ohio. Luis and General Paradiz discussed the likely scenarios as they foresaw them, along with the options I'd have for each. I found the procedure upsetting because we were, in effect, completely helpless. We didn't know exactly what had happened; we could only wait for new information and, in the meantime, prepare for the worst.

After the meeting I went back to my seat. The First Daughter was worried, so I gave her a quick summary of what I knew. She was as surprised as I to learn there was a psychic adviser aboard. "But that's *great*, Daddy!" she said. "The one thing you're short of now is like *information*, right? So, okay, like this Master Hsu could maybe see things in the cards that won't get reported for *hours* yet."

"The difference between us," I said, "is that you like playing with your tarot cards and your Ouija board and your astrology charts. I'm the president of the United States. I have to base my decisions on more scientific sources. Tarot cards are imprecise, bewildering, and completely nonlogical. That puts them squarely in the Legislative branch, not the Executive."

"Daddy, give him a chance."

"Sweetheart, in your own words, *as if!*"

"Daddy!"

The look of concern on her face was genuine. She was probably afraid I'd make some horrible mistake and go down in history as the worst president of all time. "All right," I said. "I'll have him come over here." I thought if Master Hsu could keep her entertained for half an hour—and take her mind off her anxiety—it would be worth putting up with a little mystical nonsense.

I signaled to Colonel McNeill. "Tell that psychic adviser to join me."

Something flickered in McNeill's eyes; it may have been amusement. "Yes, sir," he said.

He brought Master Hsu, and then McNeill left us alone. The old man bowed again. "Mr. President, sir," he said.

"I don't know if you've met my daughter."

"Mr. President, sir," Master Hsu said, "may I speak of security matters in front of the young lady?"

I shrugged. "Right now, she knows as much as I do about what's happening in Breulandy."

Master Hsu smiled briefly. "In a few minutes the three of us will know much more."

He sat down across from me. On his lap was a small box made of polished dark wood—the puck, I guessed. He opened it, looked inside, and his expression changed. "Ah," was all he said.

"Is something wrong?"

"My cards," he said, looking up at me. "They're not in the box where they belong. I don't know why."

My daughter spoke up. "That's cool, 'cause I've got my cards with me."

"I prefer to use my own deck," said Master Hsu.

"You *wish!* But your deck is probably back in Washington, right?"

He looked very unhappy. "Yes. I suppose we'll have to wait."

"Uh-huh," my daughter said, "but the whole *point* is you're supposed to be giving my Dad some advantage from, you know, the *psychic* world. If he has to kill time until we get home again, then you're not being very much help, are you?"

"That's true, young lady."

"So why not use my cards?"

He blinked a couple of times. "All right, I'll use them."

"Great!" She reached under her seat for her backpack and rummaged around in it for a while. Finally, she pulled out a pink-and-purple cardboard box. "Here you go," she said, handing it to Master Hsu.

He opened the box and slid out the cards, glancing at a few of them. "What are these?" he asked.

"My deck," the First Daughter said. "Well, I guess some of the cards look different to you. It's the Barbie tarot."

Master Hsu stared in disbelief at one of the cards. "Barbie?"

"Here, see that card you've got? Handbags are the suit of love and romance and stuff."

"Handbags?" Master Hsu looked by turns horrified and offended.

"Look at the *card*, okay? In the picture, Barbie's checking out this shop window, and there's all these handbags: blue ones, black ones, a green one, a yellow one, and a clear plastic one with scrunched-up newspapers in it, right? So this is *The Point of No Return*, where you've come down so far from the Spiritual World that you can't get out of the Material World and go back up. It's a decision card, on account of Barbie's got to make a choice. So, okay, one of the handbags is the *obvious* one, right? But it really *isn't*, not if you're looking real close. See the silver clasp on the clear handbag? It just won't go with her goldtone earrings and necklace and stuff. The bird on her shoulder is supposed to be this great knowledge coming from somewhere, but the bird on the sidewalk pecking at the crumbs could be advice coming from some *really faux* person, so like there's a warning to be careful. Hint, hint."

For a few seconds, the loudest sound I could hear was the whoosh of the air nozzle above my head. Then the old man slowly reached out and gave the cards back to the First Daughter. "These are not tarot," he said.

"Tcha! I guess they *are!* You just have to learn how to read them. There are like *hundreds* of different decks around, okay?"

"Yes," said Master Hsu, "and most of them are false friends."

"Oh, *right*," my daughter said. "So it's like you've got this real truth that nobody else knows, huh?"

It was time to stop her, so I reached over and squeezed her shoulder; that was the signal. She glanced at me for a few seconds—you've seen that look they get, they *know* they've met you somewhere before—and then she nodded. "Sorry, Daddy. Maybe that school in Switzerland will teach me to keep my mouth shut some of the time."

As I mentioned before, she's a great kid. "Master Hsu," I said, "what do we do first?"

"If I had my deck, I'd do a reading. The cards would indicate how you should proceed, whether to begin negotiations or use more forceful means. There'd also be information about the people involved in this situation."

"A lot of lives are at stake," I said. "Some people may already have died. I'd like to have that information, if it can be trusted."

Master Hsu's expression didn't change. "It's synchronicity, Mr. President, sir," he said. "We are of the moment, the crisis in Breulandy is of the moment, the way the cards are dealt—that, too, is of the moment. At this time, in this place, the cards can be arranged in only one way. That gives the reading its significance."

"Yes, but—"

He'd been through all this before with other doubters. "Doing the reading changes the moment, so another reading won't produce the same results. Sometimes it's a sign of bad faith to continue." He showed his brief smile again. "The cards have chewed me out plenty over the years."

I liked him. "Why the tarot?" I asked. "Why not the I Ching?"

He spread his hands a little. "Why does one person follow shotokan karate and another practice kendo?"

"Will you do a reading? With my daughter's cards?"

"I don't like them, Mr. President, sir, but if you want me to go ahead, I'll try."

"Please," I said.

Master Hsu looked through the cards for a moment, then gave

up with a sigh. "Young lady," he said, "which one of these is the King of Swords?"

"The King of Swords—that's, um, the King of Shoes. I'll find him." She took the deck and searched through it quickly. "Here he is. Brad, Christie's boyfriend. The kings are all boyfriends of Barbie's girlfriends."

Master Hsu took the card as if it were his own death warrant. He put it down on the table between us. Brad was a handsome young black man. I'd never thought about black Barbie characters before; many people haven't.

"Brad's my Dad's card?" she asked. "I don't usually—"

Master Hsu cut her off with a gesture. "Mr. President, sir, please shuffle the deck and form your question. You don't have to ask it out loud, you can just concentrate on it if you like. It's important to be clear and simple. The tarot may not reply to what you think you've asked. I mean, sir, the cards will be truthful, but they may respond to something else in your mind or heart, something personal and not political."

In law school they called that an elastic clause. It covered and absolved just about everything. I took the deck and started to shuffle. "Tell me about the crisis in Breulandy," I said.

"Now, with your left hand, cut the deck into three piles and put it together again in a different order."

I did that and gave him back the cards. "This covers you," he murmured, laying the Nine of Handbags over Brad. The card showed a plump and happy man surrounded by nine bulging purses. Master Hsu paused. "Handbags are Cups?" he asked my daughter.

"Uh-huh," she said.

His eyebrows raised a little. "It's a good card to start with, Mr. President, sir. You're going to get your wish."

"I didn't wish for anything."

"Yes, you did."

"This is about Breulandy, not me."

Master Hsu shrugged. "Let me finish and we'll see." He laid another card on Brad and the Nine of Handbags, but turned ninety degrees. "This crosses you," he said; the card was Barbie's pink Classy Corvette. There were eight more cards in the layout: beneath me was Great Shape Barbie, in leotard and leg-warmers; behind me was the Barbie Queen of the Prom boardgame; crowning me was Barbie's Little Sister Stacie; before me was the Five of Shoes; my fears were Malibu Barbie; my environment was the original #850 Ponytail Barbie, blonde, in black-and-white-striped swimsuit, NRFB (Never Removed From Box); my hopes were the Three of Handbags; and the final outcome was the Barbie Dream House.

"Mr. President, sir, I don't know what to say."

"Is it bad?" I asked.

Master Hsu shook his head. "No, I mean I don't know what to say. I don't know what most of these cards are."

"I can sort of translate," said the First Daughter.

"I'd appreciate that," he said.

"So, okay, Brad and the Nine of Handbags you know. The Corvette is the Chariot. Great Shape Barbie is Strength, and the Barbie game is the Wheel of Fortune. Stacie is the Page of Pentacles. The Five of Shoes is the Five of Swords. Malibu Barbie is the High Priestess, and the original Barbie is the Fool. The Three of Handbags is the Three of Cups, and the Barbie Dream House is the Tower. Got it?"

Master Hsu gave a little shudder. "Well, Mr. President, sir, the first thing I notice is five cards out of ten are Major Arcana. That's unusual and makes for a dramatic reading. Strength and the Wheel of Fortune are good cards, but they're not drawing my attention; neither is the Chariot, although it's a victory card. The Fool and the High Priestess are esoteric but not threatening. Generally speaking, it's a very good layout. Nine of the ten cards range from neutral to great success. Only the last card troubles me."

If he was troubled, so was I. "What does it mean?" I asked.

"If this were my deck, sir, you'd see for yourself. I don't know what the Barbie Dream House is, but in most tarot decks the Tower has been blasted by a lightning bolt, and two people are falling from it into an abyss. It's a card that can mean catastrophe, but not always. It's frightening, but like the Death card it can mean change in a good sense. I think the nine hopeful cards outweigh the Tower, especially the card just before it in the layout, the Three of Cups or Handbags, which often indicates a happy ending."

I don't know what made me think of it, but I wondered what the *Washington Post* would say if they knew I'd replaced the State Department with seventy-eight pieces of cardboard. I took my glasses off and rubbed the bridge of my nose, hoping Colonel McNeill would interrupt soon with some news from Breulandy—good news or bad news, I didn't care.

Master Hsu coughed. It was meant as a question.

I waved at him. "I'm fine," I said. "I'm just a little tired." At the conference table, General Paradiz, Luis, and a couple of the others were playing *Risk*.

My daughter squeezed my shoulder. That was our signal again, coming back at me. "Master Hsu," I said, "would you excuse us for a moment?"

"Certainly, Mr. President, sir." He got up carefully without disturbing the cards and moved toward the front of the plane.

"Daddy, remember the bird on the sidewalk?"

"No, I don't. What are you talking about?"

She heaved the sigh that kids use when they're absolutely disgusted with everything you stand for. "Hellooo? The Five of Handbags, Daddy, okay? The two birds, one of them was like warning you about *this very thing*?"

"I'm sorry," I said. "I'm thinking about hostages with their hands tied behind their backs, and you're talking Barbie cards. We're not on the same wavelength here."

She did the sigh again, this time adding a tongue click. "But like we totally *are!* So, okay, I'm *telling* you, he's wrong about the tarot layout. Things are lots worse than he thinks."

I opened my mouth to argue with her, but I didn't. Fifteen minutes ago, the very idea of a Presidential Psychic Adviser had been just absurd. Now I was about to take the man's side against my own daughter. What did I know?

Nothing. That was part of the problem. The other part of the problem was that I didn't know how much Master Hsu knew either.

"What do you think?" I asked.

"I think he's an okay guy, but like he's so wrong. Have him do another reading."

"But he said it wouldn't turn out the same—"

"Ask a different question."

Page one of my screenplay: Interior, Oval Office, Day. JFK is sitting behind the big desk with Caroline on his knee. Pierre Salinger or somebody is just leaving and closes the door behind him.

Caroline: Daddy, call Mr. Khrushchev and tell him you know he's bluffing.

JFK: (worried) I don't know he's bluffing. We could end up in a nuclear war because of what he's doing in Cuba. (He pronounces it "Cuber.")

Caroline: Trust me, Daddy, he's bluffing. My Magic 8 Ball told me.

I see myself in the role of JFK, and I'd like to get Mira Sorvino for Caroline. Maybe it needs a little work. I'll get back to you.

I felt the aircraft start a slow turn to the right, so I guessed we'd run out of continent. Far down below was Philadelphia, a city I've always found dreary. It's not politic for a president to say things like that about a major city; the truth is that Philadelphia *isn't* dull, it just seems that way because it's across the river from glamorous, exciting Camden, New Jersey.

All right, I'd given myself a couple of minutes to calm down; now it was time to get back on the job. I signaled Master Hsu to join us again.

"Mr. President, sir?" he said.

I glanced quickly at the First Daughter; she nodded. "I'd like you to do another reading."

"Yes, sir." He found the Brad card and put it on the table, then handed the rest of the deck to me. "Please shuffle again and form another query."

My daughter and I hadn't talked about the second question, but I had an intuition. I asked, "Who's in charge in Breulandy?"

"This covers you," said Master Hsu in a low voice; he put the Three of Handbags over Brad. His eyes flicked up at me; that was the same happy-ending card he'd been so glad to see in the previous spread. "This crosses you," he said, and damn if he didn't lay down the Barbie Dream House!

"Son of a bitch," I muttered.

"It still might not predict a calamity, Mr. President, sir. The card's reversed, and that could mean winning freedom for the hostages after a great struggle."

My daughter squeezed my shoulder. I just held my breath and waited to see what came next.

"This is beneath you." It was a card named Allan.

"The Emperor," my daughter said. "Allan is Midge's boyfriend."

Behind me was the Ten of Earrings; crowning me was the Nine of Shoes; before me was the Seven of Hairbrushes; my fears were the Eight of Earrings; my environment was the Ten of Hairbrushes; my hopes were Great Shape Barbie; and the final outcome was the Four of Shoes.

"Only three Major Trumps," said Master Hsu. "There's a very different feeling to this reading."

"Explain it to me," I said.

Master Hsu hesitated. "Keep in mind, sir, that these cards speak of what's happening in Breulandy. I don't believe any of them refer to you personally. The Three of Handbags still points to a successful conclusion, although the card that crosses you warns it may cost a lot, one way or another. Allan is a worldly ruler; let your intellect control your emotions in this situation. Some of the other cards support this, especially the Seven of Hairbrushes, a lone man holding off a number of enemies—grace under pressure, as Hemingway put it. The Ten of Hairbrushes shows someone who's bitten off more than he can chew; that could be you, or it could be the leaders of either side in Breulandy. Great Shape Barbie means the same as it did in the first reading: patience and perseverance. The final result card, the Four of Shoes, is ambiguous; it usually promises important insights after some creative meditation."

"Daddy—"

Colonel McNeill interrupted her. "Mr. President, we've established a telephone link to our embassy in Breulandy."

That snapped me right back to reality. "Good," I said. "Who do you have there?"

"The Breulen prime minister."

I hadn't heard the latest news yet, but it felt good just to have some movement. "I want a conference call with him and the rebels' head guy."

"We're trying, Mr. President."

"And I want you to get me Jimmy Carter on another line. He had to deal with the first big hostage situation."

The First Daughter grabbed my arm. "It's *real* important—"

"Sweetheart," I said, "I've stopped caring what the tarot says."

Master Hsu frowned. "That's a mistake, Mr. President, sir," he said.

I stood up. "It's the nature of advisers to contradict each other," I said.

I started to move out into the aisle. "Daddy, do you trust me?"

The unfamiliar urgency in her voice made me stop and turn around. "Of course I do."

"Then like it's *totally* a bad idea to do the conference now. You should talk with the prime minister first, and then you should talk with the rebels."

"Why?" Just hearing her opinion, I was giving my teenage daughter a cabinet-level position.

"'Cause." I *hate* that explanation. "'Cause Master Hsu's never even *seen* the Barbie tarot before, so like there's no *brainstorm* every time he looks at a card. No offense, Master Hsu."

"There's truth in that," he admitted.

I paused and shook my head. "Thanks, honey," I said, "but we'll be all right."

"No, we *won't!*" she cried. Everyone at the conference table turned to stare. "He's absolutely *wrong* about the Barbie Dream House, okay? It *is* a disaster. I saw it from the first card he turned—it's like the whole world in glowing *ruins* or something!"

What could I tell her? Anything I'd say would be the equivalent of "there, there." And "there, there" isn't much consolation in the middle of a shooting war. Still, I had some of the best minds in the country with me on Air Force One, and I had to trust their judgment over my daughter and Master Hsu.

I took five steps and stopped. "You think so?" I asked her.

"Daddy," she said with tears on her cheeks, "it couldn't be worse if you had ten Low-Fat Diet cards in the layout."

My heart beat maybe six or seven times; I suppose that counted as a period of creative meditation. "Colonel McNeill," I said, "cancel that conference call, but keep the prime minister on the line, I'll be with him in a minute. Keep trying to find Jimmy Carter, too."

"But, sir—" said the colonel.

"Just do what I said. Master Hsu, please stay right there. I may need to consult you again."

He bowed his head. "If you do, Mr. President, sir, I will be guided by the young lady."

"Thank you. Tell me one last thing: Where do you study to become a tarot master?"

He looked puzzled. "I'm not a master. That's my name. My mother named me Master."

"Oh." That's all I said.

What happened in Breulandy over the next few months is on record in the *Washington Post* and *Time* magazine. This is the first time the tarot has been mentioned, though, because I never told anyone all the reasons for my decisions. No one else knew what happened between Master Hsu, myself, and the First Daughter. I think it's time they both got a little credit. Especially my kid.

Days later, back home in the White House, I told her she deserved a reward. "What would you like?" I asked.

She pretended to think it over. "So, okay, like those famous movie Barbies?"

She owned some of the special collectors' Barbies and Kens, the ones packaged in costumes from *Gone with the Wind*, *My Fair Lady*, and *The Wizard of Oz*. They cost seventy-five dollars each, but they're very handsome dolls—except the Rhett Butler Ken, which is an abomination in the eyes of the Lord. "Uh-huh," I said, hearing the charges chiming on my Visa card.

"Well, buy me the *Pulp Fiction* series: Foot Massage Barbie and Ken, Pumpkin and Honey Bunny Barbie and Ken, Hypodermic in the Heart Barbie and Ken—"

I believe I went mostly ballistic. "You're *kidding!*"

"Gotcha!" She grinned at me.

Talk about striking down with furious anger. . . .

Introduction to "At the Bran Foundry"

Authors are not their stories . . . are not their novels, and yet . . . and yet . . . We're certainly in there, hidden, disguised: there you are, author, the lone, shadowy man with the mustaches looking snidely, snidely around the corner at your gentle readers; and Piglet—that's what George used to call himself thirty years ago—yes, Piglet is right here in this story.

And "At the Bran Foundry" is quintessential Effinger.

The story was published in Robert Silverberg's *New Dimensions* 3 in 1973. Thirty years ago, and for me and authors Gardner Dozois and Joe Haldeman—erstwhile members of the Guilford Writers' Workshop, of which George Alec Effinger was a founding member—those were our salad days. Those were the compressed, juicy days when everything was fast and pure, when writing was the most important thing in the world, when anthologies such as Damon Knight's *Orbit*, Terry Carr's *Universe*, and the aforementioned Robert Silverberg's *New Dimensions* were the venues for the most interesting and influential stories in the genre. In those luminous days, Gardner, Joe, Piglet, and I (among others) would gather at Jay Haldeman's old mansion in Guilford, Pennsylvania, to workshop our stories. It was the gathering of the tribe. It was hard work. It was joy.

It was where I learned the bones of my craft and met those who would become family.

George Alec Effinger . . . I remember you, Piglet, that first time I met you at Jay's. Your brown hair was shoulder length. You rushed into the living room. You wore jeans and a Yale T-shirt. You were thin, small-boned, handsome, somehow fey, smooth, and very, very cool. You were the *wunderkind*. And when we workshopped your stories, I would find myself rereading each paragraph, trying to figure out how on earth you crafted such smooth prose.

George could have—should have—written for *The New Yorker*. His prose style is New York smooth and perfectly cast. But there are plenty of writers with smooth style. What Piglet brought to his work was a brilliant and subversively cockeyed vision of the world. It was the perspective of a demonic child taking delight in . . . everything.

This story surprises in some of the same ways that J. D. Salinger's extraordinary "A Perfect Day for Bananafish" does. While Salinger's story is cozy comfortable and sun-drenched . . . at first, Piglet's story is a sort of *Boy's Life* Andy Hardy movie, complete with sound track. And the wonderful, wacky idea of smelting cereal conceals in humor what will—

Nah. I just can't give punch lines away.

But I can tell you that Piglet's genius is in this story.

Perhaps I can give you a glimpse of the writer I knew—the writer I see giggling and making faces between the lines of this story, a writer whose thought patterns seemed to dance on entirely different tracks than the rest of us. I picked up a few of his early books from the same period when he wrote "At the Bran Foundry." His salad days.

Our salad days.

And the inscription in his first novel, *What Entropy Means to Me* (his brilliant *Tristram Shandy* allegory) is pure Piglet:

> To Jack:
> *There once was a hermit named Dave . . .*
> *The rest of the novel rhymes with that line.*
> *(Have I given away anything?)*

And I found a neatly typed note inside the slipcover:

> Hey, Jack, lookee!
> Wow, ain't it something, huh?
> It's this book I wrote. Free.
> (Signed) *Yours for a cleaner vicinity, Piglet*

Piglet's voice. A kid wearing a Yale T-shirt who is slightly, slyly shocked that somehow he'd written . . . a book.

The voice is in the story that follows. May it shock and delight the hell out of you.

— Jack Dann

✝ ✝ ✝

At the Bran Foundry

IT WAS ALL SO VERY STRANGE. WE WERE TOTALLY helpless, pushed about by people who did not even seem to be aware of our existence. We began to question the reality of it all, ourselves. Where were we? Could this actually be happening to us? At times we couldn't be certain of anything; at those times, we were desperately close to madness.

It all started as the annual Key Club outing. There was "Chico" Carresquel, Robin Roberts, Don Zimmer, "Dutch" Dotterer, Bobby Del Greco, Rip Repulski, and me, squeezed into Don's Tempest. Following us were Ryne Duren, Wayne Causey, Ike Delock, Sherm Lollar, Walt Dropo, Vic Wertz, Eddy Yost, "Whitey" Herzog, Gus Zernial, Reno Bertoia, and big "Bullet Bob" Turley, in Wayne, Walt, and Reno's cars. We also had two of the Kiwanis representatives with us. The adults were Mr. Zernial and Mr. Causey, Gus and Wayne's fathers.

We left Collinwood High right after school, at three-thirty. We drove out Lake Shore Boulevard, past Euclid Beach and Humphrey's field, past Euclid, past East 222nd Street and farther. We rode with our noses pressed to the windows because we had never been to Wickliffe before. We stopped when we got to the bran foundry.

The factory consisted of many large buildings, all connected by enclosed corridors many feet above the ground. There were cat-walks that threaded the dizzy heights. The complex covered hundreds of acres; Mr. Zernial told us that part of the area used to be the old Shoregate Shopping Center. He told us how he used to go there as a child, to buy bags of plastic soldiers in the Wool-worth's.

The enormous factory was ominous in appearance; it stood there, gray and dark brick-red, hissing black smoke into the late Greater Cleveland afternoon. The various buildings stood to left and right, and the chimneys and chemical-towers stuck up like fists for a great distance behind. Immediately before us, however, was a smaller yellow building, with many windows and a low roof to give it a less gruesome aspect. We walked along a narrow flagstone path; on both sides the lawn was trimmed to an even and compulsive shortness. On the lawn just before the door to the building was a white wooden signboard with a glass door. The letters inside had been arranged to read: The Jennings Raisin Bran Corporation. Vis-itors welcome. Tours leave from the lobby 1 2 3 4:30. Personnel Office use Gate C.

Mr. Causey held the door open for us; all the rest of the guys went in, but I held back for just a moment. With the door to the lobby open, I could hear the piped music from inside. It was the sort of brisk, raucous trumpet and xylophone stuff that always meant "industry" in the Bugs Bunny cartoons that were made dur-ing the war. I looked back, across the vast parking lot jammed with the employees' cars. I saw cut-off sections of grimy buildings and tall derricks burning waste gases at the top like eternal flames of commerce. Mr. Causey was waiting, and I stepped past him into the lobby, immersing myself completely in the eager music.

We stood in the lobby for a few minutes. There were couches covered with dark-green leather, and coffee tables with copies of *National Geographic* and the house organ, *The Bran Bulletin.* Soon the bustling music built to nearly unbearable intensity, and just at the very peak, when we couldn't stand it any longer, a door marked PRIVATE opened. A personable man of middle age came out and joined us, shaking the hands of Mr. Zernial and Mr. Causey. As soon as he appeared the music quieted. Like magic, it became a divided string background to narration.

"Hi, fellows!" he said to the rest of us. He pronounced the "ow" in "fellows," smiling broadly.

Mr. Causey cleared his throat and spoke up. "I'd like to thank you," he said, "and I'm sure the Key Clubbers will join me in this; we'd like to thank you for taking time out of your busy schedule to show us around your marvelous installation here."

"Not at all, Mister, uh, Causey, is it? Yes, Mr. Causey. Well, let's get started. My name is Bob Jennings, and I am Chairman of the Board of the Jennings Raisin Bran Corporation. Come with me now, as we discover—The Wonderful World of Raisin Bran!"

The music built steadily so that during his last pause the cornets and French horns were calling through the lobby in ear-splitting fashion. Then it all hushed once more, like magic, waiting for him to make another pronouncement. It was eerie.

Mr. Jennings motioned us toward a pair of glass doors. He held one open for us, and we went through into a huge room filled with machinery making a deafening racket. Still, the background music followed us, audible over the crashing and pounding engines.

As we went through the door Walt Dropo stopped and said, "Are you *really* the head of the Corporation?"

Mr. Jennings smiled. "Yes, son, I am."

"Gosh," said Walt.

To the right of the double doors was a small, glass-enclosed office. Mr. Jennings said, "Please excuse me for a moment," and went into the office. He went up to a secretary at a desk, and spoke to her. We could hear everything that they said, as if it were being broadcast throughout the plant.

The secretary smiled; even from where we were standing I could see the perfect teeth. "Good afternoon, Mr. Jennings," she said.

"Good afternoon, Miss Brant," he said. "Is everything in order?"

"Yes, Mr. Jennings."

"Good."

Mr. Jennings came back to our group and stood by a huge, thundering machine. He put one foot up on a riveted plate, turning to us casually and smiling. From behind a massive stanchion he brought out a box of Jennings Raisin Bran. It apparently had been left there by mistake. He gazed at it meditatively for a few seconds, and then regarded our group once more.

"You know," he said, "I'm *glad* to be able to take time from my crowded working day to show you folks just how careful we are in making each and every box of Jennings Raisin Bran." The music was quieter now, playing something that I recognized as the Entry of the Gods into Valhalla from Wagner's *Das Rheingold*. It seemed to fit the ecstatic expression that Mr. Jennings made every time he said the words "raisin bran."

"Where's Walt?" asked Mr. Zernial. "What's happened to Walt?"

"Every day we get dozens of letters from simple people just like you, from all over the United States, asking me, 'Bob, how do you make Jennings Raisin Bran so good? Every box has that same homemade goodness that we have come to expect from the Jennings brand.' "

"Has anybody seen Walt?"

"I seen him," said Sherm Lollar, "last time I seen him was when we came in here. Maybe you could ask that guard over there, the one in the gray uniform."

"It's really very simple," said Mr. Jennings. "We here at Jennings Raisin Bran know how much you folks depend on the quality of every item that bears the Jennings name. And we're proud that you demand such high standards from us. It's our goal to make every box of Jennings Raisin Bran worthy of that expectation. We work hard to meet our own standards of excellence, and we're continually doing research in our up-to-date, expensively equipped laboratories to find even better ways of doing things."

"They really have armed guards right here in the plant," said Eddy Yost. "What do they need guards for?"

Mr. Causey glared at him. "Company secrets. Industrial sabotage. Now, quiet down and listen."

"For instance, let's begin with the raw materials. If you'll follow me right out these doors over here . . ." Mr. Jennings smiled, and indicated another pair of glass doors set into the side of the huge building. As we followed him I glanced around the plant, looking through the surging machines like gigantic trees in a restless steel forest. We went through a cloistered walk, and the music went with us, rising through brass or string passages, but making no progress with its exposition.

At the end of the corridor we went through some more glass doors. We were outside again; the sky was white, streaked with a heavy gray that promised rain. We were in a sort of open yard. Several railroad tracks crossed the area, disappearing quickly down avenues in the maze of buildings. Our guide went up to a group of men who were unloading boxcars on one of the sidings.

"Eddy?" said Mr. Zernial. "Now what's happened to Eddy? And has anybody seen Walt yet? The rest of you stick together. I don't want anybody else wandering off. You could get lost around here, and I don't want anybody getting hurt. Frank," meaning Mr. Causey, "maybe I should go look for Walt and Eddy."

"Well," said Mr. Causey, "why don't we just wait awhile? They'll probably find us out here. I mean, we don't want to lose you, too!"

I noticed that one of the gray-uniformed armed guards was standing to our right, leaning against one of the boxcars, trying to appear casual. Reno saw what I was looking at.

"Mr. Zernial, do they have those guards following us? Do they think we're spies from Kellogg's or something?" he asked.

"They're probably guarding the bran shipment."

"We use, first off, only the finest Laurentian bran ore. Come up closer; make a circle around here so that you can see better. I think the boys are unloading a shipment right now. Hello, Tom. Hi, Bob, Larry. Ned. Mack."

We all noticed that Mr. Jennings knew the names of all the workmen. Just like Caesar. We gathered around him in a group, watching the men break open a large wooden crate. They pried open a few slats with crowbars.

"Oh, my God! Now where's Reno? He was standing right here a minute ago," said Mr. Causey.

"Look, if they don't want to learn anything that's their business," said Mr. Zernial.

Mr. Jennings went up to the crate after his employees had broken open the top. He reached in and pulled out a handful of gritty red earth. He came back to us and indicated that we should hold out our hands; he passed the dirt among us.

"This is raw bran ore. It was recently dug out of the rich fields of ore located in the Laurentian Highlands of Quebec, or from our own Mesabi Range in Minnesota. It was shipped by ore boat through the Great Lakes right to our port on Cleveland's West Side, then loaded onto freight cars and rushed directly to our factory. To ensure freshness, the trip has taken less than two weeks from the time it left its natural rock bed to its arrival here."

"Mr. Jennings, I hate to interrupt," said Mr. Causey, "but some of our boys seem to have wandered off. I really don't want to cause any inconvenience, but perhaps I should try to find them before they interfere with some machine or something."

Mr. Jennings smiled. "No need to worry," he said. "They'll be no bother at all. I used to think these trips were stuffy, myself. Let them wander around and look at what seems interesting to them. They may learn more that way anyhow. I'll have them paged from my office if they haven't come back by the time that you're ready to leave. Now, what say we follow this shipment of ore on its way through the many changes it must make before it reaches your pantry shelf?"

We followed him into another immense building. Inside were three furnaces, black with soot and standing several stories tall. We walked by the first two; men and women in dirty overalls turned and smiled shyly as we passed. Mr. Jennings nodded and smiled at them all. The music moved easily into a pleasant *andante*, signifying a transition. Where did the background theme come from? I began to wonder what was really happening.

At the last furnace Mr. Jennings introduced us to Gary Kibling. Mr. Kibling was in charge of Furnace Number Eight.

"Thank you, Bob. Hello, boys. I guess Mr. Jennings has shown you the raw ore outside, is that right? Fine. Now, the first step in making your raisin bran is the refinement of your ore. Of course, we can't make flakes out of the impure stuff that you saw. It would taste terrible. Well, our job is to melt it all down and get out all but the very best bran content. It's actually a complex operation, but I'll try to make it as easy to understand as I can."

Rip nudged me. "They have guards in here, too," he said. I caught Mr. Jennings's eye and smiled. He smiled back.

"This," said Mr. Kibling, "is a blast furnace, very much like those in use in the smelting of iron, manganese, and paper. The basic idea is that the pure bran, having the greater specific gravity, will sink to the bottom when liquefied. Your impurities, or slag, will float and be easily removed. This slag, by the way, is useful, too. It is employed as cheap cereal filler in most of your canned and frozen meat preparations that you buy in your supermarket.

"This furnace is almost one hundred feet tall. The lower part is your crucible. It is circular on the inside, and rises up to that cone-shaped part, which is the shaft of the furnace."

"Mr. Kibling?"

"Yes?"

"Are we safe?" asked Whitey Herzog. "I mean, why doesn't the melted stuff inside melt through the furnace, too?"

Mr. Kibling and Mr. Jennings laughed. "That's very naive of you, son, isn't it? We wouldn't be here if it were that simple. No, actually, the furnace is reinforced and water-cooled, so accidents, or 'breakouts,' as we call them, are very rare."

"But they do happen?" asked Don Zimmer.

"Yes."

"It must be terrible then," whispered Mr. Causey.

"But, to continue," said Mr. Kibling. "Your raw bran is heated to temperatures exceeding twelve hundred degrees up in the shaft, in the presence of limestone and coke. The melted ore runs down into your crucible where the slag can be run off, and the pure ore tapped out as we desire. The pure bran that is formed is cast into ingots. At this stage the ingots are called 'pig bran.' They can be melted down again and again, each time being refined to higher and higher levels of purity, but we don't bother. Are there any questions?"

"Uh, it seems that Rip, Whitey, and Don have gone off somewhere with Mr. Causey," said Mr. Zernial nervously. "Did any of you notice where they went?"

"I think that they were a little shaky after that talk of 'accidents.' Perhaps they stepped outside," said Mr. Jennings, smiling. "We're going that way, too, so why don't we check?"

Again we went with him, though our number had now shrunk from twenty to twelve. Mr. Jennings stopped outside another of his buildings. The music became softer around us, and the wind grew colder.

"In here we have our own bran mills, where the pig-bran ingots are rolled into usable sheets. We find it is cheaper to do our own milling, rather than send the ingots to be made into rolls of sheet bran at one of the local mills. This is because we use the finest-gauge sheets that can be made efficiently. Most of the job mills won't handle orders for double-O-gauge sheets.

"The ingots are passed between roller presses while they are still hot from the furnace. They are reduced in thickness time and again, until they are the legal limit for flakes. The sheets are rolled up and sent by that overhead conveyor to this building here, which is the stamping plant. I think we'll skip the mill room, because there isn't actually much to see, and because we're getting a little short on time. But if you have any questions at all, don't hesitate to ask. Let's move on, though, so you can get a good look at the flake stampers."

Everywhere we went we saw the silent gray guards. Sometimes they stood in groups of two or three, but even then they did not speak. They leaned uneasily against the door frames or the walls of the buildings, fingering the holsters of their guns. The syrupy music bathed them, too, but only succeeded in making them appear more ominous.

We went into another part of the factory. This building was the noisiest yet. Here the giant, greased machines took the sheets of bran and punched out the flakes that were packaged for our consumption. The room was filled with the constant, deafening slamming.

"These," shouted Mr. Jennings above the roar, "these are the flake stampers. There are twenty-seven different flake configurations, designed by our Art Department to be pleasing in texture and shape as well as in taste. As you know, each flake may be oriented in several different ways, by turning them right to left, front to back, top to bottom, or any position in between. Thus, there are thousands upon thousands of possible flake combinations, so that when you see them in your cereal bowl they appear to be random and unique in shape."

"I didn't know that," Chico whispered to me. From the corner of my eye I saw Mr. Jennings snap his fingers and nod toward Chico. I thought nothing of it, but a moment later Chico was gone. I saw one of the gray guards coming back through a glass door. He leaned casually against the wall, nodding his head slowly at Mr. Jennings. I didn't say anything.

"From here," Mr. Jennings said over the stamping of the flake-punch machines and the louder but sweeter music, "the flakes travel down those chutes to the mixing room where they are combined with the other ingredients. I don't think we'll have time to visit the raisin-casting plant today, but you're all invited to come back again soon. In the mixing room the hand-lathed raisins and the powdered vitamins are added in carefully measured amounts. All these final operations are carried out under the supervision of a Federal Board of Food representative and our own efficiency expert. This is where that niacinamide and certified color are added. We also toss in about three percent nonnutritive crude fiber; on the Federal agent's lunch hour we get that up to twelve or fifteen percent. Then it's all shuffled together and packaged by the marvelous and expensive automated packaging machines. From there, it's only a short ride by truck to your local grocer's shelves. That's about it. Thank you for coming with me and discovering these new horizons in the continuing Adventure of Raisin Bran. Are there any questions?"

"Yes," said Mr. Zernial. "Where is everybody?"

"They're probably all waiting in my office by now," smiled Mr. Jennings.

"Mr. Jennings?"

"Yes? Speak up."

"Vic Wertz here. I was wondering about the way you glossed over the raisin part. Where do they come from?"

"They're mined in the abundantly rich Pennsylvania raisin fields, and shipped directly here by freight train."

"I think that I know what he's getting at," said Mr. Zernial. "Do you buy your raw raisin ore from the Pennsylvania strip miners?"

"Yes, sir. As much as we detest their practices, we feel that they are outweighed by the end product. We feel that we owe it to you, our customers, to use the finest basic ingredients that we can."

The rest of our group began to murmur among themselves. I looked up and caught Mr. Jennings's eye again. This time he didn't smile.

"Golly, Mr. Jennings," said Ike Delock, "we see your point, of course, but from an ecological point of view, I wonder if it is worth it. I'm going to bring this up at the next meeting of the World Affairs Club. I never realized—"

"Okay, that's it!" snapped Mr. Jennings. He looked over his shoulder; the gray guards had snapped to wary and expectant attention. "All right, get them! But save that one," he yelled, pointing his finger at me.

The guards grinned, running toward us. They drew their revolvers as they ran. They began firing at us. Mr. Zernial screamed; he fell to the floor first, and from beneath him a pool of blood began to flow, running in a stream under one of the stamping machines. We were paralyzed for the moment. My God, what was happening? Where could we go? The guards picked us off one by one, and I saw my classmates falling around me.

Mr. Jennings came up to me in the middle of the slaughter. I was crying, I think; I remember noticing that none of the employees working the stamping machines even seemed aware of what was happening. I began to pound on Mr. Jennings's chest, screaming something incoherently.

"Don't worry," he said, smiling. The music was still around me, thundering climactically. "Don't worry, they have orders not to hurt you. You're going to be okay. Just take it easy." He began fumbling with my belt. He opened the snap of my trousers. I looked up into his flushed face with amazement. "No," I cried, "don't!" I hit his hand and then I punched him in the stomach.

He turned away from me for a few seconds. He was gasping; his shoulders were hunched over and his whole body shook. When he turned around again he had a box of Jennings Raisin Bran in his hand. "Here," he said, "take this. It will get you out of here alive. I shouldn't do this, you little queer, but I love you already. Go. Get out while you can."

I took the box of cereal from him and ran for the door. I turned to look over my shoulder, remembering what was happening to my friends. They all were lying on the floor now, still and twisted in their horrible deaths. The sound had died down around them. The music had stopped, everything was incredibly silent. People moved around me deliberately, like a slow-motion movie. I saw Mr. Jennings reach into his coat. He slowly brought out a blued-steel revolver. He was grinning crazily now; I knew that he wasn't going to let me get away. His hand moved across his body, he fired the gun. A gray mist shot from the barrel of the revolver; his hand continued across his body. The gray mist spread in front of me. I felt hot and prickly inside, and I knew that I couldn't move. The grayness turned to black around me, shot with red and yellow flashes, turned back to gray, then to white. I woke up.

I was lying on the concrete driveway outside. The first thing that I could feel was the pain of the cinders cutting into the side of my face. It was beginning to get dark, and rain was falling in a cold drizzle. The noise from the factory had lessened, but I was still aware of a pounding ache in my head. As I came more to my senses I realized that I had been wounded in my arm, and from my right shoulder to the elbow my jacket was soaked dark with blood. I couldn't move the arm, and it hurt terribly. I had difficulty getting up, but I managed. I found the box of Jennings Raisin Bran on the ground near me and, remembering what Mr. Jennings had said, I picked it up and carried it with me.

I was lost among the tortuous alleys of the factory, but after some time I stumbled upon the right road. As I was leaving I passed a sign indicating that one of the dark brick buildings was the Puffed Wheat division. I knew then that I had to come back soon.

I must go back to see the cannons. I must see if they shoot the wheat from cannons, shoot it just like they say they do on TV.

Introduction to "Housebound"

Among the pleasures of knowing George were conversations about our shared interests in baseball, southern culture, and New Orleans. We got to know each other casually, in the early 1980s at conventions, and then later, quite a bit better. The several times I saw George in New Orleans we would often go on a rambling, free-form walking tour of the French Quarter and surrounding areas, with George pointing out some local business or landmark that had made its way, often in disguised form, into one of his stories.

During one of my favorite visits we spent several hours in the Jackson Square area with George pointing out various elements that had gone into his story "Beast" about the Union occupation during the Civil War. Most of the time though, our story discussions were over the telephone, particularly for the other three stories George wrote for anthologies on which I was working. Two of those were Maureen Birnbaum stories. The first was a Grail quest parody and the other a Tennessee Williams satire; both stories were as much fun to talk about as they were to read.

Among George's laments was that his mainstream work rarely received serious attention, and that as his career progressed what he was asked most often for were new Maureen stories and more Budayeen sequels. At least this was the state of things circa 1991 to 1994 when George and I were in most frequent contact. George would have liked to have written true crime books about New Orleans, but didn't want to risk retribution from local godfather Carlos Marcello. Instead he included Marcello in *When Gravity Fails* as the re-named Friedlander Bey, and was very thankful that mafia dons rarely read science fiction novels.

As an editor for the *Phobias* anthology project, one of the concerns was that the stories not duplicate each other. No less than three authors volunteered to contribute the "agraphobia" story, but changed plans when I asked them to confirm that they really wanted to write a story about the fear of farming. When I discussed the project with George, I thought he'd be pleased that this would be an opportunity to write a mainstream story, free of supernatural and SF content. He was, of course, but what surprised me was his subdued manner when he said "I hope no one has asked to write the agoraphobia story yet. There are some things I'm trying to work out right now. . . ."

On first read I thought "Housebound" to be as good as any short story George had ever written. Later, after the story was purchased and set for publication, George said to me that he also thought it was at the top with his best work. "I don't want this one to get published and forgotten," he said. "There are a lot of personal things in it, and I'd like to think someone might find it and it could help." Rereading "Housebound" now some ten years later, it still holds for me the same quiet power it did when I first read it. It's unfortunate books are not more like movie DVDs and have alternate commentary tracks so you could hear George talk about the backgrounds of his stories. Or that someone didn't have a camcorder running on one of those walks around New Orleans with George.

—Richard Gilliam

✝ ✝ ✝

Housebound

MONSTERS IN THE CLOSET TERRIFIED JENNIFER O'Casey when she was seven years old. Well, there was only one monster, but it was enough. Jennifer didn't know its name, but she knew what it looked like. It looked like a big, hulking monster, huffing and puffing way back in the blackest dark.

As Jennifer got older she learned to use her imagination. That was why, when she was ten, she realized that a monster in the closet was a dumb idea. No, any monster worthy of the name would clearly lie in wait beneath her bed, ready to bite off any foot that dared touch the ground, or any arm left carelessly dangling over the side. And Jennifer understood that the bed was big enough to shelter *many* monsters, instead of the stupid single monster in the closet.

Something had to be done. After a year or so of sheer bedtime horror Jennifer hit on the idea of forging treaties with the monsters. They were evil, but they were also reasonable. Or so she figured.

The first treaty stated that she was safe from the monsters as long as the bedside lamp was lit. The second treaty said that after turning off the lamp Jennifer had till the count of ten to get under the covers and to safety. The third treaty was a concession to the monsters. Jennifer would remain safe all night as long as the sheet and blanket were drawn up tightly around her neck, and she had to keep her hands and feet inside.

Jennifer slept every night this way, with the covers clutched in her small fists and held tightly across her neck even in the most stifling weather. She didn't break the treaties until she was twenty-four years old.

Six years later, while shopping in the Piggly Wiggly near her home, Jennifer began feeling strangely nervous and queasy. She thought she might be getting sick. As the minutes passed she tried to ignore the uncomfortable feeling. She thought she might have eaten something bad or triggered an allergy she hadn't known about before. She tossed some frozen manicotti into her cart, then found herself gasping for breath. She was having some kind of attack, and she was frightened. All she could think about was getting home, to safety. She said the hell with the rest of the shopping list, turned her cart, and headed to the checkout lanes.

The decision to bail out of the Piggly Wiggly and go home didn't make her feel any better. She guessed she was making a tremendous fool of herself in public with her anxiety and panicked reaction. She just wanted to be in the shelter of her car, on the road to her house. Instead, the shoppers in front of her dawdled and wrote checks and did everything they could to increase Jennifer's discomfort.

At last she put her groceries on the checkout belt, paid the money, and carried her purchases to her car, a cream-colored 1977 Fiat, the single most indefensible expenditure in her life. She loved the Fiat, but she felt no better behind the wheel, headed for home. She felt acutely nervous, aware of the myriad things that could happen to her in traffic. She pictured herself dying in dozens of different ways, and her own driving became timid and tentative. She knew other drivers all around her were cursing her, but she was unable to escape her sense of helplessness, her gut feeling of horrible dread.

When she arrived at her apartment building she hurried from the car, leaving the groceries behind on the seat. She rushed to her front door and unlocked it with trembling hands. Once inside she felt a wave of calmness sweep over her. She was home now. She was safe.

Still, her body was quivering with unrelieved tension. She paced anxiously from the living room to the dining room to the kitchen. It would take a while to expend all that nervous energy. In the meantime, she thought, maybe she could use a drink.

Jennifer rarely drank this early in the day, and she never drank alone, but she counted this as a special occasion and decided that anything that would mitigate her panic should be counted as medicinal.

She made a gin and tonic and drank it down in two gulps. She sat down on the davenport and waited for peace and forgetfulness. The minutes passed heavily. She got up and made two more gin and tonics. Not long after she drank them she began to feel a warm and blurry sedation creep over her. Two more, she decided, and she went back to the kitchen. She remembered nothing after that. She awoke several hours later, half on and half off the davenport, with her cheek pressed against the cushion.

There was a pool of saliva near her mouth. That was the worst thing about this whole episode—she'd been drooling. A Mount Holyoke girl like Jennifer should never be caught drooling, not for any reason at all.

Her bones creaked as she climbed back on the davenport. She had to think this through. What had brought on the panic attack in the Piggly Wiggly? She'd felt perfectly fine when she went into the grocery store. Maybe it was a warning of some kind, some tabloid newspaper kind of premonition. She desperately wanted to understand what had happened—only not yet. She had a terrible headache and an upset stomach from passing out drunk. Jennifer found it difficult to keep her mind on anything at all. Most of all, she wanted to sleep.

When Jennifer awoke the next morning she had only a small headache. A couple of aspirins would take care of it, she thought. She stayed in bed much longer than usual, still trying to figure out what had happened to her in the Piggly Wiggly. After a while she decided that knowing the truth was unimportant, as long as she didn't have another humiliating attack in public.

Good, she thought. She was proud of her self-diagnosis. The bad news was that to prevent any further emotional displays she'd have to turn into a virtual recluse. She didn't dare go out, because she was almost certain of what would happen if she did. She could have the Piggly Wiggly deliver food, but what about work? The advertising agency where she was an account executive would never allow her to work from home.

Putting those decisions off for the moment, Jennifer decided it would be a major victory to accomplish anything as complex as taking her clothes off and standing under a hot shower. She wanted to feel the water wash away the last of her fear.

It was when she realized that washing her hair was just too much to worry about that Jennifer realized she might be in some trouble. She dried herself off and climbed back into bed. She felt an odd tingling in her hands and feet. In her head there was a horrible feeling that none of this was real.

She got out of bed and went downstairs to the kitchen. She was hungry, but putting together a meal was totally beyond her. The bottle of gin was right where she'd left it on the counter. She poured about six ounces of it into a large plastic cup, then filled it the rest of the way with tonic water.

She gulped a little right there, to calm her nerves, because she was afraid that she'd spill the glass in her wobbly state. She managed to get back upstairs without any misadventures. She put the gin and tonic on her nightstand, grabbed the television's remote control, and got back in bed. Ha, she thought. Now she had everything she needed for a happy life, and all within reach. She glanced at the television; it was tuned to a network animal show. That was just fine with her. It was too much trouble even to flick through the stations to see what else might be on.

Days passed like this. She gave up on inventing new lies to tell her boss and took an indefinite leave of absence. She was living off her savings, and when that ran out . . . well, she didn't want to think about it now.

As the days became weeks she had to admit that her behavior was not normal. Calling her friend Amanda was the most difficult thing she'd ever attempted.

"You're right about one thing," Amanda said. "Your behavior is not normal. I think you should think about seeing a therapist."

"Yes," Jennifer said, "but—"

"Don't start with your objections, Jenn. To me they'll just seem trivial, but I know they're very real to you. You know that I'm subject to severe depressions and that I hate it when someone comes up to me and says, 'Hey, just cheer up.' God, do I hate that."

"Don't you see?" Jennifer said. "You're telling me to go out and find a shrink or something. My whole problem is that I can't *leave* the house to find a therapist. Now, if you know of one who makes house calls—"

"It's not that funny, Jenn. I'm not a professional, but I do know that you're going to have to make some effort, even though it may be very painful."

Jennifer paused. "I was hoping there'd be some magic pill

someone could prescribe to instantly cure my anxiety. Lithium or something."

"Another reason to find a therapist, Jenn. Maybe there *is* a pill that would help you. I don't know; the only way to find the truth is by confronting your fears long enough to get you through an interview with a trained specialist."

"I'll think about it, Mandy, but—"

"You know you're not going to feel better until you stop saying 'but' all the time."

"I know you're right."

"Good girl, Jenn," Amanda said. "Get out your phone book and make a few calls."

"I'll do that," Jennifer said, "but—"

"Bye, Jenn. Got to go."

And then Jennifer was listening to the dull burring of the dial tone.

Talking with Amanda had made her feel much better, but the good feelings fled as soon as she hung up the telephone. She knew intellectually that what her friend had told her was the truth. Emotionally, however, she couldn't face it.

Not, Jennifer corrected herself, without a little fortifying. It was just about time for the liquor store to send over another bottle of gin. No hurry, though; she had an untouched bottle of vodka to get her through tomorrow. Realizing that she didn't have to worry about panic attacks, she relaxed, took out the telephone directory, and called the number of a psychiatrist not far from her home.

The receptionist said, "Are you a new patient, or have you seen Dr. Metz before?"

"I'm a new patient," Jennifer said.

"Well, you need to be evaluated first. Can I put you down for next Friday? Ten o'clock?"

"Part of my problem is that I'm unable to leave the house. I was wondering if Dr. Metz—"

"She needs to see you in person, you know. Do you think you could overcome your fear if you were with a friend? He or she could drive so that you'd be freed from that anxiety."

Jennifer bit her nails. Amanda might be willing to drive her to the appointment. They'd been friends since college. "Yes," she said, "I think I could manage that. Next Friday, at ten?"

"That's right," the receptionist said. "We'll see you then."

Next Friday morning Amanda arrived in her station wagon to drive Jennifer to the doctor's appointment. Jennifer was waiting for her in the kitchen. Beside her on the counter was a mostly finished bottle of vodka, a tray of ice cubes, and a bottle of Rose's lime juice. She was just this side of plastered. Amanda looked at her disdainfully.

"Hell, Mandy," Jennifer said. "If I'm going to let you bully me into seeing this woman, give me a break. I'm sure the doctor's seen cases like me before."

"Maybe so," Amanda said, "but I haven't. And what I see isn't pretty."

Jennifer gritted her teeth to prevent her from saying something that might damage her relationship with Amanda. After her recent behavior, Amanda was about the only friend she still had. Jennifer wanted to tell her that constant bullying made her as angry as Amanda got when someone told her to "just cheer up."

"Well," Amanda said, "are we going or aren't we?"

"Do I have a choice?"

"Yes, you have a choice. Your choice is between going to this appointment and starting to get help, on one hand, and this sorry drunken life you've made for yourself on the other."

Jennifer glared at her friend, then came to a decision. She picked up the phone and dialed the doctor's number.

"Dr. Metz and Associates," the receptionist said.

"Hi. This is Jennifer O'Casey. I've got an appointment for this morning at ten o'clock. It looks like I won't be able to come in today. Can I reschedule?"

She could hear the tapping of the receptionist's pencil as she looked through Dr. Metz's calendar. "The best I could give you would be next Thursday at two."

"That's quite a while from now. You don't have anything sooner?"

"I'm afraid not."

Jennifer said, "All right. Thursday at two."

"Okay," the receptionist said. "We'll see you then."

"Thank you." Jennifer hung up the phone.

Amanda stood in the middle of Jennifer's kitchen. She said, "You're testing me, aren't you? You're trying to prove how miserable your life has become by chasing away all your friends. You're denying yourself help that you truly need. And you're trying to push me away, to see how much I'll put up with before I, too, walk away from you. Well, I'm going to. If ever you feel up to going to an appointment, give me a call. You have the number. In the meantime, fear or not, this is pretty ridiculous behavior." Amanda turned and went out the front door.

Jennifer watched as her friend pulled out of the driveway. Her own car was there, too, sitting reproachfully. She knew she could get the help she needed if she could just make herself go out again, but the very thought made her shudder.

It wasn't that she was afraid of open places. It was that she was horrified at the threat of making a fool of herself in public again. Realistically, she was afraid of being afraid, afraid of succumbing to a panic attack with all those people watching. . . .

Almost a week passed. In those days Jennifer woke up covered with perspiration. She just wanted to be asleep, and when she saw the clock in the morning she always groaned and rolled over. Some days she got up only long enough to use the bathroom and then went back to bed. On Thursday morning she got a call from Amanda. "Hi, Jenn. You want to go the appointment today? Or are you going to poop out again?"

"I'll . . . I'll go today. I just want this awful feeling to go away."

"Good girl. I'll come pick you up in fifteen minutes."

"Thanks, Mandy." After she'd hung up the telephone Jennifer looked around her apartment. Garbage was piling up in the kitchen, and dirty dishes were everywhere. She hadn't felt like doing the laundry either for some time. She saw how terrible her house looked, but she didn't have the energy to clean up before Amanda arrived. She wondered how much liquor she could get down before the doorbell rang.

Amanda just stood in the doorway, looking around the living room and saying nothing. She wrinkled her nose in disapproval. She knew enough, however, not to criticize Jennifer.

"Whose car shall we take?" Jennifer asked.

"Mine, I thought," Amanda said. "That way, in case you have another panic attack, you won't have to worry about getting home."

"Thanks, Mandy," Jennifer said. "I really do appreciate—"

"That's okay, Jenn. But let's get going, all right?"

"Sure," Jennifer said. She gathered up her house keys and stuffed them into her purse. When she came to the threshold she froze.

"You're making progress already. Now give me your hand and we'll go to my car. You've done that a million times, haven't you?"

"Uh-huh," Jennifer said warily. She could feel her heart pounding. She realized she was breathing in short, little gasps. She felt a panic attack coming on. "Maybe this wasn't a good idea, Mandy. What if I have an attack right out there on the street?"

Amanda looked at her closely. "Jenn, I know what you're going through. Believe me, I know. I also realize how tough this must be for you. If you want to feel normal again, you're going to have to do it the hard way."

Jennifer's mouth was dry and she could hear a loud buzzing sound in her ears. "Yes, okay," she said. "I don't like this at all."

Amanda smiled sympathetically. "Just hang on. In a few weeks you'll be feeling all right."

"God, I hope so," Jennifer muttered. And then she was strapping herself into the front passenger seat with no idea how she'd gotten there. Her hands were shaking, and she closed her eyes. She was grateful that Amanda was there with her. She was absolutely sure she could never have come even this far on her own.

"How are we doing?" Amanda asked when they arrived at the small medical complex where Dr. Metz had her office.

"Fine," Jennifer said. She was startled to hear her voice. It sounded like a croaking frog. As she followed Amanda to the elevator the feeling of unreality became ever stronger. Soon she'd be sitting in the doctor's waiting room—trapped.

"Ms. O'Casey?" the receptionist said. "Would you please fill out this sheet for our records?" She handed a clipboard and pen to Jennifer.

This much I can handle, Jennifer thought. She dreaded seeing Dr. Metz. As Jennifer filled out the doctor's form she felt a silly fear that Dr. Metz had caught her doing something forbidden and now was about to execute Jennifer's punishment. Dumb, dumb, Jennifer thought.

She sat there for some time, completely involved with her own problems. Soon she noticed how hard she was holding Amanda's hand, and she tried to relax. "It won't be so bad," she told herself. "And when I go home I'll already be under treatment. It won't be so bad."

Cold, unforgiving time passed. Jennifer tried to interest herself in one magazine article after another, but she soon realized that she was reading so intently in order to keep her anxiety at a comfortable distance. She began to tremble again when she understood what she was doing. It was kind of a vicious circle—first she was afraid, then she began to hide from the panic, and then she understood that her panic was *so great* that she needed to hide from it, and that just proved how real and intense the anxiety was.

"Dr. Metz will see you now," the receptionist said. Jennifer felt a shower of discomfort as she stood up. Her whole body was tingling in an unpleasant way.

Amanda stood and gave her friend a brief smile. "Don't worry, Jenn," she said. "I'll be here when you're through."

"Thanks, Mandy," Jennifer said in a hoarse voice. She let the receptionist lead her to an examining room.

"Dr. Metz will be with you soon. Make yourself comfortable," the receptionist said.

The examining room was large, with several shelves of books, a desk, and a comfortable black leather couch. She fidgeted a moment, then sat down on the couch.

Dr. Metz came in suddenly. She was a tall woman, prematurely gray in a rather attractive way, but all business. She glanced through the basic information on Jennifer's chart. "Yes, well," the doctor said, "what has brought you here today?"

Jennifer really hoped that Dr. Metz wasn't going to begin by minimizing her fear. She began by telling the doctor how it had all begun with the panic attack in the grocery store. Dr. Metz sat at her desk and slowly nodded her head. Jennifer discovered a new concern: Should she tell the doctor absolutely everything or hold something back?

"Do you understand the nature of your fear, Ms. O'Casey? You're describing what we call agoraphobia, a fear of open spaces, but you probably don't realize how complex and interconnected the root causes of your anxiety are. Over the years I've managed to help many people overcome their phobias. Some people come to me paralyzed by a fear of cats, of spiders, of heights, of flying—the list of possible phobias is very long. Yet a good half of those patients also say they suffer from agoraphobia."

"I don't understand," Jennifer said.

"It's very simple. If a person is afraid of snakes, for instance, he will stop going to places where there is a chance of seeing a snake. Soon this fear is generalized; the patient stays home for days, weeks, even years at a time. His house is a fortress against that which he fears."

"Are you telling me that my panic attacks could be triggered by something else entirely, maybe something in my past?"

Dr. Metz frowned a little. "I'm definitely not a Freudian, which would lead me to locate the roots of *all* your phobias and neuroses in your childhood," she said, "but his work does give good and valuable insights into this sort of problem."

Jennifer laughed nervously. "I was hoping you could just write out a prescription for me, and that would be the end of it."

"I'm sorry, Ms. O'Casey, but it's not that easy. No, if we're going to work on this together, we have to come to a common understanding of why you feel panicked. We may have to open old wounds, and sometimes the therapy is more difficult than the neurosis. You're going to have to trust me, and likewise I need to trust you, too. If you keep canceling appointments, I'm afraid there's little I can offer. It all depends on how committed you are to freeing yourself from the agony of emotional bondage. Do you follow me?"

Jennifer looked down at her feet. "I understand, Doctor. To be honest, I'm not certain that I'm strong enough."

"Fine," Dr. Metz said. "As long as I feel you're making an honest effort, I'll be willing to be here as often as you need."

"Thank you, Doctor. But isn't there some medication that would make it just a little easier?"

Dr. Metz sat back in her swivel chair. "I could, you know, write a couple of prescriptions. One for an antidepressant. That will take a few weeks to begin working. In addition, I could give you a mild tranquilizer to handle short-term panic attacks. But—and this is a large 'but'—it's no good trading one kind of emotional crutch for another. You've been drinking, haven't you? Much more than usual, I'd say. These medications, while effective, have their own sinister aspects. For one thing, they're habit-forming, and I don't want to cure your phobia and then have to treat your drug dependency."

"I've always been pretty good with medicines," Jennifer said.

"We'll see. Here's a prescription for Tofranil, which is the antidepressant, and one for Xanax, the tranquilizer. If you have trouble with side effects or anything, call the office here, and we'll try something different. Now, as to your next appointment, same day and time next week?"

"Yes, that would be fine."

Dr. Metz walked her to the door. "Let me know if the medications give you any kind of problem."

Jennifer just nodded. She still had to face the ride home, and—good God—the stop at the pharmacist. She began feeling overwhelmed again.

Amanda must have sensed Jennifer's mood, because she put her arm around Jennifer as they walked to the elevator. "You'll lick it," Amanda said.

"Thanks for the encouragement, Mandy," Jennifer said. "Right now I feel like the earth is going to open up right in front of me and I'll tumble down all the way to hell."

"Let's just get your medicine and go home. Maybe next week *you* can drive."

Jennifer gave her friend a weak and unsteady smile. "Why don't we just take things one step at a time?"

"Sure," Amanda said.

Over the next several weeks Jennifer kept her appointments with Dr. Metz, although she didn't feel as if she was making any progress at all. During one of their conversations Jennifer admitted that the most terrifying day of her life had happened when she was ten years old. Her father was at work, her mother was out shopping, and a fire started. The neighbors called the fire department, and the fire was brought quickly under control, but she had been traumatized. She never forgave her mother for not being there when Jennifer needed her. That's why Jennifer had decided never to have children, because she knew she couldn't always control what happened in their lives. She would feel guilty every time she had to leave them in someone else's care.

"Perhaps that's it," Dr. Metz said thoughtfully. "Maybe that's the root of your distress."

"I don't know. If that's the case, why did it happen when it did? Why didn't I feel the panic before, in all the years I've been living on my own?"

Dr. Metz shrugged. "I can't say, Jennifer. Maybe something triggered a long-buried memory. An odor, perhaps. You may have gone into the Piggly Wiggly and passed by the barbecued ribs, and just the right song was playing on the Muzak. It would take a lot of delving."

"But I am making progress, aren't I?"

"You're making fine progress, Jennifer, but I wouldn't go around patting myself on the back just yet. I explained to you how long a struggle it would be. Do you think it's time for you to come alone to our sessions?"

"Yes," Jennifer said, not the least bit confident.

"Just remember to stay as relaxed as possible. One other desensitizing exercise you can do is to imagine the very worst thing that could happen at every juncture. Imagine yourself getting into your car. I'd think that wouldn't pose a serious problem for you now. But turning the key and backing out of the driveway? Your serious fears might prevent you from taking back your own life."

"You don't know how difficult it is," Jennifer said.

"It so happens that I *do* know how difficult it is. I went through a period that lasted a full year, during which I couldn't bring myself even to get my mail from the mailbox."

Jennifer opened her eyes wider. She had come to think of the doctor as rock-steady and perfectly competent. "You?" she said.

"After my husband died. Do you see? It can happen to anyone. Now, if you want to make further progress, you're going to have to take small steps. You're going to have to win through to peace by confronting every stressful aspect of your life. Picture yourself accepting the challenge of getting here on your own. Imagine all the terrible things that could happen. If you work through all that, then it should become easier for you to travel about. You'll have already created scenarios far more horrible than anything that might happen in real life."

Jennifer was dubious. She wasn't sure that she could follow Dr. Metz's advice. It sounded too much like sympathetic magic to her. Live through the worst that could happen to her? Jennifer wanted something else entirely. She wanted a magic pill or a wave of a wand to free her from her escalating pain and anxiety. All right, she could admit that there were no magic pills or therapeutic wands. She'd hoped that she'd gone through the hard part, yet it seemed that every time she'd vanquished one fear, two more sprang up. At the end of the session Jennifer was deeply distressed. It seemed to her that there was always another hurdle she'd have to get over.

A few months ago it had been a joke. But life was hard. You could just read the T-shirts and find out what the rest of her generation felt about stress, fear, and helplessness. What had once been mildly amusing now appeared to be bitter truth. This made her attempt at therapy even more ironic, because she didn't really have much faith in Dr. Metz's planned renovation of Jennifer. She thought it was awfully simple to sit on the other side of the desk, nod meaningfully, and deposit a hefty check after every visit. That was not very difficult; Jennifer imagined they could train chimpanzees to do the same.

Then, yet again, Jennifer realized that she couldn't make light of this situation. She knew that unless she did what Dr. Metz suggested—confronted her fears—she'd be permanently paralyzed by them. Yet wasn't it too much to expect from her in this state?

"All right," Jennifer said to herself later that week, lying out beside her apartment building's swimming pool. "I'll just get some sun, maybe some exercise, and then I'll be better able to face Dr. Metz." She felt guilty because she hadn't performed any of the mental exercises the doctor had suggested to her.

Jennifer recalled the four stages on the way to emotional security. The first part might be the most difficult: facing up to the worst of her fears. Easier said than done, she thought. It meant no more drinking, no more hiding in bed. She couldn't fight a problem while she was still denying it even existed.

Lying in the sun, Jennifer tried to picture herself going back to the Piggly Wiggly. She imagined every step of the way, and all the bad things that could happen to her. She had conquered her fear of driving—she'd been back and forth to Dr. Metz's office alone for some time now. Of course, her fearful mind told her, she'd just begun thinking of the doctor's office as an extension of her home, a safe and secure haven. What she needed to do was extend that feeling until it took in the whole world. That was the hard part.

Later, during her appointment with Dr. Metz, she admitted that at times she could look at her fear of leaving home, and then she knew it was all stupid. There was nothing terrifying about a grocery store. No one had shown any hostility toward her there. At other times she was firmly in the grasp of another panic attack at the simple thought of the Piggly Wiggly.

"I really need your help, Dr. Metz," she told the therapist.

"I'm glad to help any way I can, Ms. O'Casey. Your true progress will begin when you realize you *don't* need my help, that everything you need in order to feel better is already there. I'm here just to show you how to fashion your own treatment."

Jennifer smiled with feigned humor. "The problem is that I can understand what you're saying on an intellectual level. I can even agree with you. But on a raw emotional level . . ." She just shrugged.

"Let me ask you a question, if I may," Dr. Metz said.

"Of course."

"Your mother . . . would you say she was strict with you?"

"She was strict, yes," Jennifer said, "but she was no demon. She just had very strong ideas about what my behavior should be like."

Dr. Metz nodded. "And did she punish you? Physically?"

Jennifer didn't have any idea what the therapist was driving at. "Yes, she punished me, but she didn't often hit me. She had other methods."

"Depriving you of something? Grounding you, that sort of thing?"

Puzzled, Jennifer let out a breath. "Yes, more along those lines rather than actually hurting me."

"One more thing before we end this session," Dr. Metz said. "You're carrying around a lot of guilt in addition to your agoraphobia, aren't you?"

Jennifer was astonished. "I suppose I am, but how did you know that?"

"It's common among phobia sufferers. You mentioned once that you resented your mother for not being with you when the house fire took place. You feel guilty about that resentment. You feel guilty about involving your friend, Amanda, in your problem. You probably feel guilt about leaving home because you're afraid something awful—a fire, a burglary, *something*—might happen in your absence. You no doubt have guilt feelings about other matters, too."

Jennifer thought for a moment. "Yes, you're right, I think. My trouble is that I can sit here and fully understand what you're saying, even agree about the sensible explanation, but I still know that I'd suffer a panic attack as soon as I set foot in that Piggly Wiggly."

Dr. Metz closed her notebook and looked directly at Jennifer. "Maybe at this stage that would happen. I think you need to do some more work on desensitizing your fear in your imagination. I know that there are a million tiny things that could bring on an attack. You could break a bottle of something in the grocery store, or you could temporarily misplace your keys—all things that you could handle perfectly well before your attacks began."

"Sometimes I have trouble even imagining those things without panicking."

The doctor nodded to show that she understood perfectly. "But that's just what you need to do. You should be totally relaxed, at home and safe. Then you can begin imagining what might happen if you went to the Piggly Wiggly. That's the next stage in your therapy."

Jennifer nodded. She'd expected something like that.

"Remember," Dr. Metz said, "plain fear can't hurt you physically. I want you to face up to it, let it completely wash over you. Let the fear have its way. Experience a panic attack and then notice that if you practice the relaxation method, the panic will gradually go away."

Jennifer gave another weak smile. "It sounds impossible."

"It may seem so now, but it's something you have to do sooner or later."

On the way home alone in the car Jennifer thought about what the doctor had said. She saw the logic in what Dr. Metz asked. She promised that she'd really begin to work at the relaxing and imagining routines—tomorrow.

The next morning Jennifer felt a little better. She put on her swimsuit, grabbed a towel, and went down to the pool. She spread the towel on the concrete apron and lay down on it. She felt the warm sun on her legs and back. She closed her eyes and pretended that she was at the beach. She imagined waves of cool water rushing up and covering her feet, then draining back, taking with them all the tension from her ankles down. When her feet were relaxed she imagined that the waves came in as far as her knees, and so on until every muscle was as relaxed as possible.

Jennifer began visualizing the Piggly Wiggly store as clearly as she could. She was amazed to see that, while she was still nervous and edgy, she suffered no panic attack. She thought about her real fear—not the grocery itself, according to Dr. Metz, but a fear of having fear in the store. That made her feel worse, so she relaxed her muscles once more and allowed the anxiety to do its worst.

It wasn't so bad, actually. In fact, she felt capable of dealing with panic on that level. When the anxiety had completely disappeared she decided to test her shaky peace of mind.

She took her towel with her as she went back to her apartment. She looked at the telephone. She reached out for it, drew her hand back, then grabbed it and called Amanda's work phone number.

"Amanda Romano's office," a secretary said.

"This is Jennifer O'Casey. Is Amanda available?"

"She should be. Hang on a minute while I try to find her." Jennifer listened to an easy-listening version of "Layla."

She thought she'd rather have silence when she was put on hold. She believed that rock 'n' roll should never be played soft and mellow.

"Jennifer?" Amanda asked. "Is that you?"

"Morning, Amanda. I was wondering if you could spend some time with me today. I want to see how far I've gotten with my therapy."

"That's great, but I can't go with you until after work. We're swamped around here. Maybe I could drop by your place later."

Jennifer said, "That'll be fine, Amanda. And thanks."

"Hey, you're my best friend, you know. Now I've got to run. See you later."

"Bye, kid." Jennifer thought she'd try going to the Piggly Wiggly with Amanda later in the afternoon. Before that, however, she decided to see what would happen if she went somewhere neutral. The post office. She needed to buy some stamps anyway.

The house was safe, the car was safe—now she'd find out if the panic attacks happened only in the Piggly Wiggly or if she was completely trapped by her phobia. If this isn't confronting your fear, Jennifer thought as she dressed, I don't know what is. She locked her front door and went to her Fiat. She still felt no particular anxiety.

That's good, she thought. Maybe she'd find out that this healthy feeling had driven her panic attacks away entirely. It was wrong to set herself up for a big letdown, yet the positive attitude couldn't be anything but therapeutic.

When she arrived at the post office she pulled into one of the parking places. She let the engine run and the radio play while she went through the imaginary beach relaxation routine. Finally there was nothing left to do but go into the post office and get in line. She turned off the radio and killed the engine. Then she marched bravely to the entrance.

There was a line of nine people ahead of her. She read a few posters, looked at the pages of men and women wanted for federal offenses, admired some new stamps. It felt very normal. Jennifer was immensely pleased with her control.

She couldn't wait to tell Dr. Metz about it.

She bought a book of stamps and went back to the lobby, happy about her victory, wanting to extend it as long as possible. She wondered what to do next. She could go uptown and have lunch—all by herself, like any normal adult. She felt as if she could do anything she wanted now.

Almost anything. The Piggly Wiggly still haunted her. She didn't dare try going there on her own. That was why she'd called Amanda.

Jennifer was further pleased to realize that she didn't have to get drunk to feel comfortable. At first the fears and guilts had mounted up to a daunting level; now the happier, more stable moments were accumulating just as quickly.

About six o'clock that evening Amanda rang the doorbell. Jennifer let her in. "Guess what I did today," Jennifer said.

"Did you do what Dr. Metz suggested? Go out and sit in your car and imagine a trip to a public place?"

"Better than that," Jennifer said. "I sat in the car, drove it down the street, and then went downtown to the post office."

"Wonderful, Jenn!" Amanda said. "I'm really proud of you. Did you go inside?"

"I sure did." She held up the book of stamps like a tiny trophy.

"Well," Amanda said, "that's some progress. Why did you want me to come over? You're not going to try the—"

"The Piggly Wiggly."

Amanda's face showed grave concern. "It might be too early to jump in the deep end."

"That's why I asked you to come with me."

"You think you can handle it?"

"I handled the post office just fine, didn't I?"

"Yes, but—"

"No buts," Jennifer said. "I'm determined."

"All right, if you think you're ready," Amanda said. Her expression told Jennifer that her friend was doubtful. There was only one way to find out.

Amanda drove, just in case Jennifer had another anxiety attack in the Piggly Wiggly. On the way there Amanda glanced at her passenger and said, "How are you doing so far?"

"So far so good," Jennifer said. She was practicing her relaxation technique.

Jennifer did feel good. That lasted until Amanda parked the car in the grocery store's lot. It was like a sudden lightning stab of fear. Amanda could tell there was something wrong. "You're anticipating, Jenn. Don't make up extra worries for yourself."

"You're right, of course. I'm afraid that I'll be afraid." She took a deep breath, held it, then let it out slowly. "Well, let's do it."

Jennifer was surprised by how weak her legs felt as she climbed out of her friend's car. She realized that she was trembling all over.

"Take your time and relax," Amanda said.

Jennifer only nodded. There was only one thing to do, or else admit defeat. She clasped Amanda's hand as they walked toward the entrance.

"There's nothing threatening in the parking lot, is there?" Amanda said in a soothing voice.

"No." Her mouth and throat were unusually dry.

"Let's go in then."

Jennifer nodded. Her face was covered with perspiration. She had to grab hold of shelves because she was afraid that she'd faint otherwise. She was in the store for less than a minute before she fell into a complete, paralyzing panic attack. "Let's go," she said in an unsteady voice.

Amanda, helped her out of the store. "We're outside again," Amanda said. "Do you still feel the anxiety?"

"Yes."

"Well, let's just go home then and make some dinner."

"All I've got is macaroni and cheese."

"Fine," Amanda said. Jennifer didn't say a word on the drive home. On top of her fear in the store she felt the humiliation of having her best friend witness a full-blown attack.

At her next session with Dr. Metz, Jennifer described in detail the day at the post office and the Piggly Wiggly. She no longer felt free to go out by herself. Her second panic attack had persuaded her that her behavior couldn't be trusted.

"I'm very glad that you made the effort to venture out," Dr. Metz said. "The trip to the post office was a good idea. I can't say the same for the grocery store. Now, there is a technique called 'flooding,' in which the patient subjects himself to the worst of his fears, with little or no preparation. Sometimes this 'once and for all' solution produces favorable results. Sometimes, as in your case, it can be disastrous. You seem to have regressed to the point where you were when you first came to me. I wish you had called me before attempting to flood your emotions by going to the Piggly Wiggly. I would've said that you're not quite ready."

"Will you continue to help me?" Jennifer said in a pitiable tone of voice.

"Of course I will. Try to master your feelings as you did when you went to the post office. When you've progressed to the point at which you decided to take your life back again, we'll work slowly on your fear of the store."

"If it's only the store I'm afraid of," Jennifer said, "maybe I'll just start shopping elsewhere."

"That's one solution. It doesn't satisfy me, however. It's like putting a bandage on a broken leg. I won't be happy until we've achieved a complete cure, and I think deep down you feel the same way."

Jennifer just nodded.

"Fine," Dr. Metz said. "You must know there's hope. Well, we begin again."

"Thank you, Doctor," Jennifer said. This time she really did know there was hope.

Introduction to "Glimmer, Glimmer"

I was at a party in Austin sometime in the early '90s where a number of science fiction fans and authors were discussing a particular habit writers have: the tendency to enter a bookstore, find one's own titles, and turn them face-out on the shelf so the next shopper will be more likely to notice them. A quick survey of the room indicated that this habit was almost universal, and that a fair number of the culprits assuaged their guilt by doing the same for books written by their friends. (On the other hand, almost as many admitted to taking books written by their enemies and reshelving them in the Abnormal Psychology section.)

This discussion segued into the thorny topic of bookstores that sell used books, and the question of whether it's good or bad for a midlist author to find his/her titles there in quantity. The consensus was that it's generally good to find one's own books for sale anywhere . . . just so long as they aren't books that have been signed and personalized to a specific individual. That, it was agreed, is pretty much the equivalent of a cold slap in the face with a shovel.

George was at that party, and when the above situation was described, he said he could top it. Once, he said, he had gone into a used bookstore . . . and of course had checked to see how many George Alec Effinger titles were there . . . and had found quite a number . . . and had then discovered that each and every one had been signed and personalized . . . to his ex-wife.

The whole room fell silent for about two seconds—until we saw the amused gleam in George's eye. And then we all exploded in laughter. George did, too.

Later, I asked him if that bookstore experience had really happened, and he assured me that it had. It had been, he said, simultaneously devastating and hilarious.

Just like so much of George's fiction.

Just like "Glimmer, Glimmer."

—Bradley Denton

Glimmer, Glimmer

ROSA TOMCZIK WATCHED HER HUSBAND BUILD UP the campfire. He dropped on a double handful of sticks and branches, and the flame blazed brighter, sending sparks into the evergreen boughs overhead. As the fire died, Rosa waited for contentment. She waited five minutes. She waited five minutes more, and she realized that she did, after all, feel something, but it wasn't contentment. What she felt was anxious suspense. Rosa had felt that way ever since her husband, Joel, had surprised her with the suggestion that they take this vacation.

Joel hadn't taken a single day off in the twelve years they'd been married; he was a workaholic, a dynamo, the *Führer* of Seventh Avenue. He had started out as a salesclerk in his father's small dress shop, and now he owned more than 300 fashion outlets in shopping malls across the country. Whenever Rosa had brought up the subject of a vacation, Joel always said that he had his empire to protect. Which made it all the stranger that he had proposed this biking trip around the countryside.

Rosa took a can of insect repellent out of her pack and sprayed her arms, hands, and face. She walked around the fire and offered the can to Joel. He sprayed himself and gave it back to her, and she went back to her pack and stowed it. Then she looked across the campfire at her husband. "So tell me," she asked, "is this trip saving our marriage or what?"

In the twilight, she saw him shrug. "It's just too early to tell," he said.

She started to reply, closed her mouth, then lay down in her sleeping bag and turned her face away from him. She didn't fall asleep for a long time; she was too busy thinking.

In the morning, over coffee, bacon, and eggs, Joel took out a creased and torn map. "There's a state forest less than a day's ride from here. We'll make the campground by suppertime. We can spend a little while looking at flowers and butterflies and stuff," he said. Rosa was irritated by his condescending assessment of her life's work in biochemical research: "flowers and butterflies and stuff."

Rosa pedaled mightily to keep up with her husband's furious pace while the land altered gradually from farms and empty fields into thick stands of pine and spruce. And then a wooden sign told them the state forest was fifteen miles farther. An hour later, they were there: a profound and unbreakable hush wrapped them almost immediately. Rosa stared at Joel's sweat-streaked back and wondered what he, the blousemonger, her off-the-rack-tycoon husband, was thinking about.

She also wondered where Joel was planning to stop for the night. They had already passed several areas set aside for campers and recreational vehicles. Her husband had made it clear that he didn't want to use these campsites; he'd rather go out into the *real* forest. And Rosa didn't get a vote in the matter.

After another hour, Joel announced, "Let's get off the trail." They dismounted their bikes and, Joel still insisting on leading the way, plowed deeper and deeper into the silent forest. They finally came to a stream, and Joel suddenly decided they had gone far enough. Rosa glanced at him; he seemed strangely elated.

That evening, after supper had been prepared and eaten and the dishes washed, they stared into the flickering flames of their fire. As usual, they had nothing to say. Rosa studied Joel's face; his new intensity troubled her. They had had a bitter confrontation previous to this trip, and Joel—livid at the prospect of losing half his hard-earned empire in a courtroom—had shouted that he would never, but *never*, stand for a divorce. Period. Then he had invited her on this trip. Maybe he had something else in mind, she thought.

"Look." Joel finally broke the silence. "Lightning bugs."

"Fireflies."

"Yeah. I love lightning bugs. You're the science expert—what makes them light up?"

"It's a chemical reaction," said Rosa. "Bioluminescence. And they're not bugs. The only insects that are true bugs belong to the order Hemiptera. Fireflies belong to the order Coleoptera."

"So big deal." Joel stared into the darkness. "Look," he said, pointing. "Look how it's shining underneath that bush. I don't believe how bright it is."

"The wingless females. Glowworms, people call them."

"Look how many there are," said Joel. "My God, I've never seen so many."

"You couldn't even describe this to anybody," she said.

"They wouldn't understand how gorgeous it is," he continued. "Everybody's seen fireflies, but not many people have seen them like this."

She stood up, went to her pack and took out a spray can labeled INSECT REPELLENT. "It's getting late, the humidity's gone up and the mosquitoes will be murder," she said gently.

"Hey, Rosa, look over there." Joel walked farther out into the woods.

Rosa looked where he was pointing. "What about it?" she asked.

"I've never seen so many lightning bugs in my life. It looks like there's a shopping center glowing behind those trees." He walked into the blackness far away from the campfire.

"If you're going out there, better spray yourself some more. The mosquitoes are fierce," Rosa yelled after him.

He walked back to her and took the can she offered. He sprayed all his exposed skin, then tossed the repellent back to her. She raised a hand to catch it but missed.

"Aw, come on. Leave the fire for now. Let's enjoy the night together. The weather is perfect and I'm feeling good," Joel said.

Rosa followed her husband a few yards farther into the forest, then stopped. Joel moved ahead of her. The fireflies flashed and flickered all around him, surrounding him. He was literally swarmed by thousands of yellow-green points of light, Rosa observed, riveted.

"There are even more of them here now," Joel called out. "Away from the glare of our fire it looks like a real swarm or something."

"It's their mating season," said Rosa.

Ten or twenty yards deeper into the woods, the fireflies were flashing brighter and faster. The insects were so luminous they looked like a bonfire. "My God," Joel murmured. He moved slowly toward the tiny lights. "At home we've got lightning bugs, but I've never, never seen anything like this. It's scary."

As Joel drew closer the insects flared brighter, melding their billion pinpoints into a fierce, greenish glow. "Rosa?"

"I'm having a nice cup of tea here by the fire," she called to him, though she wasn't. "I may even save you some." She slapped a mosquito and killed it.

Joel's figure was black against the pulsing greenish light of the fireflies. She heard him laugh, then choke. He spat and gagged. Rosa imagined what it must feel like to have a large insect wriggling in your mouth. She shuddered in revulsion.

Fireflies brushed Joel's face, formed a halo around him. His hands waved as he tried frantically to fling them away. Rosa saw him fall onto his knees. "Rosa!" he cried weakly. She remained at a short distance, watching him.

Joel was kneeling on the ground, his arms wrapped tightly around his head. He seemed to be clothed in a thick, persistent cloud of throbbing yellow-green. The fireflies covered his face and neck entirely, and his arms and hands. A mass of insects sprawled over his chest. She heard Joel whimper, then retch as he tried to clear his throat. He was choked, smothered. He rolled to the ground and thrashed from side to side, slapping his face with his hands and making queer, pathetic sounds. Rosa saw him crack his head painfully on the trunk of a tree.

"Joel," she called, and moved toward him cautiously. "Joel!" It was the strangest sight she had ever seen. Thousands of insects crawled in a glowing, undulating blanket over Joel's contorted body. Rosa stared, horrified but fascinated. In a few moments, he was unrecognizable in the midst of a vast greenish aura.

Rosa realized that her muscles were cramped and stiff from tension. Her exposed skin was ravaged by mosquito bites. She went back to the fire and took out of her pack the safe can of repellent— the one with the gray lid—and sprayed herself thoroughly. Using a latex glove, she picked up the other can of repellent—the one with the black lid—from the ground where she had let it fall when Joel had tossed it to her. She dropped this can, filled with firefly sex pheromones, into a plastic bag. She unpeeled the glove, put that in the bag, too, and sealed the bag with a twist tie. She'd dispose of it later. She left all the camping gear behind, just as any terrified and grief-stricken wife would.

Introduction to "From Downtown at the Buzzer"

It's an old expression: "From downtown at the buzzer." Ask anyone from Cleveland or Salt Lake City, where they saw Michael Jordan destroy their teams time and again from downtown at the buzzer—which means, in basketball parlance, to hit an exceptionally long shot, usually a game-winner, just as time runs out.

George loved sports. In fact, I remember that during a WorldCon in Chicago he took the day off from schmoozing editors and selling stories to go look at the old Comiskey Park (my home away from home when I was growing up on the South Side of the Windy City) before they tore it down. His goal, he informed me, was eventually to watch a game in every major league ball-park in the country.

I don't know if he felt quite the same passion for basketball (it's my favorite team sport by a country mile), but his comprehension of the game was profound. Which is to say, it almost matched his comprehension of the art of pushing nouns up against verbs.

In this particular story, George was writing on multiple levels again, as per usual. He describes basketball, suggests why blacks have come to dominate the sport, actually interests you in the outcome of the games with the Cobae—and of course the story isn't about basketball at all. (George did that a *lot*. If he'd been a football coach, his teams would have been known for their mis-direction.)

The really interesting, really Effinger thing is that although the Cobae are central to the story and everyone in it reacts to them, it isn't about the Cobae either. George just loved putting a little extra spin on the ball.

In the end, a couple of black players are laughing and high-fiving each other—and, right, it's not about *them* either.

In point of fact, like most Effinger stories, it's really about the foibles of George's favorite character: the one who kept him in business.

But read the story and you'll figure it out.

—Mike Resnick

From Downtown at the Buzzer

THERE ARE A COUPLE OF THINGS MY MOTHER will never get to experience.

I mean, there are more than a couple, of course, but there are two things that I think of immediately. First off, my mother won't ever know what it's like to see twelve space creatures in blue suits and masks staring at you while you eat breakfast and wash walls and go to the bathroom. That I know. That I can talk about. My mother can't, and just as well, I guess. But believe me, I can.

The other thing is, my mother will never, *ever* know the incredible joy you get, this feeling of complete, instant gratification, when you jump into the air, twist around, and send a basketball in an absolutely perfect arc into the net maybe twenty-three feet away. You have somebody from the other team leaping up with you, his hand right in your face, but sometimes you have God on your side and nothing in the universe can keep that ball from going through that hoop. You sense it sometimes, you can feel it even before you let go of the ball, while you're still floating. Then it's just the smallest flick of the wrist, your fingertips just brushing the ball away, perfect, perfect, perfect, you don't even have to look. You land on the hardwood floor with this terrific smile on your face, and the guy who had his hand up to block you is muttering to himself, and you're talking to yourself, too, as you run downcourt to the other end. You're happy. My mother will never know that kind of happy.

Not that I do, either, very often.

Now, this newspaper is paying me a lot of money for this exclusive story; so I figure I ought to give them what they paid for. But other magazines have paid others for their exclusive stories, and they might tell stories a little different from mine. That's because no one else in the security installation knew the Cobae as well as I did.

I'll start about a year ago, about a month before I saw my first Coba. I was a captain then, attached to Colonel James McNeill. Colonel McNeill was the commanding officer of the entire compound, and because of that I was given access to a lot of things that I really shouldn't have seen. But I saw those things, and I read the colonel's reports, and, well, I guess that I can put two and two together as well as anybody. So from all of that, there wasn't much happening around the compound that I didn't know about.

The installation was in the middle of an awful lot of nothing, in one of the smaller parishes in southwestern Louisiana. St. Didier Parish. There was one town kind of large, Linhart, with maybe six thousand people, three movie theaters, a lot of bars. That was it for the whole parish, just about. South of us were towns full of Cajuns who trapped muskrat and nutria, or worked in the cane fields, or worked in the rice fields, or on shrimp boats or off-shore oil rigs, or netted crabs. They spoke a kind of strange mixture of English and a French no Parisian ever heard. All around us, and farther north, there were only farms. We were tucked away in an isolated part of the parish, with only a small dirt road leading to the one main north-south route. No one on the base had anything to do with the Cajuns; come furlough time or weekend passes, it made more sense to go to New Orleans, an hour and a half, maybe two hours east of us.

We didn't have a lot to look at except fields on the other side of the wire fence. It was summer nine months of the year. The base was landscaped with a large variety of local plants, some of which I don't even know the names of. Everything flowered, and there was something blooming almost every month of the year. It was kind of nice. I liked the job.

I liked it a lot, until the Cobae showed up.

Before that, though, I wasn't exactly sure why we were there. We were a top-security installation, doing just about nothing. I was kept busy enough with day-to-day maintenance and routines. I had been transferred down from Dayton, Ohio, and it never occurred to me to ask Colonel McNeill what the hell we were supposed to be doing, surrounded by a lot of yam fields, between the marshes on the west and the swamps on the east. I mean, it just never came up. I had learned a long time ago that if I did just what I was told to do, and did it right, then everything, absolutely everything would be fine. That kind of life was very pleasant and satisfying. Everything was laid out for me, and I just took it all in order, doing task one, doing task two, doing task three. The day ended, I had free time, at regular intervals I was paid. The base had plenty of leisure facilities. It was all just great for me.

Of course, I was a captain.

My main outlet during my leisure was playing basketball. There were very good gym facilities on the base, and I've always been the competitive type, at least in situations where winning and losing didn't have much of a permanent effect on my life. I enjoy target shooting, for example, because there is no element of luck involved. It's just you, the rifle, and the target. But if you put me down in a hot spot, with people shooting back, I do believe all the fun would go right out of it.

Forget it. There were always a few other people on the base, not always male, who liked to get into the pick-up games. Every once in a while someone would show up, someone I hadn't seen on the court for weeks. Mostly, however, there were the same regulars. Tuesday and Thursday evenings, those were the big basketball games. Those were the games that even I couldn't get into, on occasion. They were what you'd call blood games. I enjoyed watching them almost as much as I liked playing in them. Maybe I should have been watching a little closer.

All right, it was in the middle of August, and the temperature outside was in the low nineties, all the time. Every day. *All* the time. And the humidity matched the temperature, figure for figure. So we just stayed in the air-conditioned buildings and sent the enlisted men outside to take care of running errands. It takes a while to get adjusted, you know, from mild Ohio weather to high summer in subtropical Louisiana. I wasn't altogether adjusted to it. I liked my office, and I liked my air-conditioned car, and I liked my air-conditioned quarters. But there were little bits of not-air-conditioned in among those things that got to me and made me struggle to breathe. I don't think I could hack it as an African explorer, if they still have them, or as a visitor to other equatorial places where the only comforts are a hand-held fan and an occasional cool drink.

Terrific. You've got the background. That's the way things were and, like I say, I was all in favor of them just going on like that until I felt like dropping dead or something. But things didn't go on like that.

At the end of August a general showed up, trailing two colonels. They were in one long black car. In three long black cars behind the brass were the Cobae. I think it would be a good idea if I kind of went into detail about the Cobae and how we happened to get them dumped in our laps.

As I learned shortly after their arrival, the Cobae had appeared on Earth sometime in July. I forget the exact date. They were very cautious. Apparently they had remained in their ship in space, monitoring things, picking and choosing, making their inscrutable minds up about God only knows what. A paper that crossed Colonel McNeill's desk, a paper that I shouldn't have seen, said that one Coba appeared in the private apartment of the president. How he got there is still a mystery. An awful lot about the Cobae is still a mystery. Anyway, I suppose the president and his wife were a little startled. Ha. Sometimes on silent nights I like to imagine that scene. Depending on my mood, the scene can be very comic or very dramatic. Depending on my mood of the moment, and also what the president and his wife were doing, and how genuinely diplomatic and resilient the president was.

After all, remember that the president is just a guy, too, and he's probably not crazy about strangers materializing in his bedroom. He's probably even less crazy about short, squat, really ugly creatures in his bedroom. Picture the scene for yourself. Take a few seconds, I'll wait. See?

Well, the president called for whomever he usually calls for, and there was a very frantic meeting in which nothing intelligent at all was said. There weren't contingency plans for this sort of thing. It's not often that the president of the United States has to wing it in a crisis situation. And this *was* a crisis situation, even though the Coba hadn't said a word, moved a muscle, or even blinked, so far as anyone could determine.

Okay, imagine everyone dressed and formal and a little calmed down now, thanks to things like Valium and Librium and Jack Daniel's. Now we have a president and his advisors. *They* have a creature in a blue, shiny uniform and a mask over his face. It wasn't exactly a helmet. It covered what we call the Coba's nose and mouth, by liberal interpretation. There was a flexible hose from the mask to a small box on the chest. The president doesn't have the faintest idea what to do. Neither does the secretary of state, who gets the job tossed to him because it seems like his department. The potato gets tossed back and around for a while. The Coba still hasn't done a doggone thing. As a matter of fact, no one yet has gotten around to addressing the creature (I think here I will stop calling them creatures).

Fifteen minutes after our world's first contact with intelligent life beyond our planet, someone has the bright idea to bring in a scientist.

"Who?" asked the president.

"I don't know," said the secretary of state.

"What kind of scientist?" asked one of the advisors. "An astronomer? An ethnologist? A linguist? A sociologist? An anthropologist?"

"Call 'em all," said the president, with the kind of quick thinking that has endeared him to some of us.

"Call who all?" asked the advisor.

The president, by this time, was getting a little edgy. He was ready to start raising his voice, a sure sign that he was frustrated and angry. Before that, however, he chose to ask one final, well-modulated question. "There must be one person out of the millions of people in this damn country to call," he said. "Someone best suited to handling this. Who is it?"

There was only silence.

After a while, as the president's face turned a little redder, one of the advisors coughed a little and spoke up. "Uh," he said, "why don't we hide this joker away somewhere? You know, somewhere really secure. Then we assemble a high-powered team of specialists, and they can go on from there. How's that?"

"Wonderful," said the president, with the kind of irony that has endeared him to a few of us. "What do you think the joker will do when we try to hide him away somewhere?"

"Ask him," said the secretary of state.

Again there was silence. This time, though, everyone looked toward the president. It was a head of state meeting an important emissary kind of thing, so it was his potato after all. You can bet he didn't like it.

Finally the president said, "He speaks English?" No one answered. After a while the secretary of state spoke up again.

"Ask him," said the S. of S.

"An historic occasion," murmured the president. He faced the

Coba. He took a closer look and shuddered. That was the reaction we all had until we got used to their appearance. After all, the president is just a guy, too. But a well-trained guy.

"Do you speak English?" asked the president.

"Yes," said the Coba. That brought another round of silence.

After a time the secretary of state said, "You've heard this discussion then. Have you understood it?"

"Yes," said the Coba.

"Would you object to the plan then?" asked the secretary. "Would you agree to being questioned by a team of our scientists, in a confidential manner?"

"No," said the Coba, in answer to the secretary's first question, and "Yes," to the secretary's second.

The president took a deep breath. "Thank you," he said. "You can understand our perplexity here, and our need for discretion in the whole matter. May I ask where you are from?"

"Yes," said the Coba.

Silence.

"Where are you from?" asked the secretary of state. Silence.

"Are you from our, uh, what you call, our solar system?" asked the president.

"No," said the Coba.

"From some other star then?" asked an emboldened advisor.

"Yes," said the Coba.

"Which star?" asked the advisor.

Silence.

It was several minutes later that the assembled group began to realize that the Coba was only going to answer yes-no questions. "Great," said the president. "It'll only take years to get any information that way."

"Don't worry," said an advisor. "If we pick the right people, they'll have the right questions."

"Pick them, then," said the president.

"We'll get to work on it," said another advisor.

"Right now," said the president.

"Check."

"What do we do with it in the meantime?" asked the secretary of defense.

"I don't know," said the president, throwing up his hands. "Put him or her or it in the Lincoln Bedroom. Make sure there are towels. Now get out of here and let me go to sleep."

"Thank you, Mr. President," said an advisor. The president just shook his head wearily.

I learned all of this from one of the advisors present at the time. This guy is now appealing a court decision that could send him to prison for five years because of some minor thing he had done a long time ago, and which none of us understand. He's also writing a book about the Cobae affair.

I wonder how well the president slept that night.

The next morning when they came to get the Coba, someone knocked on the door (come to think of it, what made them think that a Coba would know what knocking on a door meant?). There was no response. The aide, one of the more courageous people in the history of our nation, sweated a little, fiddled around a little, knocked again, sweated some more, and opened the door.

Twelve Cobae stood like statues in the room. The aide shut the door and went screaming through the halls of the Executive Mansion.

Later, when the advisors questioned the twelve Cobae, they discovered that only one would reply, and only with yes or no answers. It was assumed that this Coba was the original Coba who had appeared in the president's bedroom the evening before. There really was no logical basis on which to make this assumption, but it was made nevertheless. No one ever got around to asking the simple question that would have decided the matter; no one thought the matter was important enough to decide.

You know what the strange thing about the twelve Cobae was? You probably do. The strange thing about them was that they all looked the same. I mean, *identical*. Not the way that you say all of some ethnic group look the same. I mean that if you photographed the twelve Cobae individually, you could superimpose the pictures by projecting them on a screen, and there wouldn't be the smallest difference among them.

"Clones," said one knowledgeable man. "All grown from the same original donor."

"No," said another expert. "Even if that were the case, they would have developed differently after the cloning. There would be some minor differences."

"A very recent cloning," insisted the first.

"You don't know what you're talking about," said the second. "You're crazy." This typified the kind of discussion that the Cobae instigated among our best minds at the time.

When the Cobae had been around for a day or two, the president signed the orders creating the top-security base in St. Didier Parish, Louisiana. I was shipped down, everyone else on the base was brought in, and for a little while we worked in relative comfort and ignorance. Then the day came when the general and his colonels arrived, with the twelve Cobae right behind. The four black cars drove straight to a barracks that had been in disuse since the installation was opened. The Cobae were put in there, each in its (I get confused about the pronouns) own room. Colonel McNeill was present, and so was I. I thought I was going to throw up. That passed, but not quickly enough. Not nearly.

The general spoke with Colonel McNeill. I couldn't understand their conversation, because it was mostly whispers and nods. One of the colonels asked me if the Cobae would be comfortable in their quarters. I said, "How should *I* know? Sir."

The general overheard us. He looked at the Cobae. "Will you be comfortable here?" he asked.

"Yes," said the Coba who did all the answering.

"Is there anything you'd like now?" asked the general.

"No," said the Coba.

"If at any time you wish anything, anything at all," said the general, "just pick up this telephone." The general demonstrated by picking up the receiver. He neglected to consider that the Cobae would have a difficult time making their wants known, limited to two words, yes and no.

A tough guard was assigned to the building. The general and the two colonels beat it back to their car and disappeared from the base. I looked at Colonel McNeill, and he looked at me. Neither of us had anything to say. None of this had been discussed with us beforehand because the matter was so secret it couldn't be trusted either on paper or over normal communications channels. No codes, no scrambling, nothing could be trusted. So the general plopped the twelve Cobae on our doorstep, told us to hang tight, that scientists would arrive shortly to study the beings, and that we were doing a wonderful job.

It was a Thursday, I recall. After we left the building housing the Cobae, I went to the gym building and changed clothes. It was basketball night, Cobae or no Cobae.

I remember once, not long after the Cobae came to Louisiana, when Colonel McNeill asked me to show the aliens around. I said all right. I had gotten over my initial reaction to the Cobae. So had the men on the base. They were used to seeing the Cobae all over the installation. As a matter of fact, we became *too* used to seeing them. I'd be doing something like picking a red Jell-O over a green in the mess line, and there would be a Coba looking over my shoulder. I'd take a shower after a basketball game, and when I walked out of the shower room a Coba would be standing there, watching silently while I dried myself off with a towel. We didn't like it exactly, but we got used to it. Still, it was spooky the way they appeared and disappeared. I never saw one pop in or pop out, yet they did it, I guess.

With the arrival of the Cobae, our base became really super secure. No passes, no furloughs, no letters out, no telephones. I suppose we all understand, but none of us like it, from Colonel McNeill down to the lower enlisted men. We were told that the country and the world were slowly being prepared to accept the news of a visitation by aliens from space. I followed the careful, steady progression of media releases prepared in Washington. It was a fairly good job, I suppose, because when the first pictures and television news films of the Cobae were made available, there was little uproar and no general panic. There was a great deal of curiosity, some of it still unsatisfied.

I was starting to tell about this particular time when I was giving a guided tour to the Cobae. I showed them all the wonderful and impressive things about the base, like the high chainlink fence with electrified barbed wire on top, and the tall sentry towers with their machine gun emplacements, and the guards at the main gate and their armaments, and the enlisted men going about their duties, cleaning weapons, drilling in the heat, double-timing from place to place. If I had been a Coba, I think I might have written off Earth right then and there. Back to the ship or whatever, back into the sky, back to the home world.

The twelve Cobae, however, showed no sign of interest or emotion. They showed nothing. You've never seen such nothing. And all the time only the one Coba would speak, and then only when asked a question to which he could reply with either of his two words. He understood everything, of course, but for some reason, for some crazy Coba reason, he wouldn't use the words he understood in his answers.

I took the aliens through the gym building. I got one of the more startling surprises of my life. A game was going on; ten men were playing basketball, full court. It wasn't as rough as a Tuesday/Thursday game, but it was still plenty physical under the boards. I mentioned casually that this was one of the favorite ways of spending off-duty time. The Cobae stood, immobile, and watched. I began to move ahead, ushering them along. They would not move. I had to stay with the Cobae. I didn't see what interested them so much. I sighed. At that time, no one had any idea what a Coba wanted or thought. I say that as if we do now. That just isn't so, even today, though we're closer to an understanding. I had no way of knowing then that the basketball game would be the link between us and these travelers through space.

Anyhow, I was stuck with the Cobae until the game ended. After that, when the players had gone to the showers, I asked if the Cobae wished to see more of the compound. The answerer said, "Yes." I showed them around some more. Nothing else was interesting to them, I guess, because they just passed in front of everything, their expressions blank behind their masks. They never stopped again like they had at the basketball court.

Something about the game fascinated the Cobae. Of course, we've all tried to understand just what. People, who in saner days wouldn't be caught dead inside a field house, spent months analyzing basketball like it was a lost ancient art form. The rules of the game may have changed a little since its beginning almost a hundred years ago, but the style of play has altered more considerably.

There are different sets of rules, though. You have professional basketball, college ball, high school ball. Minor variations among the different kinds of basketball exist to suit the game to the various levels of competition. Professional, college, high school.

And then you have playground basketball. When basketball was first invented, and during its first few decades of existence, all the players were white. In the professional leagues, this continued longer than on the lower levels. Why? Because of the same reasons that everything else remained white until the black athlete shouldered his way into a kind of competitive position.

For basketball, it was one of the greatest things to happen to the sport. The great pro players were white in the early years. Once blacks were allowed to play against them, the blacks began dominating the game. Bill Russell, Wilt Chamberlain, Kareem Abdul-Jabbar, Julius Erving, and plenty of others have caused a reappraisal of the old strategies.

Why have blacks taken over professional basketball almost entirely? I have a theory. Sure. But it's full of generalizations, and they're as valid as most generalizations. Sort of, you know. Pretty valid, kind of.

Where do these black ballplayers come from? From ghetto neighborhoods, from poor urban and rural communities. Not without exception, of course, but it's a good enough answer. In a ghetto neighborhood, say in New York, there just isn't physical space for baseball diamonds and football fields. There are basketball courts all over though. They can fit into a smaller space. You can see a basketball rim attached to the side of a building, with groups of kids stuffing the ball into it, again and again.

Take white players. A lot of them come from better backgrounds. A white kid growing up in a town or suburb has a basketball hoop mounted on the garage. He plays by himself, or with a couple of friends.

On the ghetto playgrounds, basketball can be a vicious demonstration of one's identity. Six, eight black guys beneath a basketball backboard can turn the game into something almost indistinguishable from a gang war. Meanwhile the white kids are tossing the ball and catching the rebounds and tossing the ball. The black kids are using every move, every clever head fake, every deceiving twist of the body to show off their superiority. It's the only way many black youths have of asserting themselves.

One good way out of the slums is through sports. Mostly that means basketball. The kind of basketball you learn on a ghetto court is unlike any other variety of the sport. It's the kind of ball we played on the base. I was out of my class, and I knew it. But I could play well enough so that I wasn't laughed off the floor.

The Tuesday/Thursday games were playground games, played under playground rules. There were no referees to call fouls; there *were* no fouls. It used to be said that basketball was not a contact sport, like football. Yeah. Try playing an hour with guys who came out of Harlem in New York, or Hough in Cleveland, or Watts in Los Angeles. Those guys know just how much punishment they can deliver without being too obvious. Elbows and knees fly. You spend more time lying painfully on the floor than you do in the game. Playground moves, playground rules. Hard basketball. *Mean* basketball.

I played with black enlisted men mostly. Teams were chosen the same way as on ghetto courts. The people who show up for the game take turns shooting the ball from the free throw line. The first five to put the ball into the net are one team. The next five are the second team. Everyone else watches. Afterward the watchers could go back to their quarters without limping. Few of the players could.

I played often because I practiced my free throws. In off-duty hours I sometimes went to the gym alone and shot free throws for a while. I was good at it. I could sink maybe eight out of ten shots, most of them swishes—when the basketball went cleanly through the hoop without hitting the backboard, without touching the metal rim. All that you would hear was a gentle *snick* as the net below the rim moved.

I was a good shooter. By myself, that is, without another player guarding me, waving his arms, pressing close, without the other players shouting and running. You don't get such an open shot very often during a game. Without fouls, there are no free throws. During a game I was lucky to score ten points.

The games were an hour long, no breaks. That's a lot of running up and down the court. Even the pros only play forty-eight minutes, resting some of those minutes on the bench, with plenty of time-outs called by the coaches, with breaks for half-time and fouls and free throws and television commercials. We played harder. We felt it. But on those rare occasions when I did something right, it was worth everything I had to take. It was worth it just to hear that *snick*.

There was an unwritten law: we left our ranks in the locker room. I wasn't a captain on the basketball floor. I was a white guy who wanted to play with the black enlisted men. Sometimes I did. After a while, when I showed that I could pretty well hold my own, they grudgingly accepted me, sort of, in a limited way, almost. They gave me a nickname. They called me "the short honkey."

About September the group of scientists had arrived and began their work. It went slowly because only one of the Cobae could be interviewed, and he still said only yes or no.

"Do you come from this part of the galaxy?" asked one man.

"No," said the Coba.

"Do you come from this galaxy at all?"

"No."

The scientist was left speechless. Two thoughts struck him immediately. The Cobae had come a very long way somehow; and it would be very difficult to learn where their home was. All the scientist could do was to run through a list of the identified galaxies until the Coba said yes. And the knowledge would be almost meaningless, because within that galaxy would be millions of stars, none of which could be pinpointed from Earth. The interviewer gave up the attempt. To this day, we don't know exactly where the Cobae came from.

I had filed a report about the reactions of the Cobae to my guided tour several weeks earlier. One of the demographers thought that the interest the Cobae had shown in the basketball game was worthy of exploration. He proposed that the Cobae be allowed to watch another game.

The game the scientists chose was a Tuesday night bell-ringer. "Bell-ringer" because if you tried to grab the ball away from the strong, agile enlisted men, you got your bell rung. The Cobae were seated in an area out of bounds, along with a team of specialists watching their reactions. Of course, there weren't many reactions. There weren't any at all, while the enlisted men and I shot free throws for teams. I ended up on a pretty good team. I was set for a hard game. The first team, mine, had the ball at the start. I took the ball out of bounds and tossed it to Willy Watkins. He dribbled downcourt and passed the ball to Hilton Foster. Foster was tall and quick. His opponent stretched out both arms, but Foster slithered beneath one arm, got around his opponent, jumped, and shot. The ball banked off the backboard and into the net. We were ahead, two to nothing.

The other team in-bounded and started to take the ball downcourt. I was running to cover my defensive territory, as loose and flexible as it was. We weren't pros. We just chose a man to cover and tried to keep him from scoring. There are lots of interesting ways of doing that, some of them even sanctioned by the rules.

Anyway, as the other team brought the ball down I saw an odd sight. Five of the Cobae had stood up and were walking out onto the basketball court. The scientists had risen out of their chairs. One man turned to the remaining seven Cobae and asked if the five wanted to play. There was silence. The speaker for the group was among the five.

"Do you want to join the game?" I asked the five. I couldn't tell which among them was the speaker.

"Yes," said one Coba. Behind the masks they all looked the same. I couldn't tell which Coba had answered.

"What do I do?" I asked one of the scientists.

"Ask them if they know the rules," said one.

"Do you know and understand how this game is played?" I asked.

"Yes," said the speaker.

I stood there for a while, bewildered.

"Aw, come on," said one of the black men. "Don't let those mothers screw up the game."

"They play," said one of the scientists. The blacks were obviously angry.

"All right," I said, assuming my captain's rank again. "My team against the Cobae. You other guys go sit down." The blacks who had been put out of the game were furious, but they followed my order. I heard a lot of language that the Cobae might not have understood. At least, I hope they didn't understand.

"*His* team. Huh," growled one of the men as he left the court.

"What we goin' to do with these blue bastards?" asked Foster.

"Play them loose," I said. "Maybe they just want to try it for a while. Don't hit any of them."

"Just like my mama was playin'," said Bobby O. Brown.

"Yeah," I said. "Five blue monster mamas."

The scientists were busily talking into their recorders and video-taping what was happening. I gave the ball to Watkins. He took it out and tossed it in to me. I started dribbling, but there was a Coba guarding me. He played close. I glanced over at Watkins, who was running downcourt beside me. He had a Coba guard, too. The Cobae had started in a full-court press.

Where had they learned about a full-court press?

I passed over my Coba's head to Foster. A Coba nearly intercepted the ball. Foster put a good move on his Coba guard, twisted around, and spun back in the other direction. It would have worked against me and a lot of the others on the floor, but he ran into another Coba, who had anticipated Foster's move. Foster hit the Coba hard, but he kept dribbling. The Coba reached out and swiped the ball away from Foster. "Goddamn it," said Foster.

The Coba threw a long pass to another alien downcourt. The second Coba was all alone, and made a nice layup for the first score of the game. The aliens were winning, two to nothing. I couldn't believe it.

The game went on for the entire hour. As it progressed, my team began to play harder and harder. We had to. The Cobae were quick, anticipating moves as if they had played basketball all their lives. Our shots were blocked or our men were prevented from getting near the basket, and we had to settle for long, low-percentage shots. The Cobae were playing with perfect teamwork though. They had no difficulty finding one of their players open on offense. It didn't make any difference how we defensed them, one player was always maneuvering clear and the Coba with the ball always passed it to the open man (alien). After the first half hour, the Cobae were winning by a score of 48 to 20.

"Break," I called. "Take a rest." The black players walked off the court, muttering. All of them were glaring at me, at the aliens, at the scientists.

Monroe Parks passed near me. I could hear him say, "You can

order me around all goddamn day, but don't mess with the game, you ofay son of a bitch." I said nothing.

I changed teams. The other men played the second half. I sat down and watched. The second half was about the same as the first. The Cobae were playing a tight game, perfect defense, amazing offense. They took no chances, but they were always in the right place. The final score was 106 to 52, in favor of the Cobae.

The scientists were just as confused as I was. I didn't care, though, right at the time. I went to the showers. The men showered, too, and none of us said a word. Not a sound. But there were some mean looks directed at me.

The following Thursday the five Cobae came to the gym for the game. The enlisted men started cursing loudly, and I had to order them to stop. Five black men played five Cobae. The Cobae won the game by 60 points.

The next Tuesday, the Cobae won by 48 points.

On Thursday, there wasn't a game, because only the Cobae and I showed up.

I wonder what would have happened if I had suggested to the speaker of the Cobae that I and two of his companions should play the remaining three Cobae.

Even though there were no more games with the Cobae, the scientific team that had come to study the aliens did not stop questioning me. It seemed to them that I was closer to the Cobae than anyone else on the base. I don't know. Against the Cobae, I averaged about 3 points a game. Maybe they should have talked to Foster; he got a pretty regular 10.

Colonel McNeill received regular reports from Washington about how the program to reveal the presence of the aliens on Earth was going. He showed me those reports. I read them, and I was at once amused and concerned. Well, after all, maybe I *did* know the Cobae at least as well as anyone else, including the specialists who had assembled at our installation. The newspaper and television releases grew from hints and rumors to denials and finally a grudging, low-key statement that there were, in fact, a few intelligent visitors from another galaxy in seclusion somewhere in the United States.

The immediate response was not too violent, and the fellows in Washington did a good job regulating the subsequent reactions. The Soviet Union came forward with a claim that they, too, had visitors from beyond Earth. The ruler-for-life of an African nation tried to seize headlines with a related story that didn't make much sense to anyone, and I can't even remember exactly what he said. One of the scientists asked the Cobae if there were any more of them on Earth, in addition to the twelve in our compound. The speaker said no. So if the Soviet Union had their own aliens they were from somewhere else, and we never saw them in any case.

The Cobae showed a preference for remaining in their quarters, once it became evident that the basketball games were postponed indefinitely (read, "as long as the Cobae were around"). The researchers put their data together, argued, discussed, shouted, cursed, and generally behaved like children. Colonel McNeill and I ignored it all from that point on because we still had a security installation to run. The scientists and researchers were doing their best to bend our regulations whenever it was comfortable for them to try. The colonel and I came down hard on them. I guess they didn't understand us, and we didn't understand them.

So which group of us was better qualified to understand the Cobae?

Nobody, that's who. Finally, though, about the middle of October, the nominal head of the investigating team called a meeting to which Colonel McNeill was invited. I came along because I was indispensable or something. The meeting began as a series of reports, one by every single professor and investigator in the camp. I can't recall another time when I was so bored. Somehow they managed to make something as awesome as creatures from another world boring. It takes a good deal of skill, many years of training, constant practice, and self-denial to do a job that huge. But boring it was. The colonel was fidgeting before the first man had gone through half of his graphs. He had plotted something against something else, and I wondered where the guy got the information. He had a nice bunch of graphs, though, very impressive, very authoritative looking. He spoke clearly, he enunciated very well, he was neatly dressed and well-groomed, and he rarely had to refer to his notes. Still, I was ready to scream before he finished. I don't remember a thing he was trying to say. In the weeks that he had to study the Cobae, he apparently didn't come across a single, solitary interesting fact.

Maybe that wasn't his department, I told myself. So I waited for the second researcher. He, too, had plenty of visual aids. He took a pointer and showed how his red line moved steadily down, while his blue line made a bell-shaped curve. I waited, but he was every bit as lacking in information as his predecessor.

That's the way that it went for most of the afternoon. I think that if I had been put in charge of those statisticians and, uh, alienographers, I might have done a better job. I might be fooling myself, of course, but I think I would have tried to learn why the Cobae had come to Earth in the first place. No one could give us a clue about that. Even with yes-and-no answers, they should have been able to do that. Am I getting warm? Yes. No. Am I getting cold?

I think the idea is to start big and narrow down until you have the Cobae cornered, in an intellectual sense. Ask them if they came to Earth for a definite purpose. Yes or no. If the Coba answered no, well, they're all on vacation. If it said yes, start big again and whittle away until you learn something.

But evidently that's not the way our men and women of the study team worked. A large report was published eventually, excerpts appeared in newspapers and magazines, but not many people were satisfied. I'd still like to take my crack at the Cobae, my way. But I can't.

So, in any event, investigator after researcher after pedant after lecturer had his say. I got up after half an hour and went to the back of the room, where two enlisted men were setting up a film projector. Both men were black. One was a regular basketball player I knew, Kennedy Turner, and the other's name I don't recall. I watched them threading the film; it was only slightly less boring than listening to the presentations. I noticed that right beside me was Colonel McNeill. He, too, was watching Turner thread film. After the film was wound into the machine, the two men turned to a slide projector.

"You want to kill the lights, please?" said the woman on the platform. Turner hastened to turn off the lights. "Roll that first reel, please," said the woman. The other enlisted man flicked a switch. I watched a few seconds of a basketball game. I saw myself embarrassed by the play of a short alien. "It seems to me, gentlemen," said the woman, "that these Cobae are governed by a single mind. I don't know how I can make the idea clearer. Perhaps the mind belongs to the Coba who always answers. But the visual input, *all* the sensory input of the twelve Cobae is correlated and examined by the central mind. That was what made the Cobae so effective in this game, although we know through our questioning that they had never seen anything similar before."

"A single governing mind?" asked a man seated in the audience.

"Yes," said the woman, "capable of overseeing everything that is happening to all twelve units of the Cobae multipersonality. The basketball game here is a perfect example. Watch. See how every human move is anticipated, even by Cobae players on the opposite side of the court. One mind is observing everything, hovering above, so to speak, and decisions and commands are addressed to the individual Cobae to deal with any eventuality."

(I'm editing this from memory, of course. We didn't know they were called Cobae until much later. We just called them beings or creatures or aliens or blue men or something like that.)

"I'd like to ask a question, if I may—"

The man was interrupted by the lights going on again.

"Not yet, please," said the woman. She stopped speaking and gasped. Everyone turned around. The twelve Cobae were in the back of the room.

The Coba speaker stepped forward. "Now you honkey chumps better dig what's going down," he said. "We got to tighten up around here, we got to get down to it. You dig where I'm coming from?"

I looked at Turner and his black companion. They were laughing so hard they could barely stand. Turner held out his hands, palms up, and the other man slapped them. Turner slapped his friend's hands. They were suddenly having a real good time.

I turned to Colonel McNeill. Everyone in the room was speechless. There was a long pause. Then the colonel whispered to me. "Uh, oh," was all he said.

Introduction to the O. Niemand Stories

George Alec Effinger wrote the "O. Niemand" stories—
seven stories and a poem, actually—between 1982 and
1988, during one of the peak production periods of
his life, publishing them mostly in *The Magazine of
Fantasy & Science Fiction*, although a couple of them
appeared in *Isaac Asimov's Science Fiction Magazine*.
They consist of "The Wooing of Slowboat Sadie," the
earliest one, written in the style of O. Henry; "The Man
Outside," written in the style of John Steinbeck; "Afternoon Under Glass," written in the style of Ernest
Hemingway; "Two Bits," written in the style of Ring
Lardner; "The Artist Passes It By," the poem, written
in the style of Don Marquis of *Archy and Mehitabel*
fame; "The Day the Invaders Came," written in the
style of James Thurber; "The Wisdom of Having
Money," written in the style of Mark Twain; and "Put
Your Hands Together," the last one, written in the style
of Flannery O'Connor.

"Niemand" means "no one" or "nobody" in German, and if you knew George, you can see his sly, shy,
deceptively quiet smile behind that choice of words.

The "O. Niemand" stories are stunts, of course, fin-
ger-exercises, muscle-flexing, the sort of thing a writer of
extravagant talents and huge skills does when he's still
young, still healthy, still at the top of his game, just to
show that he *can*—and yet somehow, they're more than
that, too. They're not the work George will be remembered for, not the work that had the most profound
impact on the State of the Art in science fiction—everyone agrees, deservedly so, that that's his "Marîd Audran"
stuff, especially *When Gravity Fails*, perhaps his finest
novel. And yet, in their own way, the "O. Niemand"
stories are small marvels. Perhaps it takes another writer
to really appreciate the amount of skill that went into
them, and be awed by it.

Consider: First you have to write recognizably *in the style of another author*, without making it a parody or a caricature, crafting a sympathetic homage or pastiche rather than a lampoon—something that's hard enough to do even with highly stylized authors like Hemingway and O. Henry and Lardner, let alone quieter, more subtle authors such as Steinbeck and O'Connor. George may have been better at this than anyone who ever worked in the field, with the possible exception of John Sladek (and his stuff was more parody than pastiche or homage); many writers have tried it since, and no one has come near matching George's uncanny ear for style. But that's only part of the problem. Then—and here comes the immense leap of imagination and intellect—one must write a story believable as something that Hemingway or Steinbeck or Twain or O'Connor would have written—mimicry on a far deeper and more subtle level than mere style, mimicking attitudes and themes and concerns and styles of literary attack—*while at the same time making it a valid science fiction story*. For indeed, they all *are*, even the poem—and you sit there shaking your head and thinking that if Don Marquis ever *had* written a poem about Archy going to a domed city on an asteroid deep in space, then, by God, this is exactly the way it would have come out! I can't think of any other author in science fiction, then or now, past or present, who could have pulled that off as well as George does.

And then, after having done all *that*, you have to go ahead and make it a *good* story as well. And he managed that, too. Even the weakest of the "O. Niemand" stories are richly entertaining, clever, and slyly amusing, and the best of them—"Put Your Hands Together," "Afternoon Under Glass," "The Man Outside"—are moving as well, emotionally affecting in a way that George's work often deliberately avoided, jabbing sentiment aside with sharp little elbows of satire as soon as it came too near, and it's perhaps not too much of a stretch to speculate that writing as "nobody" enabled him to tap places inside himself that it embarrassed him to reveal when writing as George Alec Effinger. Whatever the truth of that, I'd rank those three "Niemand" stories as among the best short stories that George ever wrote, under any name, right up there with stories such as "Two Sadnesses" (which, in style and concerns, easily could have been published as an "O. Niemand" story) or "Schrödinger's Kitten" or "Everything But Honor."

So enjoy this jewel-case full of small marvels, unique, precious, gemlike, precise. In their own small way, they are unlike anything ever done in science fiction before, and you will never see their like again. In some alternate world, a luckier George, a George not cursed by Fate, a George who conquered his demons and went on to live a long, full, healthy life, wrote lots more of these little gems, as indeed George once intended to do. In this universe, alas, there are only these eight—and we must make do with them, relish them, and try not to mourn for what has been lost and never born.

—Gardner Dozois

✛ ✛ ✛

The Wooing of
Slowboat Sadie

IF YOU AWOKE ONE LUGUBRIOUS AND BLEARY-
eyed morning to the dreadful knowledge that you had, in
some manner yet only hazily recollected, lost the person of the
wealthiest and most powerful man ever to visit the domed city of
Springfield, what would you do about it? Would you inform your
superior, the overworked Captain Helfmuhn, fully prepared to
listen to his fine collection of oaths and curses? Would you explain
to him that you hadn't truly lost the Beshta Shon, that you had
merely misplaced him? Would you have the nerve?

You may weep joyful tears, for you have committed no such
blunder. But save a salty drop or two for Officer Onayly, who did
that very thing. And now you may search along with the kindly officer, who must find the Beshta Shon before lunchtime or be
assigned to a new beat out on the airless side of the great green
dome.

Officer Onayly needed to think about his problem, and when
he needed to think he always went to Thragan's for a beer. If you
don't mind having one with him so early in the day, take a place at
the bar between Thragan's regulars and the honest cop. Then you
and he may begin the day's adventure refreshed.

"Now, Onayly," said the surprised Thragan himself, "what
brings you into me place so early? I'd be thinkin' your head was too

big to be mindful of your duties this mornin'. Would you care for a short beer?"

Onayly rubbed his temples and uttered a groan of despair.

"Yes, thank you," he said. "My head feels like I rented it out all night to a pair of midget prospectors. But tell me, Thragan, how did you know my skull ached?"

"When you left here last night," laughed Thragan, "it was plain you'd be forfeitin' to the divil for the time you had." He placed a mug of sunny, foam-topped beer on the bar.

Slowly in an agony of regret to the barkeep's smiling face the copper raised his eyes. "I was in here last night, was I?" he asked.

"Aye, sure," said Thragan, "wid that little pal of yours. Don't you remember? Why, by all the saints, you must not have gone straight home like I told you."

"We saw you in the Sazerac at midnight," said a blowzy red-haired girl.

Officer Onayly was glad that he had found a clue. This was a beginning at least, even if it did come from sources that were often not wholly reliable on other matters.

"Pearl," he asked, hopefully, "when you saw me in the Sazerac, was my little friend there too?"

"Yes," she said, "that's why I followed you there. That little man knows how to spend his money. I wanted to let him know it was my birthday, but he wouldn't let me get near. He kept asking for some other dame."

"Thank you, Pearl," said the relieved minion of the law, "I owe you a favor." He gulped down the last of his beer and walked out of the bar with all the steadiness and dignity expected of a defender of public decency. His next call would be the Sazerac, a place of danger and notoriety and black intrigue, and consequently a popular little club among both hoodlums and young businessmen of great promise.

Molly, the barmaid at the Sazerac, called out to the policeman. "Onayly, I didn't expect to see you again for a week! Are you out to give your megrims the fresh air?"

"When I waked this morning, Molly, I was sorry I did. Say, tell me what happened last night. And set up a small one for me too."

Molly drew a beer on the house and put it in front of the penitent cop. "We got pig knuckles on the free lunch today, Onayly."

The officer's eyes bulged and his skin took on the color of pale jade. "No, thank you, Molly," he said, through clenched jaws.

"Who was that sawed-off little fellow?"

"Didn't I introduce you? That was the Beshta Shon himself. He came here to Springfield on a little holiday."

"What is a Beshta Shon?"

Onayly swallowed some cold beer. "If I told you what Cap'n Helfmuhn said to me, you wouldn't believe it. I myself didn't believe it when I heard it. Where he comes from, the Beshta Shon ain't just the richest man in the world, he *owns* the world, every building, every sorry stick, every square inch in the place."

Molly stared down at the polished wooden bar. "It must be grand to be that rich," she said, dreamily.

"Well, this little fellow is lonely. He comes here once a year for a bit of a party."

"And you were supposed to keep him out of trouble? They assigned *you*, Onayly? What happened, did you lose him?"

The cop nodded his head miserably. "I just got to find him," he said.

"Well, you were headin' for Slowboat Sadie's when you left here last night. That's who he was askin' for. I don't know if you made it there or not. He was attractin' attention, throwin' money around like it was last week's newspaper. I hope nothin' happened to the gentleman."

"If he was robbed," said Onayly, scowling, "I'd just as well sign myself aboard a prison ship and be done with it. But I'll find him. Thank you for the drink and the information." He finished the beer and walked out of the Sazerac, turning up the street toward Slowboat Sadie's. When he stepped inside that venerable hostelry, the bartender raised an eyebrow.

"You had some skate on last night, Onayly," Dusty Jack greeted the cop.

"So I've been informed," said Onayly. "Please, if you're after helping out an old friend, let me wet my whistle on a tittle of beer. I'm looking for my little pal."

Dusty Jack filled a frosted glass with golden ale and set it in front of Onayly. "Your pal with all the money?" he asked.

"Yep." The cop swallowed half of the beer in one great, thirsty gulp.

A tall blonde woman sitting at a table across the dimly lighted room said: "Well, say, I know where he is." This was Slowboat Sadie herself. She was the proprietor of the establishment and a friend to all her customers, most particularly the crewmen of the long-haul freighters, whence her euphonious sobriquet. Now, when Onayly turned to observe the speaker, Slowboat Sadie appeared the same as she always did. She was a striking woman, let no one remark otherwise, and she had a certain grace about her that was at least half natural, the remainder consisting of conscious effort aided by generous doses of juniper liquor, administered on the quarter hour. The blondness of her hair was only mildly encouraged by some commercial preparation, a gilding of a rare lily on this desolate asteroid. But let us not judge her vanity harshly: it betrays a refreshing modesty, a blindness to her own true charm. Yes, Slowboat Sadie was no longer so young as the girls who worked in her establishment; and, yes, perhaps it was only the dim light that flattered her so immoderately. But it was Slowboat Sadie whom the Beshta Shon came to visit, and would you be the one to tell such a man he had erred in his choice of sweethearts?

"Perhaps, Sadie," said Officer Onayly, in a casual manner, "you have had dealings with Cap'n Helfmuhn."

"Sure, and he's an old bucket of mud."

"That is as may be. But the old bucket of mud will have my shield and my head unless I find the Beshta Shon and return him safely."

Slowboat Sadie exhaled a pale cloud of cigarette smoke and took counsel with herself for a little while. She shrugged her shoulders.

"Well," she said, "it's nothing to me, but I guess I'll tell you where he is."

The grateful cop raised a hand. "Let me finish my beer first." And he tilted the glass and drained it dry with another long, deep swallow. All the while he regarded Slowboat Sadie and wondered why the Beshta Shon, with all his money and power, had come to this seedy little dive, when he could have gone to any of the posh luxurious spots that Onayly imagined must exist for the wealthy.

"You're some chaperone, Onayly," said Dusty Jack. "If ever they send a copper after me, I hope they send you. I promise we wouldn't sober up until the angels come to get us."

"Aw, climb a rope, Jack," said Onayly, in a dangerous tone.

The eponymous owner of the house left her table and came to the bar. She seated herself on the stool beside the policeman. It seemed to Onayly that she had failed to bring some of her girlish comeliness with her from the shadows.

"The Beshta Shon is safe enough," she said. "He's sleeping it off in the alley behind the building."

The cop gazed at her in wonder. "Do you know who he is? He's one of the greatest men in the—"

"I know better than you who he is," said Slowboat Sadie. She waved a hand in a bored way, dismissing Onayly.

The officer muttered a few words too low for the woman or her nosy tapster to hear. Onayly went out of the barroom through a door in the rear and found himself in a narrow alley that smelled of many awful things well past their prime. Rotten cabbage leaves, egg shells, and coffee grounds the cop saw at first glance, the effluvious sweepings and out-scourings that made a simple pallet for the magnificent Beshta Shon.

"Sir," said the officer, "perhaps you should wake up now. Let me escort you back."

There was no response from the sleeping man, unless you are capable of reading meaning in the open-mouthed snores of the gloriously squiffed. Onayly had not this talent.

"Sir," he said, nervously, "we can't let anyone find you like this. Please, sir." And timorously he shook the grimy shoulder of the Beshta Shon.

The little potentate stirred in his sodden dreams. "Wha," he declared. He opened one eye; it was the color of brick dust.

"Would you like me to help you sit up, sir?" asked Onayly.

The Beshta Shon nodded his head and immediately regretted the motion. "I was potted," he said, in a furry voice.

"Yes, sir. That's it, sit up. We must get you back before anyone sees you this way."

The Beshta Shon opened his other eye and squinted the first. He turned his head one way and another until he focused on the policeman.

"Who are you?" he asked.

"I'm Officer Onayly, sir. Don't you remember me? I was with you last night."

"Last night—I don't recall last night. What am I doing here?"

Onayly didn't have the answer to that. He decided to let the question slip away into the bright afternoon. "Let's try standing now, sir," he said. He helped the small man to his feet.

"I'm fine now, officer. I'm very grateful to you for looking out for me. Yes, I'd better be getting back. I need to take a bath and put on some clean clothes."

The great Beshta Shon, proprietor of a rich industrial world, possessor of a fortune beyond the limited imagination of a poor man like Officer Onayly, staggered just a bit as he tested his legs. In no more time than it takes a newborn wildebeest to learn the same trick, the Beshta Shon had once again mastered the art of walking. The cop gave him encouragement in a soft friendly voice. Together they made their way down the odoriferous alley.

"I shall call a car, sir," said Onayly.

"Thank you, officer."

A few minutes later, in the car, the Beshta Shon began to feel as if he might recover, after all. He sat back in the seat and uttered a long, weary sigh.

"I must apologize if I caused you any concern, officer," he said.

"No, sir, not at all."

"I have been coming to Springfield for a long time, and I always visit Sadie," smiled the Beshta Shon. "I'm in love with her, you know."

A large, fat fish falling from the sky into Officer Onayly's lap would not have puzzled him more. "But, sir, Sadie is—"

The gentleman stopped him with a gesture. "You do not need to tell me what you think of her, officer. You see only her brassy appearance. I have learned to love the beauty and gentleness that dwell beneath. Tell me, officer, do you know what this means?" A golden chain hung around his neck; on it was fixed a small golden pendant with the numerals 154 inlaid in lapis. The cop's eyes opened wider.

"You are one of the Thousand, sir," said Onayly, awestruck.

A daunting barrier rose between the two men that no amount of shared adventure could ever overcome. The Beshta Shon had paid three years of his life and a vast amount of money, and he had become immortal. The Thousand would live virtually forever, their bodies incorruptible, their minds inviolate. When Springfield itself was no more, when Onayly and all his progeny were forgotten, the Beshta Shon and the others of the Thousand would still be alive.

"You hate me now, don't you?" asked the Beshta Shon.

"No, sir." But an uneasy feeling aggravated the officer's complacency. It was the envy of one who knows he will not also live forever.

"I know what you are thinking—I have heard it often enough since I acquired this number. I have searched endlessly for someone with whom to share the lonely centuries. Whenever I found a woman whom I admired and respected, I learned that it was only my fortune she loved. Disappointment piled upon disappointment. I felt doomed to an eternity of loneliness. Then I met Sadie. She seems to be a—what would you call her? A common wench? But she is so much more than that, officer. She is the only truly honest person I have ever known. She gives everyone just the measure of respect he deserves, no more and no less. She is far more than what she looks, my friend."

"Still, she doesn't care anything for you. Perhaps if you told her—"

"I will win her in my own way," smiled the Beshta Shon. "I believe that I have already almost succeeded."

"Very well," said Onayly, dubiously. "It isn't any business of mine to begin with."

The car came to a stop before a palatial marble edifice, surrounded by gardens and fountains. A uniformed attendant helped the Beshta Shon from the vehicle.

"I want to thank you again," said the little man.

"Please, sir," objected the cop, "it was all in the line of duty. It was my privilege."

"I will return next year. Perhaps you will accompany me on my little fling again." The very notion caused a shudder in Onayly's robust, able form. The Beshta Shon reached into a pocket and pulled out a handful of crumpled bills. He chose one at random and dropped it through the window, into Onayly's lap.

"I can't accept—" protested the cop.

"Please," said the Beshta Shon. And then he turned with a bemused smile on his face and started up the long flight of marble stairs.

The officer looked at the wadded-up money. "If it's a five or a ten," he muttered, "I guess I may keep it. If it's a twenty, I will have to report it to Cap'n Helfmuhn. I'm sure he'll know a good use for it." The cop smoothed out the bill on his knee and stared at it: in the corner was the number 1000. Onayly whistled softly.

A few minutes later the driver let him out of the car at Slowboat Sadie's. Onayly felt he owed the gentleman something. Inside the barroom everything was the same: Dusty Jack was serving up beer, Sadie herself had retreated to the table in the dusky corner, the customers were bickering fiercely about nothing vital. The officer went straight to Sadie.

"I trust you found him well," said Slowboat Sadie.

"I did. He will be leaving Springfield soon."

"We will see him again next year." The woman covered a yawn with her long graceful fingers.

"Sadie," cried the cop, "how can you treat him this way? The man loves you, you know. He has true feelings. He isn't just another drunken lout for you to boot into the alley. And he has so much to offer you, if you would only listen."

244 GEORGE ALEC EFFINGER LIVE! FROM PLANET EARTH

Sadie smiled a sad smile. "Does he, indeed?" From within her shimmering blouse she pulled a golden chain. Inlaid upon the golden pendant was the figure 838.

"Great bloomin' ducks, Sadie!"

"This is what he gave me twenty years ago, Onayly. Now think on this. To live forever is fine for a man like him, who has wealth and power and an empire to manage. But what of me? Shall I spend forever in this horrible place? This life is all I know, and the only escape from it is death. Your little friend stole that escape from me."

The policeman shook his head mournfully. "If you learned to love him, you could share all that he has, as well. But you must hate him a great deal."

Onayly thought he saw a modest flush suffuse the cheeks of Slowboat Sadie—her face glowed the charming color of the palest pink crepe myrtle blossoms.

"I do not hate him," she said, softly. "I love him very much."

"But then—"

Sadie laughed. "Because, you slow-witted excuse for a cop, he has been begging me to marry him for thirty years. And if I did marry him today, what would the two of us do for the rest of forever? There are enough days for all of that. Let him come back next year, and maybe I will be sweet to him. Or if not next year, the year after. Or the year after that. I love him too much to let it go stale so soon."

Onayly looked at the woman for a moment and realized that the Beshta Shon had been perfectly correct: Sadie was beautiful. The cop was surprised he had never noticed it before. He went out of the establishment and headed back to the station; Captain Helfmuhn would be greatly pleased at the turn of events. As he walked, Onayly thought over what he had discovered that day. A little scrap of old, old poetry kept passing through his mind. "Had we but world enough and time," he recited, "This coyness, lady, were no crime." He repeated the lines to himself and smiled. Then he laughed out loud. As he strolled along, the stalwart officer twirled his nightstick in the way that made him the envy of all the rookies, and he whistled away the last bit of hangover from the night before.

+ + +

The Man Outside

MANY OF THE PEOPLE ON SPRINGFIELD ARE IN transit, although some are moving through the big dome faster than others. A certain number of them arrive on the rock in a desperate hurry to get somewhere else, looking for connecting passage to fortune or freedom or love or some other glittering fancy. They wait in clutching haste for fate to fill the inside straight of their happiness, but instead they find themselves the new taxpayers and inmates of a town under glass. The hope that loaded their hearts dwindles as steadily as the money that they put aside to buy their way into their own future.

A few will surrender easily, supposing that Springfield is as good as anywhere else they might have gone. More of them, though, fight the idea because, at first, life under the dome has a narrow look. After a while these people will see where they've made their mistake. Springfield is a green bottle full of gentle crimes and virtues, of men salty with sin and sweet with illusion.

Right up against the inside of the dome, as far to nightside as you can get from the hub of Tammany Square, there is a double handful of ancient shacks. The families that live here call the place Easy Street. The shacks have a noble history, though no one but the tenants themselves would give you a plastic penny for the whole neighborhood. When the workmen were building the dome they had to live somewhere, and they threw together a little community of self-contained shelters. The shacks were intended to be temporary and when the dome was finished over them they were abandoned. Most of them were torn down and the workmen went off to another rock and another job. Some stayed on Springfield, dreaming of the town that would eventually come to join them. So the men and women and kids of Easy Street are the descendants of the pioneers, and they own a certain liberty because their grandfathers found an edge in being there first.

All human settlements come furnished with people who don't need to work for a living, or don't want to. Some men are lazy and good-for-nothing to their wives, but happy enough with themselves. On Springfield there are the jickies who live in the hulks and wrecks of starboats in the ruins of the Old Field, people who have learned through sad experience that social contact causes sickness in their stomachs. And there are the families on Easy Street, who are unique on Springfield in their situation. They toil not, neither do they spin. They live well enough on dividends from the banks, and most of them haven't the faintest idea where it all comes from.

Only Jerome lived outside the dome, completely alone. He had lived in the little building out on the dead black rock for twenty-two of his thirty-seven years. He was average height, as fat as a puppy. His hair was pale yellow and wild. He tried to keep it under control by cutting it with a knife every few days, but it just stood up on his head like a fistful of straw. He had soft brown eyes that his mother said at the time of his birth were just a little too far apart. That was the nicest thing she ever said about him. His fingers were short and stubby, and his flesh hung on him in folds and rolls. He moved in a slow waddle around his lonely domain.

The building Jerome lived in was a monitoring station for one of the dome's power plants. It was stuck among the sharp black crags about a mile from the dome's nightside portal. Jerome had been born on Easy Street to a woman named Daisy. A lot of babies born on Springfield are named after flowers and birds that no one there has ever seen. Jerome, though, received as his only legacy the name Daisy thought belonged to his father. He had been a happy baby, happy all the time, rarely crying. Daisy thought that was very nice. Everyone remarked on how happy Jerome was. As the baby got older, the charm of Jerome's happiness began to wear off. He was too happy, even for Easy Street. He was happy when he was hungry, happy when he was tired, happy even when someone smacked him across his drooling face.

When he was fifteen years old one of the other boys on Easy Street told Jerome that a girl named Fawn liked him. Jerome was a shy boy driven into himself by his mother's words about his sluggish wits, and by his neighbor's comments about his fat little face. He knew who Fawn was. She had eyes as blue as heaven and a smile that had nothing to do with cheerfulness. Jerome felt lucky just living on Easy Street near her. He wondered that she felt the same about him.

"She's waiting for you in the shed in the alley behind Buzzy's," said Jerome's friend.

"Why?"

"She wants to kiss you."

"I don't want to."

"You got to, Jerome. She's waiting for you."

Jerome felt his face flush. He tried to think of a way to go home but his thoughts moved too slowly. He had the early flicker of an idea, but by that time it was too late. He and his friend stood outside the shed.

"Go on in, Jerome."

"I don t want to."

"Sure you do. She likes you, Jerome. Don't you like her?"

"I guess so."

"Then go on in."

Of course there were more of Jerome's friends waiting inside, along with the temptress Fawn. And what they did to him in there was supposed to be a joke, one of the common cruelties of children. But Jerome's mind was stunned by the terror and the shame, and as he ran home in tears he thought only about going away. Daisy tried briefly to learn what had happened, and made a small attempt to comfort him. Jerome had few belongings to take with him. He had a gilt wooden crucifix and a notebook.

Jerome put on a venerable pressure suit, took a bag of clothing and food and his few treasures, and went out the nightside portal. He had a secret place on the cold face of Springfield where he liked to go to be by himself. He went to the monitoring station, cycled himself in, climbed into the twisted knots of pipes and conduits, and wept, until the memory of the pain faded away.

He liked the monitoring station because there was no one there to tell him what a ball of fat he was, or how he was dumber than a bucket of mud. No one ever came to the station except Jerome. It was his favorite place.

There were several old pressure suits on Easy Street left over from the construction of the dome, but Jerome was the only person who used them. He was the only one who could bear to leave the security of the dome. Everyone else was terrified by the unenclosed space, by the blackness of the sky, by the stark shadows and loneliness. Jerome was blithely unaware of these things. If he thought about them probably he, too, would have been afraid.

So Jerome lived for twenty-two years in the monitoring station. He took care of the things he needed by making trips back to the dome. Whenever he appeared at the portal to be let in, the news spread back to Easy Street. It was always a special event on Easy Street. Everybody would run to the portal, no matter if it was dinnertime or the middle of a pinochle game. They all wanted to see Jerome. If their whole life on Easy Street hadn't already been one long holiday, his appearance would have made a nice break in their dreary lives.

When he was twenty-eight years old, after he had lived in the monitoring station for thirteen years, he came to the dome after an absence of five months. The mob of people was bigger than ever, and they were all talking and laughing as though they were waiting for a parade with bands and floats. Jerome didn't recognize anyone in the crowd. He had forgotten most of the children he had played with, and the others had changed too much. A young woman— maybe Fawn herself—stepped out of the crowd. "Daisy died," she said.

Jerome just looked at her blankly.

"Your ma. Your ma's dead, Jerome."

He just wrinkled up his brow as though he were trying to figure what to do with the news. Then he pushed past the young woman.

"Never mind," said someone else behind her. "You can't tell him a damn thing."

"Well, hell," said the young woman.

Though he lived alone and never spoke to any of the people inside the dome, Jerome was never lonely. That was because he had a friend in the monitoring station to talk to. His friend was Jesus. He had been a gift from Daisy. His mother had given Jesus to the boy without knowing what she was doing. Once, when Jerome was only eight, she said that God was going to punish him for something, for being so fat or so dumb.

"Mama?" he said.

"What you want?"

"Who's God, Mama?"

Daisy was just a little surprised. She thought she had told her son all about God. "Why, God is Jesus," she said.

"Jesus?"

"Yes, and Jesus will be with you all the time, everywhere you go. He'll watch everything you do, so be careful."

That scared Jerome, but Daisy explained that Jesus was good and kind and would send Jerome straight to Hell only if the boy did something specially dumb. So Jesus was with him in the monitoring station, and Jerome was happy to have him there. He figured that talking to Jesus kept him from going crazy.

He liked to write poems, too. He discovered poetry when he was eleven years old. The book was an anthology of best-loved poems, and it was the only book on Easy Street. It had a vital occupation: it kept Daisy's humidifier and heat exchanger level. The book had been wedged under the unit for years and years, forgotten by its original owner, ignored by everyone in all the decades since. Jerome noticed it one morning when he was lying on the floor, staring at a pattern of cracks in the wall. He replaced the book with a brick and spent the rest of the day puzzling out the poems. He could read if no one told him he had to, and he could decipher simple stories. Poems left him bewildered and charmed. Most of them made no sense at all, but he loved the flow of words and the bright, gemlike images. It took Jerome more than a year before he realized that he could invent his own poems. He had a notebook filled with them.

Once, after reading a poem by Joyce Kilmer, he sat in the monitoring station and listened to all the noises. There was a constant, regular rhythm of sound from all the machines and equipment, percussion in the pipes and ducts, clicking and banging and whirring of fans, and sudden crescendos of racket that meant something in the place had just decided to function. Jerome never heard the sounds anymore unless, like now, he felt thoughtful and unsure where to put his attention. He looked at the book again and remembered the poem about trees. He looked around the monitoring station all chrome and clear plastic and pale green walls and white ceilings and green tiled floors. There had been no trees on Easy Street, and there was nothing alive on the face of the asteroid. Jerome grasped his thick blue pencil in his fat fingers and wrote:

A Poem
By Jerome, Age 37

I think that I shall never see
A tree.

"That's real nice," said Jesus. "But it makes me feel sad."

"It *is* sad," said Jerome. "It makes me sad not to see trees."

Jesus was very kind and understanding. "But your home here is real nice, too. You don't have trees, but it's warm and clean here. You have all these blinking lights and jiggling dials to watch. No one hurts you here."

"Maybe someday I can have a tree," said Jerome.

Jesus laughed. "Sure," he said, "maybe someday."

"I don't really want a tree."

"Sure I know," said Jesus. That was another wonderful thing about Jesus: he always knew just what Jerome was really thinking.

Sometimes Jerome wondered where Jesus lived. Daisy had told him that he lived in Heaven, but she couldn't tell him where Heaven was. She always said, "Up there." Jerome didn't know what she meant. The only thing "up there" was the roof of the dome, and he knew nobody could live on the roof of the dome. And anyway, how could Jesus get from the dome to the monitoring station without a pressure suit? So it seemed to Jerome that Jesus must live in the station, and that it had been very generous of Jesus to let Jerome come to live there, too.

Not long after his verse about the tree, he was talking to Jesus about the poem. He was trying to write another one. He had written:

A Poem
By Jerome, Age 37

I like to go out in the darkness

"I guess I got to change that," said Jerome to Jesus. "You got to know how poems work. Well, I can't think of nothing that sounds like darkness: barkness, tarkness. See? I got to change it."

"I tell you what you can do," said Jesus. "What you can do is leave off the 'ness' part. Leave it just 'dark,' see? That way there are plenty of words that sound like it. 'Lark,' see? And 'snark,' and 'mark.' And maybe others."

"What does 'snark' mean, Jesus?"

Jesus looked thoughtful for a little while. "I don't exactly know," he said. "But there's somebody in your book of poems who uses it."

Jerome started the poem again from the beginning.

I like to go out in the dark.
There isn't a daisy or a lark.
There's just the rocks and the hills

"I'll tell you something else," said Jesus. "You put 'daisy' in it. That was your mama's name. Maybe you ought to of put something else there."

"Yeah, I guess," said Jerome slowly. He crossed out the word *daisy* and wrote in *flower*. "There isn't a flower or a lark," he said. "There's just the rocks and the hills."

"It's real nice," said Jesus.

Jerome looked impatient. "It ain't even done yet," he said.

"Oh," said Jesus.

"I need just one more line, and it has to end like hills."

"How about this: 'All nice and plain without no frills.' "

Jerome made a face that showed what he thought. Jesus was a good friend and he was always good to Jerome, but Jesus really didn't understand poems. "I don't know," said Jerome.

"Why not?"

"I just don't know if I like it. Maybe I want to try something else."

"Well, you go ahead and try something else, and if you don't find nothing else, you can always use it."

Jerome's expression grew sly. "I can always change hills," he said. "I can swap it for the rocks. There might be better words that sound like rocks."

"You just go ahead then," said Jesus. He looked a little hurt.

Jerome decided to put the poem away for a while. It wasn't important enough to make trouble between him and his only friend. He had other work to do. He had to make a list of the things he needed, and make another visit to the dome. He walked around his eremitic estate, checking his stores.

The monitoring station was a small, rectangular building, alone and lonely, set just inside the permanent nightside of Springfield. It had been put there to oversee the circulation of cooling water through the labyrinth of conduits of one of the dome's principal reactors. There were thousands of switches and lights and dials, thermometers and radiation detectors and pressure gauges, valves that opened or closed whole thoroughfares of pipe, valves that worked other valves, all too complex for any person, or any team of people, to comprehend. But computers did all the actual monitoring. There were accommodations in the station for a maintenance crew, but it had been a long time since anything there had needed maintenance. It had been so long that inside the dome there weren't any people who knew how to operate the machinery. Everything was written out in handbooks and manuals, though; the books knew what to do, but no people did.

There was a small dormitory in the back of the building, but Jerome never used it. He was frightened to live and eat and sleep so far from the air lock. One day, shortly after he had come to live in the station, he took his pencil and notebook and drew a picture of the control room. There was a wide, curved bank of equipment on a shielded platform overlooking the tangle of ducts and shafts. On the map he had written MY ROOM. He drew a bed and a chair that would serve him as a dresser and another chair. He dragged a mattress from the dormitory room and put it on the floor of the control room. He positioned two of the swivel chairs just as he had drawn them on his map.

The shower room was located on one side of the dormitory room, and a small service kitchen beyond that. There was a large storage area in the kitchen, and Jerome kept all his food in clear plastic containers. He always knew when it was time to go to the dome to get more.

There was really nothing else to see. There was nothing that made the place home, no pictures on the walls, not even a little rug on the floor. Everything was functional and drab, but that was the way Jerome wanted it. He wasn't threatened by drabness. And he had his poems on a chair beside his mattress, and he had Jesus anytime he needed a friend.

"So you're gonna go to the dome this afternoon," said Jesus, just trying to make conversation.

"Yeah," said Jerome. He was struggling into the old pressure suit.

"Goin' to get supplies?"

"Yeah."

"Wish I could come."

"I wish you could, too. There's not much to do when I'm walking across the rocks and stuff."

Jesus cast around for some way he could go to the dome, too. "I know what you do," he said at last. "You bring me back another suit. That way next time I can go with you."

"Can't carry no suit. It's all I can do to carry the supplies."

That made Jesus unhappy. "Then maybe sometime you can go and just get a suit, and don't worry about no supplies."

Jerome looked up. It was a good idea. "I can do that, I guess," he said. "But I don't like to go there more'n I have to."

"I know you don't. But you'd go to get me a suit, wouldn't you?"

"Sure I would," said Jerome. He was all ready to leave now. He waved to Jesus and walked clumsily to the air lock. He let himself out, and then he was all alone under the eternal midnight sky and the hard, frozen stars. The dome was a bright green glowing thing a mile away. Jerome turned toward it, and he could see lights in the ruined hulks at the Old Field. Daisy had told about the people who lived there, but he couldn't remember anything about them. He started walking. It would take more than half an hour to cross the fissured ground.

He climbed jagged rills of black stone like the jaws of monsters, and lowered himself carefully down into the flat gray plain that separated the nightside station from the dome. His fat little body labored and his breath wheezed in the suit's helmet. When at last he got to the dome's portal, he pressed the signal and waited to be let in. He knew what would be waiting for him. He knew there would be a crowd of people from Easy Street. He hated that part.

The air lock crew grinned at him but offered no other greeting. He stepped in, waited for the cycle to finish, then emerged into the greenish glare of the dome. He stripped out of the suit and hung it in the air lock's waiting room. He didn't like it in the dome, even though he was born here. He didn't like the temperature, he didn't like the colors, he didn't like the smells or the noises.

"Hey, Jerome," yelled a woman, "what you want this time? You want to get married, Jerome? I got just the girl for you!" Everybody in the crowd laughed. Jerome smiled and pushed his way through.

"Jerome," called another voice, "what you do out there all by you'self?"

"I don't see how he can stand it out there."

"Hard to b'lieve he's Daisy's. She used to be partial to company." There were some more knowing laughs.

Jerome went to the store on Easy Street and gave his order. Everything was paid for by deducting the cost from his account at the bank. Jerome didn't even know he had an account at the bank; it had been Daisy's, but since she died it was his. He carried his supplies back through the crowd to the lock, trying not to hear what the people were shouting at him. He was glad to put the suit on again and leave the dome. He was glad he wouldn't have to come back again for four or five months.

He was halfway home when he remembered that he should

254 GEORGE ALEC EFFINGER LIVE! FROM PLANET EARTH

have asked about another pressure suit. He hoped that Jesus would forgive him and not send him straight to Hell for it.

While Jerome was working his way back over the last of the sharp stone ridges, a voice spoke to him in his helmet. "Jerome?" it said.

"Jesus? Where are you?"

"What? Jerome? Is that you? This is Arency Diga, the supervisor of Reactor No. 2. We have a little problem, Jerome."

Jerome didn't understand how someone could be talking to him in his helmet. "Where are you?"

"I'm in the dome. I'm talking to you over the communicator in your suit. We need you to help us, Jerome."

"Why?" asked Jerome in a frightened voice.

"Some of the machinery in the station where you live needs to be worked by hand. It isn't anything to be worried about."

"Is this a joke? I don't like jokes. That's why I come out here."

Diga was getting impatient. "Listen to me. If you don't take care of this, we'll have to send out a crew and they'll be walking in and out of your station all day, bothering you until they get it fixed. You don't want that, do you?"

"No."

"Then let me know when you get to the station. I'll describe what you have to do."

"Okay," said Jerome. He could hear Diga talking with another man.

"Where are you?" asked the other man.

"Who are you? Where did Mr. Diga go?" asked Jerome.

"Mr. Diga is right here. My name is Meern. I'm in charge of reactor security."

"Well, I'm almost home now. What do I got to do?" Jerome started the air lock cycle. When the outside door opened, he carried his bags of supplies inside.

"There is large control box on the long dayside wall of the station." It was Diga's voice again. "There are three—"

"Jus' a minute, Mr. Diga," said Jerome. "I got to put my stuff away first."

"Jerome! Listen! This is very important. We don't have time to send a crew out there. If you don't take care of this soon, highly radioactive water will begin overflowing and flooding through the pipelines into the dome."

"All right, Mr. Diga."

"Don't go inside the station. Look for the control box—"

"I'm already in the station, Mr. Diga." Jerome put down the

bags in the kitchen. Jesus stood and watched, saying nothing, a per-
plexed expression on his face.

"God damn it," said Meern. "Jerome, you have to go back out.
As fast as you can. There's a control box—"

"Okay, okay," said Jerome. "I'm goin' back out right now."
He cycled himself through the air lock and walked around the
building. "The long dayside wall," he murmured.

"That's right," said Diga. "Do you see the box?"

"The big metal thing with the yellow stripes on it?"

"Right, that's it. Now, open the door. Just pull open the three
little latches and swing it open."

Jerome didn't have any trouble doing that. "Okay."

"Now, listen carefully, Jerome," said Diga. "There are a lot of
things inside the control box."

"There sure are." Jerome hoped that Diga and Meern knew
what they were talking about, because he knew he'd never be able
to make sense of the complicated system he was looking at.

"Do you know what a Tyler switch is, Jerome?" asked Diga.

"No."

"It looks like a little ball with shiny silver stuff in it. There ought
to be a whole lot of them in the control box. Don't touch any of
them now. Do you see them?"

"Oh, sure, I see 'em."

"Good, Jerome. Now, you see there are four sections of switches
and warning lights and things."

Jerome backed away a step and looked at the control box. If
he looked at it kind of sideways, he could see that everything was
arranged in four sections. "I see," he said.

"Now, count over to the second section.

"You want me to skip over the first one."

"That's right, Jerome. Now, about in the middle of it there will
be a Tyler switch that says Feedwater Bypass 1. Do you see that
one?"

Jerome looked carefully at the first few switches. They were all
labeled, but he couldn't make any sense out of their names. After
he read four of them, he forgot which one he was looking for.
"What does it say, Mr. Diga?" he asked.

"It says Feedwater Bypass 1. Do you see it?"

"Not yet, Mr. Diga." He went down the column. "Here it is," he
said at last. "You want me to turn it?"

"Not yet, Jerome," said Meern's voice. "Do you see, right under
it, there's one called Feedwater Bypass 2?"

"Sure," said Jerome, "and there's 3 and 4, too."

"We want you to turn all four of them, one at a time, starting with No. 1. When you turn it, wait for us to tell you to turn No. 2. Okay?"

"Oh, sure, Mr. Meern."

"Go ahead, Jerome. Turn No. 1."

Jerome grasped the crystal globe with the thick, clumsy fingers of his pressure suit. It turned easily; the silver fluid in the globe stayed at the bottom, but a little flower of electronic components rotated out of the pool. When Jerome turned the switch, a light went off in the control box. "I did it," he said.

"Good boy. Now turn No. 2." Following their directions, Jerome turned the other switches.

"Is that all you wanted?" he asked.

"Just one more thing, Jerome," said Diga. "Shut the door on the control box and go inside the station. We need you to open a valve."

"Okay," said Jerome. He shut the control box and went back inside.

"What are you doin'?" asked Jesus. He looked a little unhappy that he wasn't part of the excitement.

"The people in the dome want me to do some things," said Jerome. "I'm being some kind of hero."

"But you don't like the people in the dome."

"These people are okay. They don't talk like the people on Easy Street."

"Oh," said Jesus. He watched Jerome climb out of the pressure suit and put it in a locker.

"Jerome?" Diga's voice came over all the loudspeakers in the monitoring station. Jerome had never heard the speakers in use before.

"Here I am," he said.

"Good. Go up to the control room."

Everything inside the station was quiet and peaceful. Jerome wondered why Mr. Diga and Mr. Meern sounded so upset. "I'm in the control room," he said. He sat on one of the swivel chairs.

"Jerome, I want you to listen carefully again," said Diga. "We're going to start at the right end of the curved row of equipment panels. Do you see the big green screen with the wavy lines going up and down?"

"Sure," said Jerome. He watched it every night before he went to sleep.

"Just to the left of that are two panels with red, green, and yellow lights, and a lot of square meters with arrows in them. Do you see them?"

"Yeah," said Jerome. This wasn't much fun at all.

"Okay. Good boy. Now keep going to the left. Do you see three long rows of little silver switches? There's a sign that says Pressurized Relief Valve Intake Lines."

"It says what?"

"Pressurized Relief Valve—"

"Intake Lines," said Jerome. "Here they are."

"There should be a big metal thing, a round thing like a faucet handle, just to the left of those switches. Do you see it?"

"I see it right here," said Jerome.

"There's a sign on it, Jerome. What does the sign say?"

Jerome squinted his eyes. This was like the things Daisy used to do; when he made a mistake, she beat him. He was afraid of Diga and Meern, wherever they were. He was afraid that they'd beat him if he did something wrong. "There's a sign that says Coolant Drain Shunt. What does that mean? What does 'shunt' mean?"

"Never mind, Jerome. Turn the handle clockwise as far as it will go," said Diga.

He hesitated, his hand on the valve handle. "Do it, Jerome," said Meern. "We don't have a lot of time."

Jerome turned the handle.

A bell rang.

Almost immediately a loud, strident alarm klaxon began to sound somewhere else in the station. A whole row of lights lit up an angry red on the panel above the valve. There was a loud, furious hissing and a rapid clanking that Jerome had never heard before.

"Oh, my God!" cried Meern. "Jerome, you turned it the wrong way. You've got to close it, Jerome."

But Jerome was already running down from the control room. Jesus waited near the network of pipes and ducts. "What'd you do, Jerome?" he asked.

"I don't know." Jerome's face was drawn and white. His voice shook.

"They're gonna to be mad at you now," said Jesus, nodding his head sagely.

"I know."

There was a terrible grinding noise and one of the small-gauge lines ruptured. Water sprayed all over the floor of the station.

Another line broke, and more water flooded down on the tiles.

"I got to clean this up," said Jerome. "They'll send men out here if I don't clean this up."

"They're trying to talk to you," said Jesus. Diga and Meern were trying frantically to catch Jerome's attention.

"I don't care," said Jerome. "They'll send men out here if I don't clean this up. How'm I gonna stop the water comin' out?"

Jesus didn't dare answer.

"Jerome!" shouted Diga. Jerome looked up. "Listen, Jerome! You have to turn the valve off, or you'll pump all the water in the system into the station. We'll have to shut the reactor down now anyway, but if we lose much more water, it will start to heat up. There could be a terrible accident unless you close the valve."

"There's water all over here, Mr. Diga."

"I know, Jerome. But unless you close that valve, a lot of people in the dome may die."

"Die?"

"Yes. Go to the control room and turn the valve the other way."

"I'm sorry, Mr. Diga. I didn't do it on purpose. It was an accident—"

"Yes, Yes. Just go up there. He probably doesn't even know what 'clockwise' means."

Jerome ran up to the control room. He put his hand on the valve. "Which way do I turn it?"

Meern answered. "It will only go one way now, you son of a bitch."

Meern was right. Jerome turned the valve, and some of the red lights went out on the panel. "I don't want you talking to me like that," he said. The alarm bell didn't stop clanging, and more lights lit up on other panels.

"Is that it? Did he do it?" asked Diga.

"Yeah, finally," said Meern. "The system is pumping back up toward normal."

"I just thought of something awful" said Diga. "Jerome, don't take off your pressure suit. Leave it on. That water is—"

"I already took off my suit. Do you want me to put it back on?"

There was a long silence. Jerome went to the locker to get his suit. "I can hear the poor bastard splashing through the water," said Meern. "Oh, God."

Jerome put on his suit. Jesus watched him accusingly; Jesus still didn't have a suit. Jerome turned around so that he couldn't see Jesus's face.

"What are you going to say to him?" asked Meern.

"I don't know," said Diga. "But we owe him something. If he hadn't been there, I don't know what would have happened. We couldn't have gotten a crew there in time. We might have lost the dome. Jerome, can you still hear me?"

"Sure I can, Mr. Diga."

"He's got his suit on now," said Meern. "You can hear the difference."

"Jerome, listen to me. That water is very dangerous and you have to get out of there. You're going to have to leave the station and come to the dome."

"He can't do that, Arency," cried Meern. "He's so contaminated, he'll light up the nightside like a Christmas bonfire."

"His only chance is to get medical care as quickly as possible. Jerome, can you gather up everything you want to bring with you? You're going to have to live in the dome for a while, until we can clean up the station for you."

Jerome sloshed through knee-deep water below the control room. Jesus walked beside him with a reproachful expression. "I don't want to live in the dome," said Jerome.

"I know that," said Diga, "but you have to. You'll get very sick if you stay there."

"I will? What about Jesus?"

There was a long silence from the dome. "Jesus?" asked Meern.

"Yes" said Jerome. "What about Jesus?"

"Is Jesus there with you now?"

"Yes," said Jerome.

There was another pause. "We'll send a surface car for you," said Diga. "We'll take care of Jesus later."

A third voice interrupted. "I won't authorize any of our cars to go," it said.

"But we owe him something—"

"We're just going to have to write off that station. It won't cool down until this whole rock is nothing but radioactive dust floating around in space. He saved some lives and he cost us a monitoring station. We're going to have to shut down Reactor No. 2 until we can build another. I'd say we were even with him. If he wants, he can walk here."

"That's crazy!" said Meern. "He's—"

"Did you hear that, Jerome?" asked Diga. "You're going to have to get here on your own. Can you do that?"

"I don't think I want to. Not without Jesus." Jesus smiled at him; Jerome was glad Jesus wasn't angry.

Diga didn't know what to say. "I told you we'd take care of Jesus. And we'll take care of you."

"Do I have to go back to Easy Street?"

"Not unless you want to, Jerome," said Diga.

"I don't want to." Jerome went up to the control room and took his book of poems and his notebook and his gilt crucifix; then he came back down to the air lock.

Jesus looked mournful. "I'll never see you again," he said.

"Sure you will," said Jerome. "But we got to go live in the dome."

"I don't see how come."

Jerome never lost his patience with Jesus. He knew that sometimes Jesus had a hard time understanding some things. It was up to Jerome to explain them. "Because the water is poison water," he said.

"I won't drink none," said Jesus.

"Well, it ain't just that. It's bad water, and they said they're going to bring a surface car for you and a suit and everything. I'll wait for you inside the dome, and we'll find someplace to live where nobody'll bother us. Maybe we can go live out at the Old Field. People can live out there, you know."

"Maybe," said Jesus. He didn't seem very happy about the idea.

Jerome waved good-bye and left the station. He started the long walk across the sharp-edged rocks that separated him from the nightside portal. In a while he began to feel very sick. His head began to throb and his whole body hurt. His skin felt like it was burning, as if someone had sandpapered it until it began to bleed. He got very weak. The dome towered above him, not a quarter of a mile away, but Jerome had to sit down right in the thin gray dust that covered the plain. "Oh," he said. It seemed to take all his strength.

"Jerome? Are you still there?" It was Meern. He sounded surprised.

Jerome paid no attention. "Jesus loves me, this I know," he sang in a small voice. " 'Cause my mommy told me so."

"Jerome?"

After a few minutes he stood up and continued walking. Only a few yards from the portal, the awful nausea began. Jerome vomited in his pressure suit. He fell to his knees just outside the portal, and retched until it felt like his eardrums were going to burst. He saw flashes of red and white light like stars exploding before his eyes. He was finally able to stand and stagger the short distance to the portal. He pushed the signal.

There was no response.

"Hello!" he called. "It's me, Jerome. Let me in."

No one answered. He looked up, and a man turned away from the port pretending not to see him.

"Let me in!"

At last a voice spoke in his helmet. "Jerome," it said, "why don't you go back to your station? We'll send a surface car for you as soon as we can. We're very busy right now. We can't let you in because we're just so busy. Go back to your station and we'll send a car just as soon as we can."

"Did you send a car for Jesus?"

"What?"

"It *was* a joke, wasn't it? I *said* I didn't like jokes." Jerome sat down in the dust beside the portal. He was in terrible pain. He didn't understand why he hurt so much. He wanted to cry, but Daisy always slapped him when he cried. He just sat in the dust and tried to breathe. It even hurt to breathe.

"We'll send a car, Jerome."

"You won't, will you? You won't send a car." There was a click in his helmet, the noise of the communications link being broken. From then on, there was nothing for Jerome to listen to but the sound of his own breathing.

✛   ✛   ✛

Afternoon Under Glass

THE HOTEL WAS SMALL BUT CLEAN AND GOOD. It was on Long Street, a red brick building between two tall steel and glass office buildings. Across the street was a small park with concrete benches where the workers in the offices sat and ate their lunches. There were only three couples stopping at the hotel. There were the Merbeks, who had been waiting on Springfield more than three weeks for a fast boat to Shannon. There was an old man named Stone, who was traveling with a pretty young woman. There was a couple from Smalt named Essuan, who had rented the room across the hall from the Merbeks for two days.

In the afternoons the Merbeks had nothing to do, so they walked across the street. On one side of the park there was a small place called the Café Solace. Sax Merbek decided that he hadn't had quite enough to drink at lunch. When the waiter came, he ordered rye whiskey for himself and white wine for his wife.

"I'd like just coffee," Mrs. Merbek said. "I've had enough wine already this afternoon."

"Bring her the wine," Merbek said. The waiter looked from the man to the woman. He left without saying a word.

"You're not going to do it again today, for God's sake. Sax, please, it's our last day here."

"Do it again?" he asked. He stared at the green dome overhead.
"Do what again?"

"Let's not talk about it, shall we? Let's just not even talk about it."

"That's fine."

The waiter brought the drinks. He put the whiskey in front of Merbek and the wine by the woman. Each glass had its own white china saucer.

"I shouldn't think it was good wine," Merbek said. "Taste it and tell me."

"Give me a cigarette, please, Sax."

"Try the wine, Elaine."

She made a gesture of annoyance. "Are you going to drink too much today, Sax? Are you going to get tight and start a row again? Am I going to have to get you safely back to the hotel by myself?"

"You don't have to worry. That's the hotel just across the street."

"Let's not even talk about it."

Merbek finished the whiskey and signaled to the waiter for another. "I think I'll have one more," he said. "You haven't even tried the wine."

"If you're so curious about it, you drink it."

"Oh, look. It's those people from Smert." The Essuans were crossing Long Street.

"Smalt. They're from Smalt. I hope they don't see us."

"Of course they see us."

"Then I hope they don't sit with us."

"Why? Have I embarrassed you enough for one day?"

Elaine stared at her husband for a few seconds. "That's it. That's just it."

The couple from Smalt came toward them. "Oh, hello," Mrs. Essuan said. "Eileen and Sax, am I right?"

"Elaine," Merbek said. "My wife's name is Elaine."

"Yes. Do you mind if we sit down?"

"Please. And you're—"

"Tom and Christina Essuan. From Smalt." When the waiter came over, Tom Essuan ordered two coffees.

"So you're from Smalt," Merbek said.

"I say, yes," Essuan said. There was an uncomfortable silence.

"Don't you think Elaine has a smashing face?" Merbek said. "Lots of men think she has a smashing face."

Essuan looked at Merbek. "Yes, she's very attractive."

"Lots of men think so."

"That's enough, Sax," Elaine said. "Why don't we see if we can find the hotel?"

"There's nothing to do in the hotel. That's why we came over here. What are we going to do in the hotel?"

"What we can do in the hotel, darling, is not make an ass of ourselves in front of these nice people from Smalt."

Christina Essuan drank some of her coffee and reached across the table to put her hand in her husband's.

"The coffee is just lovely," she said.

"That boy never brought me my drink," Merbek said.

"I am going back to the hotel," Elaine said.

"Then you just do that. You take your smashing face back to the hotel. Waiter, another rye."

"I say, dear," Essuan remarked, "I didn't know it was so late. Isn't it time for that show you wanted to see?"

"Yes," she said. She stood up.

"Stay," Merbek said. "Don't let Elaine's nerves drive you away. You haven t even finished your coffee. And I want you to tell me about Smalt."

Elaine sipped some of her wine. She looked up at Christina.

"Oh, do sit down. There really isn't anywhere else to go. I know all about that. We've been here for three weeks now."

"Smalt is rather nice, really," Essuan said. "We've lived there for a year. I have a little fault-shielding contracting business in two of the larger cities."

A young man waved from the sidewalk. "Look," Merbek said, "it's your young fellow. My wife has a fellow, did you know that? This young man here, I forget his name, you know, but he thinks Elaine is simply smashing. He's one of her damn fellows." The waiter brought another rye whiskey and another white saucer. Merbek began a stack of the saucers.

"Now I do think it's time to go back," Elaine said. The young man hesitated for a moment, then came toward the table. Christina looked at her husband. He drank his coffee and shrugged.

"Mrs. Merbek," the young man said pleasantly. "How nice to see you."

Her hands fluttered on the table.

"Sax, this is Perez Teyjad. He's a waiter at that restaurant we went to. You know, the one with the—"

"I know which one."

"Yes," Elaine said. "Perez, this is Tom and Christina Essuan. They're from Smalt. They're stopping at our hotel, too."

"Very nice to meet you," the young man said. Without being invited, he drew up a chair to the table. He was tall and lean and sunburned from the hours he spent beneath lamps for just that effect. He spoke in a quiet, earnest voice, pitched low so that the women leaned toward him to catch his words.

"My wife enjoys the food at the place where Mr. Teyjad works," Merbek said. "She's suggested that we eat there several times in the three weeks we've been on Springfield. In all our travels, she seems to like that restaurant best. I wonder why that is." He finished his whiskey in one long swallow, looking at Teyjad over the glass. He signaled the waiter to bring another.

"My husband is jealous, you see. He used to be a very athletic young man himself. I fell in love with him in those days. He thinks that because he is not so young and not so athletic, I don't love him any longer."

"Mr. Teyjad is the very image of myself at his age," Merbek said. "Except that I was something better than a waiter."

"Let's see about that show," Christina said.

"Why not just stay where you are," Merbek said in a harsh voice.

Essuan was angry. "I say, Merbek, that's my wife you're speaking to."

"You must understand my husband," Elaine said, and laughed. It was a forced laugh and rather unpleasant. "When he was an athletic young man, he used to win all sorts of competitions. All sorts of them, didn't you, dear? I hope to God he did. I really don't think he ever came in second. His daddy wouldn't allow it, so Sax won all the time." She sipped some more of her wine and she was surprised when she finished it. "Naturally, that was all a long time ago. May I have another glass of wine?"

"Waiter," her husband called. When the waiter came, Merbek indicated the empty wine glass.

"All a long time ago," Elaine said. She smiled brightly.

"I still win, Elaine. I still won't come in second."

"Which competitions are these, darling? I can think of a few games in which someone, oh, like young Mr. Teyjad, for instance—"

"Damn your young Mr. Teyjad!"

"I was only pointing out, darling, that time catches up with us all." She looked at the Essuans. "That shouldn't be such a difficult thing to believe, should it?"

"It's very sad," Christina said.

"Very sad, she says," Merbek said. The waiter brought the glass of wine and the glass of rye whiskey. He put another saucer on Merbek's stack.

The young man stood up. "I have to go now," he said in a cold, furious voice. "I have to be at the restaurant soon."

"Wait a minute, Mr. Teyjad," Merbek said. "Young, strong, athletic Mr. Teyjad. My wife, who certainly knows an athletic young fellow when she sees one, has told me more than once just how young and athletic you are. Well, then, are you? Athletic, I mean. We can all see how young you are."

"You're just slightly tight, Mr. Merbek," Teyjad said. "I'd enjoy speaking with you another time."

"Isn't he generous?" Merbek said. He looked around the table happily. "Essuan, isn't the young man generous? Well, we'll see how athletic he is. I have a thousand right here that I'm willing to wager."

"Sax!" Elaine said.

"A thousand. You've never even seen a thousand, have you, Mr. Teyjad?"

The young man said nothing.

"Can you run, Mr. Teyjad? I imagine you can. My wife was suggesting games, and when you play those games you get very good at hiding under beds and running with your trousers down around your ankles. Can you run a mile in fifteen minutes, Mr. Teyjad? Without the usual encumbrance of trousers around your ankles?"

"Are you betting me a thousand that I can't finish a mile in fifteen minutes?"

Merbek waved a hand in the air. "Oh, but do let me set some conditions, or it wouldn't be a true contest. If you don't have a true contest, you can't win anything worthwhile. What I'm saying to you, Mr. Teyjad, is that I have a thousand that I'm willing to stake against your being able to cover a mile across the face of this asteroid within fifteen minutes."

Christina Essuan gasped. There was a long silence. Elaine looked from her husband to Teyjad.

"As I said, I have to go," the young man said.

Merbek laughed. "I'm glad at least you aren't easy. Five thousand, then."

"Sax, stop it!" Elaine said.

"Ten thousand," Merbek said.

They all looked at Teyjad. "I know what he's going to say," Christina whispered. "He's going to do it."

"He's going to try," Merbek said. "Aren't you, Mr. Teyjad?"

"I'll do it, for twenty thousand."

Merbek looked at the young man, and then he looked at Elaine, and then he turned and stared for a few seconds into the dark part of the café's bar. When he spoke there was wonder in his voice. "Could I have been wrong about him, do you think? Could she have been right all along?"

"What do you say, Sax?" Elaine asked.

"Of course, Christ, of course. Twenty thousand." Merbek took a thick black wallet from the inside of his jacket. He took out several bills in large denominations. "We want a pressure suit with fifteen minutes of oxygen in the tank. You'll drive out a mile from the dome in a surface car, get out, and make it back as fast as you can. Mr. Essuan, here is twenty thousand. Would you do us the honor of holding it?"

Essuan accepted the money. "I hate the idea of having anything at all to do with this."

"And would you be so kind as to make the arrangements, Mr. Essuan?" Merbek said.

Essuan looked helplessly to his wife. She was excited now by the wager. "Do it, Tom," she said. "Go into the bar and hire a surface car."

Essuan shook his head and got to his feet and walked into the bar. He came back in a little while. "Anytime," he said.

"When shall I leave?" Teyjad asked.

"Whenever you like," Merbek said. "But do go soon. It's almost dinnertime."

"I'll go now, then. That way I'll be able to collect the money and get to work on time." There was a bit of contempt in his voice.

"You must have a real calling," Merbek said. "Essuan, you will have to accompany him in the surface car. I will trust you to make sure this is carried out fairly and honestly."

"I want to go, too," Elaine said. Her eyes were very bright.

"Yes, no doubt you do," Merbek said in a tired voice. He massaged his forehead with one hand. "Stand on the sidelines with your paper pompom. Cheer the young fellow on to victory and all that."

"Then let's go," Teyjad said.

The young man, Elaine, and Essuan waited for a taxi to take them to the dayside portal. It did not take long for the taxi to come. Merbek and Christina sat at the table and watched as the others got into the car and drove away.

"Well, this is certainly an interesting way to pass the afternoon," Christina said.

"Do you think so?" Merbek asked.

"Why, yes. Your wife was quite right about there being nothing to do in the afternoon. There really is nothing. And you've been here for three weeks. It must be simply awful sometimes. I say, do you do this sort of thing often?"

"What sort of thing?" Merbek looked at her and frowned. "Sit in a café and have too much to drink? Yes, I do that rather frequently."

"No, I meant wagering such huge sums of money. I must say, even though Tom, my husband, has a rather tidy income and we live comfortably enough, I don't believe he'll ever pick twenty thousand out of a wallet and put it at risk like that."

"He ought to try it. It can be damned invigorating." Merbek turned away from her and looked into the bar.

"This café is simply grand," Christina said.

"Except that you can't get the waiters to bring you a drink. Would you like another coffee, or a drink?"

"I would simply adore a gin fizz."

Merbek signaled to the waiter and ordered two drinks. This time the waiter brought them quickly.

"Thank you," Christina said. "Very nice of you."

"I hate to drink alone," Merbek said. "Well, bung-o."

"Bung-o."

There was a long silence. "I apologize if I spoke rudely to you before," Merbek said.

"Oh, never mind about that." She laughed.

"Elaine's right, you know. About the way I get when I've had too much."

"Well," Christina said.

Merbek and Christina sat on the terrace and watched the people walking by on the sidewalk. There were people wearing the odd costumes of their home worlds, and other people who did not want to be taken for tourists, and occasionally there were natives of Springfield who did not want to be taken for natives. The traffic in this part of the city was made up mostly of taxis and buses filled with tourists stopping at the hotels. Now and then a sidewalk annie strolled by, shrewdly looking over the crowd in the café. Merbek caught the eye of one pretty young woman and quickly looked away.

A taxi pulled up at the café and Elaine and Essuan got out. Essuan paid the fare and the cab drove away. "We're back," Elaine said.

"I suppose he got out all right?" Merbek said.

"Just fine," Essuan said. "I say, it was interesting to ride out across the surface. We all had to wear pressure suits because he was getting out. The suits are supposed to be cooled, you know, but it was damned hot. He'll have more of a contest than he expected."

"I'm sure," Merbek said.

"There's a flat plain all around the dome," Elaine said. "But it's dreadfully torn up with craters and ridges and things."

"And damned hot," Essuan said.

"Yes, it was hot," Elaine said. "What time is it?"

Essuan looked at his watch. "Well, we let him out at twelve minutes past four, and then it took us twenty minutes to get here. It's 4:32."

"Then he is already in the air lock," Christina said.

"But you have no idea of how bad the traffic is in the city at this time of day," Essuan said. "He won't be here for twenty minutes or half an hour more."

"I know something about competition," Merbek said. "I used to be rather good in my day, you know. I used to be a runner, a damn fine runner." He swallowed some whiskey.

"A sprinter?" Essuan asked. "Or distance?"

Merbek smiled. "Both," he said proudly. "I used to run the hundred meters, the two-hundred, the four-hundred, the eight-hundred, the fifteen-hundred, and the five- and ten-thousand. I never took up the marathon, though. Always thought it was more theatrical than athletic."

"And you always won?" Christina asked.

"At the games on Virtu I won seven gold medals in those events. No one else has ever won seven gold medals in one competition."

"Then why didn't you go out to watch him run?" Christina asked. "I should have thought you'd be interested."

"I couldn't do that. You compete only when you have something left to prove. I am no longer the competitor. I am now the challenge. It isn't the running that will test him. I must wait for him to come to me, because he is trying to conquer me, not the distance." He finished the whiskey in his glass and laughed. "I am the contest, and Elaine is the prize."

"I say, in any event he ought to be here soon," Essuan said.

"Then let's have one more round before he does," Merbek said. "I'm sure I'll need it." He called the waiter and placed the order.

They talked and watched the traffic pass by the café. Teyjad still hadn't arrived when the waiter brought the drinks.

"What time is it now?" Elaine asked.

"I say, it's already four minutes past five," Essuan said.

"If he used the full fifteen minutes to get back to the dome, that would make it 4:27. He should have been here by five o'clock," Elaine declared.

"The traffic," Essuan said.

"Yes, of course," Christina said. They watched the street, waiting for Teyjad to step from every taxi that paused in the slow-moving knot of vehicles on Long Street.

"Christina, you know what you've been told about too much excitement," Essuan said. "This suspense is bad for you. I'll take you back to the hotel, and for dinner we'll go to the restaurant where the young man works. He'll tell you all about it later."

"If you think that's best," Christina said.

They stood up and Christina walked away from the table. Essuan reached into his pocket and took out the twenty thousand. He gave Merbek a black, reproachful look and dropped the bills on the table. Then he joined his wife. They waited for a break in the traffic and crossed the street and went into the hotel.

"What are you going to tell him when he gets here?" Elaine asked.

"Why should I tell him anything? I'll give him the money. I don't see why I should be gracious about it, too."

"Sax, don't think he doesn't know that you're using him to make some silly point. He's a smart boy."

"They're all smart boys at that age."

"When he's old enough, he'll realize that you humiliated him."

"The twenty thousand will bind his wounds. That's something else I learned a long time ago. What do you want me to say? 'Congratulations, you're the better man. Take my wife and my money. I'll just go up to my room and put a shawl around my shoulders?' I won't do that."

"Don't talk rot, Sax. He's just a pretty boy. He never meant anything at all to me."

They sat in silence for a long time. The lights in their hotel went on and the workers began to leave the office buildings. In a little while the artificial twilight began to lengthen the shadows. A taxi stopped beside the café and a young man and a girl got out, laughing as if it were the most natural thing in the world. Merbek and his wife had finished their drinks, but the waiter did not disturb them. They watched as the cars on Long Street switched on their headlamps. In a little while no more people came out of the office buildings, and the traffic in the street thinned.

Elaine put a hand over her eyes so that Merbek would not see that she was crying. He saw anyway. After a while she got up from the table. Her face was as drawn and drained of color as Merbek had ever seen it. She ran out of the café and through the cars and into the hotel.

Merbek stared after her. For a long time it was as though he were dreaming. Then he called to the waiter. "Bring me one more rye," he said. The waiter nodded.

The waiter came with the whiskey and put it on the table.

"You've been very patient," Merbek said. "I'd like to buy you a drink."

"I'm very sorry, sir," the waiter said. "The manager doesn't permit us to drink while we're working."

"No? Then what time are you finished? I'll buy you a drink when you're finished."

"Seven o'clock, sir."

"I'll wait," Merbek said. He drank the whiskey quickly and stood up and went out of the café.

The waiter watched him walk unsteadily across the street. When he saw that Merbek had reached the other side safely, he went to clear away the things on the table. He saw a small pile of money lying beside the stack of white saucers. They were all large bills. "*Meu Deus*," the waiter whispered. He looked up and saw that Merbek had gone into the hotel. The waiter folded the twenty thousand and put it into the pocket of his apron. Then he picked up the whiskey glasses and white saucers and went back into the bar.

✝ ✝ ✝

Two Bits

WELL, I BET YOU THOUGHT YOU WAS NEVER goin' to see your 5 hundred again but the fight supprised us just like it supprised a lot o' folks. Now we are on our way on this rattletrap bucket of a ship somewheres called Peachtree where Two Bits will fight the great Suzavod. Who is Suzavod or really what is a Suzavod I hear you ast, and believe me I ast the same damn thing. I suppose we'll find out when we get there, just like we found out all about Kid Jupiter hisself.

Now you know when I come bustin' in again sometime with a hot tip you ought to do like I says. If you had went with 1 or 2 thousand instead of your measly ½, you would be rollin' in the dough. I wisht I had follored my own advice and then I would be rollin' in it to. Now I know I can lissen to Mick and even to Perbidge hisself. I can promise you that if they tell me Two Bits is in good shape I will put up 1 or 2 thousand o' my own funds against the great Suzavod and will write to you so you will have the chanct to double your money all so.

When we come to Springfield I and Mick never knowed o' Jendin Perbidge nor any other fighter there and we was both supprised to hear that they was a contender right in Springfield. When Mick says we wanted to find a fighter and this fella Perbidge turns up, I and Mick didn't put no stock in it when he says he was the number 1 welter contender. Mick give him a look in the gym, and Perbidge seemed like at least he had saw the ring from both sides o' the ropes, so Mick says to me that we ought to take him on.

Now old pal you recall where we come from a fighter with a handle like Jendin Perbidge would of never got a bout with a 1 legged grandmother, so I said to Mick, "We got to find a good name for him."

"What's wrong with my name?" ast this Perbidge.

"It don't sound right enough by ½," I says.

"Don't worry," says Mick, "we'll come up with somethin' good. How's about Black Death Perbidge?"

"Naw," says our boy, "it makes me sound like a fry cook on a ferryboat. My name was O.K. with my pa and it was O.K. with my ma and all my brothers has never said nothin' that it was a bad name, so I guess I'll just stick with it a wile longer. I guess I know what my own name ought to be. You can't just take a fella and tell him that from now on his name is goin' to be somethin' different and he ought to hurry up and get used to it. I can throw a right cross just as good as Jendin Perbidge as I can anything else, and if yo boys don't like my name the way it is and won't honor our contract, you can just do the other thing with it."

Mick thought a wile and then he said:

"How's about Butcher Perbidge? We ain't had no Butcher in a long time."

"Sounds all right to me," I says.

"Naw," says Perbidge. "You couldn't get away with callin' me anything like Butcher on account o' my ma. She never liked for me to be no boxer in the 1st place and so I promised her that I would never hurt nobody unless they was hurtin' me. So I say I don't see why my own name ain't good enough. My ma would think I wasn't keepin' my word if she come out to the fight and everybody was callin' me Butcher. An' another thing. Rosie—that's my girl—Rosie would hate it right off the reel. She says she likes me just the way I am and probily couldn't never set around and talk with no joker called Butcher. They's a hole lot o' reasons and if you give a minute I will think up 1 or 2 more."

I give Mick the wink and I says, "Our boy likes to get his value from his two bits worth."

All of a sudden I seen Mick's eyes have lit up. "That's him all right," he says. "Two Bits Perbidge, the welter champeen o' the universe."

Well old pal Perbidge looked like he smelt somethin' funny and he says, "Say, what kind o' crack is that?"

And Mick says, "It ain't no crack a tall."

"Then how come it sounds like a crack to me?"

Mick give me the wink back and says, "Two bits is what you give the porter to put out the lights, get it?"

Well it looked to me like Perbidge don't get much o' nothin', so I says, "Just like you put out the lights of everybody you fight," and I guess he liked that all right.

"But how come I got to have any nick name a tall?" he ast.

" 'Cause Jendin Perbidge sounds like a wash woman is why," says Mick.

For a second I thought our boy was goin' cut loose on Mick's chin, but the boy cooled down some and finally agreed as long as all the posters used his real name to. That was in case some iggorant stranger might mix him up with all the other Perbidges around, and so you saw all the posters that said Jendin "Two Bits" Perbidge and I guess to this day he don't know how come he got that name. You could probily visit him on Springfield and he'd be glad to give you his two bits on any subject you care to mention.

Well it was about this time that they was lookin' for a new welter champ of everywhere on account o' they hadn't been none ever since the old champ, Kid Hoegemenimer, was ate just after his fight with Foyg on Blue Skies. So they was no welter champ and all the contenders got to take each other on and the 1 that licked 'em all would get the title. Two Bits give out the information that these other guys think they could be champ but the most o' them should ought to of stayed barbers or waiters or what they was before. It wasn't only that Two Bits got an opinion on everything and everybody, but that he liked to talk both your ears off and your nose tellin' you about it. When he started gettin' in shape he didn't like nothin' about the food or the hotel or all the work, and he kept talkin' until I and Mick couldn't lissen to the sound o' his voice no more. I slipped the mouthpiece in and he talked some more, and wile he's circlin' his sparrin' partner he's still yakkin'. "Hit him a couple in the face," Mick says to the sparrin' boy. "Maybe that will shut his yap." But it didn't.

One day this promoter name o' Dugel come into the gym. He watched Two Bits dancin' round for a little bit and then he says, "Is that the boy you're aimin' at the welter title?"

Mick nodded but didn't say nothin'. We run into this Dugel before.

"I got a boy workin' out all so," says Dugel.

Nobody says nothin' for a wile.

"The way I sees it," says Mick, "Perbidge here has got as good a chanct as any of 'em."

"Well," says Dugel, "I like my boy pretty good."

They was another minute or 2 when neither o' them says nothin'. Finally Dugel says:

"Your boy got to fight my boy sooner or later if he wants to be champ."

Mick says, "What's your boy's name?"

"Kid Jupiter."

I and Mick looked at each other. "I ain't never heard o' your boy," says Mick.

"An' I ain't never heard o' yours neither," says Dugel. "They mustn't be only a few fighters that knowed o' Kid Jupiter, but I bet oncet they are carried out o' the ring they don't forget him."

It went on like that for a wile, but before Two Bits is done workin' out Mack has signed a contract for him to go up against Dugel's Kid Jupiter. Dugel just happened to of had a couple blank contracts in his pocket.

Mick told Perbidge about the fight and Two Bits says that he never knowed o' no Kid Jupiter on Springfield nor anyplace else. Mick looked at me and says:

"You got to look up that boy in the book to-morrow to find out how many fights he has and how many knockouts. We got to know what we're up against."

"Sure," I says and I made a note to see if Kid Jupiter got the goods or not.

And then Mick wanted to know if Two Bits hisself got the goods.

"Perbidge," he says, "how many fights you been in?"

Two Bits got a look on his face which on somebody else might mean they was thinkin' hard but on his pan it was like a shadow a little cloud might make. They was never nothin' behind it. He says, "46 countin' the time they brang a big paper bag and I boxed my way out of it to settle a bet."

"And how many times did you happen to win?" says Mick.

"37," says Perbidge.

"Does that count the paper bag or don't it?" I ast.

Well, Mick decided that we had a shot at Kid Jupiter no matter how good that boy was, as long as Two Bits stood away from the skirts and the drinkin'. We figgured his girl Rosie would take care o' that for us. This Rosie was one that didn't nobody want to tangle with 'cep' Perbidge hisself. Mick talked to her and fixed it up that she should look out for her darlin' until after the bout. "Ain't nobody goin' to have no fun till after he flattens Kid Jupiter," Rosie complained.

Mick nodded and says, "That's the way it is. All's fare in love," and she wants to know what of it. Mick says, " 'Cause every time you look around you got to pay somehow," and she knowed what he meant right off.

At supper it was somethin' to see Two Bits dig in. He et like all the air in Springfield was leakin' out through a hole in the dome and he got to leave the table in a minute. The funny part was that he didn't never stop talkin'. I saw him put ½ a steak in his yap at one time and go on about his pa or 1 o' his bouts or somethin' else didn't nobody want to hear about. He talked from the time he set down till he almost et the shine off his plate. I and Mick learnt to appresiate his talkin' so we never lissened to a word of it, but his girl Rosie payed attention to every single thing like they was somethin' special in it for her. Generally he always et the last bit o' food and was walkin' away yammerin' to Rosie before I and Mick even got the forks to our mouths oncet.

The big news was the next day when I learnt all about Dugel's boy.

"This is goin' to be some fight," I says to Mick.

"I'm pretty glad to hear it," he says. "How come you say that?"

" 'Cause Kid Jupiter ain't no boy."

I thought Mick's jaw was goin' to drop clean off the way he was lookin' at me. "You mean Two Bits is goin' to fight some girl?" That didn't bother him so much 'cause didn't neither of us have no trouble picturin' Perbidge givin' the wallop to some dizzy skirt. It wouldn't of bothered Two Bits none either.

"No," I says, "this Kid Jupiter ain't even a person."

Mick kind o' covers his eyes with a hand and asts in a real tired voice, "What is he then?"

And I says, "He's a big worm. A Jovian flameworm."

"Some day I'm goin' to murder that Dugel, you just see if I don't," says Mick. "Does our boob know yet?"

"No," I says.

"Well I got to tell him. We shouldn't ought to of come here in the 1st place. Have you even saw 1 o' them flameworms fight? Ain't no man alive can beat a flameworm if it's trained. I wisht I knowed how Dugel managed it."

It was a real tough spot. A Jovian flameworm is a thing can't no person whup it 'cause it's to dumb to know it's hurt. They was only 1 other flameworm in the fight game a long time ago and it never oncet lost or drawed a match. It was finally kilt by a angry crowd and cooked in butter and garlic and so retired undefeated light heavyweight champeen. They ain't more o' 'em boxin' 'cause they are generally all so to dumb to learn the rules.

Mick looked like he had a idear. I hoped he did have 1, 'cause I knowed I didn't. "Jendin," he says, and Two Bits ought to of tumbled that somethin' was up 'cause Mick didn't never call him Jendin. "I just learnt somethin' that will make you happy and your poor old ma to."

Perbidge looked interested. "What's that, Mick," he ast.

"I learnt somethin' about this Kid Jupiter. He ain't a boy exactly. He's 1 o' these flameworms that you see sometimes givin' kids rides out to the zoo."

Two Bits thought this over and he didn't go for it a tall.

"I ain't gettin' in the ring with no worm," he says. I couldn't blame him, and Mick felt the same way 'cep' for the signed contract he got with Dugel. "I ain't afraid to go up against nobody," says Perbidge.

"If you come to me and say I got to fight the heaveyweight champ o' the universe, well I'd give it a shot. I ain't scared o' no man 'cause I figger no matter what he's got, I got somethin' all so and I can come back at him. I got the wallop and alls I need is the chanct to unload it. I got a Sunday punch and then some. But none o' that means a bug in a brick factory to a Jovian flameworm. I heard all about that other 1 that got et and somethin' tells me that's the only way to get a flameworm to lay down quiet." Two Bits went on for a wile but Mick must of thought to let the kid get it out o' his system.

"But look at it this way," says Mick. "You can't hurt him no matter how hard you try. They got skins that fixes theyself up real fast. If you cut it, the cut closes up in a couple o' seconds and it's like you never layed a glove on it. You can't knock its wind out and it ain't even got no jaw to clip."

"My ma will be happy to know that," says Perbidge. "But then how'm I s'posed to lick it?"

Well old pal you can see how Two Bits cut right to the meat o' the trouble. Mick thought for a second or 2 and says, "Leave that to me. We need some kind o' fancy stragety."

O' course, Perbidge talked about this and that for another long wile, but he couldn't make no decision on his own. Before he said yest or no he looked to his girl Rosie. Rosie didn't care if Two Bits clumb into the ring with a Jovian flameworm or her great-aunt Elsie. "It's a welterweight, ain't it?" she says.

"Yes," I says.

"Then Jendin will knock its block off." I and Mick declined to tell her that flameworms come generally without no blocks a tall.

We had 3 more weeks till the fight with Kid Jupiter but Two Bits didn't hardly need no more work. He was sluggin' the heavy bag and rattlin' the speed bag and bustin' his sparrin' partners like he was already champ. Nobody said much about Jovian flameworms and slowly but surely the day o' the fight come closer. You remember old pal how the bout was moved from the Civic Gym to the St. Bernard Auditorium on account of all the interest in our boy goin' up against a Jovian flameworm. None o' that made Perbidge nervous. I think that's when Mick and I decided we really liked this kid 'cause he didn't scare none or else he was plain bug nuts.

Mick said he was goin' to think up a stragety for our boy but ½ hour before the bout he still hadn't come up with nothin'. We was gettin' Two Bits dressed an' I was rubbin' his arms off when Rosie come in to wisht him luck. She was no bear for looks but I guess lots o' guys could of went for her when they got to know her some. Two Bits was wearin' maroon trunks with a white stripe and Rosie wanted to know what Kid Jupiter was wearin'. Didn't none of us know and I don't think we care to much neither. Rosie kist her boy and told him she'd be back after the fight with all the money. I guess she was bettin' all they had but I couldn't say on Perbidge or the worm.

"Well," says Two Bits, "you said you was goin' to give me a secret plan so's I don't get kilt by this worm."

Mick gave him a smile and says a lot o' nothin' about keepin' his guard up and not lettin' Kid Jupiter have no openin'. Our boy knowed real fast that Mick didn't have no plan a tall. Perbidge started his yammerin', goin' on about how Mick was sendin' him helpless into the ring against some kind o' creature which didn't care if Perbidge got kilt or not or wouldn't know the difference. Two Bits talked and talked till they was only a minute before it was time to leave the locker room.

"All I can say," says Mick, "is they has got to be a way to beat 'em. Even flameworms don't live forever."

"They don't?" ast Perbidge.

"Well," says Mick, "I guess they do."

They come for us and we beat it out o' there through the tunnel and up into the crowd. Everybody in the place was cheerin' for Two Bits and I don't think the worm had a friend in the crowd 'cep' for Dugel hisself. Our boy clumb in through the ropes and I and Mick went with him and we plunked him down in his corner and started in to workin' him up. Mick gave him advice and I rubbed his neck and shoulders.

Then they was a big yell and I seen the flameworm and Dugel comin' up the isle. They wasn't nobody happy to see the worm and they all hooted when Kid Jupiter had trouble gettin' through the ropes. Them worms can squinch theyself into any shape they want, and Kid Jupiter was walkin' on 2 short legs as big around as sewer pipe, with 2 long arms with boxin' gloves on the ends and not much of a head to speak of. Dugel had a pair o' green trunks on it with a yella stripe.

Some fella innerduced them and they was a big cheer when he says, "From Springfield's own 9th Ward, wearin' maroon trunks an' weighin' 144 pounds, our own Jendin 'Two Bits' Perbidge." They yelled and screamed and maybe they would of never settled down 'cep' the fella turned to Kid Jupiter and then they wasn't nobody much interested.

The referee called the fighters to the middle o' the ring and give 'em the rules. Two Bits touched gloves with Kid Jupiter and come back to the corner. "It give me a shiver just to touch him," he says. Then the bell rung and they was at it.

I'll give Perbidge the nod for looks. He got out there and started circlin' the flameworm and bobbin' and weavin' right out o' the book. Kid Jupiter just stood there and waited for Two Bits to bring the fight to him. I and Mick knowed that was the bunk. The only chanct our boy got was to stay away from the worm. But if Perbidge didn't start nothin' they wasn't nothin' goin' to get started, 'cause Kid Jupiter was to dumb to know he was in a fight. So the referee says somethin' to Two Bits and the boy says somethin' back and moves in on Kid Jupiter. The worm put up his dukes and even though they was worm's dukes I and Mick was worried about our boy.

Two Bits scored the 1st point, a terrible uppercut to the body that ought to of flattened the Kid but nothin' come of it. Two Bits danced back a bit and watched. The worm follered him round and jabbed with its straight right. It done that 'cause to a Jovian flameworm it don't make no difference if it leads with its right or left. Perbidge busted it a few in the body and swung a left hook at its knobby little head. Even though our boy hit a couple o' good ones it didn't bother the worm none. A Jovian flameworm can shake off a hurt in 4 or 5 seconds. They was some more dancin' and then the 1st round come to an end.

"It's like punchin' a paper sack full o' ice cream," says Two Bits. I was flappin' a towel to cool him off and Mick was rubbin' the boy's arms.

"If you stay out o' his way for 10 rounds," says Mick, "you're goin' to win on points for sure."

"I couldn't face my pa if I don't give it all I got," says Two Bits.

"Now I know you got the nerve," I says.

Our boy kept talkin' about how he got to fight so as his pa would know he was no lily liver. Two Bits talked till the bell rung. Kid Jupiter come out o' his corner and the referee was callin' Perbidge out and still he talked, right into Round 2. If you remember old pal Round 2 was all the worm's. It was a awful round, a specially 'cause Two Bits catched one blow after another and he didn't never stop conversin'. I don't think Kid Jupiter was payin' much attention and I know the referee didn't care nothin', and I and Mick couldn't hear good but Perbidge didn't clam up just the same.

Kid Jupiter whammed him good in the stumach and then hit him again so hard Two Bits ought to of set down and thought the hole thing over but he didn't. The worm cut off the ring and Perbidge didn't have nowheres to go. He kept his gloves in front o' his pan and Kid Jupiter whammed him in the stumach again. Two Bits dropped his hands and Kid Jupiter walloped him on the chin.

"The Kid sure fixed up his map that time," says Mick.

When the flameworm started in on Two Bits, his girl Rosie came up to where we was. "What's he doin' in there?" she ast.

"He's givin' your boy a beatin', girlie," says Mick.

That wasn't what Rosie ast a tall. "What's Jendin doin'?" she says.

"He's yappin', what else!" I says.

It looked to me that Two Bits hardly knowed where he was, and Kid Jupiter was fixin' to wham him good but the bell rung. Mick ought not to of went out there to bring Perbidge back to the corner 'cause that was my job, but Mick was worried sick.

"I never seen nothin' like this Kid Jupiter," says Two Bits. "Can't Foyg nor any man stand up to me when I am right. You hit this worm and his skin turns green for a wile and then it's like you never hit him a tall. And if you bust him in the stumach it don't do no good and if you bust him in the head it don't do no good neither. I hope you got that secret idear ready 'cause if you don't we're goin' to be in big trouble. This Kid Jupiter is plenty tough and then some. You better tell me what to do or I ain't lastin' here only another round."

"Say, kid," says Mick, "I got the idear right here."

"Well, what is it?" says our boy. I wanted to hear it to.

"What you got to do is keep after him. I saw in the 1st round before you set up as Kid's punchin' bag that every time you busted him he went green. If you bust him real fast again he turned greener. Try bustin' him one two three and don't let up and we will see what happens. Maybe they's a limit to how fast he can shake it off."

Perbidge would rather of kissed Mick than lissen to his idear. "You want I should clinch with the worm and wham him?" he says.

"Wham him good," says Mick.

The bell rung for Round 3 and Two Bits got Kid Jupiter in the middle o' the ring. First thing I seen is our boy in close and wham he busted the Kid in the body. The worm went green. Wham went Perbidge and the worm went greener. Wham wham wham. The flameworm looked like he ought to of went somewheres to get sick. He was the color o' the stuff that floats on the top o' Lake Lee. But Perbidge didn't stop. Wham wham wham. Two Bits keeps bustin' the worm till I and Mick knowed Mick was right. He was supprised 'cause he didn't hardly think what he said would of really worked. Kid Jupiter wobbled around and then bam he's down and the hole place was yellin' and screamin' like they was little flameworms eatin' everybody in the cheap seats.

Rosie was smilin' and Mick was laughin' but I was worried on account o' Two Bits was still in the middle o' the ring makin' a speech to the referee. He was probily tellin' about how this was all Mick's idear and all the credit should ought to go to Mick and what not. O' course this ain't by far the 1st Long Count in boxin' history but it was the only one I knowed that was a specially nuts. Mick figgered Two Bits trimmed the worm and he wasn't appresiatin' what was happenin', 'cause he was still cellabratin' with Rosie. The referee was pushin' Perbidge towards the nutral corner but our boy got to talk. The flameworm got overloaded or somethin' but it didn't take only 15 seconds and Kid Jupiter was back up ready to go. Two Bits was still goin' on and the referee looked to give it up. Now Mick seen what happened and he don't say nothin', he just looked madder'n a bee on a hot iron. The referee separated Two Bits and Kid Jupiter and then they went at it again. First thing wham the flameworm knocked Perbidge down and ought to of layed him out for the night but Two Bits is just as dumb as the worm and all so don't know when he is hurt. Then the bell rung and I guess you thought you could of kist your 5 hundred good-by.

It was a uphill battle for Two Bits just then, Mick said that he should of stood with bustin' Kid Jupiter till the flameworm gone down again, but Perbidge come back with the information that he was seein' stars and hurtin' from Round 3, but our hero as you might call him was strong enough to talk us into the ground so as we were glad when the bell rung again to start Round 4. "If he loses to a damn worm then won't nobody give him another fight," says Rosie and I guess she knowed what she was talkin' about. We watched Two Bits come up to Kid Jupiter to bust him like Mick said, but the flameworm gave him a wallop on the chin and Perbidge went down. Dugel give a loud whistle and didn't have no trouble gettin' the Kid to go to a corner. Mick looked sick and Rosie turned away but I seen our boy jawin' with the referee and I knowed he was O.K. When the count got to 8 Perbidge got up and shaked his head. The sap ought to of stayed away till the end o' the round but he went in on the Kid and the worm give him another wallop and the bell rung. We went out to collect our boy and drug him back to the corner.

"You want I should throw in the towel?" I ast but Mick says no.

"Jendin," says his girl Rosie, "I don't hardly think I can marry nobody that loses to a worm."

"And you ain't goin' to neither," says Mick. Then it was Round 5 and Two Bits knowed what he got to do. He all most run acrost the ring and give Kid Jupiter a swell wallop and the worm went all over green. Wham Perbidge give him another and wham another still. Two Bits busted that flameworm 1 after another till the Kid got as green as the Springfield dome. Our boy hit him with uppercuts again and plop the worm went to the canvas. This time Two Bits shuts hisself up long enough to go to a nutral corner.

"1, 2, 3," says the referee and the flameworm was healing fast.

"4, 5, 6," goes the count and the green was fadin' and Dugel was yellin' to Kid Jupiter to git to his feet.

"7, 8, 9, 10, Your out!" Everybody in the place screamed and our boy Perbidge is a winner by a knockout. His girl Rosie run out and give her boy a hug and kiss. Mick breathed easy and I was pretty happy myself. Then Kid Jupiter was all right and got up and shook hands with Two Bits and I seen it give the boy a shiver all though he ought to of been used to it by then.

We had a wingding afterwards in a place acrost from our hotel and Dugel and Kid Jupiter come up to us. "You know you ought to buy me a drink," says Dugel, "'cause oncet you knowed my boy's secret they won't never be no more Jovian flameworms in the boxin' game. You have ruint me."

I and Mick laughed at that. "You won't never be ruint," says Mick. "Not as long as they is 1 fighter left that will lay down for 50 big ones."

Dugel got a kick out o' that to. He had a drink with us and they brang Kid Jupiter a awful lookin' bowl o' somethin' and he slurpt it all up. All of us 'cep' Dugel won a pile o' money and we had a great party, a specially as how every time Two Bits looked like he was goin' to start yammerin' his girl Rosie kist him on the mouth to shut him up.

Two Bits wasn't lyin' when he said can't no other man lick him when he's right. Now we are goin' to Peachtree to find out about this great Suzavod. Our boy is in swell shape so if the great Suzavod ain't worse'n a Jovian flameworm I guess you will hear soon that Perbidge is the new welter champ o' the universe. And if you don't put no more'n 5 hundred on our boy then you are as cheap as they say.

+ + +

the artist passes it by

boss here i am
on springfield
this big green dome
on a rock in the middle
of nowhere
don t ask me
how i got here
i was just looking
to get in out of the rain
and the next thing i know i
am spending three months
in the belly of a freighter
tiptoeing through space

i ran into our friend
the bohemian lady cat
in this place here
they call the old quarter
the old quarter of what they
won t tell me or where
they ve thrown the other three quarters
but anyway
it won t surprise you to learn
that the old quarter

is where the feline dancer
has taken up residence it
reminds me of her digs at home
only shabbier dirtier and more
odiferous
i have nosed around here says
the lady cat
it s a stimulating place
for an artist like myself
but i think i ll go home
in a while

first i saw a place
she says
that claimed it was the
ultimate dining experience i
sampled of their cuisine
in the garbage in the alley
it made me sad to think
flameworm chowder
will always be downhill
from there
another place advertised the
ultimate in holodot fidelity
well says she
you know that fidelity
has never been
a major concern in my
pursuit of happiness so
i walked on
until i saw
in fiery big letters
metasense
the ultimate experience

* * *

i didn't go in sniffs
our feline friend
if i want
to be disappointed
by the ultimate experience
i will just wait
for my next honeymoon
toujours gai kid toujours gai

✝   ✝   ✝

The Day the Invaders Came

SOME READERS HAVE WRITTEN TO ME ABOUT THE
way I portray my grandfather in these stories. They complain
that he's shown as a cranky, cantankerous old galoot, and that he
was shut up in the attic just because he sometimes forgot what year
it was. "You're awful cruel, son," wrote one correspondent, "so let
that nice old codger out from the attic for a change!" Well, I suppose there is some truth in the accusation, although it was never
I who put him up there—mostly grandfather retreated to the attic
when the rest of our excitable family started to give him the nervous jimjams. He came downstairs often enough when he felt
better, and whenever he did he caused some kind of ruckus. That's
what happened the day he defended Springfield when the invaders
came.

We were living in a big white house at 154 State Street, about
a half mile from the wall of the dome. We were so close to the
dome that from the attic window, which we could look out of only
when grandfather was out of the house on one of his mysterious
errands, we thought we could see beyond to the lifeless black face
of the asteroid itself. My father tried to explain that we simply
couldn't see craters from our house, because the dome was tinted a
deep green and the artificial sunlight made it impossible to see out.

That didn't stop me from believing that I could see craters. My younger brother, Parren, told a story for years about the dinosaur he had glimpsed creeping among the rills and ridges beyond the dome. We all told him that was impossible, too, but he just got stubborn and maintained that he'd seen what he had seen. My mother had the experience once of imagining that she'd observed a large three-masted sailing vessel scudding across the barren landscape, sails billowing full in the wind. My father almost went berserk. "There isn't any wind out there," he argued. My mother just shook her head defiantly. She said that she had awakened Parren, who slept in the same room with her, and pointed it out to him; but Parren reported that nothing of the sort had happened. My mother tried to make a deal with him, offering to believe in his dinosaur if he'd believe in her ship, but Parren didn't care about such a thing. He knew he had seen his dinosaur, and he didn't need mother's insincere testimony to support his claim.

Grandfather was also fascinated by the forbidding territory beyond the dome. He disappeared sometimes, and when he returned he brought back wild tales of his adventures out on the nightside of the asteroid. He generally had one of two kinds of stories: either he prospected among the low hills, certain that gold and jewels and other riches were just waiting to be discovered; or else he fancied that the treacherous Cycladians were planning a sneak attack on Springfield, and that he had to hurry to his observation post. Grandfather had been in the army during the war with the Cycladians, but that had been more than sixty years ago, and peace had been made with them a long time ago. Even during the war, they had never come nearer to Springfield than four or five light-years. Grandfather had never seen any Cycladians in his entire life. He didn't even know what they looked like.

Still, every few months he borrowed father's groundcar and raced across the asteroid to an abandoned shack near the dayside. That is what happened on the morning of the day the invaders came. Our maid, Mella, came into the kitchen with a tray. "The old gennamun he ain't there," she said. She put grandfather's breakfast on the table, and my older brother, Rys, who had finished his own, began to eat grandfather's.

Mother's expression grew worried. She looked at me. "Go tell your father," she said. "Wake him up and tell him that grandfather's gone again." I didn't like the job of waking my father, but you didn't argue with mother about things like that. You didn't argue with her about anything.

My father's reaction was less concerned. He had been through all of this many times before; it just meant renting another ground-car and fetching grandfather home again. Whether grandfather was poking around for gold or keeping a weather eye out for the Cycladians, our task would be long and tiresome.

My brothers and I always looked forward to these expeditions, but my mother continued to fret and my father was just plain annoyed. We climbed into the rented groundcar, my parents in the front and the three of us behind them. Mother, as was her habit, gave my father directions in an appalled tone of voice, convinced of the imminent destruction of her entire family and her with it. My father, in retaliation, kept growling that we should lay off the arguing and wrestling in the back seat. And so the time passed as we emerged from the nightside portal and hurried toward grandfather's fortress.

We did not get outside the dome very often, so these drives were something of a treat, although the truth was that one part of the asteroid looked exactly like any other part. The darkness and the silence frightened my mother, I know, and my father was never enthusiastic about leaving the dome, either; but my brothers and I always stared with wide-open eyes at the grim terrain. "Here's where the dinosaur was," said Parren at one point. I heard my father sigh.

"How can you tell?" demanded Rys.

"I can see its tracks," replied my younger brother. We were all tired of hearing about his dinosaur, so no further inquiry was made. We weren't far, in any event, from our destination.

We checked each other's pressure suits and climbed out of the groundcar. Father led us through the shack's airlock, and when we were safely inside we shucked out of the heavy suits. Grandfather was astonished to see us, but it put him in good spirits. "Boy howdy," he cried, "reinforcements!"

"The Cycladians are coming again," said my mother sadly.

"I smell them varmints," said grandfather. "They'll attack at dawn."

One of grandfather's other little crotchets was his distrust of certain modern conveniences. He had no truck with any sort of power that came out of atoms. The shack was equipped with nuclear-generated electrical lights and heat, but grandfather had long ago supplied the place with lanterns and a pot-bellied stove. We looked at each other in the flickering dimness and knew there was nothing we could do until grandfather's mood changed. He grasped his ancient rifle, ready to prevent any of us from leaving the outpost. He always was a strict one for discipline, even among green recruit reinforcements like us.

My father, knowing that it was very likely a hopeless task, attempted to reason with grandfather. "This asteroid has a nightside and a dayside," he said. "There isn't going to be a dawn. Ever."

"Ye be as skeered as a duck in thunder," cried grandfather. "Don't worry, boy. They can't creep up on me."

"But if you stand there looking out that port and waiting for the sun to come up, you're going to have a long wait!" shouted father in exasperation.

Grandfather gave a short, courageous smile. "They reckon they're goin' t' ketch me unawares, but I know they're comin'. That's my secret, boy."

"I'm hungry," said Parren.

"You new men air purt near allus hungry," said grandfather sternly. "We're on short rations here. It's your skin ye ought t' be worried about, not your stummick."

"And I'm cold, too," complained my younger brother. There was a small box filled with coal, and Parren scooped some of the black lumps into the stove. The fire flared and the temperature in the shack fluttered up a degree or two.

Father had made no progress with his calm approach, and he had no more success with any other. Mother joined him in begging grandfather to come home with us, but the old coot only became angry. "Ye're askin' me to desert my post!" he shouted. "What air ye, spies for them varmints? Is that it? Just think o' your mothers and sisters, dependin' on ye at home!"

"We don't have any sisters," said Rys. "And mother's here with us."

"All the more reason," snarled grandfather. He turned back to his duty. The hours passed, the shack got colder, and dawn was as far away as ever. Eventually Parren got tired and fell asleep in mother's lap. Rys threw the rest of the coal into the stove and huddled up against me for warmth. Father glowered by himself in one corner, and grandfather stood wakeful and watchful at the shack's single port.

When we awoke we had no idea what time it was. It was still night, of course, but several hours at least had passed. It was very cold in the shack, because the fire in the pot-bellied stove had gone out. Grandfather sat on the floor beneath the port, his rifle beside him. He was studying us closely. "It's time ye woke up," he said.

"Didn't you sleep, Pa?" asked mother.

"How could I sleep?" demanded grandfather. "It's colder'n a freezer full o' shorn sheep."

"Put some more coal in the stove," said Rys, yawning and shivering.

"Coal?" asked grandfather. "Air ye crazy? What coal?"

Father explained that the previous night Parren had dumped a boxful of coal into the stove; and, he asked, was there any more? Grandfather grimaced and made some remarks about how weakminded the younger people were these days. He usually didn't spend very much time in the cold shack, he said, because he'd rather be out in the hills, looking for gold and jewels. It was very obvious to all of us that grandfather had forgotten all about the Cycladian menace, and this was good news all around. It meant that we might be able to go home soon.

Grandfather had similar suspicions. "Ye come out here t' honeyfogle me back t' the goddam dome with ye," he snapped.

Father wore a strained smile and he patted the air in what he must have thought was a reassuring gesture. "It's cold here," he said, "and it's nice and warm at home."

Grandfather snorted. "But d'ye have gold and jewels layin' about at home?" I was going to point out that grandfather didn't have gold and jewels laying about here either, but I kept my thought to myself. I learned at an early age that in a situation of this delicacy, sense and logic have little place.

It developed in the end that grandfather, in his less militant frame of mind, was easily persuaded. We let him think that he might slip away from us another day, and that the gold and jewels weren't going anywhere. At last, mummified once again in our pressure suits, we made our way from the old shack to the groundcars. Grandfather wanted to drive, but my mother wouldn't allow it. Father drove his own car, and Rys drove the rented one.

The trip home was made in relative peace; grandfather lapsed into a sulky silence, and Parren and I dozed. Just before we arrived at the nightside portal, however, grandfather said something that roused us. "What was all that flummery about coal?" he wanted to know. Mother repeated the story of the night before, but grandfather shook his head vigorously. "Don't ye know where coal comes from, girl?" he cried. "There ain't ever been anything alive on this goddam asteroid. Ye'd be as like to find coal here as tits on a boar hog. It'd be worth more'n its weight in gold and jewels." We just looked at each other. Back in the dome, the coal would have made everyone change their ideas about where Springfield had come from. Maybe our chunk of space debris had once been part of some larger world. It was too late for idle guesses now, though. We'd burned every bit of evidence.

Later we tried to find out where grandfather had found the coal, but he refused to admit that it ever existed. He got so tired of the argument that he never went prospecting again. From that day on, whenever he disappeared, it was to go fight the Cycladian invaders. That made it even more difficult to fetch him home, and soon my father didn't want to have anything more to do with the matter. My older brother, Rys, took over the job of going after grandfather.

My mother, however, only let out a wistful sigh now and then. "It sure would have been nice to've saved a piece of that coal," she would say. "It sure would have been nice to be rich." She was probably right about that.

✛ ✛ ✛

The Wisdom of Having Money

1

THE FASTBOAT ON THE SPRINGFIELD RUN HOVE itself out of true, integral space and into the smooth black sailing of incremental space. The pilot turned to the lazy bench and considered the two young men sitting there, who in their turn watched the pilot's every move with all the attention a caterpillar gives the first hungry robin of spring. The pilot's calm, stern expression did not change as he looked over first one cub—his own son— and then the other, his nephew, the son of his dead brother. The pilot cast a quick glance back at the screens—although there was barely a need to do so, as there hadn't been as much as a squawk from the graysmen—and once more sized up the boys, with eyes squinted just a bit as if he'd struck an idea. By and by he called out smartly:

"Halan!"

His nephew hopped off the bench as if his behind had been singed. "Yes, sir, Mr. Yolney!" Down on the hurricane deck or in the main saloon it was "Uncle Grather," but in the pilothouse it was always "Mr. Yolney, sir!" The other cub had it no better; his own father was "Mr. Yolney" to him when the pilot's hands were on the pad and his eyes on the screen.

"Halan, come here, boy." Mr. Yolney watched the play of black space and white space on the forward screen; he didn't like what he saw; and he made the slightest correction with the pad that a human eye could discern. Poor Halan hadn't yet arrived at that exalted level of understanding that explained what in d-mnation his uncle had just done, or why he had seen fit to do it.

"Yes, sir." Halan wondered what bothersome business the pilot was going to plague him with now.

Mr. Yolney pointed to the starboard screen, where a great eddy of swirling white space was eating away at the calm and empty blackness. "Tell me, boy, what's this?" His long, pale-skinned finger aimed deep into the heart of the disturbance.

"Why, that'll be Ipimay 209." Halan hadn't been a 'prentice on the *Smoky Mary* for a full year without picking up a little useful information along the way. He even let himself stand with something like the cocksure posture he'd observed on all seasoned pilots.

"Right you are, my boy. Now, looky here at t'other and tell me what it is." The pilot's hand swung across to the portside screen, which should have shown no white space at all, and everything should have been peaceful, black, and a deal of easy running. Instead there was a small white blotch at the very edge of the screen, with rippling gray lines shoaling against it, like the tickling wavelets on the shore of some worldly ocean, as you may say.

Halan had to swallow, but his throat was too dry. He didn't have enough of a reply to wake a baby. "I don't know, Mr. Yolney." His posture went from confident to puzzled to scared; and he stared and stared at the screen; but the white blotch just did not want to disappear.

"Lively, boy, make speed! To lay away from that white space on the stabboard, we're going to have to cramp the boat full up to that other little piece of trouble you don't know nuthin' about. Take the pad, now."

It took a moment for Halan to find his voice; in the silence he heard his cousin, Thysix, laugh softly. Halan swore that he'd make Thysix pay for that laugh, even though Thysix was a year older, a head taller, upwards of twenty pounds heavier, and had laid over Halan in every one of the hundred fights they'd already had. Halan was crushed to hear the quavering in his raspy voice:

"Take the pad?"

Mr. Yolney did not deign to reply—he merely stood back from the screens and the pad. If Halan didn't take over the *Smoky Mary*, she would soon be at the mercy of 'cremental space. Even an iron-jawed old hand like Mr. Yolney didn't understand all the shifting, mysterious features of 'cremental—but Mr. Yolney would never admit that. It was policy aboard the *Mary* that Mr. Yolney knew as much about making way in the Fourth Derivative as the Unseen Powers that had put it there in the first place.

Halan rested his hands lightly on the pad. His fingers trembled and his palms felt sweaty. He looked anxiously at the forward screen and saw the lightening grayness of looming danger. His eyes moved from the starboard screen to the port screen—doom and destruction on the first, merely deadly disaster on the second. Halan couldn't see any advantage in either prayer or action, but by and by he said:

"I'm going to come off ten points to labboard." There wasn't conviction worth bothering about in the tone of his voice. He waited for an eruption of scorn and dismay from Mr. Yolney—there was only silence except for Thysix's continued giggling. Halan blinked his eyes and squeezed them tight shut; he took a deep breath; and he tapped the keys on the pad. Presently the great white subspace pattern of Ipimay 209 fell away somewhat; but the impossible thing on the port screen swung directly into the cali-brated center circle. There shouldn't have been any danger at all here, yet there it was: a rock, a snag, a sunken wreck on the bottom of space. Halan asked helplessly:

"What do I do now, Mr. Yolney, sir?"

There was no reply except from the port graysman:

"One point oh, Mistah Halan!" The call meant that the fastboat would tear herself apart if she held on that course much longer. There was still time to save her, if the cub knew how.

Halan didn't even dare to take his eyes from the screen to see if his uncle was frowning or nodding in approval. How many nights had Halan fallen asleep to the glorious dream of booming along in a fastboat under his guidance through the white- and black-banded perils of 'cremental space? Now he was having his chance. He must show what he was made of in front of Mr. Yolney and Thysix. Halan himself had got to learn what he was made of now, too. It was a question that had vexed him for a long time, and to which he had never dared to make an answer. He would know that answer very soon.

Halan hoped that the whirling white thing on the port screen might be an electronic failure, or a phantom trick of the engine-room strikers, who liked to hide away in their holes below decks and think up mean dodgery to play on the uppity ones in the pilot-house. Halan hoped it might be anything at all but a true dire peril

—that was too many for him. Behind him even Thysix had fallen silent. Halan lifted a fingertip.

"What are you fixing to do?" came Mr. Yolney's deep voice.

"Call for everything and lean her hard to labboard."

"She'll never make it." The pilot moved in closer but did not take back control of the fastboat. "Looky here. You have to gauge the strength of these treacherous gray bands. You'd never get her clear of that rock—the bright white tells you that, the depth of those gray shadows. Fetch her back to stabboard—easy, easy now."

On the port screen the brightness fell away a bit. The gray ripples that marked the calamity and ruin around Ipimay 209 crept back on the starboard screen.

Said the port graysman:

"Oh point nine."

Said the starboard graysman:

"Oh point one."

No one else said a word. Halan stood up on the heading, although it was ever so obvious to him that he, Mr. Yolney, and everybody else on board the *Smoky Mary* were headed straight for a sudden and fiery end. The starboard graysman called out:

"Point three."

The deadly rings that reflected Ipimay 209's position in true space commenced to blaze in the screen's scaled markings. If the graysman's call reached point five now, so near the danger, there would be no further reason to read the changes—the crew would be again at peace. They would all be dead and therefore, by many accounts, at peace.

"Point four."

Halan nearly swooned on the bridge; but his fingers rested lightly on the pad; and he waited orders from Mr. Yolney. Halan hoped the orders would come tolerably soon, because the fastboat was beginning to settle pretty low in the unforgiving grayness. Said Mr. Yolney at last:

"When I give the word, heel her round to labboard with all she's got. Hold her steady."

"Aye, aye, sir," said Halan. He felt fear clutch at his heart; minutes ago—or were they only seconds?—he had wanted to perform the same maneuver and skirt the smaller white blotch to leeward; but now it was too late for that. Now Mr. Yolney was ordering him to throttle up the fastboat and ride straight into perdition. The forefinger and middle finger of his right hand touched the two buttons that would fetch up every ounce of thrust the old tramp had to spare. His left middle finger lay on the key that would alter course. Mr. Yolney never looked down to see that his fingers were on the right keys—but Halan knew now for certain how far he had to travel before he was good enough even to carry Mr. Yolney's cap. He glanced down and was satisfied that when the call came, he wouldn't hit the wrong buttons and send them all to Jericho.

Suddenly Mr. Yolney cried:

"*Now*, boy, stand on her! *Stand on her*, blast you, you tin-plated excuse for a pryanian!" With one prodigious wallop the pilot knocked Halan away from the pad and against a bulkhead, nearly staving in the boy's skull as a bonus. When Halan's senses returned, he saw Mr. Yolney calmly skinning the port screen's threat to windward as close as white on snow. A minute passed, and another; and then all three screens showed nothing but deep, safe blackness.

Halan had tried to go around the danger, but his timidity would have cost them all their lives; Mr. Yolney had the nerve and the sureness to pass between the two white spots of death, near enough to the smaller of them to spit in its eye as they passed. Halan knew that it would take some earthquaking heroics to refurbish his pride and self-respect. The question at the moment was if Mr. Yolney would ever again trust Halan at the pad.

The answer to that, until they came out of 'cremental space, was No. Halan fooled away his watches on the lazy bench. Mostly Mr. Yolney held the pad; sometimes it was his partner, Mr. Sackess; and sometimes it was that conceited flathead, Thysix, who always made sure that Halan noticed how fearlessly he tapped the keys. Halan noticed only that Thysix never faced a choice betwixt the devil and the bright white night. Perhaps if some unexpected white speck reared up on one of the screens and the graysmen started their frantic singing, *then* everyone would learn with what sort of ticking young Thysix was padded out. However, no such hazard evidenced itself the rest of the journey; and day by day Halan grew more restless on the bench. He was only moderately thrilled when by and by Mr. Yolney laid the fastboat in her marks and brought the *Smoky Mary* out of the solid blackness into true space.

2

Springfield was an asteroid in the middle of nowhere that could have been a perfect jewel of a moon if there had been a planet hard by for it to revolve around. It was large enough to have gravity comfortable to some of its visitors, but too weak or too strong for others. It was near enough to an unremarkable star to give it a bright face and a permanently dark side; and that's almost all that could be said about its features. There was a city on the rock—a domed city also called Springfield. Inside the dome there were artificial days and nights; air to breathe; expensive water to drink; expensive food to eat; expensive places to sleep; and the skillful scavengers, swindlers, and other industrialists who were found wherever human civilization put down its irksome roots.

Aboard the *Smoky Mary*, Mr. Yolney switched the screens from "derivative mode" to "true space mode"—although no pilot ever said "true space." At the pad, the proper words were "integral" or "zero-exponential space." The screens became telescopic scanners. Halan and his cousin pressed behind the pilot to see the distant, unblinking star snap back into view; and they watched the unpromising lump of lifeless matter that was Springfield gradually grow larger on the forward screen. From a distance of fifty thousand miles, Springfield looked like a dead rock painted dull black across half of its worthless real estate. The green-domed city was not visible at all.

By and by Mr. Yolney gaped and stretched; his watch was coming to an end; and he knew it as all pilots know it, without the need of consulting a clock. When he was relieved by Sackess, he said:

"Fifty thousand and closing handsomely."

Mr. Sackess nodded but did not reply. He moved toward the pad. Mr. Yolney said, almost as an afterthought:

"I'd ruther Mr. Halan made landfall." The casual remark had an audacious effect on everyone in the pilothouse. Cried Mr. Sackess:

"But he hain't never had the experience!"

Mr. Yolney merely raised a hand to wave away his partner's objection. After all, Mr. Sackess was the junior pilot aboard the *Mary*, and as such his opinion counted little more than that of one of the deckhand rousters. "This is how he will get the experience."

Halan stammered:

"But—but—Uncle Grather—" The notion of taking the *Smoky Mary*'s yawl down on his own hook scared him out of his wits. He had a dreadful clear vision of bringing the boat aground a mite too handily and smashing it into worthless, twisted rubbage—incidentally murdering all the paying passengers and himself into the bargain.

Mr. Yolney departed the pilothouse as if no one had spoken; and he was not seen again during the remainder of Mr. Sackess's watch. Halan glanced at Thysix, who looked wonderfully eaten up with envy. Halan would have been overjoyed to pass along the honor to the other boy, but Mr. Yolney's word was law.

Mr. Sackess said:

"I will shape her into her parking orbit. When we are cleared by the port authorities, Mr. Halan, you will take command of the yawl. Is that clear?"

"Aye, aye, sir, Mr. Sackess."

"Until then, please stow your scabrous carcass in your quarters. I will send for you in due time."

"Aye, sir."

With that exchange the junior pilot restored his temporary sovereignty at the pad. Both cubs were relieved of duty, and they retired to their tiny cabin in the forecastle. They missed nothing exciting as the *Mary* hove toward the asteroid. It was a tiresome bit of time because there was nothing for the pilot, the graysmen, or anyone else to do until the Springfield harbormaster challenged them. Halan had something to eat; he caught a few hours of sleep; and he was roused by the second mate in the middle of a vague but troublesome nightmare.

Directly, Halan brought himself to the cockpit of the fastboat's yawl and seated himself at the console. There was a control pad much like the one in the *Smoky Mary's* pilothouse; but there were no screens—taking a boat down from orbit was done mostly by computers. If they failed *and* their backups failed, screens or windows would serve no purpose at all: watching the ground rushing up at a fatal velocity is no more helpful than it is diverting.

Halan glanced at the second mate, who had the responsibility for putting the yawl through its preflight checkout. "Everything snug?"

"All green, Mr. Halan, taut and shipshape."

Halan punched a row of diagnostic keys and saw all their lights flash green. Then he called the Springfield harbormaster and asked permission to come ahead.

A computer's synthetic voice answered from the asteroid's surface:

"You will be set down on landing area 117. Please switch control of your craft to remote guidance."

Halan pressed the appropriate button. His function as pilot was now ended, unless a catastrophe happened and he must override the automatic systems—but Halan did not wish to think about such a thing.

There was no sensation of motion as the yawl left the *Smoky Mary*'s docking bay and approached the asteroid. There was only the steady regaining of the weight—at least some of it—that Halan had sloughed when the yawl left the fastboat's artificial gravity. There was a soft bump when the boat grounded; and then the electronic voice spoke again over the radio:

"Stand to and prepare to receive boarders." These would be Springfield's customs clerks, who would check over the *Mary*'s manifests and passenger list. Halan tapped off all the keys on his pad, letting the second mate remain behind to watch over the life-support systems. All in all, Halan felt a good deal of success; he hadn't killed a single passenger—he hadn't so much as maimed a limb.

A flexible tube led from the yawl's air lock down into a large receiving area, so Halan got no quick look at Springfield when he left the boat. The passengers hurried through the tunnel and the low-ceilinged, echoing chamber, but Halan ambled along curiously. He had listened to stories of Springfield all his life—wild tales, bawdy tales, fearsome tales—and he meant to savor every detail. When he returned home again famously, he would add his own stretchers to the stale lot he had heard so often. He showed his 'prentice pilot's papers to a bored and sleepy woman in a gray uniform. She said:

"Pilot's wardroom is through there." She pointed to a large door made of glossy black wood brought from some far-off world, and bright as glory with polished brass fittings.

"Now this is something *like*," Halan thought. He took a moment to adjust his cap so that it listed a trifle to starboard, just as Mr. Yolney wore his. Then he nervously grasped the gleaming doorknob, pushed open the heavy door, and went through.

To his surprise, no one stopped him or questioned his right to be here in the fraternal clubroom of the pilots' association. Halan felt a crazy elation. He was *one of them!* He was a *pilot*—of sorts. Back home on Bouligny, many dreamed of leaving that placid world and flashing hither and yon through the universe, but few ever played that trump. Yet here Halan was: not merely off world, not just on Springfield itself, but here as a kid-gloved *pilot*, who merely by the grace of his profession's grandeur alone would probably someday be offered a reserved loge seat among the Heavenly Elect.

Halan was awed by the others in the common room, all laughing and cursing and trading lies. He suspected that he did not truthfully belong among the quality; he felt suddenly like an intruder—a tiny one at that—like an ant using among mammoths. He took off his cap, put it back on, took it off a second time and ran his hand through his short brown hair, and fitted the cap on the very crown of his head. The swaggering set of it was gone along with his confidence. Halan felt conspicuous and meager; he sought a chair where no one might see him, where no one might offer a greeting or ask a question. He found a place in a dim corner, on the far side of the room from the bar where the pilots mostly congregated.

"What are you drinking?" came Mr. Yolney's voice.

Halan jerked around, startled. He said:

"Uncle Grather! Nothing—I mean—I'm not drinking—I mean . . ."

Mr. Yolney smiled in a friendly way; the voyage was behind them now. It was time to collect their pay—and spend it. Beside him stood his son, Thysix, whose cap was still tossed at an arrogant angle. The pilot asked again:

"What are you drinking?"

"Nothing, sir."

"You don't drink?"

"No, sir."

Thysix said with a wicked grin:

"He dasn't, Pa. Aunt Leofra would whup him ragged."

Mr. Yolney looked amused. "You've *never* had a drink?"

"No, sir."

"Ah, well-a-well, I promised your mother that I'd make a man of you or slaughter you, whichever seemed easiest. You're learning the piloting trade as fast as ever a numskull saphead like you can, so I suppose I must do the whole thing from hell to breakfast. You'll drink what I'm drinking—bingara."

Halan started to object, thinking of his ma's prohibitions against such vices; but she and her world were a tolerable long way off; and if he was to become a man, Halan must chart those vices and steer by them without her. He couldn't grow to maturity behind his ma's skirts. "I thank you kindly," he said.

Mr. Yolney turned to Thysix. "Bingara for you, too, boy?"

Thysix's grin wavered just a little before he answered:

"Well, sure, Pa."

The pilot led the two cubs to the bar and ordered the drinks. Then he announced to the assembled company:

"I give you my son, Thysix, and my nephew, Halan: the two

302 GEORGE ALEC EFFINGER LIVE! FROM PLANET EARTH

most promising cubs to come out of 'cremental space since my own initiation." All the other pilots laughed appreciatively. Mr. Yolney threw his drink down at one go.

Halan looked at Thysix, who looked back at Halan; both boys emulated Mr. Yolney and threw their drinks back with something of his dash and flair; but their reactions need not be described at length. It need only be reported that the pilots' merriment increased to an uproarious level.

One of the other men questioned Mr. Yolney about the *Smoky Mary's* run. Said Mr. Yolney:

"I'll say it was peaceable enough. That is, it was until I began making real speed. I slipped down from Second Derivative to Third and then to Fourth, and we were just a-boomin' along until we come to the reaches around Ipimay 209."

Another pilot, a short man with the wan complexion of a wax dummy, the mark of these men on whom no sun ever shines, remarked:

"Ipimay 209? I'm bound through that stretch."

Mr. Yolney laid a finger alongside his nose. "Then you'd be wise to lay in a deal of caution. I had that star hard on my stabboard beam where I wanted it, when I spied a white flare off to labboard that hadn't ever been there before. There warn't barely room enough betwixt 'em to whisper a kind word."

"Bosh. There ain't nuthin' around Ipimay 209—not a planet, not an asteroid, nuthin'. Never has been."

"A comet?" another man offered.

Mr. Yolney shrugged. "I don't give a rat in a rain barrel *what* she was; she was setting there making me choose which of two quick deaths I'd ruther."

The short pilot demanded:

"What did you do?" Everyone at the bar was now hanging on Mr. Yolney's every word.

He ordered another drink first to fire up their interest some, tossed the bingara down, then looked around at all the other faces and smiled. He said:

"I turned the pad over to my cub." He pointed a finger at Halan; then he grasped the two boys by their arms; and he hurried them out of the clubroom while the pilots exploded in consternation behind them. Someone called after them:

"If that ain't all the brass-bound nerve!"

Once outside, Mr. Yolney let loose a loud guffaw of his own, very pleased with himself. "They'll be yelpin' over that one for another year!" Halan didn't know what to feel, remembering keenly how the incident had actually happened; he was aware that Thysix was seething now with something more than envy. He was giving Halan a look that threatened a reckoning not far in the future.

Mr. Yolney laughed again and said:

"Time's running thinner by the minute, boys. Here we've been on Springfield the best part of an hour and we ain't yet been tattooed nor let our pay ride on the backs of a pair o' crooked dice."

"We hain't got our pay yet, Pa."

"That's where we're heading directly, son, and *then* I'll show you rapscallions the splendidest time a body ever seen who managed to stagger out alive afterward. It takes more'n walking away alive from your first landing on Springfield to turn out a man from a boy, and that's what your mothers don't understand."

Thysix's face flushed with excitement. "We even goin' to try metasense, Pa?"

"That's right, boy—we'll amp our brains till they're all over glowing."

"What else, Pa?"

Mr. Yolney laughed at his son's impatience. "We'll get ourself anchored in Sot's Bay and fool away half our money in a cutthroat game of old sledge and then bust our knuckles in a drunken brawl; but first I got to make *men* of you, though I can do that in less'n half an hour."

Thysix look dumbfounded at the very notion, but said:

"Less'n half an hour, Pa? How you fixing to do that?"

Mr. Yolney cocked his cap a tad more to starboard and said:

"We're going to sign on wives, boys."

Wives! The very evil horror of the notion hit Thysix hard, so that his grin of anticipation wandered rudderless until the boy looked like he could no way keep from jumping ship. Old Thysix was wonderful anxious to try his hand at buzzing his skull with electricity and bar liquor; at gambling; and at tawdry port-town women taken aboard according to ancient tradition and maritime statute—that is, you pay the wharfage fee and lay alongside, you unship your cargo, and you hoist sail afterward to make way for another vessel. A *wife*, howsomever, well, that was just too various for Thysix. Young Halan, to his silent discomfiture, found himself in shocked agreement.

3

The office of the Perseid Queen Line was in a building a few blocks from the terminal, and Halan nearly died three or four times as he stared at the gaudy and uncommon sights that passed him by in the short space of five minutes. Why, he saw men and women and creatures and things so powerful fine or so powerful ugly that he knew he couldn't put them in his tales for the folks at home—all his old friends would think that Halan had sold them for sure, taken their willing credence and left them with nothing but booming nonsense.

Mr. Yolney didn't bother to rap on the door to the Perseid Queen Line's office—he just threw it back as if he owned the whole corporation from carpet tacks to starboard thrusters. And blamed if they didn't just treat him as if he did, too! He swaggered up to the desk where a lovely young lady was sitting, and he commenced to talk about one outrageous thing and another until she most bust from laughing. Then all of a sudden he laid off his carrying on; and he put on his solemn face; and he asked the young lady:

"Has the cap'n been in yet to collect his pay? Have I missed dear old Captain Cazareen?" Captain Cazareen was the coffee-and-cake captain of the *Smoky Mary*, and there never was much love lost betwixt him and Mr. Yolney on account of Cap'n Cazareen got to wear the uniforms with the braids and brass buttons, and get piped aboard so's everybody could watch, and had the terrible job of walking up and down the decks reassuring the ladies and making certain they wouldn't faint when they were sure they heard the creakings of black holes and astrophages and whatnot in 'cremental space where there wasn't nothing to hear in the first place, except in the pilothouse where it wasn't fit for no lady to listen anyways.

"The captain was here not more than a quarter of an hour ago, sir."

Mr. Yolney smiled at his son and his nephew and said:

"Last on the boat and first off every time, he is, and first to nail down his hard-earned pay! Why, if I had to promenade in those fine suits and listen to the miseries of those rich widows and talk over the hard life with every tiresome old rip who wisht he'd 'a' gone into space ruther than sell ribbons or rakes or whatever he done, I'd be low and gritless myself when the boat sets down. It's the pitifulest life, bein' a space captain, boys—and never you forget it, nuther." He looked around to make sure that everybody in hailing distance was catching the full length and breadth of his bullyragging. A good pilot like Mr. Yolney earned eight or ten times as much money on every trip as the ship's captain, despite the captain's gold-leaf uniform and parlor manners.

The young lady nodded at Mr. Yolney's taking on and said: "The captain did leave these for the boys." She gave two sheets of paper to the pilot.

Mr. Yolney read one aloud:

"'This is to testify that I, Thodoleus Cazareen, contracted captain of the Perseid Queen Line's vessel *Smoky Mary*, do hereby attest that the ship's apprentice pilot, Thysix Yolney, performed his duties admirably and with full consideration for the safety and comfort of the passengers and his fellow crew members. I therefore recommend that he be inaugurated as a full pilot with all the privileges pertaining thereto.'"

"Well, I'll be hanged!" cried Thysix.

Said Mr. Yolney as he tore the document in half and crumpled the pieces:

"It may well come to that, son. You'll be a pilot when *I* say you're a pilot, and not a split nano-never before." Thysix went from a-whooping and a-hollering to as low as ever a living body could be. Then Mr. Yolney took the other piece of paper, which Halan reckoned was his own advancement; and the pilot performed the very same act of destruction to it; and blamed if Halan didn't feel just as tromped to mush as Thysix. Said Mr. Yolney:

"Cap'n Cazareen's word don't stand no show and it ain't worth spit to no other pilot, nor to no other shipping line looking to *hire* a pilot." And *wasn't* he calm as the torn and twisted pieces of paper fell to the carpeted floor. Thysix looked at Halan again, and both cubs tried to size how long it might be before Mr. Yolney would soften down and give them *his* official endorsement, and if they might strike it so lucky as to live that blessed long.

Mr. Yolney observed his charges' low demeanor and said:

"It's blooming high time to find you wives—your mournful faces are just about awful to see. I learned a long time ago that if it's one thing that can make you forget a rattlin' bad trouble, it's *another* trouble worse'n the first. And they ain't yet run up against nuthin' more plaguey than a wife."

"Then why do we want to get one, Uncle Grather?"

Said he:

"Because every once in a while—when the devil's mucking

about elsewheres—a wife can suddenly be the most uncommonly splendid thing going. Take them all round, wives are inspiration and tonic, if you pay no mind to their blattering and bawling and whatnot."

"But why must we *marry* them, Pa? Why don't we just take up with some fine young women the way creation intended, the way civilized folks do? Wives is illegal and immoral and just generally looked down on back home on Bouliny and every other respectable place I know of."

The pilot smiled and said:

"*That's* why you must try it now. Marriage is allowed on Springfield, son; married people from jerkwater worlds pass through here every day; and don't nobody give 'em so much as a squinty-eyed look, nuther. Everybody gets to hankering after the things they can't have, it's only human nature. If you went home and settled down with some tolerable woman, you'd always wonder what it would be like to *marry* her. It would get at your mind and d—mn near drive you mad, most. Now is your chance to find out all about it and why it's a perversion of everything that's good and proper, and a flat-out embarrassment amongst decent folk."

Thysix's grin returned as he considered the imminent, illicit, and undefined delights of marriage; but Halan was still of a mixed mind. "I still don't see how marrying a woman is different than building and sharing a home with one in the regular way."

Mr. Yolncy nodded his head solemnly, as befitted the wellspring of wisdom and the voice of experience. "You'll see. It just ain't what you can explain to a body in words. You have to study it out for yourself."

The wife shop was on Long Street, at the worn-downedest end of that grand boulevard near to the barrier of the green dome itself. The shop didn't look respectable from the outside—but then it wasn't pretending to be a church or a union hall. It was slid in betwixt two luridly disreputable establishments that offered any and all vices unobtainable in the more specialized wife shop shouldered up against them.

The pilot led the way into the shop bold as brass; and his son followed only a pinch less confident; but Halan was in a dismal quandary, though he kept his objection unspoken. This, he reckoned, was also part of his pilot's training; but for his very soul he couldn't fetch up on a likely reason why it should be so.

4

Now, Mr. Yolney didn't fancy the gorgeous outfits or high hats or diamond stickpins that many fastboat pilots encumbered themselves with when they went into the town. His suit was cut just like his plain pilothouse uniform, only all of a soft, cream-colored calfskin; it had silver buttons, and pale blue trim the hue of his home world's sky at sunrise; his cap was like his pilothouse cap, but cream-colored, too, with his pilot's insignia in gold. He wore shirts of modest cut and color—but of the finest silk and other fabrics, so that a body might know that Mr. Yolney *could* 'a' trotted around a diamond stickpin—huge precious rings, and boots that cost a month's wages. A covey of pilots found in a Springfield taproom was usually plumed in every color of the rainbow and two or three besides, each man trying to outdress and outsplendor and lay over all the others; but even in such an assemblage Mr. Yolney was remarkable, because he got considerable show from his quiet elegance, and he knew it.

The pilot stopped just inside the door of the wife shop and waited for the proprietor to come to him. At first the shopkeeper noticed only Thysix and Halan, and he let his gaze glance off them and toward what other worthless motes of dust had drifted into his store. By and by he spied Mr. Yolney in his fine suit, and the merchant's expression changed. He moored in place that canny grin you see on starving wolves, and on folks who want to tell you how interesting their lives have been, and on other such predatory creatures.

Meantime, Thysix and Halan looked about the shop, wonderfully thunderstruck by the merchandise on display. There were many glass-walled boxes; in every one stood a perfect vision of a wife, each more beautiful than the last; and the very meanest of them was prettier and more precious than anything the boys had ever seen. The wives in their unadorned cases did not move or blink or breathe; they were unclothed but for a small orange plastic necklace that fitted tightly around their perfect throats; they gave no sign that they might be alive or, at the worst, but recently deceased; yet they were so lovely that if they were real or holographic models or only clever plaster counterfeits, it made no sort of difference to Thysix and Halan. The boys stared first at a tall, gentle-faced sample with a fine lavender cast to her skin; then they went all to smash over one the color of a rain cloud, with hair as shimmery as mother-of-pearl, and eyes of copper and steel-blue flecks; and then they commenced to run from one case to another, calling out in astonishment or delight or disbelief.

Just when they had got jamfull of beauty and the particular feelings that it may arouse, the pilot and Mr. Cosgred, the shopkeeper, flanked them to starboard. The two men were beaming as if they'd been bully friends ever so long, and as if Mr. Yolney had charted the *Smoky Mary* to Springfield just to renew this old acquaintance. Mr. Yolney observed Thysix's excitement and said:

"You set your mind yet, son?"

"One of *these*, Pa? I must pick one of *these?*"

"Ain't they fine enough for you, boy?" The two older men whooped, though it was plenty knotty enough for Thysix and Halan to see what they were laughing about.

"Blazes, Pa! Every one of 'em's in bloom and likely as t'other! I just reckoned—I judged—maybe they was *too* fine and ruther fancy for me. I mean, for a *first* wife, you know."

Mr. Yolney put on a serious face and considered a moment, then said:

"These are the rarest, beatenest wives on Springfield, boys; I wouldn't let you fall up against nuthin' but the best—I owe that much to your mothers, and I owe it to your departed pa, Halan. But thunderation! D'ye want to traipse around escorting a wife with a horse-face and a stagger and a bray like a swozzled stricker's boy? Every consarned gaff-line mate or mud-clerk which passed by on the street would have a wife to make yourn look like the pitifulest thing out; and then every time I struck another pilot, why, he'd laugh his bones loose about it; and then all my years of work and dedication wouldn't be worth bothering about—the association would prob'ly exterminate my license to save their pride. And every man jack of 'em'd be taking on about it from here to Nevermind! No! I *won't* have it! Take which one you'd ruther and let's us get the marrying done; and remember who has command around here, and who still must step lively."

Halan figured that his Uncle Grather was only trying to act the pilot and a deal of an outrage, too; and that little, if any, of that speech—splendid as it had been—was anything but lies or at least powerful stretchers. But then Mr. Yolney said:

"Mr. Cosgred, I believe I will marry Miss Lyjia." The shopkeeper looked as satisfied as a cat at a fish fling, and turned to the two boys.

Thysix fetched up when he saw this wasn't but a show or a casual rumble, but the very preliminaries to a set of three sure-enough flagrant matrimonies. He said:

"Well, Pa, as this is my first wife, I s'pose nuthin' will do but that she must be the best, but I hope to gracious if I kin make such a choice."

Mr. Yolney nodded solemnly and turned to Mr. Cosgred. "The *best*, sir."

"That would be Miss Melcie."

Thysix's face went all over pale. "Miss Melcie," he whispered. He glowered at Halan as if it was the younger boy's fault that all this was happening. Said the merchant:

"And the other young man?"

"Well, if Miss Melcie is the best, dadfetch it, I'll just have whichever comes right next after her." He glared back at Thysix, determined that he would get out of this gloomy mess with his pride untarnished further; and his body still alive, if possible.

The shopkeeper plated on his blank, serious, well-meaning look again. Halan tried to remember where he'd seen another display like that; and by and by it struck him that it was on the face of everybody standing around the grave of his pa, when the box had been set in the ground and people were tossing in their little clods of dirt and flowers and sad poems and whatnot. It made Halan all of a tremble to think of that. Mr. Cosgred said:

"There is Miss Varenia, who is quite perfect in her own way. Please step over here." He led the way to Miss Varenia's case.

"Miss Varenia," said Halan, trying her name on his tongue for size. "She's never been a wife before? I mean—I was only thinkin' that—well, after all, she's next best to Miss Melcie—and she might prove out too audacious for me, being only a cub, you know—and, heck—" Halan might have gone on in that skittish way until the artificial day lit up the streets at dawn, except the salesman patted the air in his soothering way. Still, Mr. Cosgred was insulted, and he ripped out and said:

"*None* of them has *ever* been a wife before. If all you're wanting is a night of middlin' fun with a woman, they have got annies all over town for that, and they ain't so difficult to locate, nuther. I reckoned you boys for some sort of refinement, and when the honorable pilot wisely chose Miss Lyjia, I knowed I warn't goin' to have to put up with no such foolishness as I get all the livelong day; gawpers all boggled, and smirkers and suchlike saps who come in here just to peek at these yer wives, and then they swift clip out to tell their right down friends what they seen."

Mr. Yolney eased the air a bit by declaring:

"I've been married a time or two in the past, as you well know, my friend, but my young hands are making their first passage through the straits of wedlock, as you may say; so I'm sure you'll forgive their disgustful iggorance."

The proprietor dropped his insulted air so fast, there wasn't no more hurt to him than there is to a snowball. He glanced from Mr. Yolney and Miss Lyjia to Thysix and Miss Melcie, then to Halan. He said:

"Let us connect your bride and proceed with the formalities, the civil whim-whams obliged upon us by our public servants." It was just like the moment of uncomfortableness had never happened at all. And blame it! That Mr. Cosgred had *style*, according to Halan's way of thinking; though it was a different sort of style than Uncle Grather's; and just maybe a tad less grand, in its own admirable way.

The shopkeeper twirled a round color lock on the side of Miss Varenia's case, and lifted aside the glass lid. Within the box, Miss Varenia looked mighty sleepful, like Snow White or Lenin, like there wasn't anything in nature that could rouse her; and that maybe she plain *couldn't* be waked, and that she was as demised as ever a body was; and that got Halan all quivery. But nothing come of it, because as soon as Mr. Cosgred carefully stripped off the orange plastic necklace, Miss Varenia was all connected again in a flash and filled with life and stepping softly and sweetly from her casket, blushing and carrying on mighty shy and pretty, though just like Miss Lyjia and Miss Melcie, it didn't seem to make no mind to her that she didn't have no more clothes on than a handful of red beans. The store owner took advantage of the moment when everybody was just too struck stupid to say anything; and he gave a little regular speech about the official business of getting married and what it meant and what the city of Springfield expected and the different kinds of marriage he had to offer and all that sort of bother. Mr. Yolney, he knew all this foolishness from before, but Thysix and Halan were both looking at Miss Melcie and Miss Varenia and didn't hear a blessed word of it, so the pilot reckoned he'd have to take the boys in hand and steer them through the treacherous course of legal and nuptial matters.

The merchant looked at Mr. Yolney and said:

"I assume you'll be taking your usual one-year lease?"

"That's right."

Thysix frowned. "*Lease*, Pa? Why, I reckoned to sign on Miss Melcie permanent, unless you judge she's nigh unboatable and should ought to be spied out from cam cleats to keelson."

Mr. Yolney said:

"I'm sure she's as going and spry a wife as you could find, Thysix; and I'm just as sure you run no risk giving your custom to my old friend, Mr. Cosgred. He's leased me a wife or two in our time, hain't that the truth?" The store owner just smiled modestly. Mr. Yolney continued: "I was just advising you, Thysix, that it's a sight less irksome to lease, and there are a heap of other advantages, too. For one thing, you don't have to worry none about repairs and maintenance, which I can promise you I learned about to my sorrow before you was even a nagging notion in my jubilant mind. If something unlucky served Miss Melcie—and fate preserve her from anything of the sort—Mr. Cosgred would gladly give you the loan of another wife just about as likely as yourn. And then, when the year's come to an end, why, you just bring Miss Melcie back to Mr. Cosgred's emporium, and you lease yourself whichever new soft-voiced, dadblamingest wife that takes your fancy."

Thysix listened, but it was plain that he suspicioned it was nothing but traps and hiving. "The truth is, Pa, that at the end of the year you don't own but *nuthin'*; and after payin' all that money, and trainin' a wife so's she acts civilized and just so; and feedin' and clothin' and paradin' her around, then you wants to pay a whole *nuther* deal of money on a *second* wife you don't know from Joshua's niece's cousin, and start the whole pison-long business *again*. And you don't never strike a day when you actually own a rattlin' *thing!*" He looked as if his father was trying to smouch some awful, childish foolishness past him for some reason.

"When I was your age, Thysix, I thought the same things; and I made the same mistake you're sure enough about to make. But, as I says, I judge this is all part of your growing up. I could mention that a leased wife don't depreciate like a boughten wife does, nor must you pay certain taxes and levies that otherwise remain the responsibility of Mr. Cosgred. But this is where I stand back and let you take the pad and control of your own private future, as they call it." He folded his arms and turned to Miss Lyjia, and the two of them commenced an acquaintance that showed every bit and grain of cordiality, and bid fair to grow into deeper understandings yet to be.

Said Thysix:

"Then I'll *buy*, ruther than throw my money away and have nuthin' but expired contract papers to show for it. Halan?"

Mr. Yolney turned to look at his son and said:

"Leave him alone for that. He can cipher his own mind." And Halan spoke up himself:

"Oh, well, I s'pose Uncle Grather knows more than Thysix and me lumped together about this wife business, but I judge buyin' is pretty good enough, too." He just couldn't let Thysix leap out to some imaginary promotion. The boys glanced at Mr. Yolney, wondering if his advanced years and the dreadful responsibilities in the pilothouse made him look for easeful answers during his occasional time ashore in such places as Springfield.

"Fine," said Mr. Cosgred. "I'll have the papers ready in a few moments."

Thysix gave Halan a nudge and pointed toward his winsome Miss Melcie. "This ain't bully nor nuthin'! I reckon not! This must be the biggest boss dodge of all!"

Halan, for his part, however, wanted to shin it out of the wife shop before anything even more troublesome happened; and he wished that he hadn't let the pilot begin this tour of Springfield and all its ruinations. Halan, he was just ready to slip out, when the proprietor came back with three sets of contracts. Mr. Yolney signed his lease, and Miss Lyjia daintily set down her name; and then Mr. Cosgred gave the two boys their papers. Thysix and Miss Melcie signed theirs as quick as a sneeze through a mitten; but Halan hung back, pretending to read this clause and that emendation and one other proviso and a rider. Thysix laughed and said:

"You look scared most to death, Halan!"

"Lord A'mighty, no!" Halan signed his name, and so did Miss Varenia. Thysix arranged them all, with Mr. Yolney and Miss Lyjia betwixt the younger couples, Thysix himself and Miss Melcie on one side, and t'other couple on t'other. Thysix asked:

"Is there much ceremony? I get uncommon fidgety in ceremonies."

The salesman examined the contracts and collected his fees. He said: "No ceremony. As soon as I give you your receipts and enter this data in Springfield's data base for vital records, you will be wedded couples. I hope to do business with you all again." They had their receipts in a tolerable short time, and then Mr. Yolney led them back out onto the dreary street. Thysix leaped right in with:

"Gamblin' now, Pa. Metasense next?"

The pilot stared at his son for a moment. "It's your *weddin'* night, boy. That ought to hold you until breakfast, at least. A good pilot needs lightning judgment and quick reactions, but above all else he needs stamina during the long and perilous watches. You must test that tonight. Sometimes there's just no way I can understand you, Thysix; it's like you packed a deal of Bouligny's rich black mud behind your eyes for when you got lonesome. Now we must find rooms."

Mr. Yolney's pay, many times more than what the cubs earned, left him with enough spending cash to hire a lovely suite in a good hotel, even after the cost of his wife's lease had been deducted. The boys, however, were not in such handsome condition. They had little of their wages left, and had to take rooms in a low part of town, some distance from the pilot's splendid hotel. As they parted, Mr. Yolney said:

"Remember men—for men you have become—your education has only barely *begun*. All that flummery aboard the *Smoky Mary* was just work, common labor. Now you must find out what *life* is all about, and life will lay out flummery every time. It's up to you to see that you turn out worthy of your folks, and the others home on Bouligny. I plan to put in here in Springfield maybe six months or more, but I s'pose you don't have *that* kind of fortune put by. Don't ever forget that you can come to me for advice anytime; but not a loan nor asylum from the law." He led his Miss Lyjia up to the hotel, leaving his charges staring after and watching the gaudily uniformed porters and other fancy hands hopping to their duties; and then Mr. Yolney disappeared inside. Halan felt his heart slump down towards his stomach somewheres—he hadn't sized on learning all about *life*, at least not for a considerable number of years yet to come. Now he had the burden of a legal wife—a notion that was just beginning to skaddle its horribleness around in his brain. He said good night to Thysix and Miss Melcie; and then Halan went with Miss Varenia to their meager suite—to their new home.

Though it may be true that he had all the grit of a colicky puppy, howsomever Halan was fit for it, life for him had begun.

5

The prettiest surprise to Halan was he *liked* being married. Varenia was tall and slender and beautiful, as many of the wives in Mr. Cosgred's shop had been; she had fine hair of a medium length and a delicate claret color; her eyes were long and heavy-lidded and as bright as polished brass; her voice was low and loaded to the gunwales with humor most times, with honest interest or sympathy or what else might be needed t'other occasions. She was helpful and loyal and such, just as Halan had expected when he laid his money down; but it was more than that—she wanted a home, not just a place to live; she was determined to see that they

were happy, not just satisfied; and Halan was always striking delighted discoveries of little, thoughtful things she had done for him.
He found himself spying out ways to let her know how much she
meant to him, too. It wasn't long before he told her that he loved
her. He was still a mite shy about speaking aloud of such things,
but he said:

"I've been fond of you, Varenia, but it's doggone well past
that point now. I feel as if I'd found you on Bouligny myself and
courted you and we'd agreed to a five-year temporary contract,
ruther'n getting . . . getting—"

"Married?" Varenia smiled at him.

"Well, yes. What was such a splendid woman as you doing in a
wife shop anyways?"

She studied that out for a moment and said:

"I always wanted to go into one of the helping professions. I
thought about being a nurse when I was younger."

"I mean, what if you'd been picked by some pitiful, lowdown
rip you couldn't hardly abide?"

"I'm protected by the contract you signed. If a husband does
anything contrary to the contract, a wife can easily get a divorce;
and the penalty to the husband is severe enough to catch his attention. And dear old Mr. Cosgred has the interests of the wives
near his heart, as well as the interests of his customers. If he hadn't
'a' judged you'd be responsible and kind, he wouldn't 'a' taken your
money."

"I'm glad to hear that. And I'm glad he *did* take my money,
sweetheart." Halan embraced his wife and kissed her.

Varenia pushed him away after a little while and smiled. She
said:

"Your cousin isn't so happy now, though, is he?"

Halan was astonished. He said:

"Why, how you talk! How could he *not* be happy, with such a
wife as Miss Melcie to do for him?"

"Melcie's as good and sweet as a body could wish, but that may
not be enough for Thysix. Melcie visited me yesterday, and I do
believe she was nigh onto tears, Halan. I was hoping you'd visit
them and see how it all lays, and if he's treating her all right, and
everything."

"Naturally, Varenia, if you reckon I should. I'll go on by there
tonight."

"Melcie was my best friend, till I met you. It would put me at
ease to know she's comfortable and glad with Thysix."

After supper Halan walked through the eternal springtime of the domed city to the building where Thysix and Miss Mclcie had taken up residence. His feelings were all bothersome for no reason that he could figure. Thysix's apartment was not in the least way grand, nor was it mean and shabby; put beside Halan's own, no nearsighted man could tell the two apart. Yet regardless there was a different air within Thysix's place—a mood of unsettlement and imperfect peace. Halan wished mightily that he had not agreed to come, or that he had brought Varenia with him; with those two wishes ungranted, he hoped only that he could foot it out of there as quick as may be.

Both Thysix and Miss Melcie were polite as pie to him and invited him to have something to eat, which he declined, saying that Varenia had whupped up a special dinner for him that night; then Miss Melcie engaged Halan in a pleasant talk about how he and Varenia were getting along and how they were settling into married life. The chat was amusing enough, but by and by Halan saw that Thysix had allowed Halan and Miss Melcie to share the sofa, while he sat sullen-faced in an old and faded armchair nearby; and the only decorations Thysix put on the conversation was an occasional essay at a joke—but that the joke was always more than halfways bitter and always drew a look from Miss Melcie as if she was fit to bust out crying. She tried to cover up, but Halan could see her wince and shrink back whenever Thysix let fly with one of his peevish dismal remarks. Presently Halan could stand it no longer, and he said:

"Thysix, I come here tonight for to speak with you private about something that's troubled me for a month, most. Why don't you and me light out for a beer and talk it over? That is, if Miss Melcie won't mind her dear husband going off to some den of thieves with me for a spell."

"Miss Melcie won't mind. I reckoned you'd fetch after my advice sooner or later, Halan."

The two boys stood, and Thysix led his younger cousin to the front door. Halan looked back over his shoulder, making a sort of unspoken apology. Miss Melcie gave him back a weak smile. Before they left, Thysix looked at his wife and said:

"Give me a little money, won't you?"

Miss Melcie went to a desk in one corner of the room, pulled down a drawer and took out a box, and selected a few bills. She carried them to Thysix, who took them without a word. After Miss Melcie closed the door behind them, Thysix explained:

"I give over all the accounts to her. She's good at sums, and I'd ruther not have the bother. I can size up if she's skinning me any, and I judge I'll know how to bring her thinking around if she fancies she can come any such game with *me*."

They left the building. It was still evening; it was still spring-time. They headed toward a saloon nearby. Said Halan:

"I'm sure Miss Melcie ain't the kind to skin you none, Thysix. She's every bit and grain as devoted as my own dear Varenia."

Thysix stopped on the sidewalk and said:

"Melcie tops Varenia every which way, Halan, and don't you never forget that, nuther. I asked for the *best*, and I sure have got myself the best."

"I hope to gracious, Thysix, I 'member it all exactly. So she's as uncommon honest as she is uncommon pretty." Thysix only grum-bled and shoved his way into the crowded barroom.

They drank a beer in silence. Thysix didn't have anything to talk about, and Halan was trying to lay out a course towards what he wanted to ask. They had another beer, and then Thysix spoke up of a sudden:

"Bein' married ain't so much," says he.

"I'm finding it tolerable enough so far."

Then Thysix, he swallowed some more beer and shrugged and said:

"And that's just the very wust of it! 'Tolerable!' Just as tolerable as rotting away here in Springfield, when I could be in some pilot-house, a-working for my license. I can't see no advantage in waiting for Pa."

Halan commenced to see what Thysix's problem was—he was getting the fidgety fantods about fooling away another five months or so, till Mr. Yolney signed on with another fastboat. Halan asked:

"Are you fixing to sign on without your pa? With another pilot?"

Thysix frowned into his beer and replied:

"God A'mighty, that's a perfect awful election to make, but I've considered and considered, and I hain't come up with one other idear."

"And you could stand leaving Miss Melcie behind for a spell, too."

"Aw, she's plenty sweet enough, Halan, just as you say. It's mainly that bein' married ain't so much, that's all; it ain't what I thought it would be."

"Talk to your pa, Thysix, an' tell him what you told me. He'll give you the proper heading—he was a cub hisself, once. Tell him how you're just itchin' to get back into space. You have got to trust your pa."

"Ain't *you* itchin' to get back into space?"

"Not so's a body'd notice, Thysix. I'm wonderful happy with Varenia; when Uncle Grather is ready to ship out, I'll ship out with him. I'm in no hurry."

Thysix shook his head and muttered:

"I been lookin' and I been lookin', and I hain't seen nary a trace of it yet. And this is *Springfield*, blame it!"

"What you been lookin' *for*, Thysix?"

Then the older boy's face turned all dismal and sad, and he said:

"I'll be blast if I know!" Right then all the anger and resentment Halan had ever felt towards Thysix went out of him, and he was freighted up with another feeling, something he couldn't put a name to. It would be awhile before Halan judged it was pity.

The next day, Thysix talked it all over with Mr. Yolney; and the upshot was that perhaps Mr. Yolney wouldn't stay on Springfield six months as he had said, and that perhaps Thysix could hold out a sight longer and keep himself from busting with ambition. Thysix allowed as he would give it a try, and everything went back to normal for a bit.

By and by, official letters arrived at the homes of Thysix and Halan, and they caused no end of grief. They were bills from the Springfield Public Service Commission, for the first month's matrimony tax. Halan took one gander at the bill and 'most swooned— the city wanted a full quarter of all the money Halan had left after the wedding and paying the month's rent on the apartment. He showed the bill to Varenia and asked:

"They a-going to send a bill like this every month?"

"Shucks, yes, of course. Getting married is an unnecessary luxury, like getting your body tattooed all over. It ain't like eating and sleeping and breathing—people won't die if they don't get married, though sometimes they judge that they must. Most folks take out temporary contracts for one bit of time or another. It lets out all the risks; you never know what sort of traps and jimcracks a body will bring with him into a marriage. In some places, I've been told, marriage is actually illegal. It's been outlawed on the far, frontier planets; Mr. Cosgred could never explain to us just why those people need a law to protect them, ruther'n just plain common sense. Mr. Cosgred's mail-order business would be more'n he could keep up with, otherwise."

"Never you mind all that! I can't afford to pay this much every month, luxury or no luxury."

Varenia commenced to let tears fall. "Then you *don't* . . ."

Halan said quickly:

"Oh, *don't* say that I don't love you! Hang me if I don't love you, dear—it's just this bill! We don't have much money."

"I know that, Halan."

"I'll have to see Uncle Grather. He'll have to sort this out for me." He felt all empty inside.

"Per'aps this is one reason why he didn't just rip out and buy Miss Lyjia. He leased, you know, and so *he* doesn't get a reckoning every month. Your uncle is an experienced man that has studied what to do with his money. I judge he's middling wise about most things, besides just piloting a fastboat through white space. Go see him and ask his help."

Halan looked glum. Said he:

"Uncle Grather knowed this would happen to Thysix and me. He *told* us to lease a wife as he did, ruther'n buy; but Thysix wouldn't have none of that, and I up and followed like a dad-fetched saphead. I s'pose my uncle will give me hark from the grave when I tell him about this, but there's nothing else for it." Halan kissed Varenia good-bye, and he walked through a bleak Springfield to Mr. Yolney's gilt-edged foofaraw of a hotel.

The pilot listened to Halan's story without asking questions or showing an opinion until the boy had finished, ten full minutes by the watch. Directly, then, Mr. Yolney *did* give him down the banks for Halan's flatheadedness, at great length and volume and with the fine look to detail a body might expect from a fastboat pilot. He said:

"Looky here, I reckon you want me to overhaul your breached hull for you, boy; but just think on what I once said to you—I'll furnish all the counsel you need, but no loans. You won't amount to much of a man if I fetch out my money and make all your trouble disappear. Why, d-mnation! There'd be one more numskull triumph after another for you if I did! You must study making your own bed, Halan, and then you must study lying in it, and then shaping it up again in the morning."

"Aye, aye, sir, Uncle Grather; I know I reckon I gone up on my own. I'm not asking you to give me money. I have got to do whatever must be done on my own hook, sir, but I need you to tell me where and how to commence upon it."

Of a sudden, Mr. Yolney settled some and stopped his bullyragging. He said:

"That is truly a fine thing to hear, Halan. Your spineless cousin —my own son, if it comes to admitting that scurvy fact—was here just a tad afore you; and his only scheme was to hive me out of the money with one lame alibi or t'other. I sent him back with his lines all a-fouled, you may have a good deal of certainty about *that*; and *wasn't* he flinging a blizzard fit! No, I'm glad I took the wrong notion, as far as you are concerned. If you mean to get the money —from a body besides myself—then you have got to earn it. You must find a job of some sort here in Springfield, to help you and your powerful lovely bride live restful till we lift off again in a few months. It will be tolerable easy for me to find you such a position, though it won't be grand employment; but I judge you don't give a sow's sidesaddle for wearing gaudy uniforms to work, or suchlike foolishness."

"No, sir. Any decent work would answer for us."

Mr. Yolney clapped the boy on the back and said:

"It heartens me to hear it, Halan—and it will hearten your mother, too. Avast worrying, boy. Anyways, it's my bounden duty to help you this-a-way. I'll give you the news soon. Present my better wishes to your Miss Varenia—you see, I save all my *best* wishes for my own Lyjia. Just remember this precious sentiment, which my own dear ma learned me many years ago: It *is* true that two folks in love may live as cheaply as one—it's only unfortunate that it costs five or six times as much."

And so with good hopes, Halan bent his course homeward along the way that had magically been made shorter and more pleasant in every respect.

6

One day followed the other into history, and Halan judged that he had never been so contented. When he married Varenia, he had reckoned on recreation and titillation and delectation and perhaps even satiation. He had never figured on exhilaration; he had never figured on happiness. The only source of worry was the money the marriage was costing. Mr. Yolney discovered that there were a considerable number of fine positions available for Halan—in six months. It was unlawful on Springfield to hire a body who was not a resident. In six months, Halan would have his choice of attractive jobs; of course, in six months he would likely be in space again with Mr. Yolney; in six months, unless Halan struck some other plan, he would be in debtor's prison, Varenia would be disconnected or returned to Mr. Cosgred, and the trouble would be settled with no profit in it for nobody. Halan was reminded of the urgency of the problem one day when he received another bill from the Springfield Public Service Commission:

> We sent you an itemized statement of your account and still have not received payment for this amount due. We ask for your prompt payment. If this is not done, will take stronger action that could not only affect your continued service, but your rating with an intersystem credit-reporting agency as well. If payment has recently been sent, thank you. Otherwise, send it without delay.

Halan read the notice and felt himself shiver. He said:

"They are threatening to interrupt service. What do they mean?"

Varenia gave him a wistful smile and said:

"Do you remember when you first saw me? I was wearing an orange plastic necklace then, because I was disconnected. The Public Service Commission can disconnect me again anytime, if we're late in our payments."

"I'll be blest! I'd ruther die than let something like that happen to you, dear."

"It's not so bad, Halan. It's like falling asleep and not dreaming. I had a headache when I was reconnected, but that was the worst of it."

"No, dear, the worst of it is not having the money to stop them from doing such a terrible thing. Per'aps Thysix was right; per'aps I should sign on with another pilot as soon as I can. I'll see Thysix today and find out what success he's had."

The climate was more cheerful in Thysix's apartment. The older boy declared that he had found a pilot who would take him on for a cub. Said he:

"My worries will be over, Halan. Mr. Safroth is a friendly man and, by all accounts, a good pilot. He offered to pay me more than even my pa paid me."

Halan watched his cousin scrouch about the parlor all satisfied with himself. Presently Halan said:

"Your pa's feelings will be hurt, Thysix."

Thysix frowned. He let himself drop down into his favorite armchair. "Hang it, I know that; but I lay Pa will understand. He knows how much it means to me to get my license. Ain't *you* in a hurry, too?"

"Cert'nly I am, but I'll wait for Uncle Grather."

"Suit yourself, Halan."

"Though I can't get any other work and Varenia and I may starve to death before your pa is ready to ship out."

Thysix made an indulgent gesture and said:

"I'll take care of you, my boy. I can take an advance on my wages and loan you enough to see you through."

Halan's eyes opened wide. "You'd do that for me?"

"Shucks, why not? We're flesh and blood, after all." Halan suspicioned that it made Thysix feel good to get him obliged, to make Halan seem even more pitiful. Said Halan:

"Thank you kindly, Thysix."

"Come back tomorrow and I'll have your money for you."

Halan said good-bye to Thysix and Miss Melcie and took his leave. He walked homeward slowly, wondering if he was more glad to have his problem fixed, or more unhappy to be under Thysix's thumb. As he fetched up on his building, he judged that he was glad. It meant that he didn't have to worry about Varenia being disconnected; that was worth all the dreadful gratitude he'd have to show Thysix from now on.

The gladness gave the day mainly a hopeful glow; however, it vanished quickly when Varenia showed Halan another message from the Public Service Commission.

> Urgent!
> Our records show your account to be past due. If we do not receive your payment *in our office immediately*, you will force us to disconnect your service. If disconnected, we cannot assure you that service will be restored until the *next working day following receipt of full payment* of the amount due plus a reconnect charge and a cash deposit, if required. Remember, *you* are our most important resource.

"Blame it!" murmured Halan. He folded the notice and put it in his pocket. He was scared most to death. He hoped Thysix remembered his offer. He gave Varenia a quick kiss, and once more hurried to his cousin's house. Halan was surprised to see his uncle there; Mr. Yolney was soothing Miss Melcie, who sat on the sofa, a-weeping into a lavender-scented handkerchief. Halan took a quick look around and asked:

"What's happened?"

The pilot said:

"It's Thysix. He's been disconnected." Mr. Yolney gave his nephew an amused look. The pilot wasn't in no sweat at all.

"Thysix? But that's terrible!"

322   GEORGE ALEC EFFINGER LIVE! FROM PLANET EARTH

"Oh, he won't suffer worse'n a little banging in his head. Maybe he'll learn suthin' from this."

Halan had trouble ciphering the business. He said:

"I reckoned it was Miss Melcie they must disconnect."

Mr. Yolney grinned. "'Twas Miss Melcie paying the bills. The accounts were in her name, so they disconnected my sapheaded son."

"What are we going to do?"

"Oh, I'll take care of his debt, I reckon. I can't leave him like this. Maybe I threw a little too much growing up at him all at once. He just ain't as rattlin' clever as I was at his age, or else per'aps he is. I'll sign on with the next fastboat what needs a pilot, and you boys can draw advances on your pay to leave with your wives. You'll get your licenses after one more trip, I judge; and then you boys can take up your lives howsomever you want. The first thing, though, is getting Thysix's brain to working again. Maybe when the Public Service Commission jump-starts him again, he'll wake up with more sense and less cockiness in him."

Halan looked at Thysix's monstrous still body, then at Miss Melcie, and finally at his uncle. Said Halan:

"Uncle Grather, sir, I think I'd ruther stay here on Springfield with Varenia. As soon as I can, I'll find myself some sort of job. I purely love going into space and traveling about the worlds, but I love Varenia more. I've only just found her, and I don't think I can leave her behind so easily."

Mr. Yolney gave his nephew a shrewd look. "Are you sure of that, boy?"

"Yes, sir, and I hope you can forgive me. I don't mean to seem ungrateful."

"By no manner of means! I'm pleased for you; and I know your ma will be, too, even though you went and got married. She'll take the notion a sight better in time. Looky here: any thick-skulled baboon can learn to be a pilot; all it takes is some common sense and good judgment and a fine knowledge of when to bluster and when to 'vast blustering. Finding happiness is a deal more difficult; but if you've struck it already, why, you'd be a fool to throw it away. Stay here on Springfield, Halan. I have some help for you, too—a little money, a last gift from your pa. He told me to give it to you when I judged you wouldn't just fool it away on fribbles and wuthless trifles. It ain't much, but it'll keep you till you can pay your own way."

When Halan went home and told Varenia what had happened,

she was surprised as a calf staring at a new gate. "You'd really stay here with me instead of going back into space?" she asked.

"We're *always* in space, dear. We're in space on the bridge of a fastboat or here under the dome in Springfield, or even in the fields on Bouligny. Space is always around us. That's the real beauty and the real mystery of the universe. Now, Thysix can't seem to *see* that; that's why he's so all-fired eager to ship out as soon as may be. To me, though, the romance of being a pilot got lost somewheres, hidden per'aps by the bothers and trials of learning the art. I've found more wonder here with you—the wonder of falling in love. Thysix can't fathom that, nuther. If he'd 'a' knowed the life of a cub on a fastboat wasn't so much for romance, I reckon he'd never 'a' left Bouligny. He's looking ever so hard for something, and I'm tolerable certain he won't never find it."

"I feel sorry for him, then."

"So do I, Varenia. The thing is that you must shed the pretty kickshaws of life so you can live the real article; and Thysix, he can't seem to turn loose of his ideas of adventure and romance. He always dreamed of a gorgeous life and glory, so he's bound to be disappointed—by both piloting and the ups and downs of love."

"But piloting *is* grand, after all, isn't it? And I know that love is, too. Thysix is looking for some kind of imitation grandness instead."

"He's not much older'n I am. Per'aps he'll figure the difference soon."

Varenia looked sad and said:

"I just hope he doesn't lose Melcie before then. Oh, Halan, we got another message while you were gone." She gave it to him and he read it:

> THIS IS TO NOTIFY YOU THAT THE ACCOUNT SHOWN HAS BEEN PLACED FOR IMMEDIATE COLLECTION. IT IS EXTREMELY IMPORTANT THAT THIS ACCOUNT BE PAID IN FULL WITHIN TWENTY-FOUR HOURS. PROPOSED FINAL ACTION WILL BE CANCELED IF YOU REMIT AT ONCE IN FULL.

Said Halan:

"Well, we can pay it now."

"I guess our problems are over, thanks to your pa's wisdom."

Halan smiled. "I don't s'pose our problems will never be over—that's part of what makes real life harder and more lovely than gaudy dreams. But we'll take up the problems as they happen, and we'll work together to solve them, and that will stand us considerable show. We have the whole future together; a body can do a mess of fine living in a lifetime, if he allows hisself the privilege."

"Are you sorry you married me, Halan? Instead of just leasing?"

"My uncle had suthin' like a good idea, I reckon; at least he doesn't have to worry about the bill every month. Still and all, I'd marry you again if I must and gladly pay the tax. But remember, dear: when we visit my ma on Bouligny, we must pretend we *aren't* married. Those folks are dismal old-fashioned, and my ma would never live down the scandal!"

✛   ✛   ✛

Put Your Hands Together

MRS. SMYLES DIDN'T CARE MUCH FOR THE NEWS channel, but she liked to read the bulletin board and hear about all the things that were happening in the dome. She didn't like the people in the dome, but she liked what they were doing. Mrs. Smyles was a tall woman, as thin and hard as a rake handle, with a withered arm and eyes that were always squinted in disgust at the sin and evil of this life. She was proud that she woke up every morning knowing where everything was and how everything ought to be, and she was amazed that nobody else ever seemed to know where anything was and how anything ought to be. Even in Bucktown, where her neighbors were more level-headed than the people in the dome, Mrs. Smyles was sure that they'd all have long ago gone to the devil if they hadn't had her to keep them straight.

Her own sister, Ormanie, had this same peculiar blind spot. Ormanie was ten years younger than Mrs. Smyles and she had a curly-haired boy called Alphabet. Everybody called him that because he was named P. G. T. B. Kologhad after his daddy. His daddy had run off to live in the dome and he might as well be dead, as far as Mrs. Smyles was concerned. Nobody missed P. G. T. B. Senior much. The only good thing he had ever done was to trade some salvaged navigational equipment for a new hymnal and a straw hat with pink and yellow flowers on it. He gave the hat to Ormanie and the hymnal to Mrs. Smyles. He forgot to get something for his boy, Alphabet.

Mrs. Smyles and Ormanie lived in Bucktown, a tumbled heap of junked and ruined spacecraft left behind on the Old Field when the domed city of Springfield built the New Field. The sisters shared the large pressurized cabin of an obsolete yacht, a ship that would never sail again through the eternal night. The Old Field was connected to the dome by a tunnel a mile long built on the surface of the asteroid. Alphabet was always begging his mother to take him to the city, but Mrs. Smyles argued that only bad things could come of it. Alphabet was too young to see all the wickedness and corruption of the dome people. That would be terrible enough, but the worst was the possibility that he would come back to Bucktown with a secret liking for Springfield, and that someday he would go back there to stay, just like his daddy.

One morning Mrs. Smyles was watching the holoset, reading the notes on the bulletin board, when she called out, "Ormanie, honey, you come here and look at this!"

"I'm fixing breakfast," Ormanie said. "Alphabet didn't eat hardly nothing last night for supper."

"Well, this is something I think you ought to see. Hurry up before it goes away."

Ormanie let her breath out loudly and wiped her hands on a towel. "I'll be there terrectly," she said.

"It's high time you introduced Alphabet to the mysteries, sister. It's not right for a boy to grow up without knowing who made him."

Ormanie stared glumly at the holoset. "I made him, Verilee," she said. "Me and Mr. Kologhad." She sat on the arm of Mrs. Smyles's chair, her right leg crossed over her heavy thigh.

"Looky here. It's going to be a camp meeting in the dome today, at the St. Bernard Civic Auditorium. The preacher is Reverend Bobby Laws. I been hearing about him for a long time. I believe I'll go witness, and I'll be glad to take Alphabet with me. You don't have to come, Ormanie. I know how you feel about God." Mrs. Smyles gave her sister a look that was stiff with compassion.

Ormanie didn't want to get into an argument about God again. "You don't know how I feel about God," she said. "You don't know anything about it at all."

"You're one of the Lord's stray lambs, sister, that's all. You just haven't seen the light, but I still pray for you every day. Someday you'll welcome God into your heart and you'll be saved and all my praying will be rewarded, and I'll be the happiest person in Bucktown."

Ormanie let out a groan but didn't say anything. She stood up and went back into the kitchen. The bacon was done cooking, so she took it out of the skillet. She cracked three eggs into the bacon grease and fried them. Then she spooned some grits onto a cracked yellow china plate, added the bacon and eggs, then threw a cup of strong coffee into the leftover bacon grease and mixed it up. She poured the gravy over the grits and brought the plate to the table where Alphabet was waiting with a peeved look on his face. "What's this?" he asked.

"It's redeye gravy," said Ormanie. "You like redeye gravy."

"No, I don't." He picked up a piece of bacon and crushed it between his teeth. Ormanie waited, but Alphabet didn't give her any more trouble about the breakfast.

"What do you think?" asked Mrs. Smyles.

Ormanie looked at her. "What do I think about what?" She told herself that she needed the patience of a saint to live with the boy and her sister. They were lucky she didn't just put on her long, brown cloth coat and leave them. She wasn't so old yet. She could find somebody who would marry her, somebody who would appreciate her cooking and how hard she worked. Nobody would blame her if she did.

"I been saying I'm going to this camp meeting, and I'll take Alphabet along if you want."

Ormanie said she didn't care one way or the other about the camp meeting. She said she didn't think Alphabet did, neither, but if Mrs. Smyles wanted to take him, Alphabet would probably enjoy going to the dome. "Well, Verilee," said Ormanie, "you're asking for trouble. The boy can be a pack of mischief when he wants to be."

"Nobody ever said the Lord's way got to be easy," said Mrs. Smyles. She didn't look at Ormanie when she spoke. She was still reading the messages on the holoset.

"I don't want to go to no camp meeting," said Alphabet. He had tiny white teeth and his eyes were too close together, but otherwise he was a good-looking child.

"You never been to one before," said Mrs. Smyles. "You don't even know what they're like."

The boy turned in his chair. He had a mouthful of grits jammed into his cheeks and he looked like a greedy animal storing up food for winter. His eyes were narrowed and sullen. "I do too know about camp meetings," he said. His words came out smothered and hard to understand. "It's praying and preaching and getting baptized and whatall. I'd rather stay to home."

"You never been baptized," said Mrs. Smyles. "It can't hurt you none."

"What do you know about it?" asked Alphabet. He put another spoonful of grits and gravy into his mouth.

"I know more than you do," said Mrs. Smyles. She gave him a look that was supposed to let him know she was at perfect peace and contentment, thanks to her undying faith in the Lord.

"You do not," said Alphabet. He turned his back and picked up another piece of bacon.

"Ormanie, you shouldn't let the boy talk that way to his elders," said Mrs. Smyles.

"I can't stop him, can I?" she said. "I can't punish him before he says something, and after he says it, it's too late."

Mrs. Smyles opened her mouth to say something, but then decided against it. Ormanie allowed her boy to sass back if he took a mind to it, and there was nothing Mrs. Smyles could do about it. She could see right off that Alphabet was growing up just like his daddy, and he'd probably run off to Springfield and desert them both as soon as he got old enough.

Ormanie wasn't afraid of that. She always told Mrs. Smyles not to worry about it. "You know what will happen?" she said. "I'll tell you. Someday Alphabet will go to the city by himself. He's a normal boy, he's got a normal boy's curiosity. When he gets to the city, though, everybody's going to make fun of him. They're going to say 'Why, look at the jicky from Bucktown. Who let this jicky in here?' And poor Alphabet will come home crying, and he'll be proud to be a jicky and he'll never go to the dome again to his dying day."

"That what happened to you, Ormanie? People make fun of you? That why you never go to Springfield?"

Ormanie looked at her sister with a solemn expression. "Verilee," she said in a low voice, "I never told you all of what happened to me there, and I never will. You can just use your imagination, but I'm sure you couldn't think of half the awful things I saw."

Mrs. Smyles shook her head. "And those city folks made you proud to be a jicky," she said.

"Well, yes."

"The city's a terrible place, all right, but a good Christian ain't afraid to go anywhere. A good Christian knows he walks in the protection of the Lord. If you was a good Christian, things would've been different."

"How, Verilee? All them people would've said the same things. All them people would've done the same things."

"Yes," said Mrs. Smyles with a look of a woman who has taught and taught and knows every lesson has been in vain, "but in the protection of the Lord none of the evil would've touched you. You would've come back home praising His name."

Ormanie looked at her and blinked a couple times. "Alphabet," she said, "you finish your grits and change your shirt. Your Aunt Verilee is taking you to the camp meeting this morning."

"She'll have to find me first," said Alphabet.

"Don't you mind him," said Ormanie. "He always talks like that."

"Don't I know it," said Mrs. Smyles.

While Ormanie packed some cold collard sandwiches for lunch, Mrs. Smyles put on a long black dress with a string of small plastic pearls and a broad-brimmed black felt hat with a white ribbon. She carried her hymnal and the sack of sandwiches in her good hand. Alphabet had on a pair of jeans and a red shirt that said Old Field Trash And Proud Of It.

"Are we ready?" asked Mrs. Smyles.

Alphabet rolled his eyes. "Mama, do I gotta?" he whined.

"You go with your Aunt Verilee and be good," said Ormanie. "If I hear you was a bad boy, you'll spend the night down in the dark engine room where the bogeyman lives. Now go have a good time."

"Don't you give him another thought," said Mrs. Smyles. She led Alphabet out of the cabin and through the airlock into the long tunnel that pointed toward the green dome of Springfield. "Alphabet," she said, "you carry these sandwiches for me. I only have one arm, you know, and might need to use it. Take the book too."

"I'll go to the camp meeting with you," said the boy, "but I won't pray. Nobody can make me pray."

"That's right," said Mrs. Smyles, "nobody can make you pray. You don't have to pray if you don't want. But maybe when you get there and see how glad everybody is, how happy they all are praying, why, maybe you'll just join right in. Miracles still happen."

Alphabet was already peeking into the brown paper sack at the sandwiches. "She only made four, two for you and two for me. When are we going to eat?"

"After the prayer meeting. Now close up that sack. When I was a girl just about as old as you are, it was coaches that ran along this rail here. You could ride for free, and the coaches ripped along without making a sound. If you closed your eyes, you didn't even know you was moving. It was like an angel carrying you between the Old Field and the dome."

"You been praying a long time, Aunt Verilee?"

"All my life, I hope to tell you," said Mrs. Smyles. She gave Alphabet a warm look of satisfaction, the same look she wore at Easter Sunday service until her joints began to ache.

"And you're still waiting for an answer."

Mrs. Smyles's satisfied look went away. "Oh, I've had my answers," she said coldly. "I've had my answers. I don't need to pray for myself anymore, Alphabet, on account of I welcomed Jesus as my personal Savior. I pray for other people. *Other people*, Alphabet, who haven't learned yet how easy it is to be saved and how terrible it will be if they ain't." She shook her head sadly. "I expect some-day my prayers for *other people* will be answered too, but it ain't nothing more I can do but pray for them."

They passed through a large, abandoned lobby and climbed up a frozen escalator. Before they stepped out onto the crowded street, Mrs. Smyles glanced at her reflection in a mirror. She straightened her black dress and tugged at her floppy hat. She tried on a blissful smile and a pious expression. She decided on a serious look that wouldn't invite conversation from strangers during the walk to the auditorium. "We can stop and look at all these store windows after the meeting," she told Alphabet, "but I don't want to be late." Alphabet didn't say a word. He had already promised himself that whatever happened, he wasn't going to be impressed by anything in Springfield. He was going to be bored by it all.

When they got to the St. Bernard Civic Auditorium, they found a sign directing them to Gate C. "C for Christ," said Mrs. Smyles.

The admission was free, but Reverend Bobby Laws's deacons were asking for a love offering to help in his good works. A deacon looked at Mrs. Smyles and Alphabet and said, "It's all right, sister. Just pass on through."

Mrs. Smyles said, "I don't have much money, young man, but what I do have is for the Lord to use in His way." She dropped a few coins into a basket half full of many-colored paper bills. The deacon gave her a heavy paper fan decorated with a picture of Jesus the Good Shepherd.

A large green and white striped tent had been set up on the floor of the auditorium. It was warm and still in the tent, and people were stirring up the air with their Good Shepherd fans. An usher helped Mrs. Smyles and Alphabet find seats.

"What are all these folks here for, Aunt Verilee?" asked Alphabet.

There were hundreds of people waiting on hard benches in front of a raised wooden pulpit. "They're here because they love God," said Mrs. Smyles. "Or else they're terrible sinners who've been brought here to be washed."

"Washed how?"

"In the blood of the Lamb."

"Yuck," said Alphabet.

A man in a plum-colored suit sat next to Mrs. Smyles. He took off his hat and leaned forward in a little bow. "Name's Doggett, missus. Vessel Doggett. I trade in valves and gaskets of all kinds, retail and to the trade, had my own business now for fifteen years."

"How do," said Mrs. Smyles.

"I see you've got a withered arm."

"You see right," said Mrs. Smyles.

Mr. Doggett looked at her and closed one eye to let her know he was speaking in absolute sincerity. "It's one true thing you can say about life, and it's everybody's got a cross to bear. You got your withered arm. I got a back it won't let me do no lifting nor carrying and a wife at home with inflagrations of every bone in her body. I'll bet your boy here got something wrong with him too."

Mrs. Smyles looked at the man in the plum-colored suit, blinking and frowning. "He ain't my boy," she said.

Mr. Doggett said, "I didn't mean nothing by it, lady. He sure is a good-looking boy."

"She ain't my mama," said Alphabet. "She's my Aunt Verilee."

Mr. Doggett smiled. "Verilee. Now I think that's just the prettiest name." He closed his eye again in a wink.

Mrs. Smyles's expression grew sterner. "I'll thank you to watch how you talk. That's just how my husband started on me, and I ain't fool enough to listen to it from you too."

"Your husband must be a powerful lucky man."

"Last I heard, he'd taken up blerd ranching on Shukran. Mr. Smyles knows less about ranching than my daddy's dead cat. Serve him right if he spends the rest of his days sweeping out barns."

"You don't keep blerds in barns," said Mr. Doggett.

"A lot I care," said Mrs. Smyles.

Alphabet tugged on her sleeve and pointed. "What's that?" he asked, nodding toward a low canvas pool beside the pulpit. "Is that for the baptizing?"

"Yes," said Mrs. Smyles. She watched as two men set up a stepladder beside the pool. She remembered her baptizing, forty years ago, how she'd felt as if all her sins had come off in the water and had floated away. As she got older, new sins blackened her and were harder to wash off. She knew that God pardoned her every sin, but she never again felt as clean and pure as after her baptizing. She never felt really forgiven. "Maybe you'll hear the call today, boy. Maybe today's the day you'll open yourself to the Lord and be baptized. It would make your mama so happy."

"My mama don't give a damn about it," said Alphabet. Mrs. Smyles pressed her lips together hard and looked back at the front of the congregation.

In a little while a minister came into the tent and climbed up on the platform. "Is that him?" asked Mrs. Smyles. "Is that Reverend Bobby Laws?" She thought the man was too thin and nice-looking to be much of a preacher. Bobby Laws was supposed to be able to strike divine fire from his first word to his last.

"No," said Mr. Doggett in a low voice, "that's the Reverend Vriner. He's a pretty good preacher and he's hard on backsliders, but he ain't no Bobby Laws."

"I guess I can see that," said Mrs. Smyles. She fanned herself and settled back to listen to Reverend Vriner. The meeting was just beginning, and men and women were still coming into the auditorium. The people on the benches were whispering and coughing. Mrs. Smyles looked around with disapproval. She hit Alphabet on the back of his head and said, "Sit still!" although he wasn't making any noise. He was just the only person she could reach.

Reverend Vriner let his gaze travel from one side of the gathering to the other. He had a fierce look in his eyes, as if he had been sent out single-handed to convert a world full of Christian-eating savages. "How many people we got here today who'll give the Lord their vote? Say amen!"

There was a mild "Amen!" from the assembly.

Reverend Vriner smiled sadly and shook his head. "Seems the Lord ain't got many friends here in Springfield. I said how many people here today'll give the Lord their vote? Say amen!"

The response was a good deal louder this time. Mrs. Smyles shouted it out. Alphabet sat slump-shouldered on the bench with a weary look on his face.

"It's some better," said Reverend Vriner. "I can see we got our work to do. I want to tell you what it was like being lost and ignorant. I want to tell you what my life was like before I met up with the Reverend Bobby Laws and found God."

Someone in the crowd yelled "Hallelujah!" Reverend Vriner smiled and said, "Glory! Praise Jesus, brother! I used to be like some of you. I thought I knew what preachers meant when they said salvation. I thought I knew it all. But I'm here to tell you I didn't know. I'm here to tell you that you don't know, neither. No, not until the power of God lights your heart can you see the truth. That's the first gift you get from God, the knowledge of how wrong you been. Once you seen that, my friends, once you seen how terribly wrong you been, then it ain't nothing to do but come and get cleansed in the holy tears and blood of Jesus Christ."

"Yuck," said Alphabet.

"Pay attention," muttered Mrs. Smyles. "The man is talking to you."

"I ain't heard my name yet," said the boy.

The man in the plum-colored suit leaned over and whispered, "If you'll excuse me, missus, it seems to me that your weazened arm ain't the half of your troubles."

Mrs. Smyles sat up straighter. "The boy ain't no trouble," she said. "One day he'll hear the Word of the Lord, and it will give me so much joy, it will all be worth it."

Mr. Doggett looked at her silently for a moment. "You really fancy the preaching, don't you?" he said at last. He seemed astonished, as if a camp meeting was the last place he'd expected to meet someone like her.

"I haven't missed saying my prayers, morning and night, in more than forty years," said Mrs. Smyles.

"And you're proud of it too!" The man's surprise had turned to amusement.

"If you ain't here to testify," said Mrs. Smyles coldly, "what are you here for?"

Mr. Doggett winked at her. "Christians need gaskets every bit and grain as much as normal people," he said.

Mrs. Smyles turned away and paid the man no more attention. The minister finished his exhortation and began inventing a hymn, thinking up one line while the congregation repeated the last one. "We'll suffer not in Glory, we'll leave our cares below," he sang. "We'll know but joy and comforting, when to Paradise we go."

Mrs. Smyles put her fan on her lap and clapped her hand on her leg until the improvised hymn ended. She called out "Amen!" and picked up her Good Shepherd fan. Her peaceful expression faded again as she gloomily contemplated the sinful company around her.

Reverend Vriner raised his arms high over his head. "Brothers and sisters, I want you to put your hands together! I want you to put your hands together one time, because now we're going to bring out somebody who *knows* how to rock your soul, somebody who *knows* how to lift your heart! Put your hands together one time for the Reverend Bobby Laws!"

"Now you're sure going to hear something," said Mr. Doggett. "Now you're going to hear some real preaching. If it's any sinful secret you don't want folks to know about, you best get aholt of it tight, because Bobby Laws can drag it clean out of a body."

"Sinful secret," said Mrs. Smyles contemptuously.

The people on the benches near the pulpit began to clap their hands. Mrs. Smyles leaned forward to see, but a woman in yellow overalls jumped up and blocked her view. She reached forward and tapped the woman on the arm. "Pardon me," she said. The woman ignored her. Mrs. Smyles tapped her again. "Pardon me," she said in a louder voice.

"Stand up, Miss Verilee," said Mr. Doggett. "Won't none of these people sit down 'til Bobby Laws lets 'em sit down."

"It ain't right for a preacher to stir such a ruckus," said Mrs. Smyles. She stood up and pulled Alphabet to his feet too. She could see the pulpit if she looked over the shoulder of the woman in the yellow overalls. "It's the gospel should get the welcome, not the man."

"Aunt Verilee," said Alphabet, "it ain't no man."

At last Mrs. Smyles caught sight of the Reverend Bobby Laws. He was a humanoid creature with skin the color of the water in Lake Lee in City Park. His legs were very long and thick, like tree trunks. His arms were attached at strange angles to his small body, and his hands hung down to his knees. His blue face was smiling, but the glitter in his black compound eyes frightened Mrs. Smyles. "Dear Lord," she murmured.

"Hee hee," cackled Mr. Doggett. "I just love to see the looks on their faces! Surprised you, didn't he? You should see the look on your face!"

"Sweet Jesus, he's a prytanian," murmured Mrs. Smyles. She sat down slowly on the bench. Her Good Shepherd fan fell to the floor.

The alien preacher held up his hands for quiet. "I'm Bobby Laws," he said. "I've preached on twenty worlds in the last month, and now I'm happy to be here on Springfield. What can I do for you folks?" He was well-spoken but a little hoarse.

Mrs. Smyles sat on the bench feeling as if her throat were closing up. She watched the woman in yellow overalls lift herself up on her toes, then come back down, then lift herself up again. People were shouting on all sides. Bobby Laws's words soared over the clamor and came to Mrs. Smyles as if they were aimed at her alone. He sounded more intelligent than most prytanians, but one look had been enough to convince her that he was an ungodly mockery of a human being, a fraud and a wicked impostor.

Mrs. Smyles sat on the edge of the bench with her good hand pressed tightly in her lap. A part of her wanted to stand up and march out of the tent and out of the auditorium, but another part of her was mesmerized by this blue creature that called itself a minister of the Lord. "Blaspheming the holy Scriptures," she muttered.

"Here comes a miracle, missus, hee hee!" Mr. Doggett was enjoying her distress. "The convicted and the afflicted, they're fighting each other to be first. Maybe you should come forward too. Maybe you should take your awful old arm on up and let that there Bobby Laws speak some words over it."

Mrs. Smyles did not relax her stiff posture. "I thank you to stop mentioning my arm, Mr. Doggett."

"You can just call me Vessel, it ain't no reason we can't be friends." He looked at her with his head tilted a little. "What I tell you? Hee hee! Here comes the miracle, just like I said!"

The Reverend Bobby Laws came down from the pulpit and raised his hands for quiet. "It won't be no miracles," said Mrs. Smyles. "It's all profanity and swindles."

The woman in the yellow overalls turned around and gave her an angry look. "If all you jickies come for was to scoff," she said, "why didn't you just stay to home?"

Mrs. Smyles felt her face grow hot. "I surely didn't come to scoff, but it's my Christian duty to protect this boy. It ain't no camp meeting, it's an abomination in the eyes of the Lord."

Two deacons carried a stretcher up the aisle to the front of the gathering. An old brown woman lay on the stretcher, frail as a bundle of dry sticks. Bobby Laws knelt beside her, and she lifted her head to whisper in his ear. The preacher stood up and looked out at the assembly. "This good woman is eaten up with cancer," he said. "She believes in the power of God. She doesn't know a thing about the power of Bobby Laws. My friends, let me tell you one secret: Bobby Laws don't *have* no power. No sir. Y'all came to see Bobby Laws work wonders, but now you got to hear the plain truth: Bobby Laws *can't* work no wonders. This woman has cancer, and I truly wish I could heal her. I wish I could just lay my hands on her and make her whole, take away her pain, give her back her strength and spunk. But I can't, brothers and sisters, because I'm only a preacher, and preachers can't do miracles."

"Shoot," said Mr. Doggett. "This ain't what I come to see." He spat on the floor.

"I'm only a man," said the Reverend Bobby Laws, "and men can't do miracles."

"He ain't no man," said Mrs. Smyles angrily. "He ain't no preacher and he ain't no man. Men are created in God's image, men and women, but not blue-skinned devils that quote Scripture when it serves their purpose. It's a sin just to listen to him. He can talk, but that don't make him human. Prytanians don't have souls, just like beasts and birds and serpents don't have souls."

"You best hush up, Miss Verilee," said Mr. Doggett. "I'm warning you for your own good. Lots of folks around here come to hear him talk."

"You tell her," said the woman in the yellow overalls. "You ought to tell your friend to shut her goddamn mouth."

Mrs. Smyles was furious. "How dare you talk to me that way?" she cried.

Bobby Laws glanced toward the disturbance. "It's only God that can do miracles," he said. "Only God in His infinite love can work a healing. But sometimes, my friends, God chooses to work through a poor sinner like me." He rested his three-fingered hand on the old woman's forehead. "Sister, do you believe in the power of the Lord? Do you have faith, not in me, but in Him? I'm asking you to forget everything you've ever heard about Bobby Laws, because Bobby Laws is just a speck in the Lord's great plan. Do you love Jesus, sister? Do you trust in God?"

The sick woman lifted a hand and let it fall back to the stretcher.

Bobby Laws bent close to her. "Jesus told the paralyzed man, 'Rise, take up your pallet and go home.' And he rose and took up the pallet and went out before them all, so that they were all amazed and glorified God, saying, 'We never saw anything like this!'"

"This is sacrilege," said Mrs. Smyles.

The brown, shrunken woman on the stretcher clutched Bobby Laws's arm and slowly pulled herself up. Tears sparkled like diamonds on her dark face. Shouts of "Hallelujah!" came from the crowd.

"It's a trick!" said Mrs. Smyles. Her fist was clenched, ready to battle everything in the world she hated and feared. "It ain't no healing! It's a lie and a cheat!"

With Bobby Laws's help, the weak invalid woman got to her feet. She was as unsteady as a newborn deer, but her eyes shone with wonder. "I don't hurt," she said in a quavering voice. "Praise Jesus!"

Mrs. Smyles was numb with outrage. "He's a devil and it's all fakery!" she said.

The woman in yellow overalls slapped her and Mrs. Smyles reeled back. Mr. Doggett got to his feet and slapped the woman in yellow. "It ain't no cause for you to hit her," he said. The woman's husband, a little man with thin black hair and sullen eyes, tried to grab Mr. Doggett around the neck.

"Who . . . do . . . you . . . *think—*" demanded Mrs. Smyles. She swung her good arm and struck the woman a light blow on the shoulder. Deacons and ushers hurried to break up the scuffle. The woman in yellow pushed Mrs. Smyles, and she fell over onto Alphabet. Mr. Doggett helped her up. "Don't pay her no more mind," he said. "Maybe you best go on home."

"I'll go," said Mrs. Smyles breathlessly, "and it'll be a cold day before I come back here."

"Missus," said one of the deacons, "your boy is hurt."

Alphabet lay on the floor between the benches, an ugly dark line of blood running from his head. Mrs. Smyles gave a stifled shriek and bent over him.

"He ain't breathing, ma'am," said an usher.

Mrs. Smyles straightened and pointed at the woman in yellow. "You killed my sister's boy," she said. "He's dead and you killed him."

"Missus," said the deacon, "he like to talk to you."

Reverend Bobby Laws came up to Mrs. Smyles. She stared at him in mute rage. His faceted eyes made him look like a demon that had come to snatch poor Alphabet down to Hell. He murmured some comforting words that didn't fool her for a minute. Slowly all the horror leaked out of her, and she just looked at him and couldn't say a word.

"Are you all right?" asked Bobby Laws.

"What am I going to say to Ormanie?" asked Mrs. Smyles.

"Do you believe in the power of the Lord, sister?"

Mrs. Smyles gave him a thin smile. "I believe in the power of the Lord, all right," she said. "What I don't believe in is you."

Bobby Laws nodded solemnly. "If you want me to, I think I can give you back your boy."

Mrs. Smyles gasped. "Resurrect the boy? Raise the dead? Like Jesus?" The blasphemy of the suggestion overwhelmed her.

"He done it before, missus," said the deacon. "I seen him."

"Sometimes God works through me," said Bobby Laws, spreading his hands. He shrugged.

Mrs. Smyles took a step backward. "I've never heard nothing so evil," she said.

The preacher looked into her eyes. "You're not afraid of me, sister," he said softly. "You're afraid of the real greatness of God. You're afraid there's more to the mysteries than just singing songs and saying prayers."

"You can have the boy back," said the deacon, "good as new."

"I'm a good Christian," Mrs. Smyles insisted.

"You ought to ask yourself if you really believe in anything at all," said Bobby Laws.

Mrs. Smyles covered her mouth with her hand and turned away. She pushed through the people and ran out of the tent. A block from the auditorium she found a small coffee shop. She went in and sat in a red vinyl booth. She stared out the window, and tears ran down her cheeks.

"Can I get you something, lady?" asked the waitress.

"No," said Mrs. Smyles, "thank you."

"Something wrong? You're crying."

Mrs. Smyles dabbed at the tears. "Nothing," she said. "I lost my book of hymns. I left it behind. I been having that book for years." The waitress let her sit in the booth without ordering anything. Mrs. Smyles watched the traffic go by in the street, and after a while her tears just stopped falling.

Introduction to "Seven Nights in Slumberland"

George Alec Effinger . . .

. . . who I met first of all when I was fourteen, in a Fafhrd and the Gray Mouser comic—he wrote an eight-page origin story for the Mouser, I remember. That was before I read any of his books or stories, so for me he was always a comics guy.

When we first actually met, twenty years later, he seemed touched that I'd noticed, and that I'd remembered.

Let one meal stand for all of them; let one conversation stand for all of them.

We're in a Chinese restaurant, somewhere in America, me and George (I never learned to call him Piglet, for which he always seemed rather grateful) and the lovely Barbara Hambly. The Chinese restaurant is vast and, except for us, completely empty. The food is excellent.

We are talking about writing: the craft, and narrative, and building books, and making magic using only words. This is only unusual because mostly writers talk about money. To make up for it we also talk about money, and the hospital bills that meant that, for several years, he would only write "sharecropped" stories in other people's worlds—the hospital he owed money to was claiming that they owned his copyright material. We talk about story. We talk about books. He apologized that there were no transvestite waitresses; if only we were eating at night, rather than during the day, we would have gone to a restaurant that there would have been. Somewhere in there we decide that he will one day tell the story of Dracula from Renfield's point of view. I no longer remember exactly why. It would have made him rich, possibly beyond the dreams of avarice. And the hospital could have done little with characters already belonging to other people.

And we talk about the food. And I learn things.

I think that was what I liked best about talking with him: I learned things.

I don't think we talked about this story then, but we did another time, and we're letting this meal stand for all. How he took my characters and folded them into the landscape of Winsor McCay's Little Nemo. "Seven Nights in Slumberland" is a Little Nemo story, in which Nemo meets the Endless (from my "Sandman" series) —in order of age, though not of appearance: Destiny, Death, Dream, Destruction, Desire, Despair, and Delirium.

It is, like all of his stories, beautifully written and constructed, a bravura performance, in which comics' two best-known dream-worlds are finally united. I like to think that he would have written it anyway, even without the strange threats from the hospital that meant that he was forced into "sharecropping." I think he would. He seemed proud of this story, after all, and with good reason.

—Neil Gaiman

✦ ✦ ✦

Seven Nights in Slumberland

THE FIRST NIGHT:

THE YEAR WAS 1905. LITTLE NEMO WAS SIX YEARS old, and he was having trouble falling asleep. He wore a long, white nightshirt, and he lay between stiffly starched and ironed muslin sheets in his wooden bed with the high headboard. He said, "I hope I can get to the palace in Slumberland tonight. I do so want to meet the Princess again. Yes! I hope I don't wake up before I get there."

The lonesome Princess had sent many of her servants and subjects to lead Nemo to the royal palace of her father, the King of Slumberland, but almost every night some accident or adventure caused the boy to waken before he arrived. Every night Nemo's papa and mama were roused by the sound of his tumbling from his bed in the throes of his dream struggles. Every morning they wondered what ailed the boy, and determined that he should never again be allowed to eat cheese toast at bedtime.

On this night, the Princess of Slumberland had sent a special courier with wonderful news to Nemo. The courier's name was Lopopo, and he was a tall, thin man with a tuft of red hair and a wide, friendly grin. He was wearing a fine purple coat with wide lapels, green tights, and green boots, and he had a very high, green hat that came to a point. "Oh, Nemo," he said politely, "the Princess herself has sent me with this invitation. It is for you, yes!"

Nemo took an envelope from Lopopo and opened it. Inside were a pasteboard ticket and a brief note from the Royal Box Office of Slumberland. "This is for me?" the boy asked.

"Yes, yes. There is to be a special baseball game played for the entertainment of the Princess. That ticket is for you. You will join the Princess at the stadium, and after the game I will present you to His Majesty."

"A baseball game! Oh, I am excited!"

Lopopo led Nemo down a flight of stairs that had never before existed in the boy's bedroom. "Yes, it will be a thrilling contest, I have no doubt, a game between the New York Giants and the Pittsburgh Pirates. They are the two best teams in the National League."

Nemo was so pleased that he clapped his hands. "The New York Giants are Papa's favorite! He will wish that he had come with me. Oh!"

At the bottom of the stairs, Nemo discovered that they were in a low-ceilinged tunnel. Torches mounted along the sides of the tunnel gave a smoky light, and it glittered on the facets of many colored gems that decorated the walls.

"This cavern will lead us to Slumberland, all right," Lopopo said. "It is only about a thousand miles long. Then it is but another five hundred miles through the King's realm to the Slumberland Stadium. We will be there soon, ha!"

They walked for a very long time, and Nemo was surprised by all the bizarre and wonderful sights to be seen in Slumberland and its outlying reaches. He was beginning to grow tired, though, and he stopped and stretched. "Will we ever get there?" he asked.

Lopopo laughed. "Come along, Nemo! You do not wish to disappoint the Princess, no! Everyone in Slumberland knows how much she has missed her playmate."

They walked another hundred miles, and then another. At last they climbed a very long, very broad set of marble stairs, from the underground cavern up into the fresh, flower-scented air of Slumberland.

"Hurry, Nemo!" Lopopo urged. "We have five hundred miles more to walk, and we have only a few minutes!"

"Oh, I am walking as fast as I can!" Nemo said.

They hurried through wide, tree-lined boulevards, where crowds of Slumberland's citizens cheered the boy who had become their beloved Princess's new friend. They passed by grand, imposing buildings in which the affairs of Slumberland were debated and ordered. After a while, Lopopo pointed. "There! Nemo! The Slumberland Stadium!"

"Good," Nemo said. "I do not think I could walk another hundred miles."

"Now, you have not lost your ticket, have you, Nemo?"

The boy held up the envelope. "I have it right here."

"Then give it to the man in the blue uniform and we will go right in. It is almost time for the baseball game to start!"

The Slumberland Stadium was the biggest Nemo had ever seen. He and Lopopo began walking up the marble ramps toward the special box of seats reserved for the King of Slumberland, his daughter, and their guests. At last they emerged, and Nemo could look down at the baseball diamond laid out below.

"Oh! It is so beautiful!" he said. "I have never seen grass so green!"

"This way, Nemo," Lopopo said, directing him to his seat beside the Princess.

"Oh, come to me!" the Princess said. "I have missed you! You will enjoy the baseball game. It will be grand!"

Nemo bowed to the Princess, then sat beside her. He looked down at the field again, where the game was about to begin. "Oh, it is 'Matty'!" he said. "Mathewson is pitching for the Giants! 'Matty' is Papa's favorite player. He will wish he'd come, gracious!"

The Princess looked through her field glasses. "And now it is Honus Wagner batting for the Pittsburgh fellows," she said.

"He is a very good hitter," Nemo said. "'Matty' will have to be careful."

Mathewson pitched a hard fast ball and Wagner swung at it. He hit a foul ball that sped like a rocket toward Nemo and the Princess.

"Aha," Nemo said. "'Dutch' Wagner is sending us a souvenir!"

"Oh, I'm afraid it will hit us!" the Princess said.

"I will catch it," Nemo said. The ball began as a little white speck down on the playing field, and as it came nearer it grew larger and larger and larger. Soon the ball seemed the size of a melon, then it was as big as a house, and then Nemo could see nothing at all except the gigantic baseball that was screaming toward him.

"Oh!" he said. "It will crush us! Help!"

And the next thing Nemo knew, he was tangled up in his bedclothes on the floor of his room. His papa had come to see what was making the boy shout aloud in his sleep.

"Pshaw!" Nemo said. "I wish I'd seen the rest of that game!"

"Go back to sleep, Nemo," his papa said. "And stop that dreaming!"

THE SECOND NIGHT:

Nemo was fast asleep in his bed when a noise made him sit up in astonishment. Once again he saw a strange man in his room. This fellow was dressed as a clown, with a white face and a broad, red grin painted around his mouth. He wore a tiny, cone-shaped hat on his smooth white head, and a baggy clown suit decorated with purple, yellow, and green circles. He held his right hand out before him, and a small bird perched on his forefinger.

"Have you come from Slumberland?" Nemo asked.

"Yes," the clown said. "I am Doopsie the Chief of Clowns. The Princess sent me to fetch you. She has a special surprise planned, you see! You will meet the Spirit of Heart's Desire."

"It is such a long walk," Nemo said, yawning. "I am always so tired before I get there."

"Do not worry, no!" Doopsie said. "We will not need to walk tonight." He knelt down and let the bird hop onto the floor of the bedroom.

"Oh!" Nemo said. "It is Budgie, Mama's pet!"

"Yes, and he will carry us both quite safely to Slumberland."

As Nemo watched, the little bird began to grow. In a moment he was so big that his feathered head brushed the room's ceiling.

"Oh, mercy!" Nemo said. "He will never get back into his cage now! I hope Mama will not be too unhappy, no!"

Doopsie mounted the giant bird's back and held out a hand for Nemo. The boy climbed up behind the clown, and Budgie spread his huge wings. Then they soared upward, smashing through the ceiling, flying through the upstairs room where Angelus the Negro maid slept, and then breaking through the roof of the house into the cool, sweet, moonlit sky.

"Papa will not be pleased with the hole in the roof, I guess," Nemo said. He clutched Doopsie around the waist.

"It is a long way down, but don't be afraid, Nemo," the clown said.

They circled over Nemo's house, then flew away across the city. Nemo laughed when he recognized his school, the church, and his friends' houses far below. "Wheeo! This is much better than walking, yes!" he said.

"Hold on tight," Doopsie said. "We will be in Slumberland soon."

As good as his word, the clown steered Budgie up into the clouds, toward the shining spires of Slumberland. In a few minutes the bird descended, and at last came to a gentle landing in the courtyard of the Princess of Slumberland's palace.

"Yes, we are here, Nemo," Doopsie said. He jumped down and lifted the boy from Budgie's back. The bird began to shrink again immediately. When it was its normal size once more, it flew back into the air and disappeared.

"I hope he goes back to Mama," Nemo said.

"Look, Nemo," Doopsie said. "It is your dear friend, the Princess."

"Yes," Nemo said, "but oh! Who is that with her?"

Doopsie said, "That is the Spirit of Heart's Desire. I am sure the Princess will introduce you." The clown made a low bow to the Princess and another to Nemo, and then he backed quickly away.

The Princess smiled. "I am so happy to see you again, Nemo!" she said.

"I am glad I did not fall off that bird's back."

"I want you to meet the Spirit of Heart's Desire," the Princess said. "Desire is the most beautiful of all in Slumberland. Don't you think so, Nemo? Yes?"

The dark-haired Princess was herself very beautiful, and Nemo was about to tell her so when he was interrupted by a sudden commotion. Someone had burst into the very palace of the Princess. "Heart's Desire, pshaw!" the ill-mannered intruder said. "I can not even tell if it's a beautiful girl or a beautiful boy! What sort of a game is that?"

"Oh!" the Princess cried. "It's Flip! If my father hears of this, he will be very angry!"

Flip was a sour, unhappy person with a green face and a huge cigar stuck in a corner of his mouth. He wore a long, black tailcoat, green trousers, and a very high stovepipe hat with a broad hatband. Written on it were the words "Wake up!" He was jealous of Nemo; he always did his best to interfere with anything the boy and the Princess had planned.

"If you cause trouble, Flip," Nemo said, "then you and I are for it, and you will have to take a lickin'!"

Flip glared at Nemo. "I don't care two shucks for that. I may call my uncle, the Dawn Guard, to bring on the sun and melt all of Slumberland into daylight! Just see if I won't."

The Princess looked unhappy. "Oh, Nemo, we will pretend he is not even here. Now listen, because the Spirit of Heart's Desire must ask something of you."

Desire gave Nemo a charming smile. "You see, Nemo, it is this. I have lost something very valuable to me, and the Princess said only you could find it. Will you help me? Yes?"

Looking into Desire's golden eyes, Nemo was glad to be of service. "I will do anything I can for you," he said.

Desire smiled again. "Yes, I know you will." The Spirit's voice was sweet and melodious.

"So what are we looking for?" Flip asked. "I am coming along, too. It is no use leaving me out of this."

Desire glanced at Flip, then turned again to Nemo. "I hope you will find my golden bottle. It has a stopper carved from a beautiful diamond. It is a small thing, and Slumberland is a very big place."

"I will search everywhere," Nemo said. "What is in the bottle?"

"It is dream dust," Desire said. "King Morpheus himself gave it to me."

"Come along then, Flip," Nemo said. "We won't come back until we have found it."

"Oh, Nemo, good luck! Yes!" the Princess said.

"You will have a special reward when you find it," Desire said.

Nemo and Flip left the palace and began their quest for the golden bottle of dream dust. "I guess I am stumped, kiddo," Flip said. "Where will we look first? The jungle? The desert? The frozen north?"

They turned down a narrow street between two great domed buildings. "Gracious," Nemo said, "this may take all the rest of the night."

"Well, ahem, what is this?" Flip said. He had lifted the lid of a metal trash can and was peering inside.

"Come along, we don't have much time, no!"

Flip reached down and lifted something from the trash can. "I guess it is a golden bottle with a diamond stopper! I guess it is!"

"Oh my!" Nemo said, astonished.

Flip was very pleased with himself. "They say it is always in the last place you look, but not this time, eh?"

"Now we can take it back to the Spirit of Heart's Desire. We will get our reward, sure!"

"Oh," Flip said, "I will keep this for myself. I found it. Yes."

Nemo tried to pull the golden bottle away from the green-faced rascal. Flip would not let go, and they wrestled for a while until Flip called out to his uncle. "Uncle Aurora, help me! Bring on the sun and send this kid back where he belongs!"

Suddenly, all of Slumberland was flooded with bright sunlight. "Oh no!" Nemo cried. "I am falling sound awake!"

And then he turned over in his bed. His mama had come into the room and was shaking him by the shoulder. "Come along, Nemo," she said. "It is nearly time for Sunday school, yes!"

THE THIRD NIGHT:

Dressed now in a pale blue coat with brass buttons, blue breeches, shiny black leather boots, and a peaked military cap with a black visor, Little Nemo wondered where the Princess of Slumberland's city had gone.

The palace had completely vanished. The maze of streets, the carefully tended parks, the vaulting marble edifices had all disappeared like the cool morning haze. Nemo stared in astonishment. There was nothing to see except a grass-covered plain. Not even a tree stood between him and the distant horizon.

"Oh, dear!" Nemo said. "This is all Flip's doing! When I find him, I will make him sorry! Yes!"

"You know," a young woman's voice said, "what happens sometimes is there are just some people you can't make sorry. Um, like my brother. One of my brothers. At least one."

Nemo turned and saw her. She was not much taller than he, and she looked a little bewildered, and he decided that he liked her even though she was the most unusual-looking person he had ever seen, even in Slumberland. She had skin as white as bone, and wild hair that was long in places and cropped short in others; sometimes the hair was blond and sometimes it was pink or purple or orange. She wore earrings—little white skulls—but she also had a ring through one nostril and another in her upper lip, like savages in Mama's picture-books. She didn't look like a savage, though; she looked nice. She wore a jacket made of heavy, black leather, and a short, black skirt. She had one blue eye and one green eye and she was staring over Nemo's head at absolutely nothing.

"Excuse me, ma'am," Nemo said, "but I am looking—"

"He called me 'ma'am'," the young woman said. "The last time anyone called me that—um, I forget."

Nemo tried again. "I am looking—"

"You're looking for a golden bottle with a diamond stopper."

Nemo raised his hat and scratched his head. "How did you know that?"

"I don't know how I know, I just know," she said. "Don't you know when you know?"

"Don't I know what?" Nemo asked.

The young woman gazed at him for a moment. "Here," she said at last. "I can help you find what you're looking for. We'll use my cards."

"Mama and Papa like to play cards."

"Let's sit down on this nice, red grass," she said. "Now, shuffle."

Nemo sat beside her, but he didn't say anything, because there was only one single card, and he didn't know how to shuffle one card.

"That's good enough," she said. "Now turn it over." She touched the grass, and tiny, fire-breathing dragons in many bright colors began to crawl around.

Nemo watched for a moment, then he turned the card. It was the four of hearts.

"Ah," she said. She smiled. "The six of pentacles. A nice card. Um."

"What does it say?" Nemo asked.

"How can a card say? I can tell you what it means. A card can mean. Um, wait a minute. It means that this is a really, really good time to help somebody. So that's why I'm helping you."

"Thank you, yes!" Nemo said. "I must find that bottle!"

"Now shuffle again."

Nemo turned the four of hearts over so the back of the card faced up—it was from a deck of Delta Airlines playing cards. Then he turned it over again. Now, somehow, it was the jack of spades.

"Oh, wow," she said. "It's the Little Nell card. That's a *horrible* card. It means lots of grief and suffering, and sometimes as much as you want to help someone, you just *can't*, you know?" She stared over Nemo's head again. "Well, um," she said, standing up, "in that case, good-bye."

"Oh! Oh!" Nemo cried. "Please don't leave! No!"

The young woman sat down beside him again. "Okay, we'll try it again. Turn the card over; but if it comes up Hiroshima or the King of Anchors or something, I'm gone."

Nemo nodded and turned the card: the deuce of diamonds.

"I'll bet that even felt better, didn't it?" she said. "It's all about freedom and happiness and, well, goldfish, I guess, if you want goldfish. I like them until they're, you know, dead. You're going to have a wonderful future and you're going to have a good friend, a tall, pale man who lives far away from the city. Oh. *Oh*. I'll bet I know who that is!"

"Who is it?" Nemo asked. "Tell me, do!"

"Um," she said.

"Shall I turn over another card?"

The young woman raised her eyebrows. "There *aren't* any more cards," she said.

"Then how will I find the golden bottle?"

She sighed. "All right. Take this string." She lifted the end of a long piece of white string and gave it to Nemo. "The other end is tied around your golden bottle. All you have to do is follow it."

"Thank—"

"And, um, hope that somebody bad doesn't untie it before you get there."

"Thank you, ma'am," Nemo said.

"He called me 'ma'am'," she said happily, as she vanished.

Nemo opened his eyes and found himself back in his bedroom. He heard his papa calling him: "Nemo! Sleepyheads don't get breakfast in this house! No!"

THE FOURTH NIGHT:

Little Nemo realized suddenly that the healthy grass of Slumberland was gone. Swirling patches of fog had appeared while he'd followed the string, and now he could barely see the ground.

"Oh, gracious!" Nemo said. "Where am I now? What is happening, eh?" He wasn't out under the bright blue sky any longer. He was in some dimly lighted, dank and echoing room. He still held the string, and he walked and walked and walked, but he didn't seem to be getting anywhere. He couldn't see walls on any side of him; he couldn't see the ceiling or the floor. There was just the fog, getting thicker and thicker.

And there was a rat, a huge, gray rat the size of a large dog. "Oh my!" Nemo said. "Maybe that awful rat won't see me in all this fog. I hope!"

"I do see you there," the rat said. It had a rough, rasping voice.

"Oh! Oh! It is a talking rat!"

"What are you doing in my realm, Nemo? I don't get many visitors, and they're usually sorry they came here."

Nemo felt a cold emptiness within him. "I must wake up!" he said. "I must go home to Mama and Papa!"

The rat made an unpleasant growling sound; it may have been laughter. "You won't ever go home, Nemo. Look at your string."

Nemo glanced down at the string in his hand. It had been chewed off, and the end of it dangled uselessly from his fingers. He became even more frightened. He sank to his knees, searching in the impossibly thick fog for the other end of the string.

"You won't find it, you know," the rat said. Its voice was barely above a whisper, but it was compelling nonetheless. "You'll never go back to your home or your family again. Just this easily, hope turns to despair."

Hot tears ran down Nemo's cheeks. He stood again and looked wildly around himself; he saw only the fog and the rat. "Mama!" he cried.

"She can't hear you."

"Why is this happening? Why am I here? Eh?"

The rat showed its long, crooked fangs. "Your task, Nemo. You haven't found the golden bottle with the diamond stopper. Desire is waiting for you, and you haven't even begun to look."

"I have looked for it, yes," Nemo said hopelessly. "I would look some more, but how can I find it here?"

"There's an important lesson, then: Yearning may lead only to unhappiness. A wise person knows when to stop searching. It's time to quit, Nemo; it's time to give up."

Little Nemo blinked and the rat became an ugly old woman. She had skin like a cold, dead thing and eyes the color of a bitter morning in December. Her short, black hair was caught together with a dirty piece of cord, and she had on no clothes at all. On her left hand, where Nemo's mother wore her wedding ring, this woman had a ring with a barbed hook, and with it she ripped at the flesh of her own face. Nemo watched the blood trickle downward toward her chin. He shuddered, and then he shuddered again.

She reached for him. "Come, boy," she said in her low, disquieting voice, "I will show you how you'll end."

Little Nemo ran. He could hear the blood roaring in his ears. He felt prickly and hot. He ran through the fog; it twirled and twisted around him, but it could not hold him. There were many window frames suspended in the air. Nemo wondered what he might see if he stopped by one, but he was too afraid to look.

"Oh, why can I not wake up now?" he said. He ran some more.

He had run a thousand miles, and he had not gained a single step on the ugly woman, who was still chasing him.

He ran along a narrow, muddy path where, here and there, someone had set down wooden planks. "I am in a deep ditch," Nemo said. Now there were walls made of dirt, and they reached a few feet higher than his head. There were sandbags piled on top of them, and ladders going up. He could not see where he was, and he could not see where he was going, but he did not stop running. The way turned and crossed itself, and Nemo quickly became confused in a maze of intersecting channels.

"A dozen years from now," the ugly woman said, "you'll die here in the trenches."

Nemo heard her as if she were beside him, whispering into his ear. "The trenches?" he said.

"The next twelve years—the rest of your life—mean *nothing*. You'll end here in the cold, in the mud, with all the others. The sound of the maggots will be like winter wind rustling the dead straw, except there will be no one alive to hear it. Why do you even—"

Nemo felt a sharp pain in his side just beneath his ribs. It hurt too much to run, so he continued walking as fast as he could. He turned into a trench that crossed to the left, and then into another leading back to the right. After a while he no longer heard the voice of the ugly woman, but he did not stop hurrying away.

At last, a long time later, he needed to rest and catch his breath. He looked behind him and saw two bright points of red. "Oh, I can see the eyes of the giant rat," he said. "I must get away, that's all!"

He had gone only a few more steps when he tripped over a rock embedded in the muck. "Oh!" he cried. "That did hurt my toe, oh!"

Nemo discovered that he was home again, but that he'd fallen out of bed and now lay on the floor twisted up in the sheets. "I guess I was dreaming again, Papa," he said.

His father shook his head. "Dreaming, eh? I wonder what you do dream about!"

THE FIFTH NIGHT:

"I hope the Princess sends another messenger for me tonight," Nemo said, sitting up in bed. "He will help me find the golden bottle with the diamond stopper, I know! It is lost somewhere in

Slumberland, and I must return it to the Spirit of Heart's Desire."

"Then you must look for it in Slumberland, Nemo."

"Who said that, eh?" Nemo looked around his bedchamber and saw a young girl somewhat taller than he. She was dressed like the older school-maids he knew except that her sailor-dress was black rather than blue, and she wore black cotton stockings, black, high-button shoes, and a sort of silver cross around her neck. "Oh, you are very pretty! You are as pretty as King Morpheus's daughter, the Princess, yes! You are almost as pretty as my mama!"

The girl smiled. "You're sweet, Nemo."

"Do you go to my school? I think I have seen you there."

She shook her head, laughing. "No, we haven't met before. For most people, one visit from me is more than enough. Now, if you like, I can show you the way to Slumberland. It's just through that door."

"But there is no door there! Oh, oh, now there *is* a door!"

The girl opened the door that had just appeared in the wall. Little Nemo stepped through, still dressed in his nightshirt and slippers. He was outdoors again, beneath a bright blue sky. He was unhappy to see that he'd returned to the awful trenches.

"What's the matter, Nemo?" the girl asked.

"I don't like it here. The ugly woman said to me—"

His amiable companion smiled again. "I know what she said to you, and now *I'll* tell you something: She doesn't always know what she's talking about."

Little Nemo shivered even though the sun was warm overhead. "Who is she?"

"She's my sister. My younger sister."

Nemo was confused. He didn't believe she could possibly be the sister of the ugly woman who'd chased him—and it was even more unlikely that she was the older of the two. "Why did she bring me here?" Nemo asked.

"She thinks if people get a look at how they're gonna die, it'll tip them over the edge into despair. She doesn't realize that there are worse things around than death. *Lots* of worse things."

Nemo felt afraid. "How does she know what will happen to me?"

"She *thinks* she knows."

"Will I really die here in twelve years?"

"Maybe," said the girl. She looked more closely at Little Nemo and shrugged. "And maybe not. I think my sister could use a good lesson."

She took Nemo by the hand, and they walked a little farther. He thought she had the palest complexion and the blackest, most disheveled hair he'd ever seen. "What is that, eh?" he asked after a while. Nemo pointed to the heavy silver pendant the girl wore on a chain around her neck.

"It's an ankh."

"An ankh, is it, eh?"

She smiled and lifted it up. "I have a brother who insists on calling it an ansate cross. Ansate means having a handle, like a long-haul driver on the CB."

"What—"

"Never mind. Now, I want you to look up there." She pointed to a wooden ladder raised against the wall of the trench.

"Shall I go up that?"

"Yes, Nemo, and tell me what you see."

He was glad to climb the ladder and look out of the trench. "Oh, it is a lovely garden!" he cried. "Have we found our way back to Slumberland? Is the palace of King Morpheus near? I do hope it is!"

"Just follow the path through the hedges," she said. "And give the Princess a kiss for me when you see her."

"If I never do anything more as long as I live," Nemo said, "I *must* find that golden bottle. I would do *anything* to please the Spirit of Heart's Desire."

The girl frowned. "I know," she said. "Almost everyone would. I hate the way people are punished for the crime of falling in love with Desire. Now, get yourself up that ladder—and be careful up there."

Nemo scrambled over the top of the ladder. In his haste and excitement he caught his feet in the coils of barbed wire, and he fell sprawling to the muddy ground.

"Nemo!" said his mother, shaking him by the shoulder. "If you kick off the covers every night, you will soon catch your death of cold!"

THE SIXTH NIGHT:

There were hedges and gravel paths, a sundial and an iron bench. The garden—if it was a garden—went on and on.

"Now where am I, eh?" Little Nemo said. "Is this Slumberland?"

Just as he'd been lost in the maze of trenches, Nemo was now lost in a labyrinth of tall hedges. The shrubbery towered over him; as before, it was impossible to see where he had been or where he was going. Every twist and turn in the maze brought him to a place that looked exactly like all the other places Nemo had seen there: There was the carefully groomed lawn and the trimmed hedges and a green-painted bench.

And the statues—Nemo had never seen so many statues, of men in overcoats or business suits, women in gowns or servants' uniforms, even children sitting at desks or at play. The statues weren't particularly heroic or even memorable. Then Nemo followed an avenue of the maze and came upon a statue that looked familiar. "Oh gracious!" he said. "It is my Uncle Alexander! I wonder why there is a statue of Uncle Alexander in this place."

He walked along some more, beginning to feel both tired and hungry. He said, "I do hope the Princess will send someone soon to find me. Yes!"

A moment later—a dream moment that may have lasted seconds or hours or years—a man appeared from beyond a turning of the way, perhaps in answer to Little Nemo's wish. The man wore a long, brown robe and his face was hidden within its cowl. He walked along the path, studying a large book. Nemo saw that there was a chain around the man's wrist, and the book was attached to the other end of the chain.

Nemo didn't want to disturb the man in the brown robe, but he was very curious. "What is that great book you are reading, eh?"

The man gazed at Little Nemo for a moment. "It is a book that contains everything that ever happened, and everything that *will* ever happen." He had a calm voice, like a churchman or a librarian.

Nemo was astonished. "Does it tell how the world was made?"

"Yes, it does." He turned to a page about a quarter of the way from the beginning. "Here it is, in this chapter."

Nemo was puzzled. "If this is when the world was made, what is in all those pages that come before it?"

"Things that happened before there was a world," the man said.

"If there wasn't a world," Nemo said, "where did they happen?"

"You may read it if you wish."

Nemo looked at the book, and although the words were in English, the pages didn't make a particle of sense to him. He shook his head. "And does it tell how the world will end?"

The man nodded his cowled head. "Here," he said, indicating a page about three-quarters of the way through the book.

"What will happen after the end of the world?" Nemo asked.

"You may read it if you wish."

"Thank you, sir," Nemo said, "but if that book tells about everything that will happen, does it say if I find the golden bottle with the diamond stopper?"

Without a word, the man opened the book to a certain page and showed it to the boy.

"Now I must find my way to the palace of King Morpheus," Nemo said. "Can you tell me—"

The man didn't even look up from his reading. He just pointed to a path.

"Thank you, sir!" Nemo said. He turned to hurry away, and stumbled into a wall of hedges. "Oh, pshaw! I will be tangled in these bushes now!"

He fought with the branches for a moment, until he realized that he was fighting with the sheets and his pillow. "Oh, Mama!" said Nemo. "I was only dreaming again!"

THE SEVENTH NIGHT:

Little Nemo woke and sat up in his wooden bed with the high headboard. He'd heard a noise in the room, but he saw nothing out of the ordinary. "Was that you, Leo?" he asked the family's cat. "Did you meow?"

"Yes, Nemo," the cat said. "The Princess is eagerly waiting for you. Do hurry!"

"Oh, now you can talk, Leo!"

Leo stopped a moment to lick his paw. Then he went on: "The Spirit of Heart's Desire wishes to have the golden bottle with the diamond stopper returned. Nemo, you are to rush to the palace as quickly as you can. All of King Morpheus's loyal subjects are expecting you, yes!"

"Will you come to Slumberland with me?" Little Nemo asked.

"Yes, I will go with you. And Captain Jack the Soldier will go to protect us, and Bobby Bear, too!"

Nemo took off his nightshirt and put on his clothes. "How will we get to Slumberland, Leo?" he asked.

"Hobbyhorse will take us easily, you will see!"

Little Nemo climbed onto Hobbyhorse's wooden saddle. He carried Captain Jack in one arm and Bobby Bear in the other.

"Oh my!" said Leo. "Is there enough room for me?"

"Yes, yes! Jump up here, Leo!" The small, gray cat leaped onto Nemo's lap, and the boy began rocking back and forth on his Hobbyhorse. Soon, as if by magic, they were racing across meadows and fields, leaving the town far behind.

"Gracious!" said Leo. "I have never ridden so fast! It is making my head spin!"

"We will be in Slumberland in no time," said Captain Jack the Soldier.

"I can see the domes of King Morpheus's palace!" said Bobby Bear.

"Tell me when we get there, for I will shut my eyes until then," said Leo.

In less than a minute, Hobbyhorse came to a stop at the bottom of the grand marble staircase that led up to the palace gates. "We will come back soon," said Little Nemo, "and then we will go home again."

"I will be here, yes!" said Hobbyhorse.

Still carrying Captain Jack and Bobby Bear and with Leo following behind him, Nemo began mounting the marble stairs. From his previous visits he knew there were exactly 1,234,567,890 steps; he had counted them often. It took a long time to climb the staircase, but when they arrived at the top, the Princess's special courier, Lopopo, was waiting for them.

"I see you have brought your friends to Slumberland, Nemo!" Lopopo said, grinning. He took off his pointed, green hat and bowed. "The Princess asks you to wait for her in the Ice Cream Chamber. You may have as much ice cream as you wish!" Lopopo bowed again, and then he went to tell the Princess of Nemo's arrival.

The Ice Cream Chamber was a room as big as a castle, and in the middle of it was a mountain of ice cream. "Oh, that is grand!" said Nemo.

"There is enough ice cream to freeze an ocean!" said Bobby Bear. "This has got me winging!"

"I will have some," said Captain Jack the Soldier. "All that riding made me hungry!"

"Oh, what kind of ice cream is it?" asked Nemo.

"Ah! Ha! It is rum raisin!" said Captain Jack.

Before Nemo could eat even a tiny bit of the ice cream, the bad-tempered, green-faced Flip threw open a door and strutted into the chamber. "Huh!" he said. "You thought you could have a party without me!"

"It is that Mr. Flip," Leo said.

"Flip," said Nemo, "you may leave now! We don't care if you do!"

"I'll show you something," said Flip. "I'll fill this flubadub with ice cream and have some all day and all night!" He held up the golden bottle with the diamond stopper.

"Oh! I have been searching for that!" said Nemo.

"I know it, kiddo! I guess if I give it to the Princess, she'll like me and forget about you anyway!"

Little Nemo felt a terrible fury, a passion greater than anything he'd ever known before. "I guess you will give it to me!" he said fiercely.

"Wait, Nemo!" Flip said, astonished by the boy's grim expression. "For mercy's sake!"

"Let it go, or you'll be worrying!"

Nemo tore the golden bottle with the diamond stopper from Flip's grasp. As soon as he touched it, Nemo was filled with a profound happiness. "Gracious!" he said in a quiet voice. "This must be the most wonderful thing in the whole world!"

Captain Jack the Soldier said, "Now you must take it to the Princess and the Spirit of Heart's Desire."

"I . . . oh!" Nemo said. He didn't want to give it to anyone. He ran out of the Ice Cream Chamber, chased by Captain Jack, Bobby Bear, Leo, and Flip. They shouted at him to stop, but he just ran and ran. He didn't know what was inside the golden bottle with the diamond stopper; he just knew that it was *his* Heart's Desire as much as anyone's.

"Come back, Nemo!" called Captain Jack. "That does not belong to you! No!"

"I will not let them have this," Nemo told himself. He dashed out of King Morpheus's palace and began running down the 1,234,567,890 steps; halfway down, he came upon two people. "Mama! Papa!" he exclaimed. "You are here in Slumberland!"

His papa reached for the boy's treasure. "I'll take that now, Nemo," he said.

Nemo woke suddenly in his bed. "Um! Ooh!" he said. "I was dreaming! You weren't really chasing me, Leo!"

The gray cat did not reply.

"I'll take that now," said the Spirit of Heart's Desire.

"Hurrah! Look!" said Little Nemo. "I still have the golden bottle with the diamond stopper!"

"Yes," said the Spirit, "and now you must return it to me."

Nemo felt his heart beating faster. He didn't want to surrender his prize.

The Spirit of Heart's Desire sat on the bed beside Nemo, holding out one hand. "Don't you love me, Nemo? I won't love you anymore if you don't give it to me."

Nemo felt like crying. He wanted the Spirit to love him, but he didn't want to give up the golden bottle.

Someone else came into Nemo's bedroom. He was tall and very thin, and he was dressed all in black. "I will take that now," he said.

As soon as the gaunt man took the golden bottle from him, Nemo felt a great relief. "I must still be dreaming!" he said.

The man in black turned to the Spirit of Heart's Desire. "How *dare* you use one of my dreamers to steal the illusion of Heart's Desire!"

Desire gave Dream a mocking laugh. "His desires are under *my* jurisdiction—or have you forgotten about that?"

"It is not right for a child to desire something that strongly. Get out." In an instant, Desire vanished.

Dream stood beside Little Nemo's bed. He put a hand on the boy's forehead and looked into Nemo's eyes. Then, like Desire, Dream also disappeared. Later, Nemo could never quite recall what the King of Dreams had said to him that night. Nemo didn't wake up because he was already awake. He lay in his bed and watched as the sunrise flooded his room with soft, golden light. Soon his papa and mama would call him to breakfast.

Introduction to "My First Game as an Immortal"

Even in Paradise, playing football with angels and heroes, George sees himself as managing to lose a yard. But he's there. . . .

— Barbara Hambly

My First Game as an Immortal

I took the ball from Uriel
and I thought Why
don't he run it himself, I
sure don't have no
terrible flaming sword
but I run it to the left
and there was Hadraniel
who had struck Moses
dumb with awe,
whose every word
looses 12,000 flashes of lightning
and he was muttering up a storm.
Where is my blocking? I thought, but
I run the other way
and there was the great Jim Thorpe, smiling—
you don't fool nobody in Paradise.
So they stopped me behind the line
for a loss of a yard
and the shouts of the Heavenly Choir
poured down from the cheap seats
like a blessing.

Two thousand copies of this book have been printed by the Maple-Vail Book Manufacturing Group, Binghamton, NY, for Golden Gryphon Press, Urbana, IL. The typeset is Electra with Bergell display, printed on 55# Sebago. Typesetting by The Composing Room, Inc., Kimberly, WI.

"The book that wowed me more than any other in 2003 is *Budayeen Nights* (Golden Gryphon) by the late George Alec Effinger. *Budayeen Nights* serves as a beautifully evocative postscript to Effinger's trio of Budayeen novels (*When Gravity Fails*, etc.). The stories featuring the novels' protagonist, Marîd Audran, are the most effective, but the whole book is wondrously sensuous, seductive, witty, and thrilling. Effinger's creation, the Muslim underworld of the Budayeen, is one of my favourite settings in SF, and revisiting it for this final outing was a moving experience."

—Claude Lalumière, The Best SF and Fantasy Books
of 2003, *Locus Online*

Available from Golden Gryphon Press
ISBN 1-930846-19-3, Cloth, 235pp, $24.95